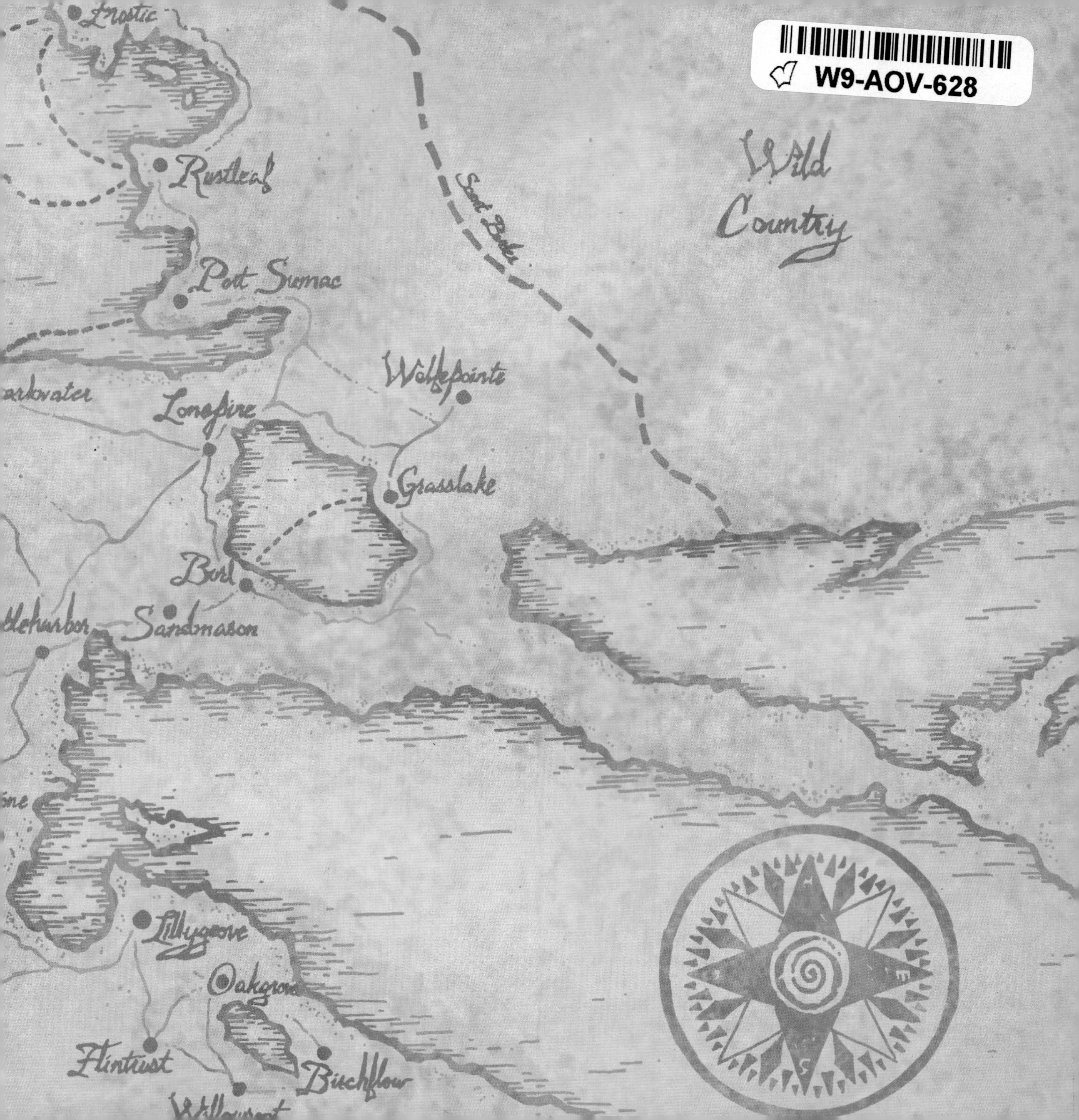
Rustleaf
Port Sumac
Wild Country
Wolfepointe
Grasslake
Lonepine
Burl
Sandmason
Lillygrove
Oakgrove
Flintrust
Birchflow

MOUSE GUARD™
FALL 1152

ARCHAIA ENTERTAINMENT LLC
WWW.**ARCHAIA**.COM

FOR MY WIFE JULIA

AND IN LOVING MEMORY OF
GILBERT AND DORIS PETERSEN

MOUSE GUARD™
FALL 1152

STORY & ART BY
DAVID PETERSEN

For this Edition

Paul Morrissey, *Editor*
Scott Newman, *Production Manager*

Archaia Entertainment LLC

PJ Bickett, *CEO*
Mark Smylie, *CCO*
Mike Kennedy, *Publisher*
Stephen Christy, *Editor-in-Chief*

Published by **Archaia**

Archaia Entertainment LLC
1680 Vine Street, Suite 1010
Los Angeles, California, 90028, USA
www.archaia.com

ARCHAIA™
NEW STORIES. NEW WORLDS.

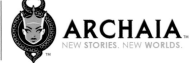

MOUSE GUARD: FALL 1152 Collected Edition Hardcover. April 2012. FOURTH PRINTING.

10 9 8 7 6 5 4

ISBN: 1-932386-57-2
ISBN 13: 978-1-932386-57-8

Printed in **Korea**.

PREFACE

IN THE FOLLOWING PAGES YOU WILL FIND THE FIRST IN A SERIES OF ADVENTURE STORIES I CONCEIVED OVER TEN YEARS AGO. ON A SCRAP OF PAPER I HAD QUICKLY SCRATCHED "MICE HAVE A CULTURE ALL THEIR OWN; TOO SMALL TO INTEGRATE WITH OTHER ANIMALS." THIS SCRIBBLE LED TO MORE THOUGHT ABOUT HOW MICE WOULD SURVIVE AS CHARACTERS IN SUCH A HOSTILE WORLD POPULATED WITH PREDATORS: "HIDE THE CITIES, MAKE THEM SELF SUFFICIENT AND SPREAD APART FROM ONE ANOTHER" FROM A STORYTELLING PERSPECTIVE, IT MEANT THE MICE WERE PRISONERS OF THEIR OWN HOMES.

SKETCHES FOLLOWED OF THREE MICE, SAXON, KENZIE, AND RAND, DESTINED TO PLAY THE ROLES OF PATHFINDERS FOR THEIR KIND. AS MOUSE GUARD RATTLED AROUND IN MY HEAD, THE WORLD BECAME POPULATED WITH MORE CHARACTERS, TOWNS AND VILLAGES, AND A HISTORY OF ITS OWN, UNTIL 2005 WHEN IT BEGAN SPILLING ONTO PAPER

I AM VERY HAPPY TO BEGIN SHARING THAT WORLD.

I WISH TO EXPRESS SPECIAL THANKS TO MY PARENTS, JESSE GLENN, MIKE DAVIS, EMERSON JONES, SEYTH MIERSMA, JEREMY BASTIAN, MAIJA GRAHAM, NATE PRIDE, RICK CORTES, MARK SMYLIE, AKI LIAO, BRIAN PETKASH & GUY DAVIS.

David Petersen

DAVID PETERSEN
MICHIGAN 2007

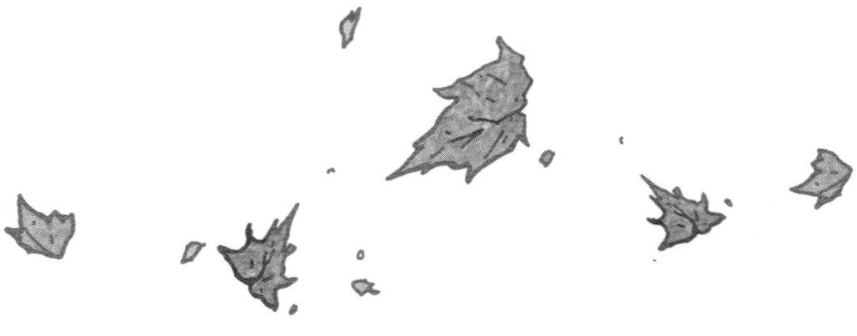

CONTENTS

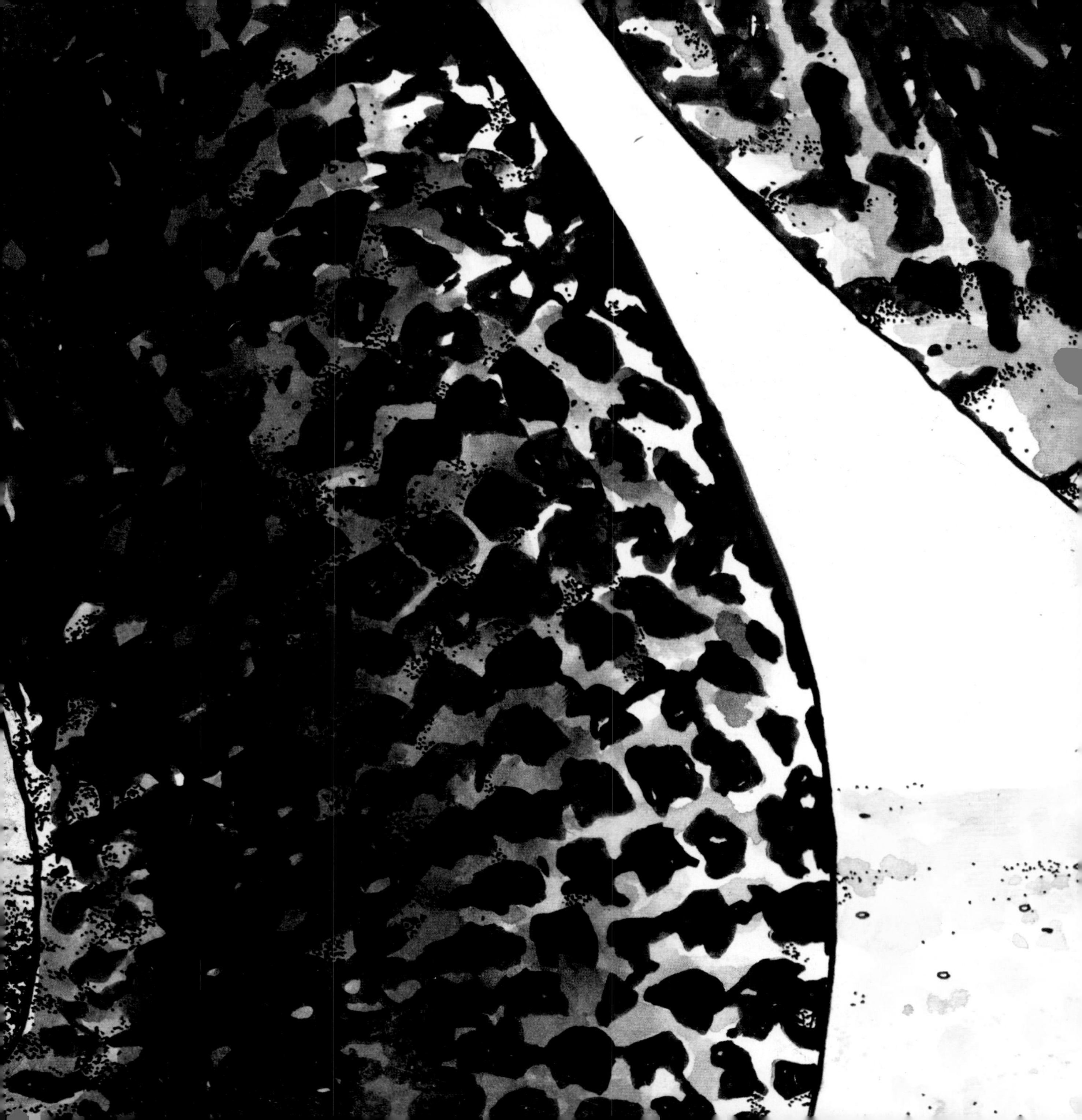

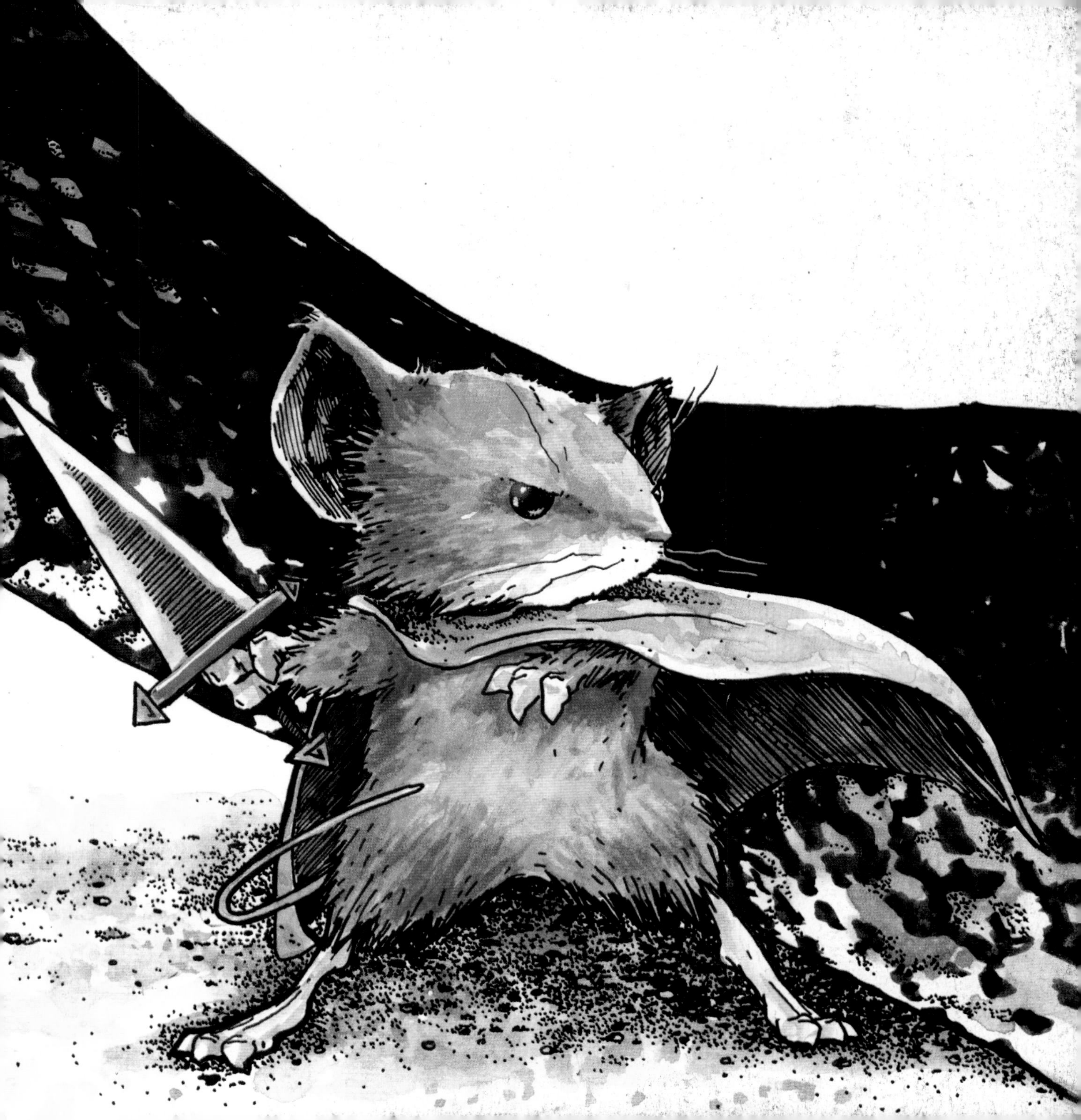

CHAPTER ONE

BELLY OF THE BEAST

The mice struggle to live safely and prosper among all of the world's harsh conditions and predators. Thus the Mouse Guard was formed. After persevering against a weasel warlord in the winter war of 1149, the territories are no longer as troubled. True, the day-to-day dangers exist, but no longer are the Guard soldiers, instead they are escorts, pathfinders, weather watchers, scouts and body guards for the mice who live among the territories. Many skills are necessary for the guard to keep the borders safe. They must find new safeways and paths from village to village, lead shipments of goods from one town to another and, in case of attack, guard against all evil and harm to their territories.

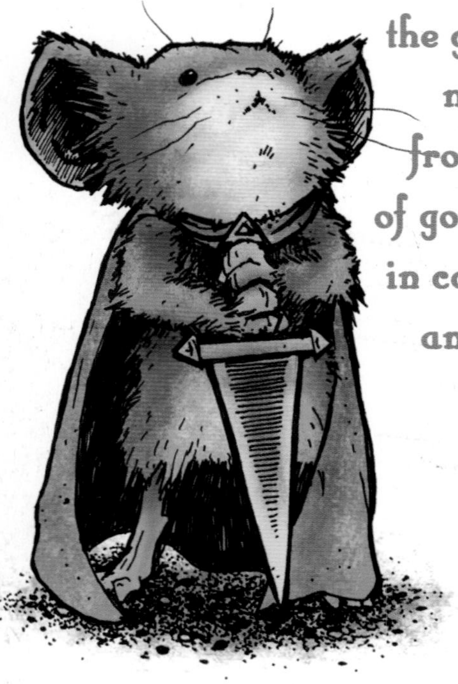

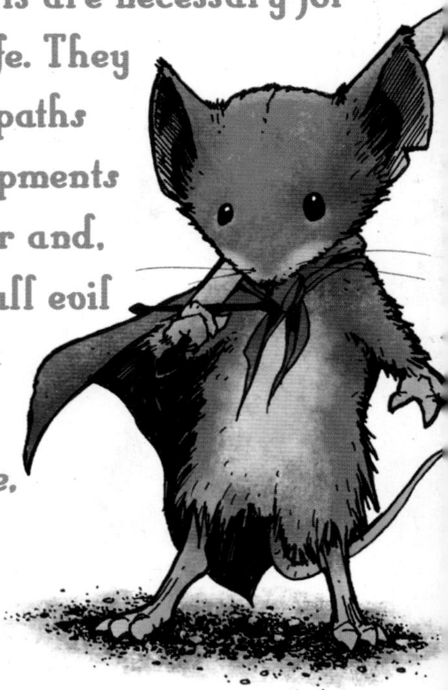

'Hail all those who are able,
any mouse can,
any mouse will,
but the Guard prevail'

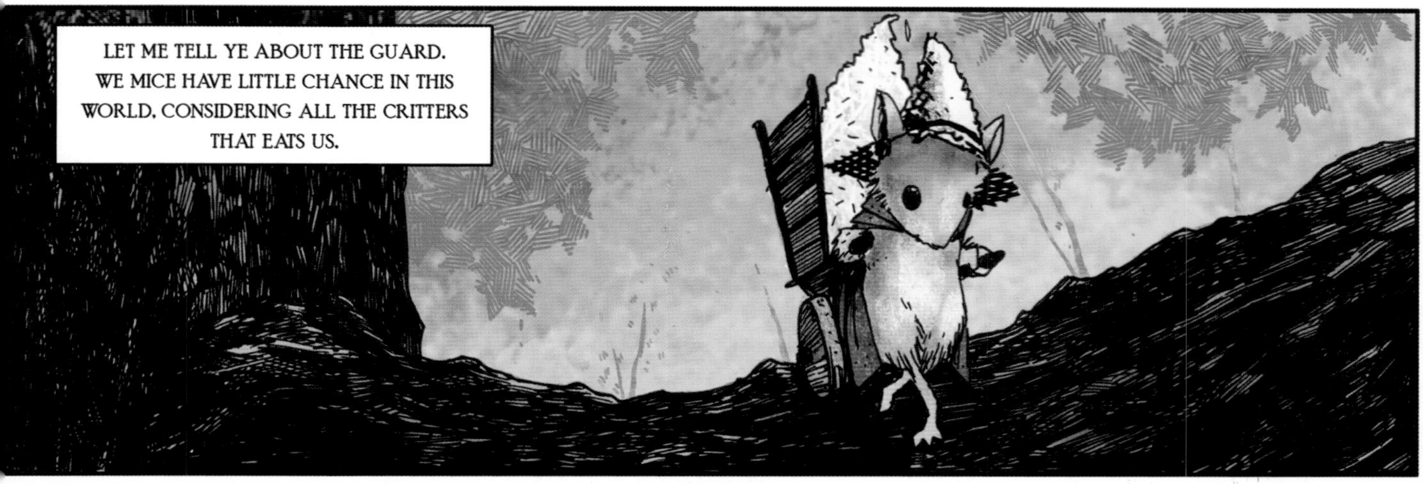
LET ME TELL YE ABOUT THE GUARD. WE MICE HAVE LITTLE CHANCE IN THIS WORLD, CONSIDERING ALL THE CRITTERS THAT EATS US.

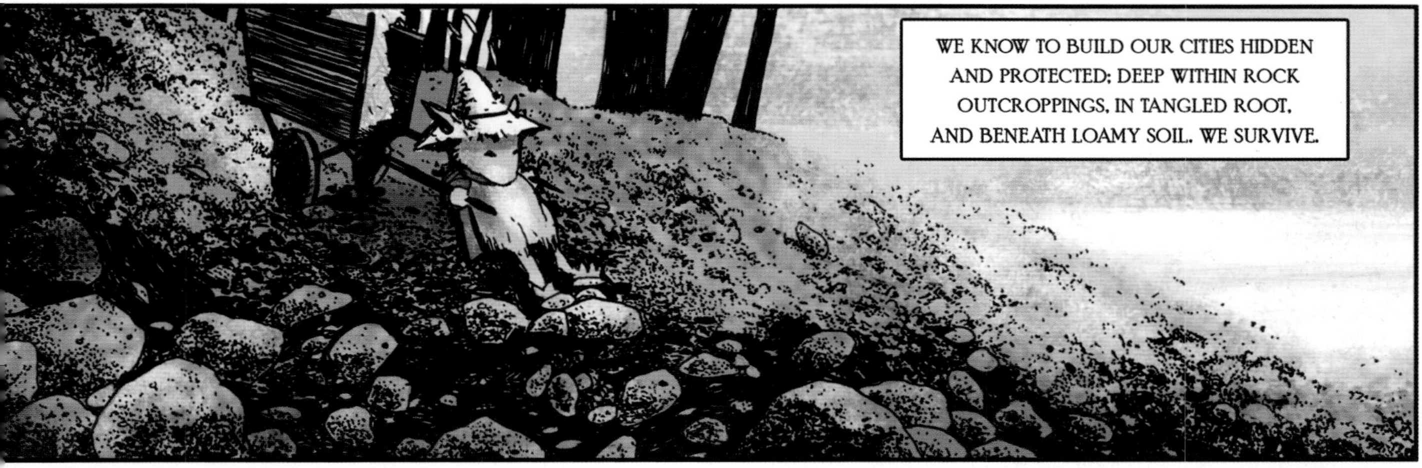
WE KNOW TO BUILD OUR CITIES HIDDEN AND PROTECTED: DEEP WITHIN ROCK OUTCROPPINGS, IN TANGLED ROOT, AND BENEATH LOAMY SOIL. WE SURVIVE.

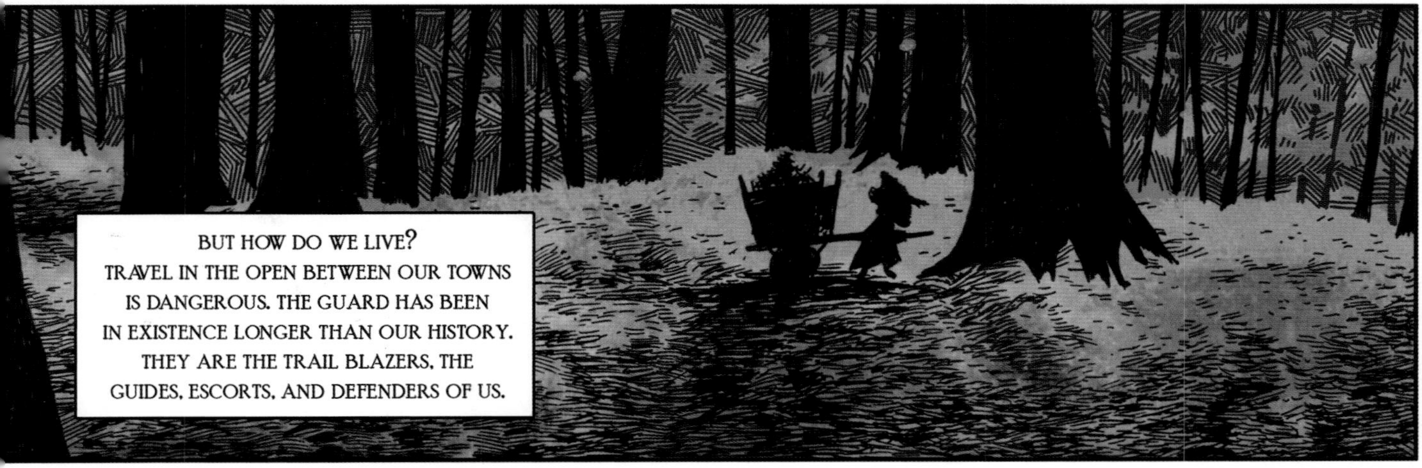
BUT HOW DO WE LIVE? TRAVEL IN THE OPEN BETWEEN OUR TOWNS IS DANGEROUS. THE GUARD HAS BEEN IN EXISTENCE LONGER THAN OUR HISTORY. THEY ARE THE TRAIL BLAZERS, THE GUIDES, ESCORTS, AND DEFENDERS OF US.

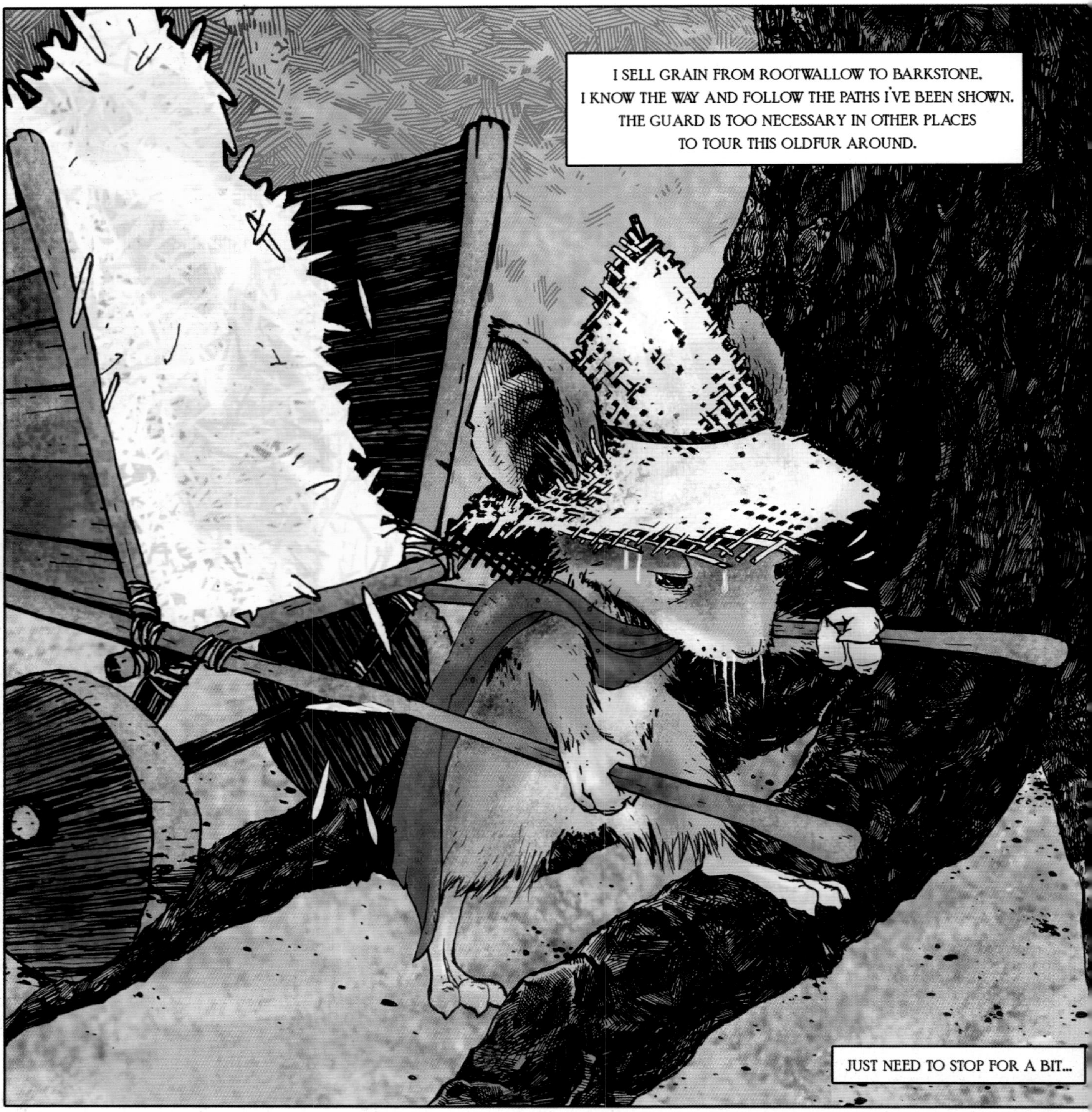
I SELL GRAIN FROM ROOTWALLOW TO BARKSTONE,
I KNOW THE WAY AND FOLLOW THE PATHS I'VE BEEN SHOWN.
THE GUARD IS TOO NECESSARY IN OTHER PLACES
TO TOUR THIS OLDFUR AROUND.
JUST NEED TO STOP FOR A BIT...

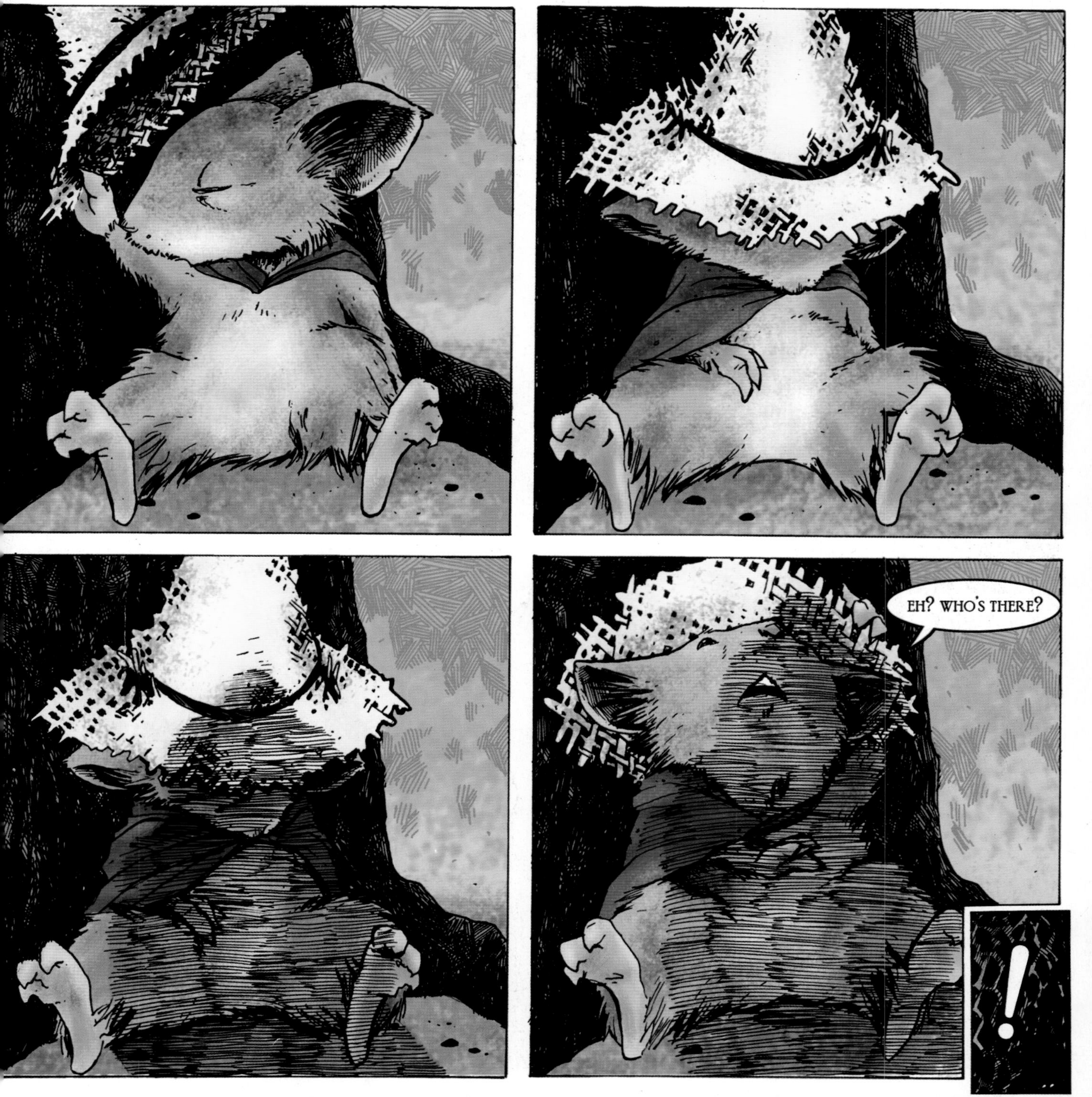
EH? WHO'S THERE?
!

Mouse Guard:
Belly of the Beast

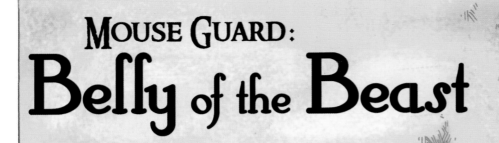

GWENDOLYN SAID YOU WOULD BRIEF US ONCE WE WERE ON THE TRAIL, KENZIE. SO TELL US, WHY HAVE THREE OF THE GUARD'S FINEST BEEN DISPATCHED?

LIEAM

A MOUSE PEDDLING GRAIN TOOK THE PATH FROM ROOTWALLOW TO BARKSTONE ALONE.

WE NEED TO FIND THIS MISSING GRAIN MOUSE... SEEMS HE NEVER ARRIVED AT HIS DESTINATION.

KENZIE

WE WON'T AT THIS RATE... IT'S STILL QUITE A WAY TO BARKSTONE AND NO SIGN OF THE LOST FOOL YET.

SAXON

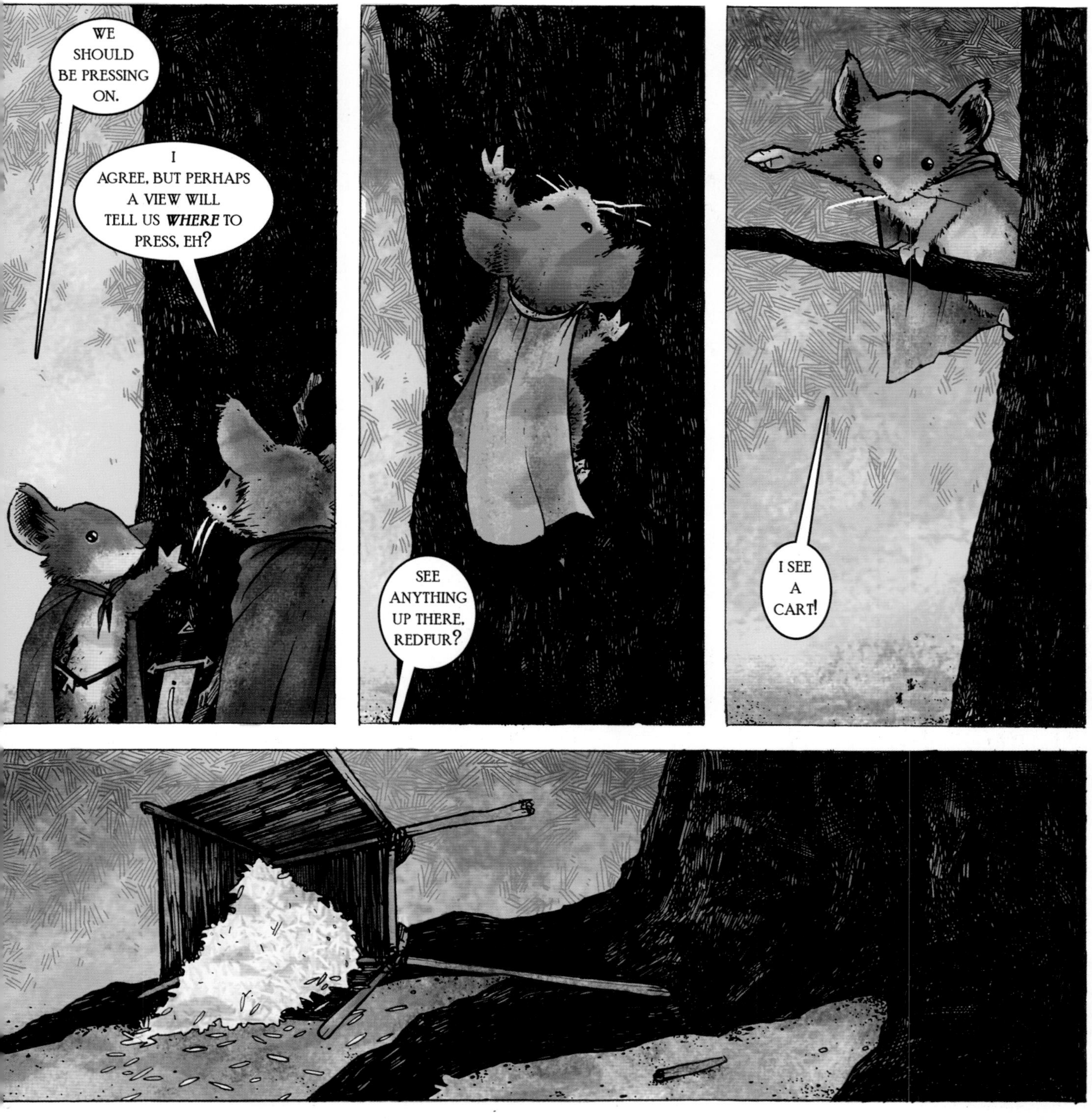
WE SHOULD BE PRESSING ON.
I AGREE, BUT PERHAPS A VIEW WILL TELL US *WHERE* TO PRESS, EH?
SEE ANYTHING UP THERE, REDFUR?
I SEE A CART!

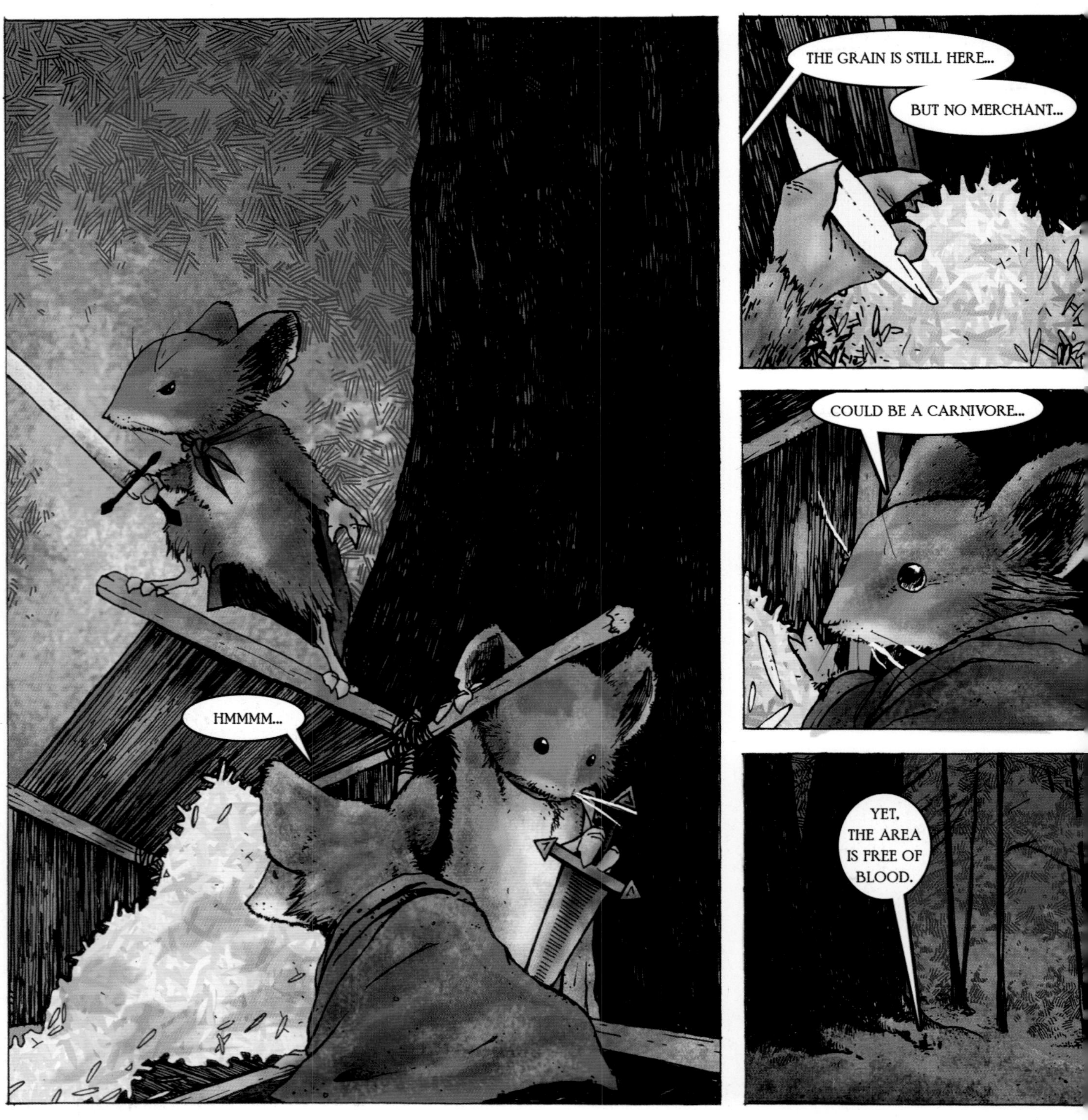
HMMMM...
THE GRAIN IS STILL HERE...
BUT NO MERCHANT...
COULD BE A CARNIVORE...
YET, THE AREA IS FREE OF BLOOD.

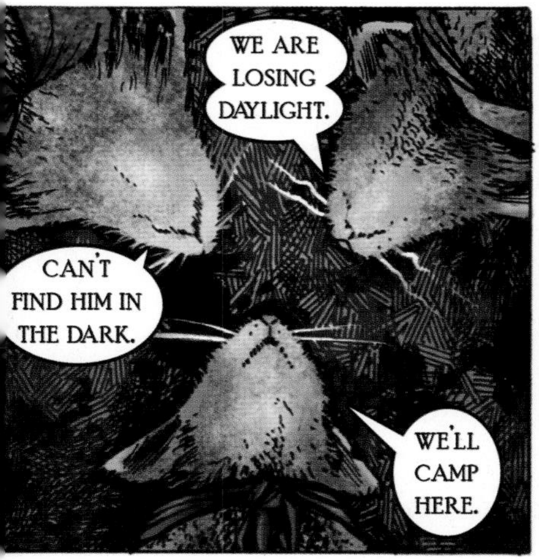
WE ARE LOSING DAYLIGHT.
CAN'T FIND HIM IN THE DARK.
WE'LL CAMP HERE.

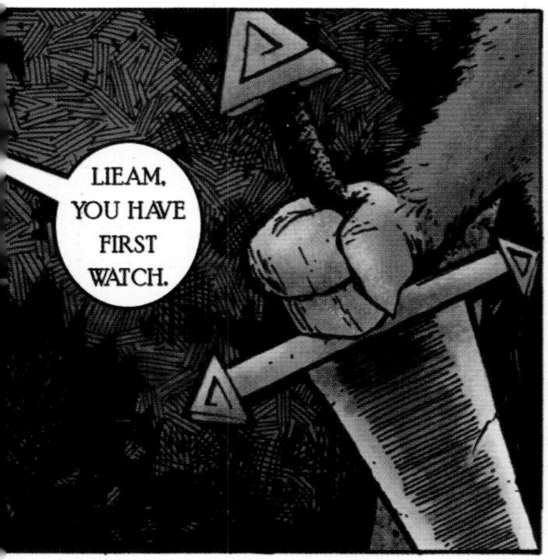
LIEAM, YOU HAVE FIRST WATCH.

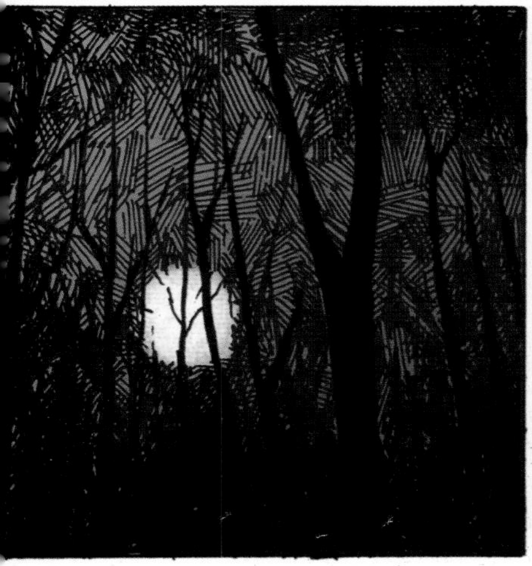

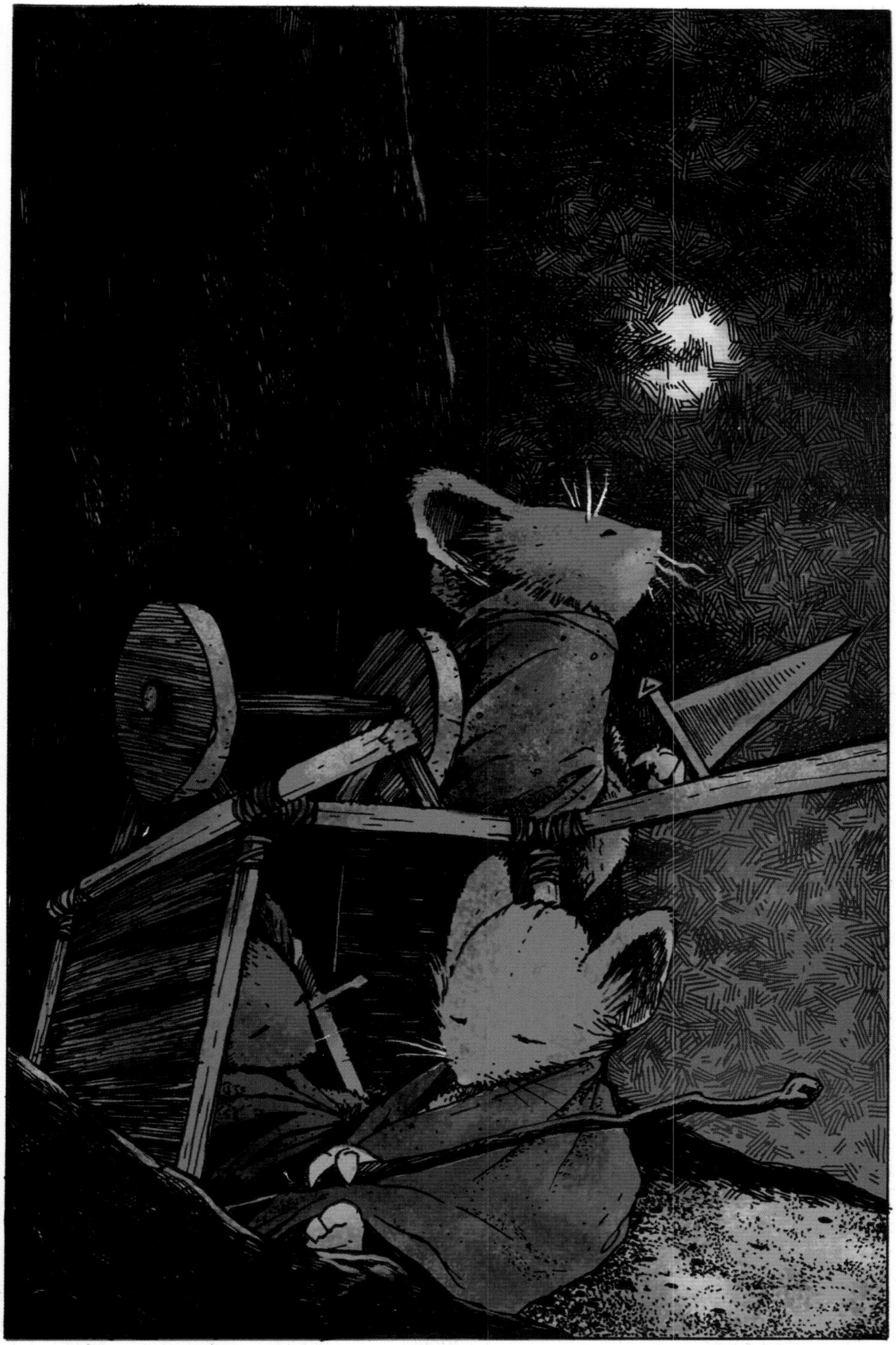

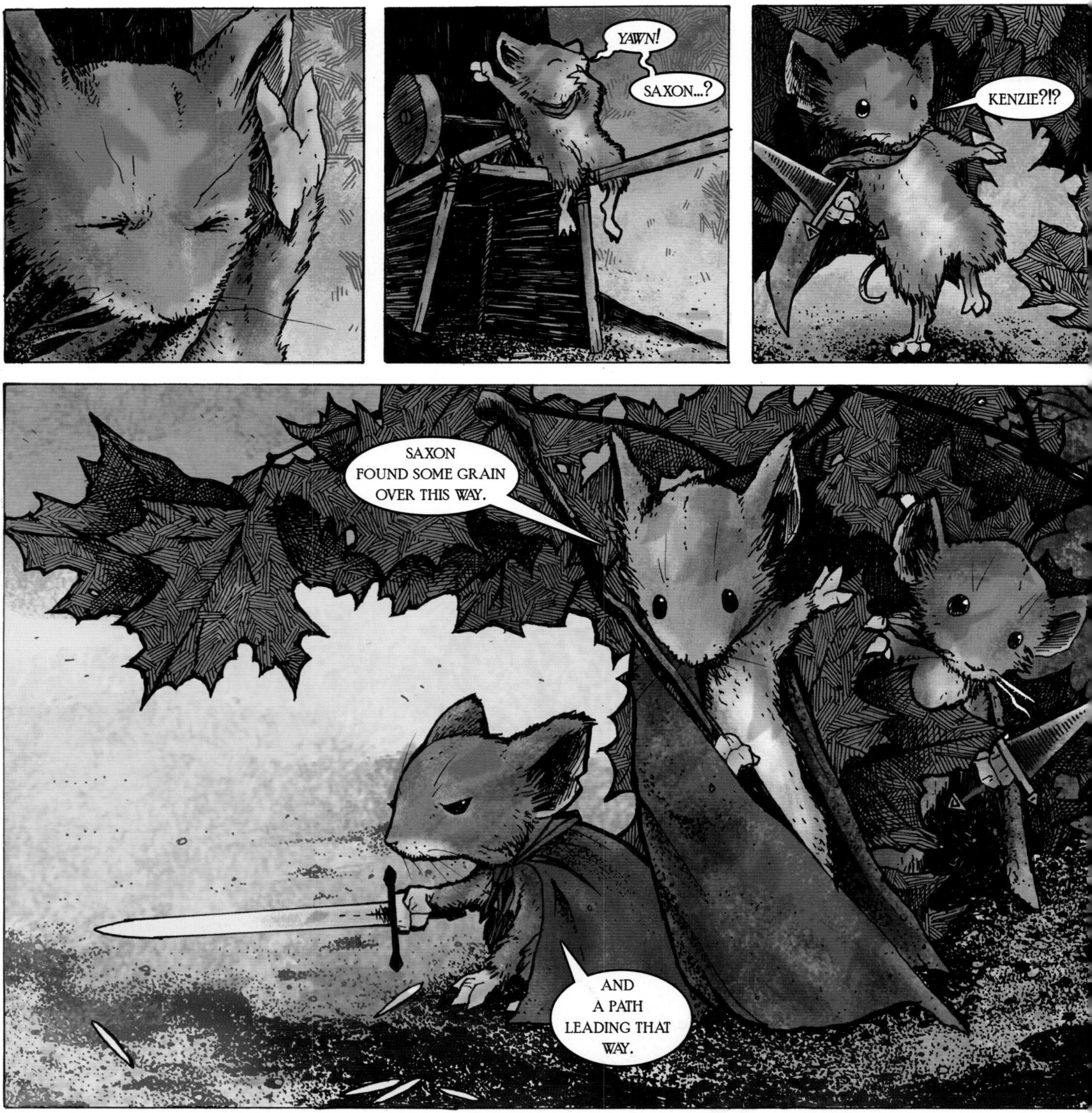
YAWN!
SAXON...?
KENZIE?!?
SAXON FOUND SOME GRAIN OVER THIS WAY.
AND A PATH LEADING THAT WAY.

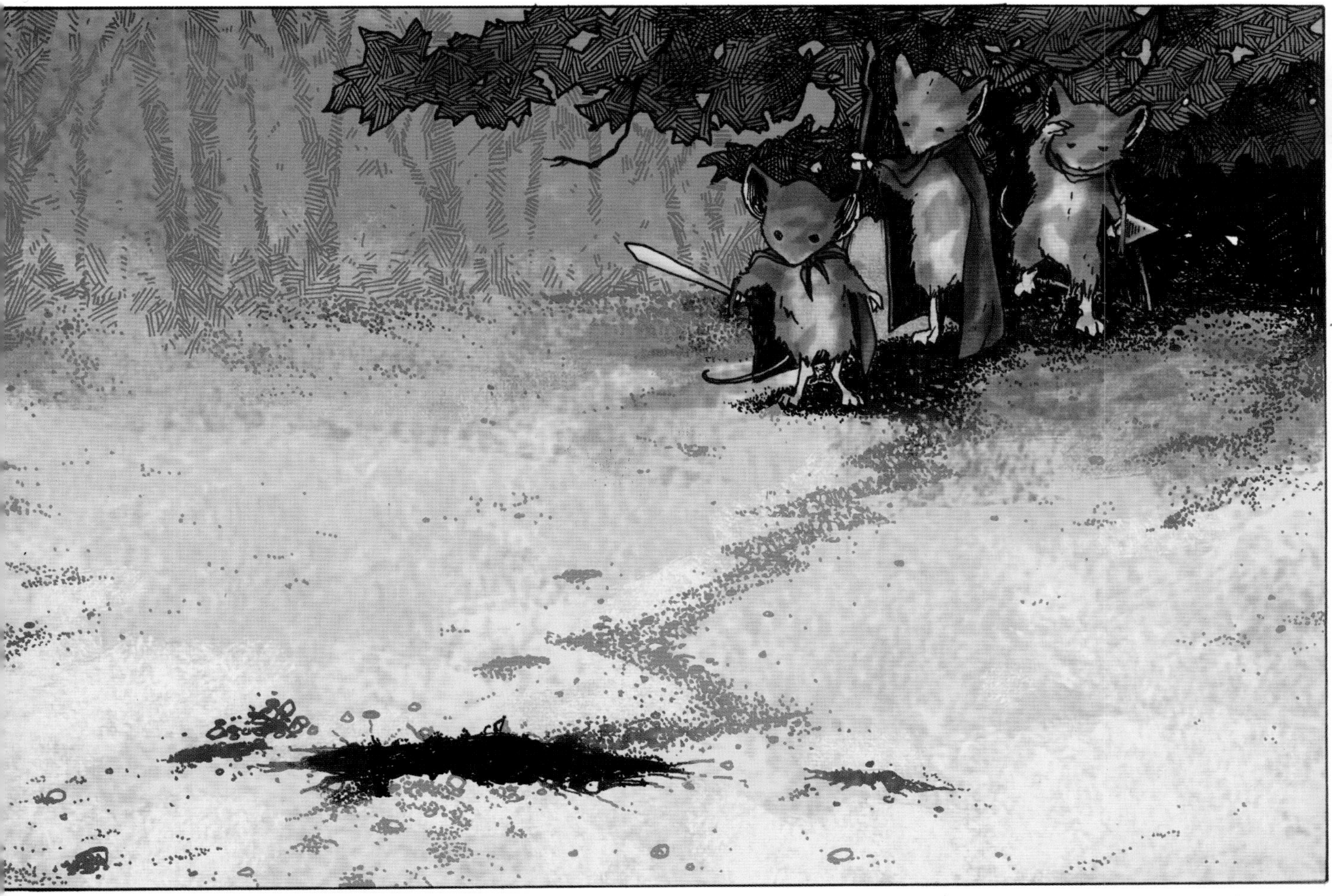

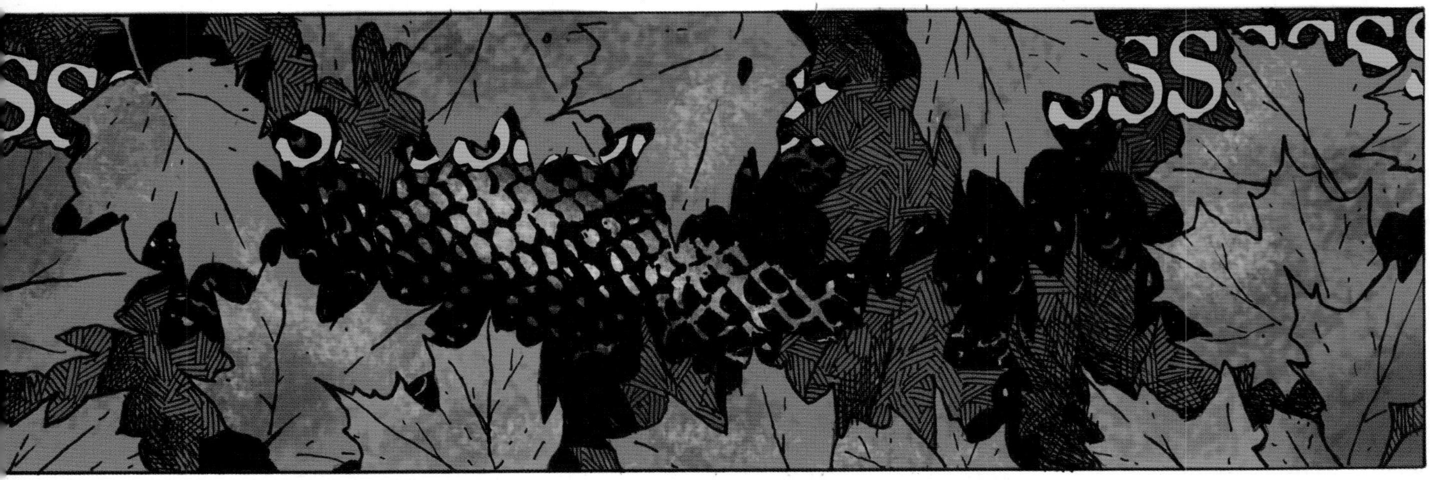
SS
SSSSS

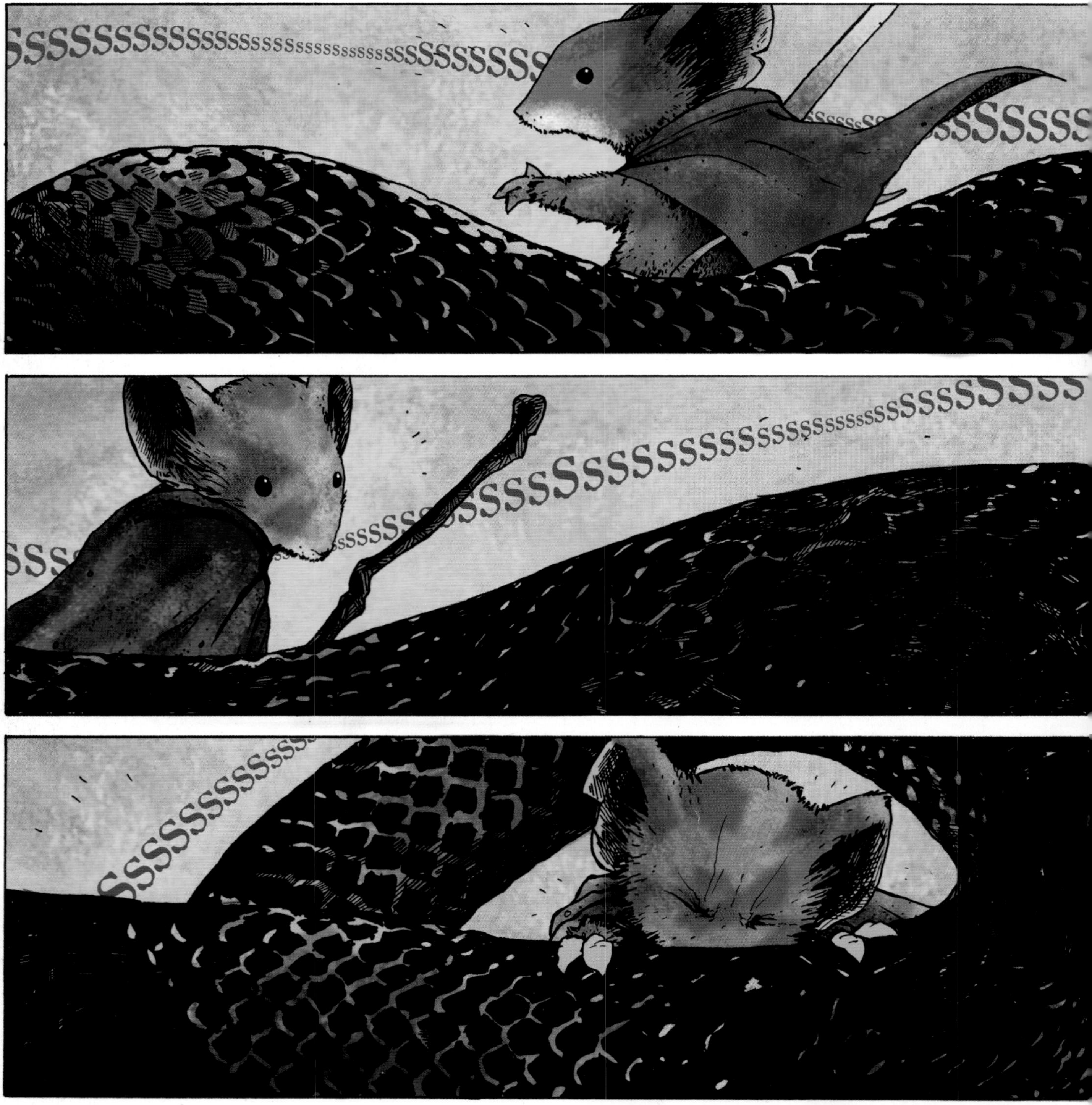

SSSSSSSSSsssssssssssssssssssssSSSSSSSS
ssssssSSSSSS
SSSssssssSSSSSSSSSSSSSSsssssssssssSSSSSSSSSS
SSSSSSSSSSSsssss

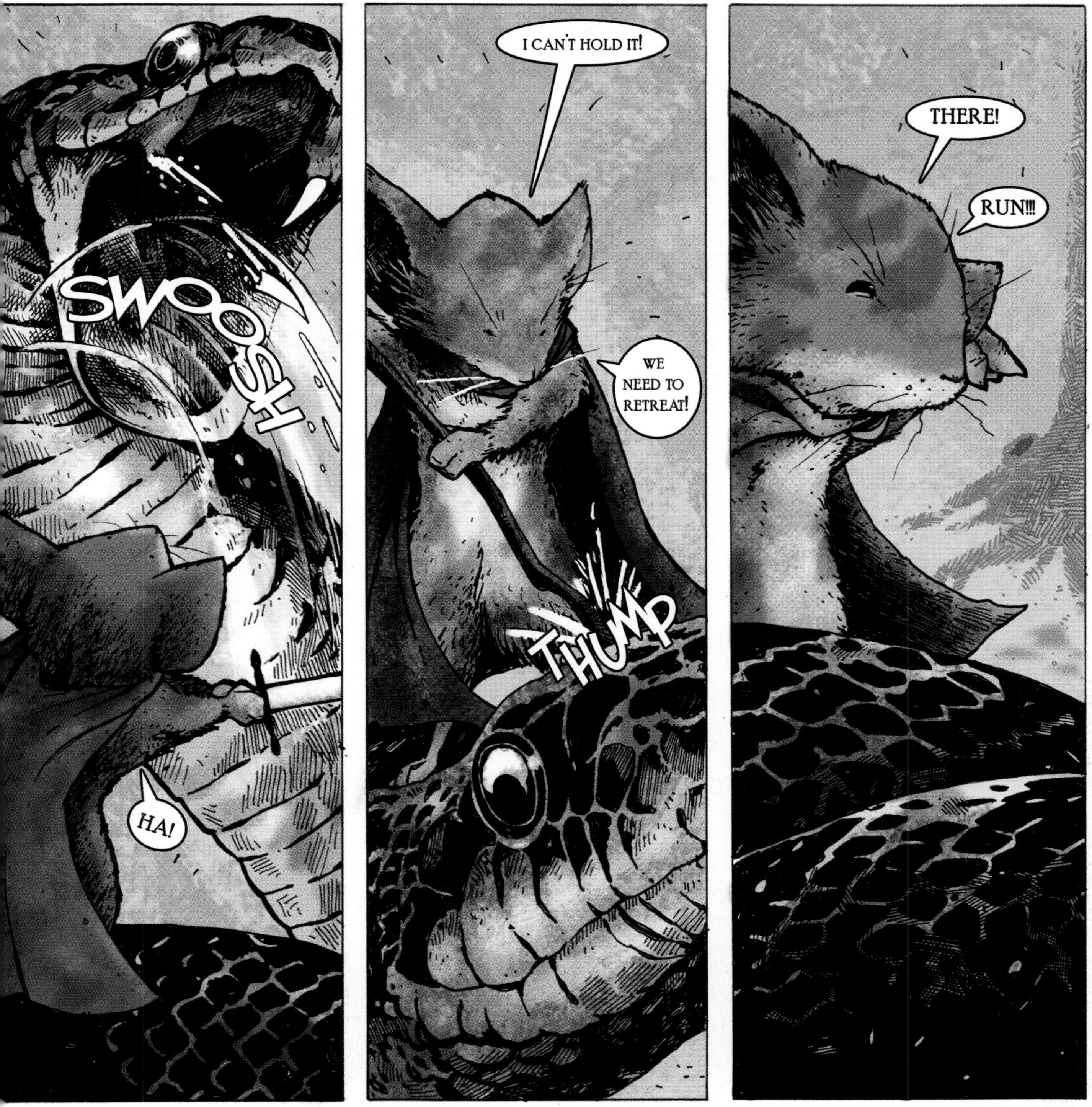
SWOOSH
HA!
I CAN'T HOLD IT!
WE NEED TO RETREAT!
THUMP
THERE!
RUN!!!

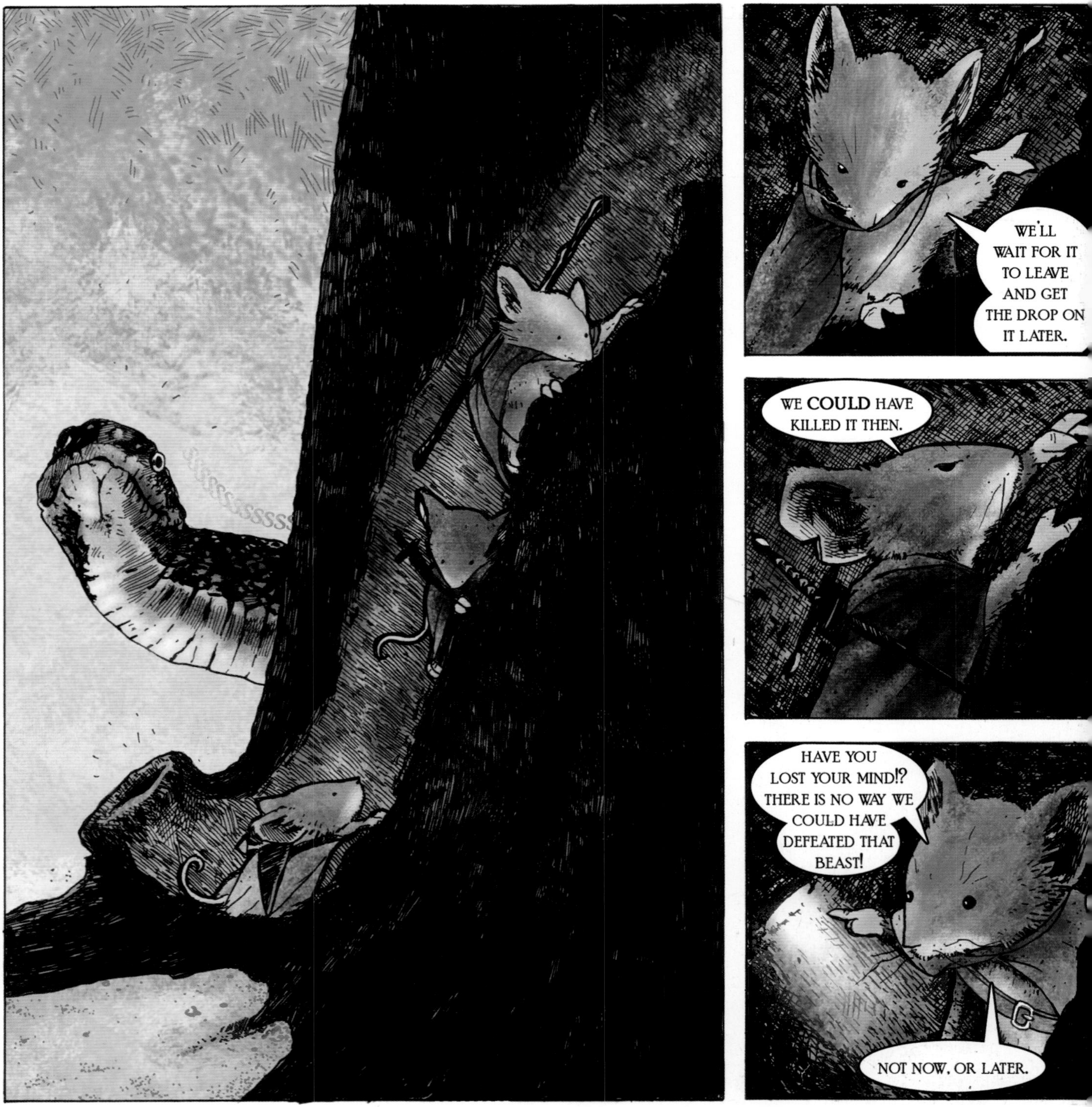
WE'LL WAIT FOR IT TO LEAVE AND GET THE DROP ON IT LATER.
WE **COULD** HAVE KILLED IT THEN.
HAVE YOU LOST YOUR MIND!? THERE IS NO WAY WE COULD HAVE DEFEATED THAT BEAST!
NOT NOW, OR LATER.

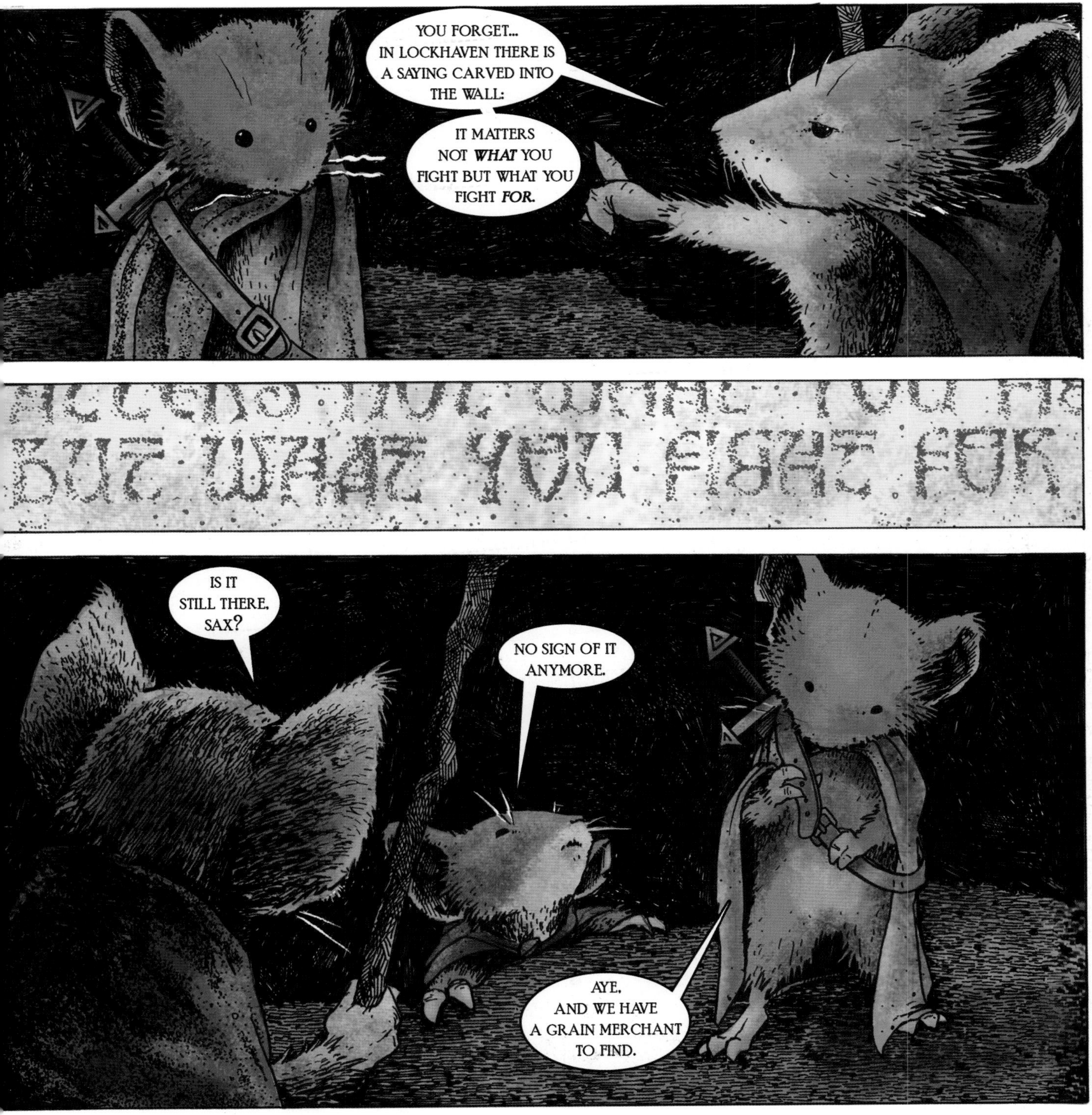
YOU FORGET... IN LOCKHAVEN THERE IS A SAYING CARVED INTO THE WALL:
IT MATTERS NOT *WHAT* YOU FIGHT BUT WHAT YOU FIGHT *FOR.*
BUT WHAT YOU FIGHT FOR
IS IT STILL THERE, SAX?
NO SIGN OF IT ANYMORE.
AYE, AND WE HAVE A GRAIN MERCHANT TO FIND.

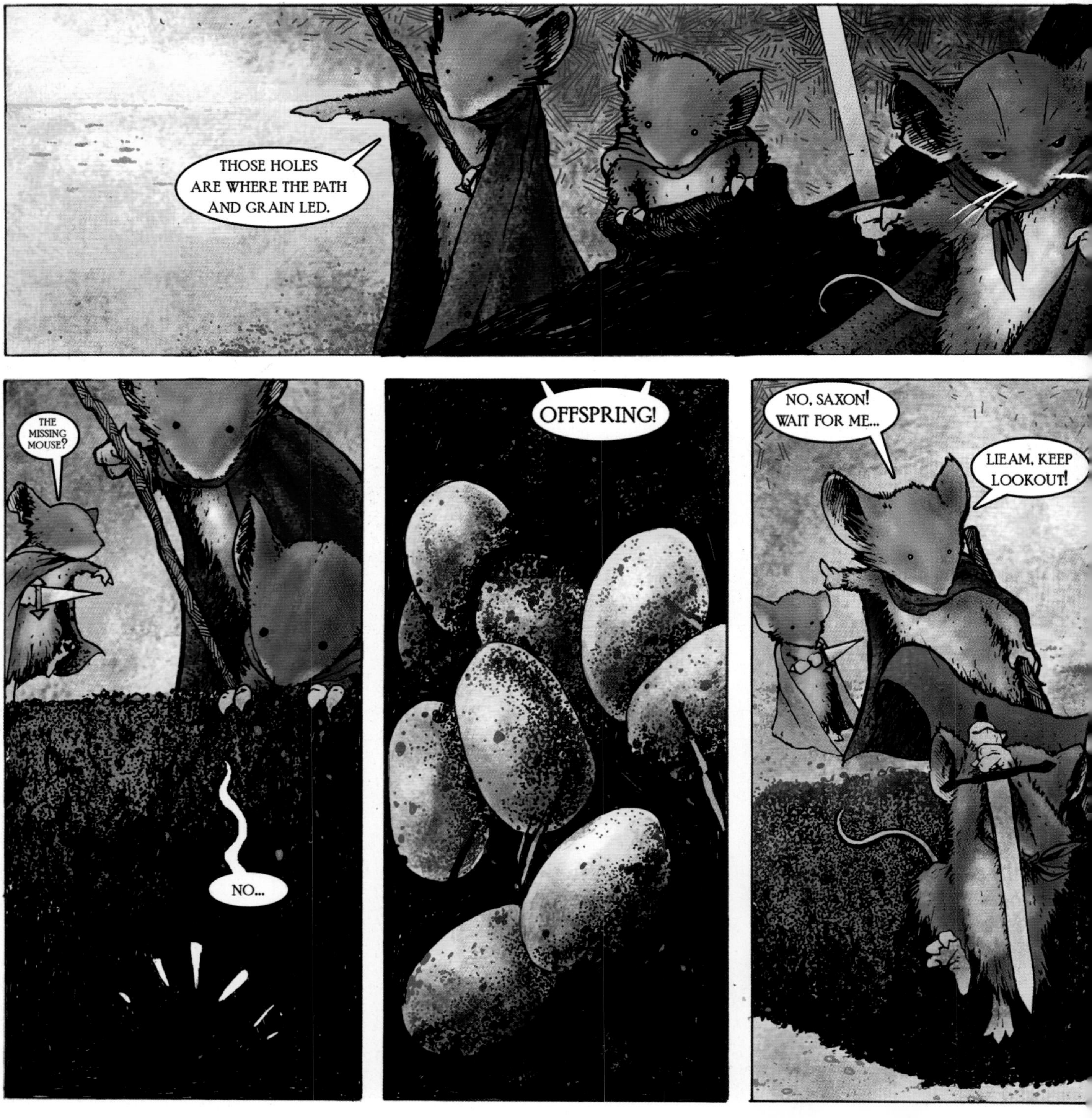
THOSE HOLES ARE WHERE THE PATH AND GRAIN LED.
THE MISSING MOUSE?
NO...
OFFSPRING!
NO, SAXON! WAIT FOR ME...
LIEAM, KEEP LOOKOUT!

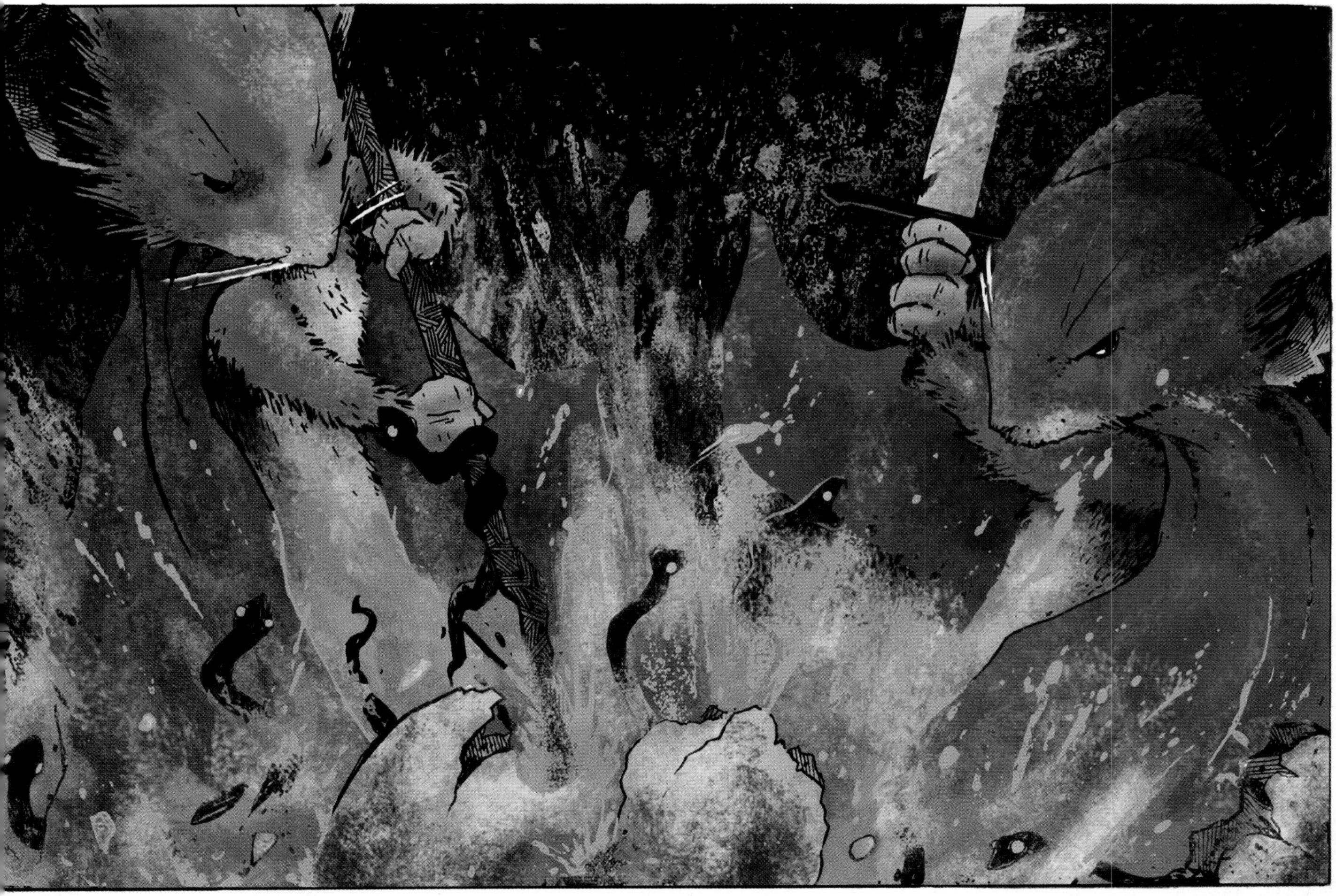

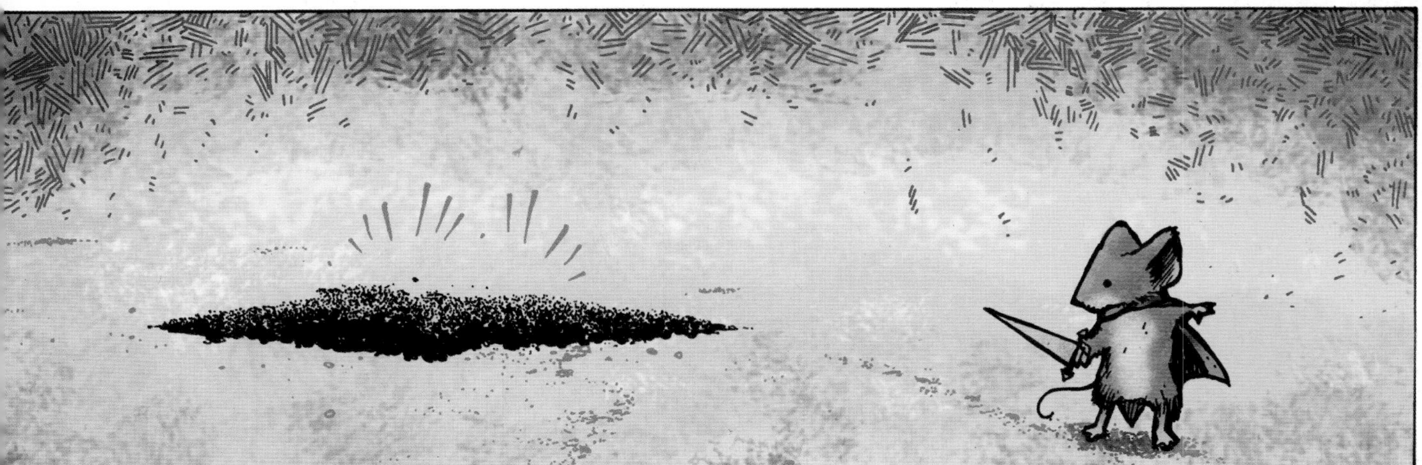

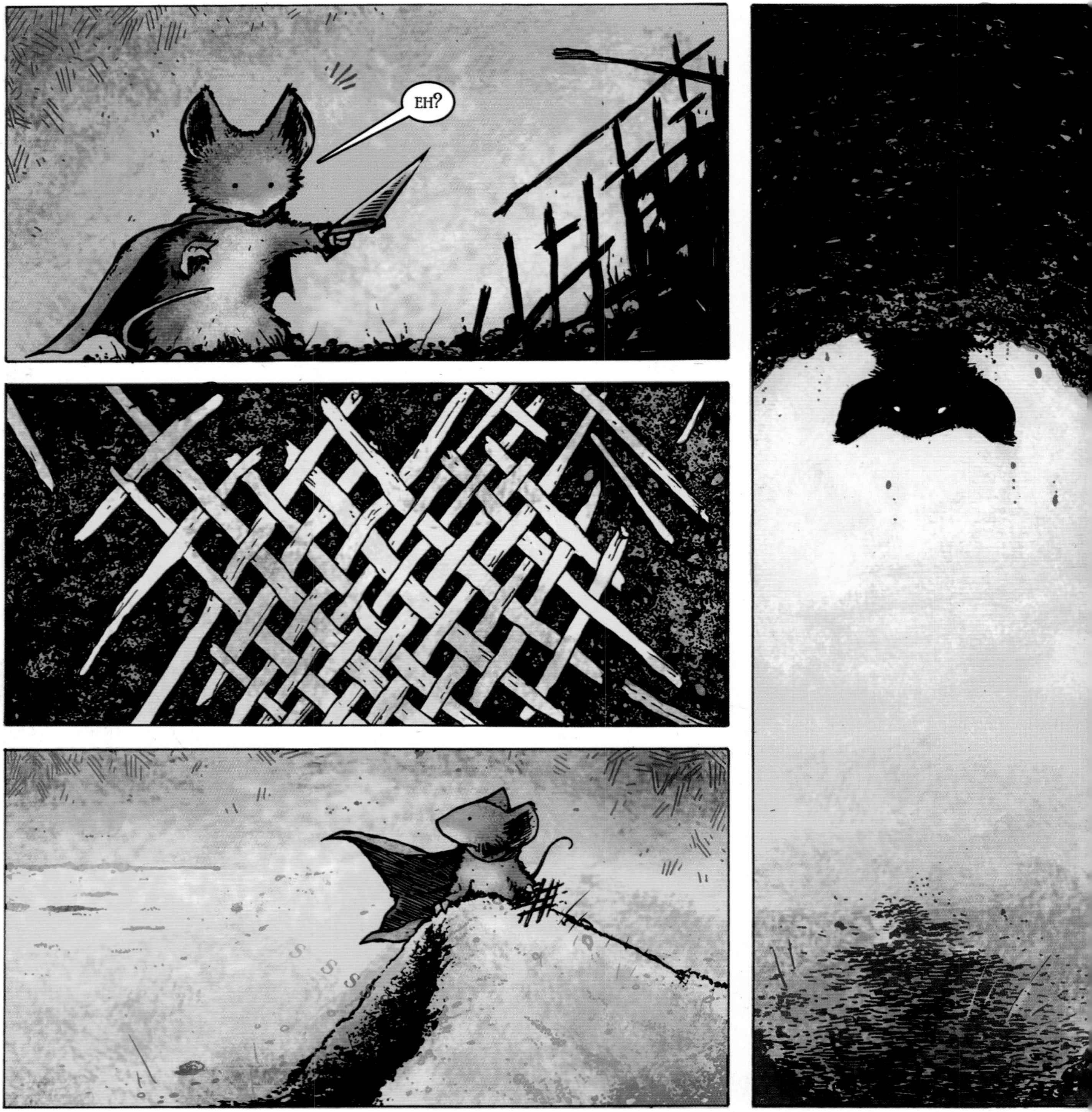
EH?
S S S

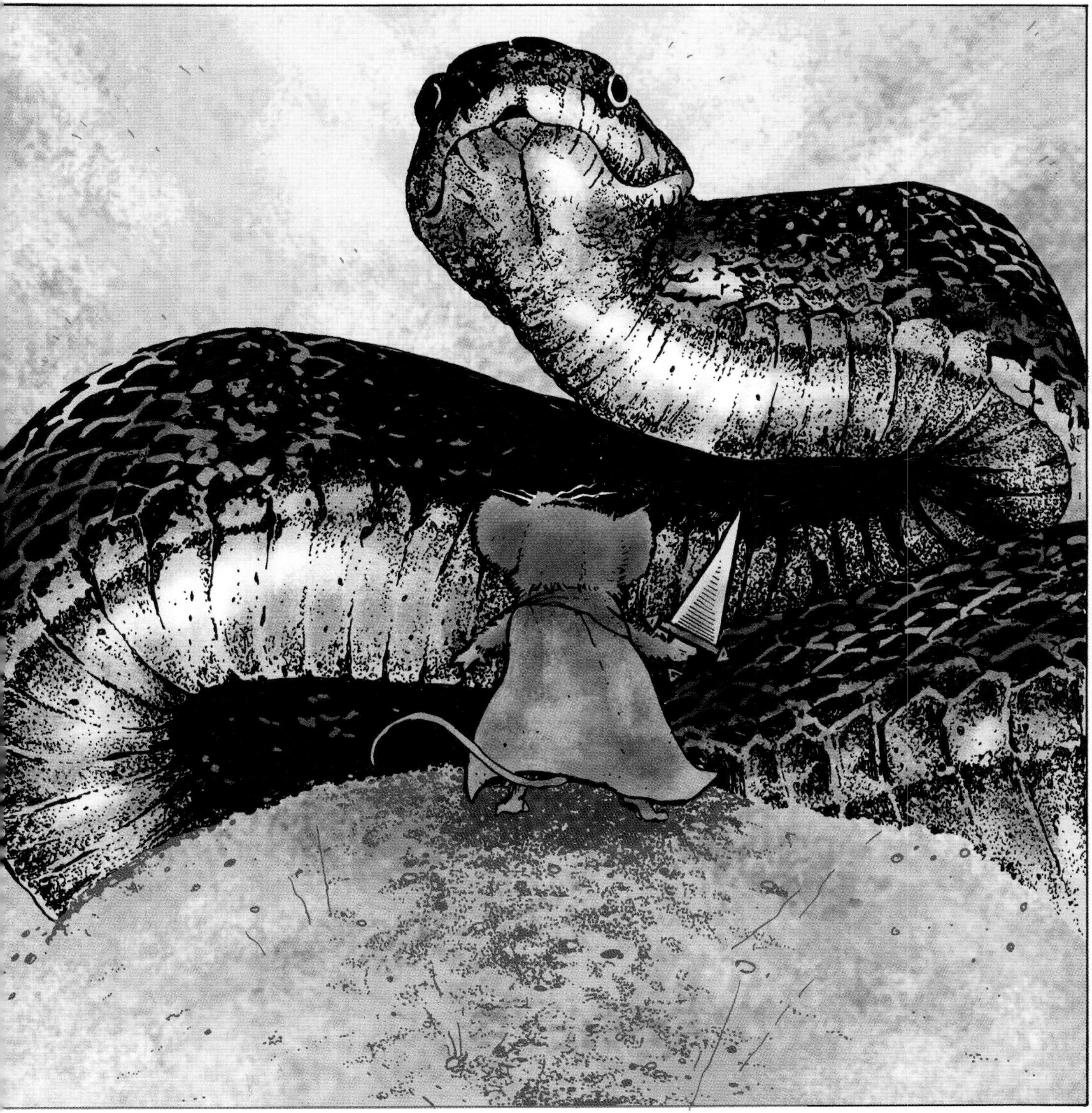

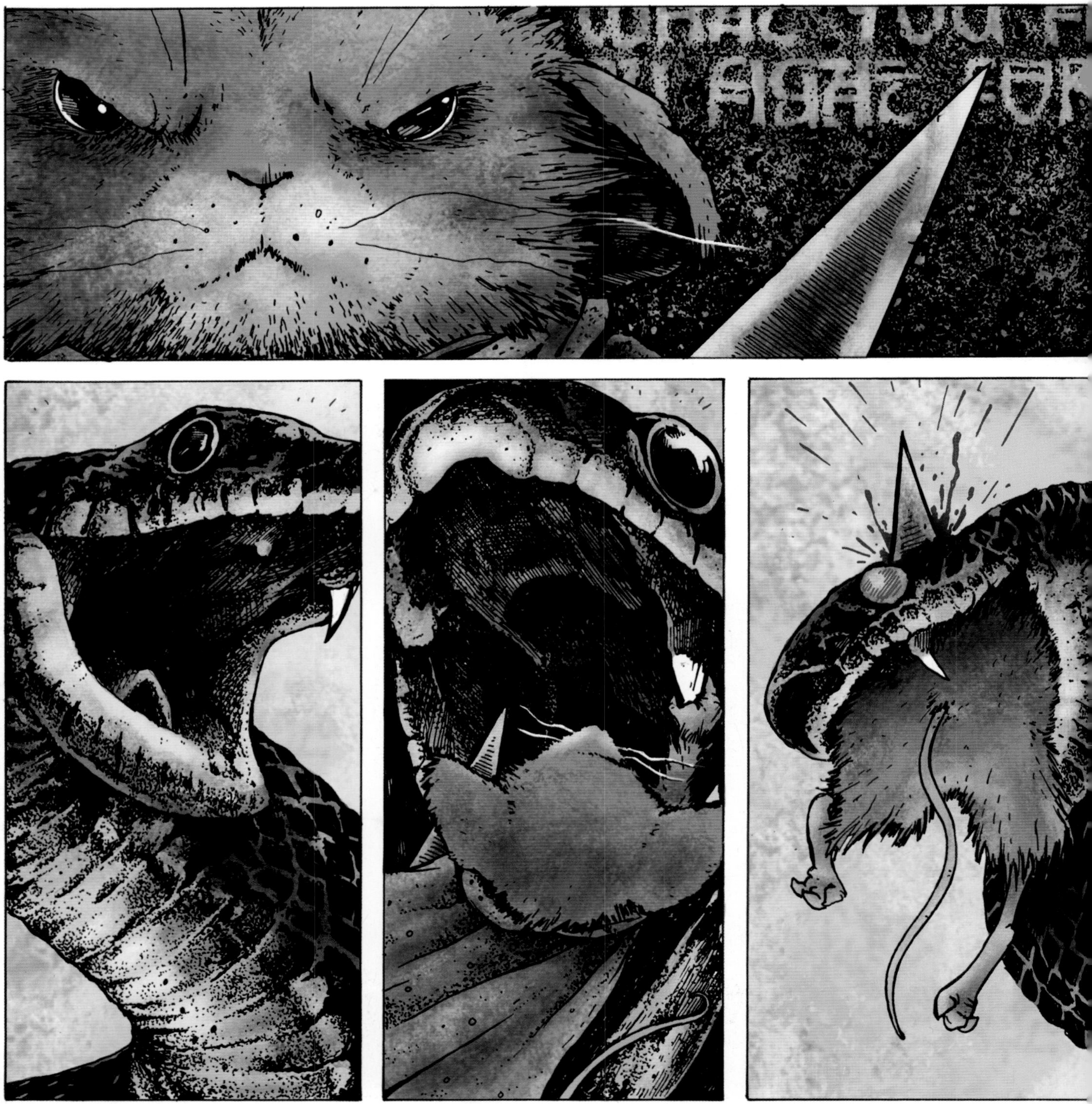

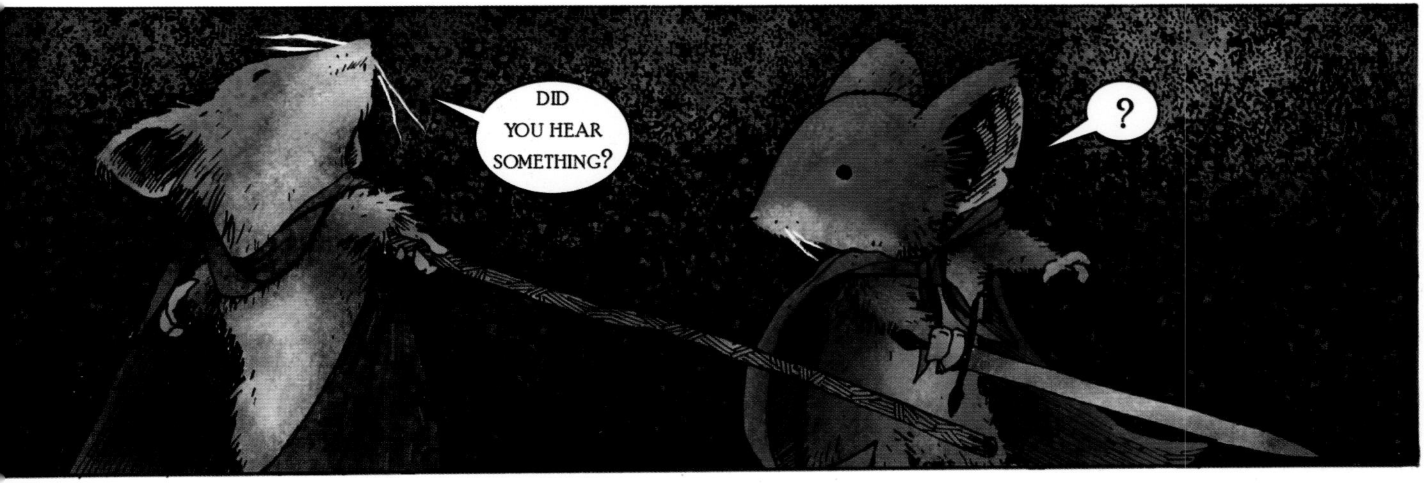
DID YOU HEAR SOMETHING?
?

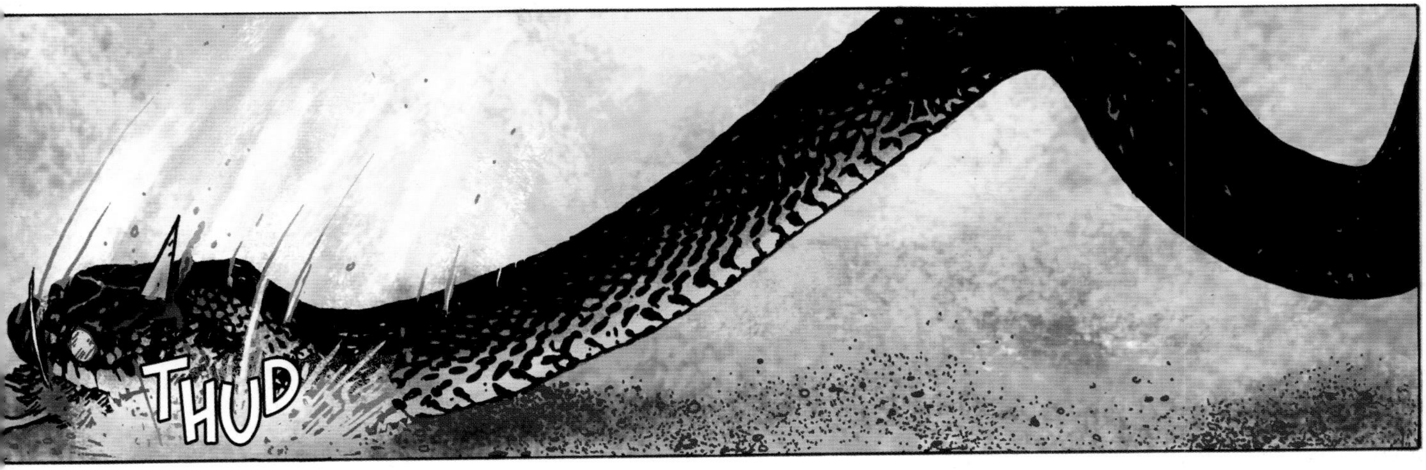
THUD

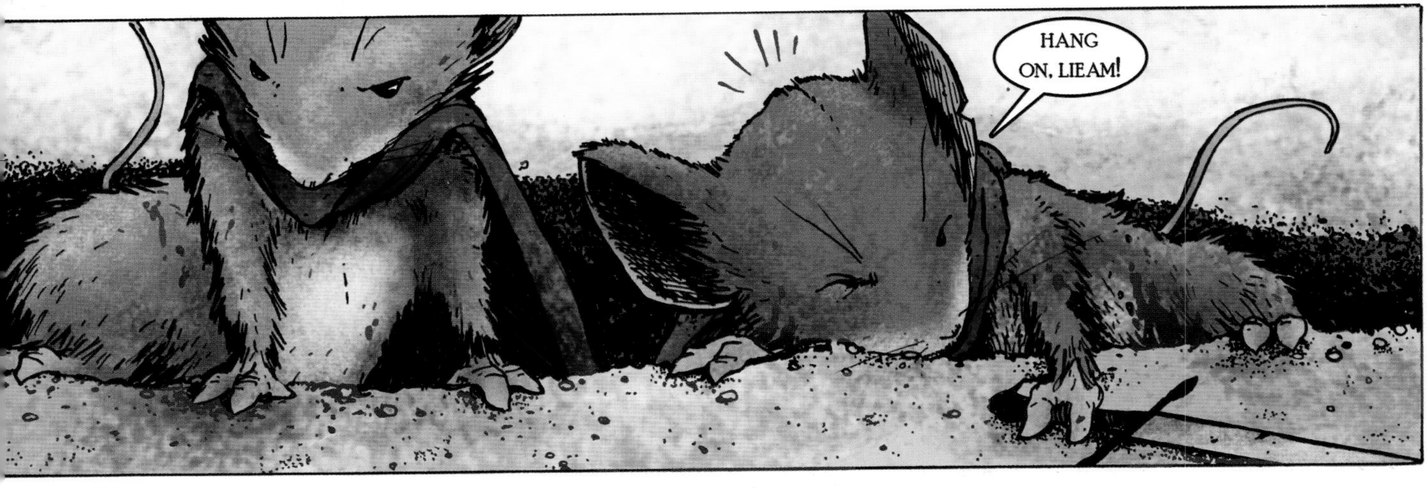
HANG ON, LIEAM!

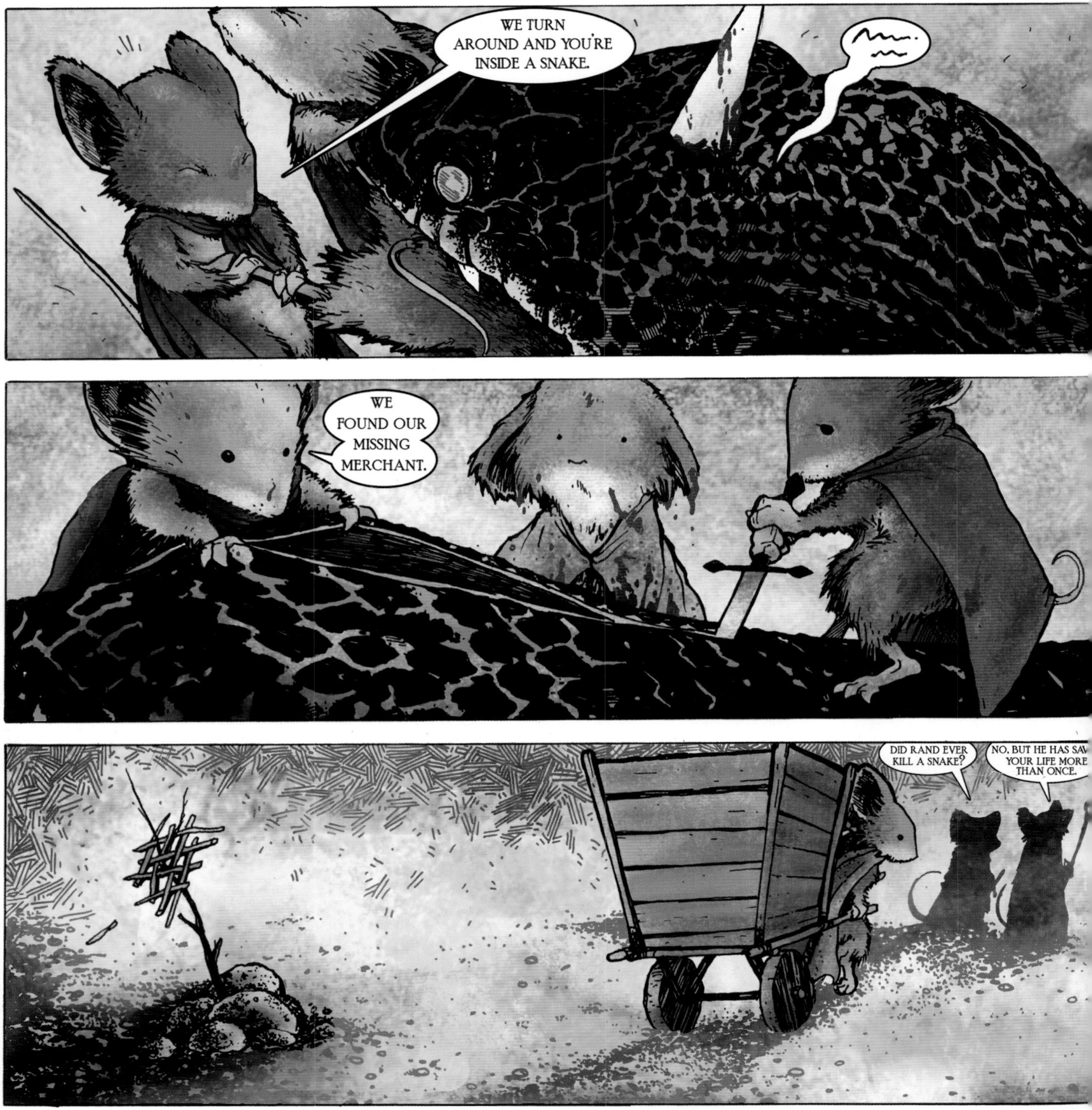
WE TURN AROUND AND YOU'RE INSIDE A SNAKE.
WE FOUND OUR MISSING MERCHANT.
DID RAND EVER KILL A SNAKE?
NO, BUT HE HAS SAV YOUR LIFE MORE THAN ONCE.

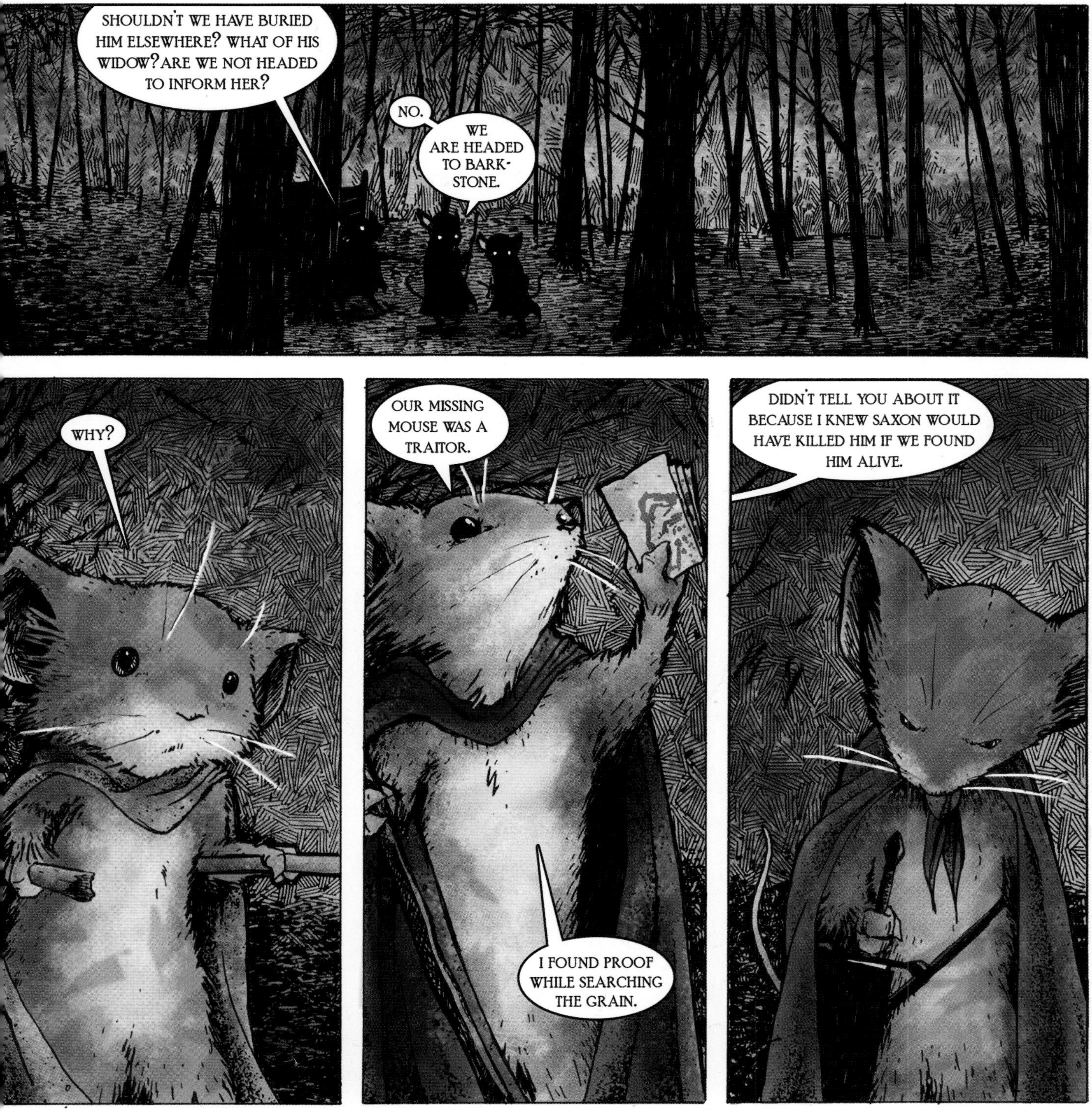
SHOULDN'T WE HAVE BURIED HIM ELSEWHERE? WHAT OF HIS WIDOW? ARE WE NOT HEADED TO INFORM HER?
NO.
WE ARE HEADED TO BARK-STONE.
WHY?
OUR MISSING MOUSE WAS A TRAITOR.
I FOUND PROOF WHILE SEARCHING THE GRAIN.
DIDN'T TELL YOU ABOUT IT BECAUSE I KNEW SAXON WOULD HAVE KILLED HIM IF WE FOUND HIM ALIVE.

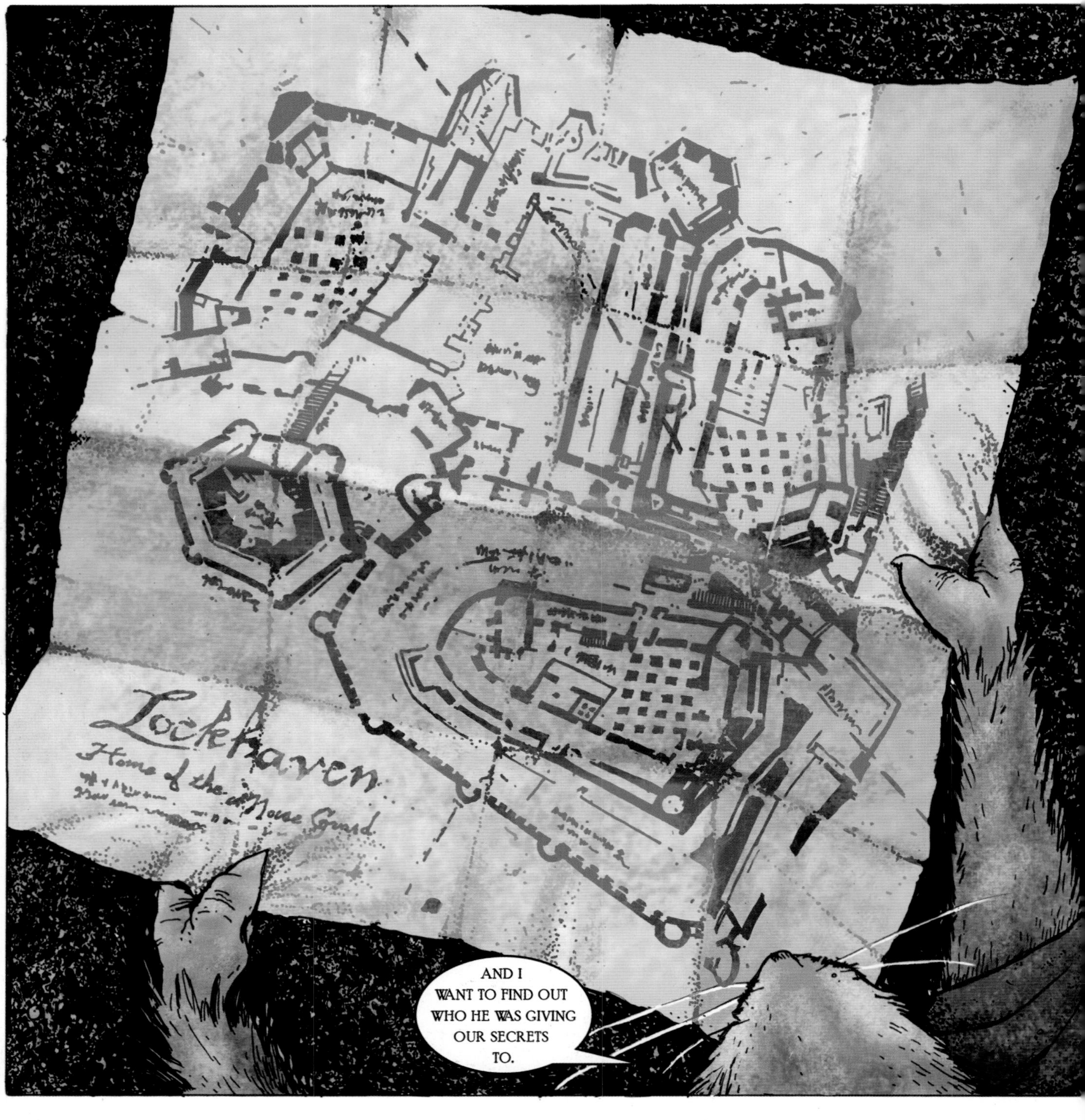
Lockhaven
Home of the Mouse Guard
AND I WANT TO FIND OUT WHO HE WAS GIVING OUR SECRETS TO.

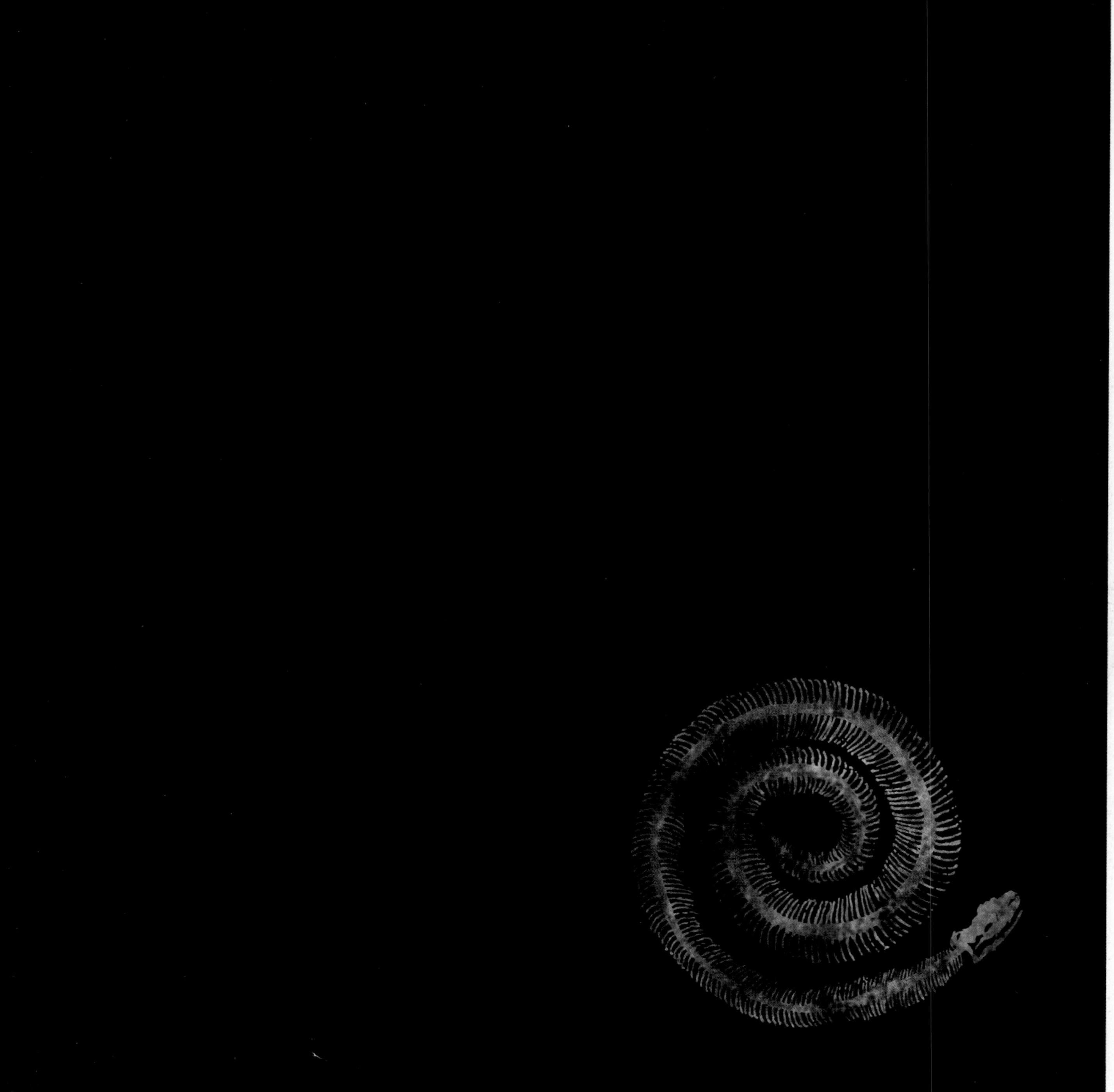

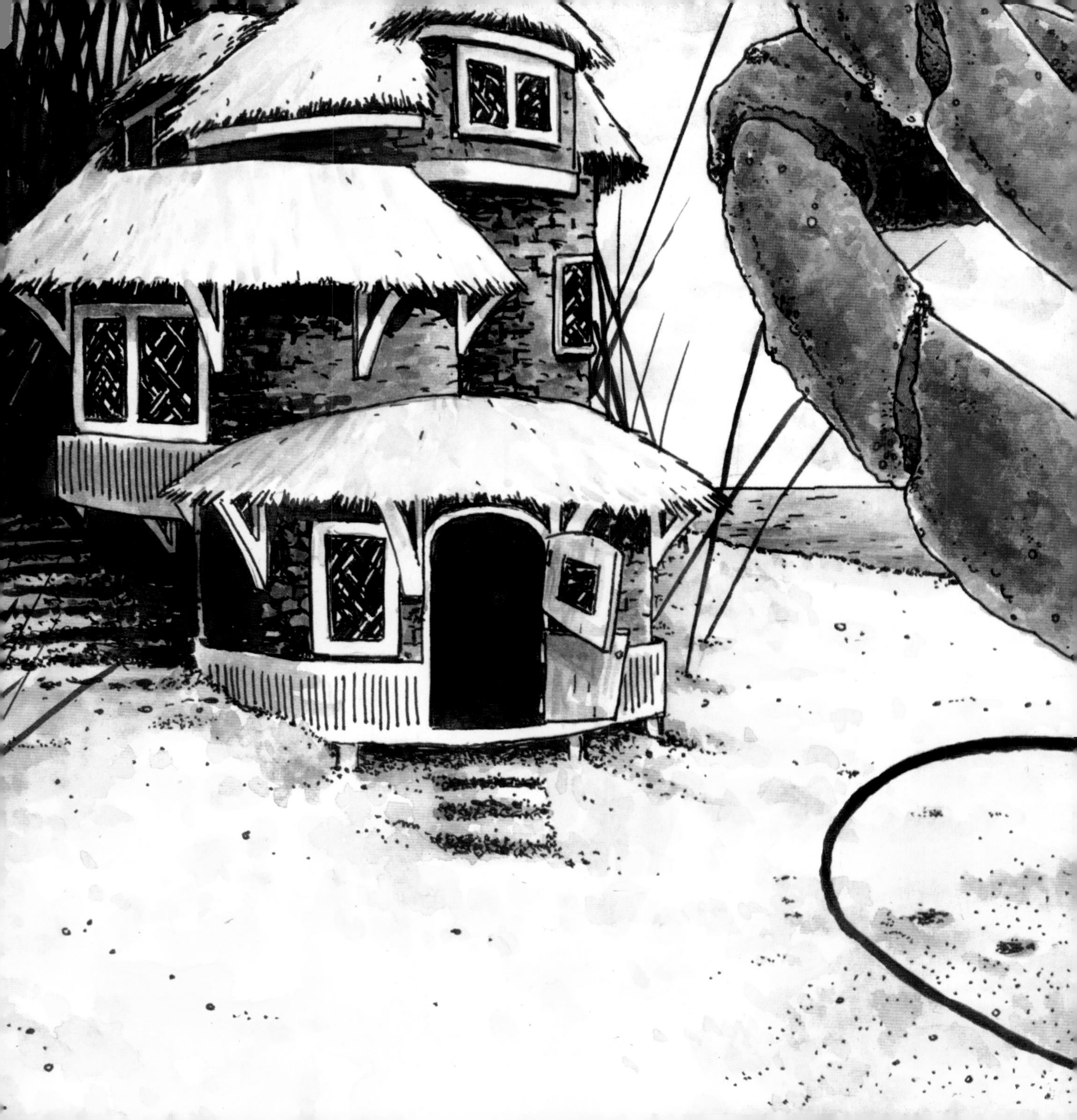

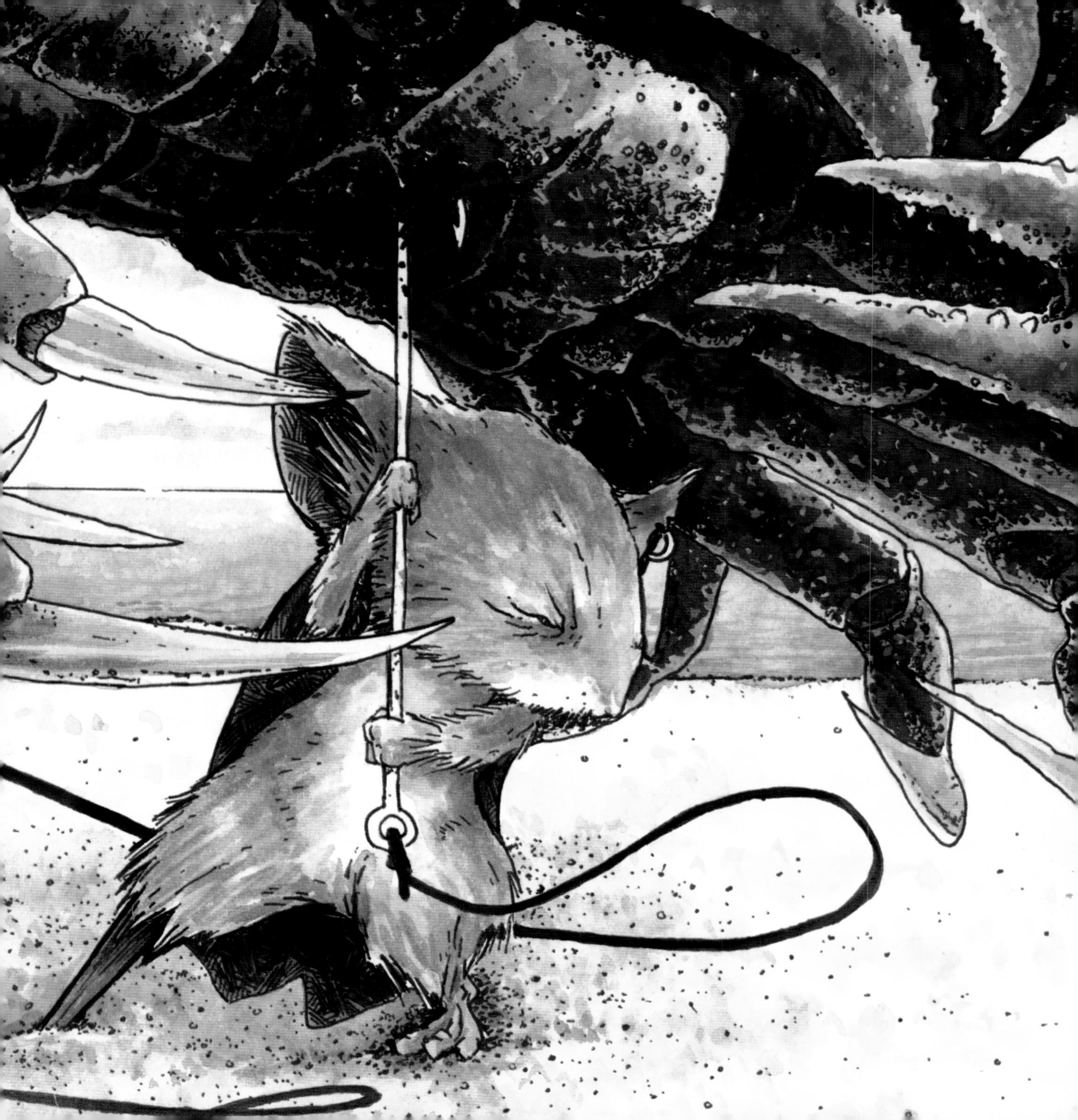

Chapter Two

Shadows Within

While Saxon, Kenzie, and Lieam were tracking the path of the grain merchant, Gwendolyn, head of the Mouse Guard, sent word to Sadie. Sadie, who once watched a shoreline region of the Mouse Territories, has been asked to make contact with another missing mouse, Guard member Conrad. There has been no outgoing communication from his shoreline dwelling, Calogero, and the Guard fear the worst...

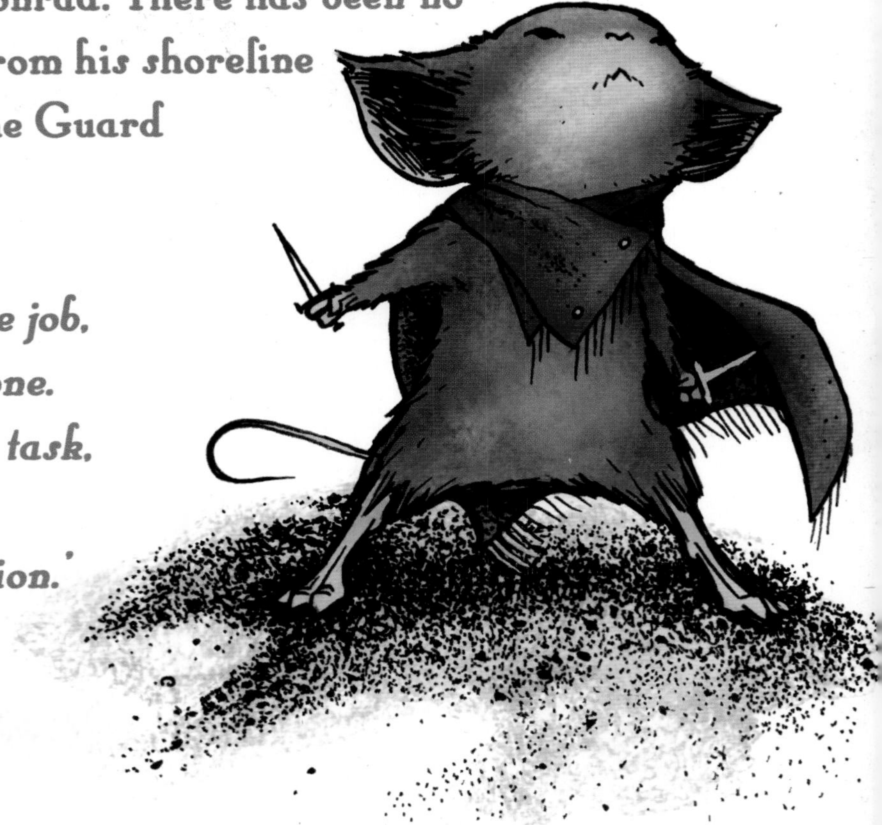

'Send any mouse to do the job,
it may or may not be done.
Ask the Guard to do the task,
even death cannot
prevent it from completion.'

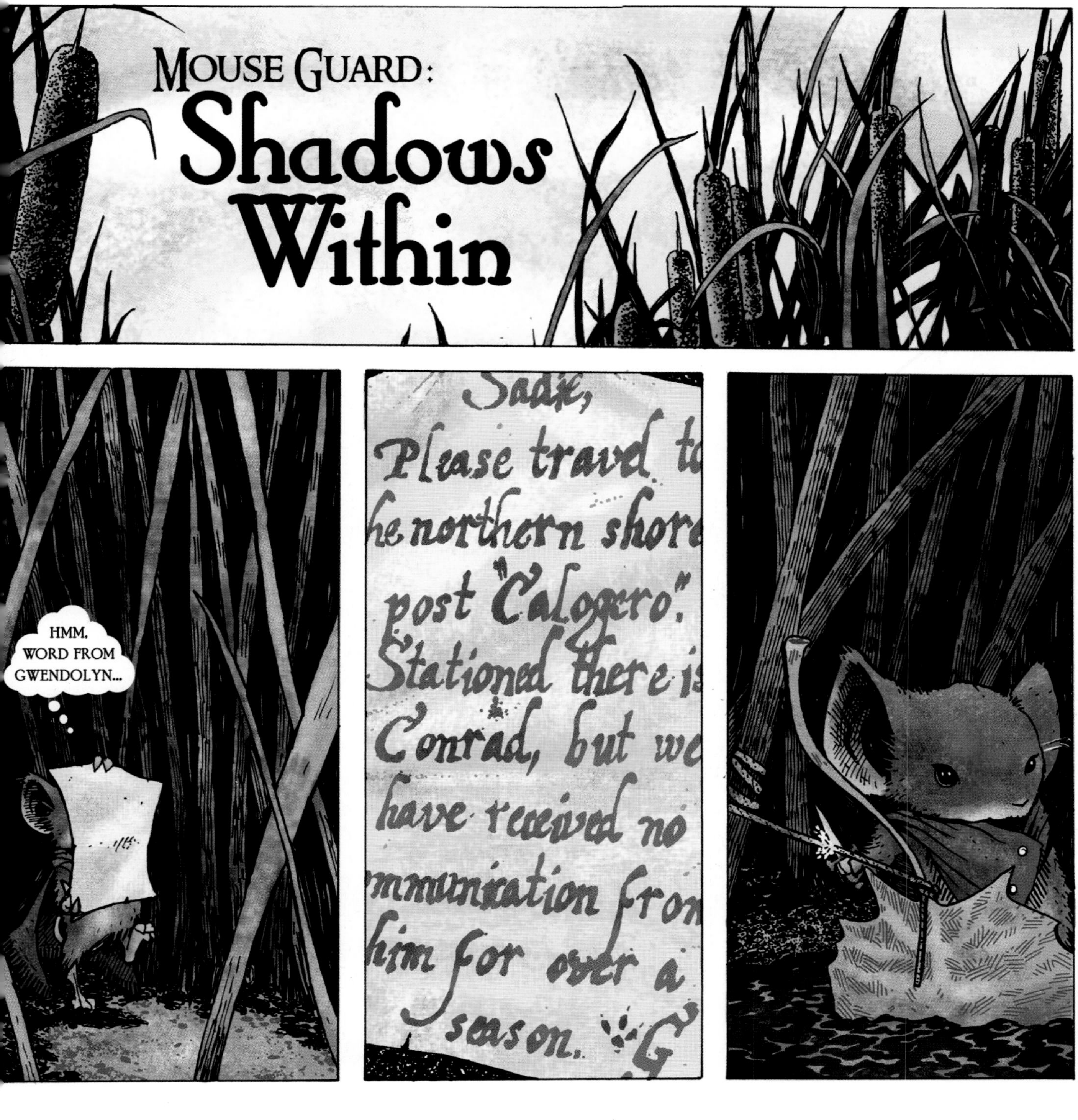
MOUSE GUARD:
Shadows Within
HMM, WORD FROM GWENDOLYN...
Sadie,
Please travel t
he northern shore
post "Calogero".
Stationed there is
Conrad, but we
have received no
mmunication from
him for over a
season. G

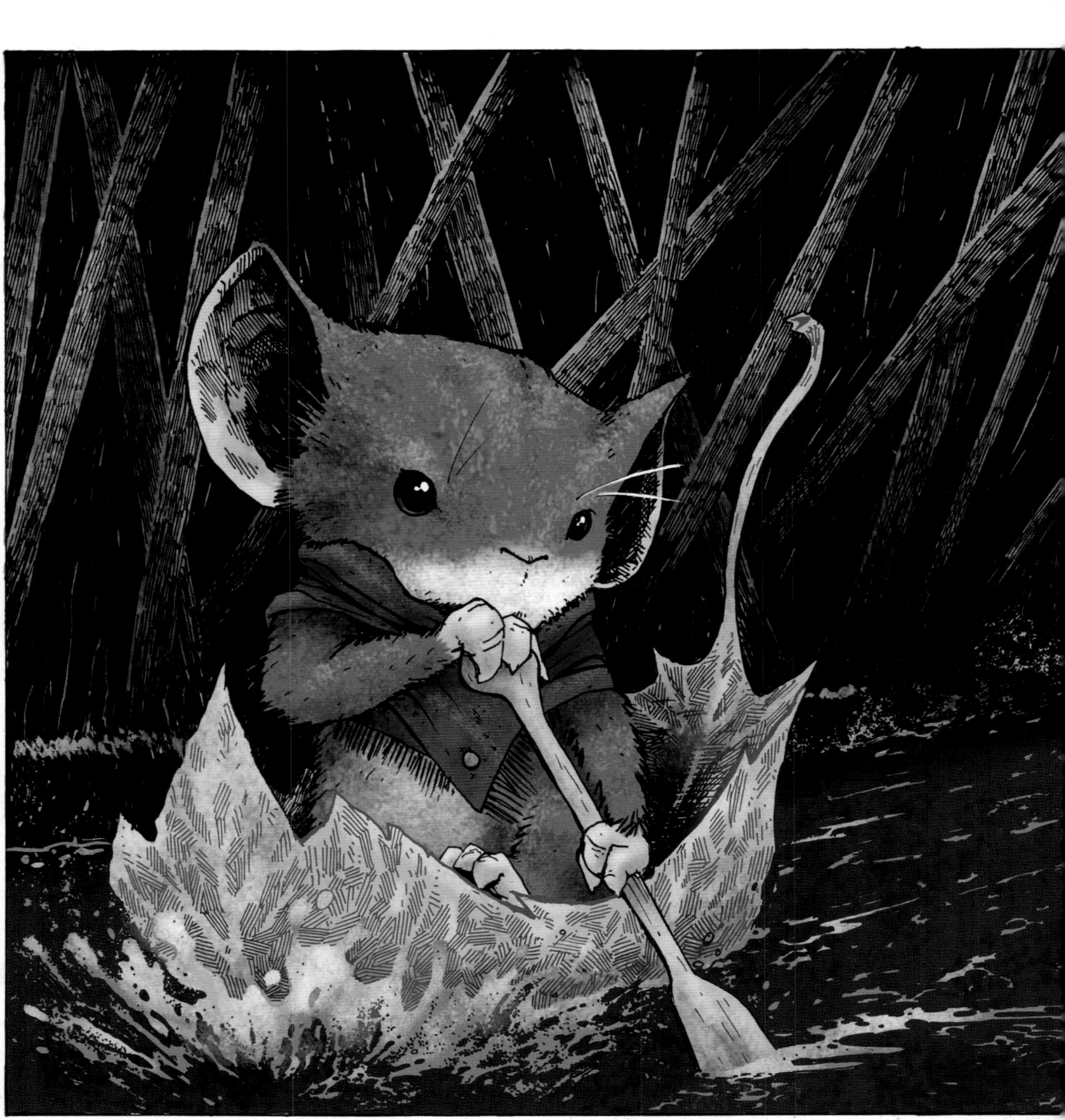

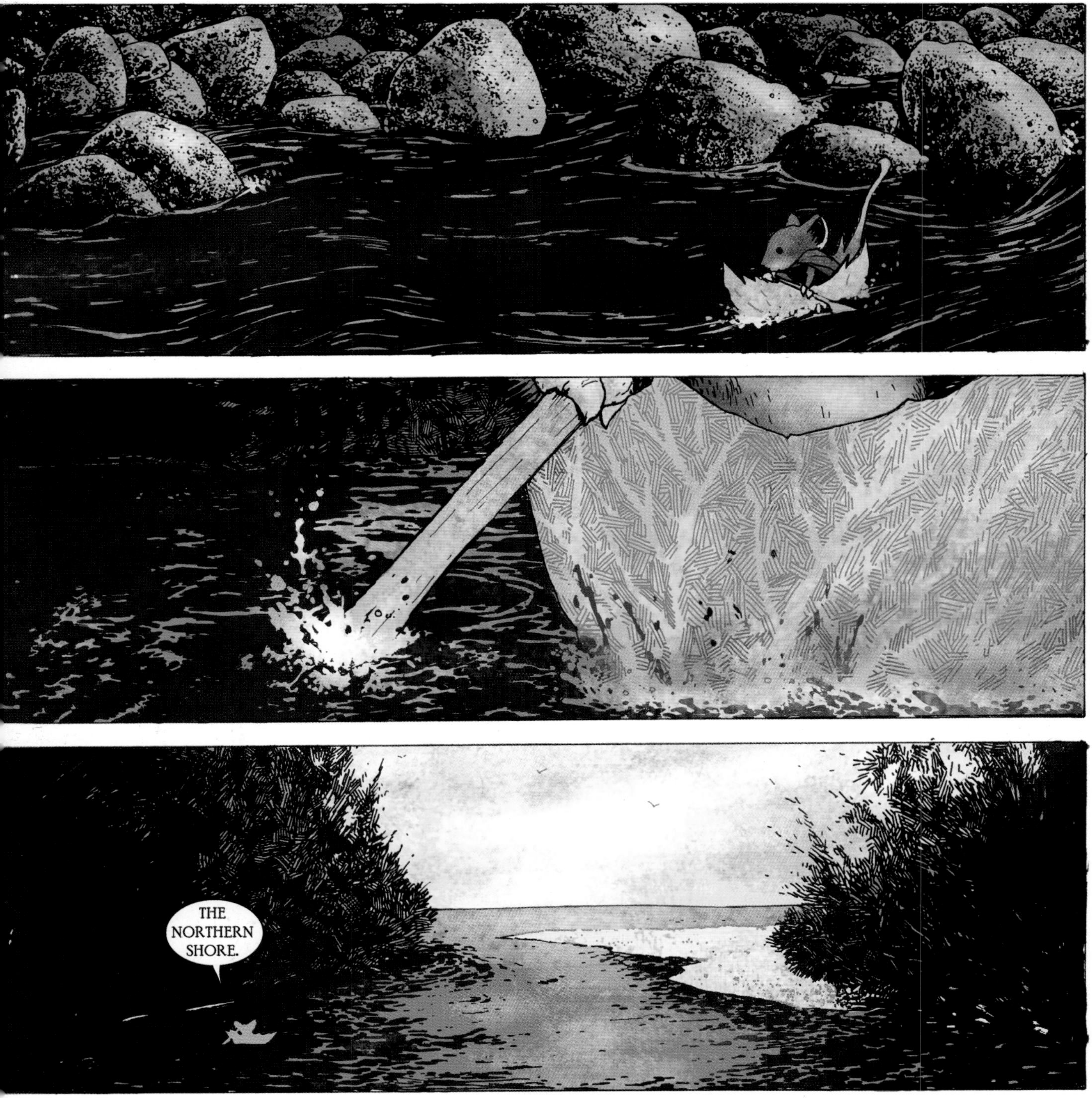
THE NORTHERN SHORE.

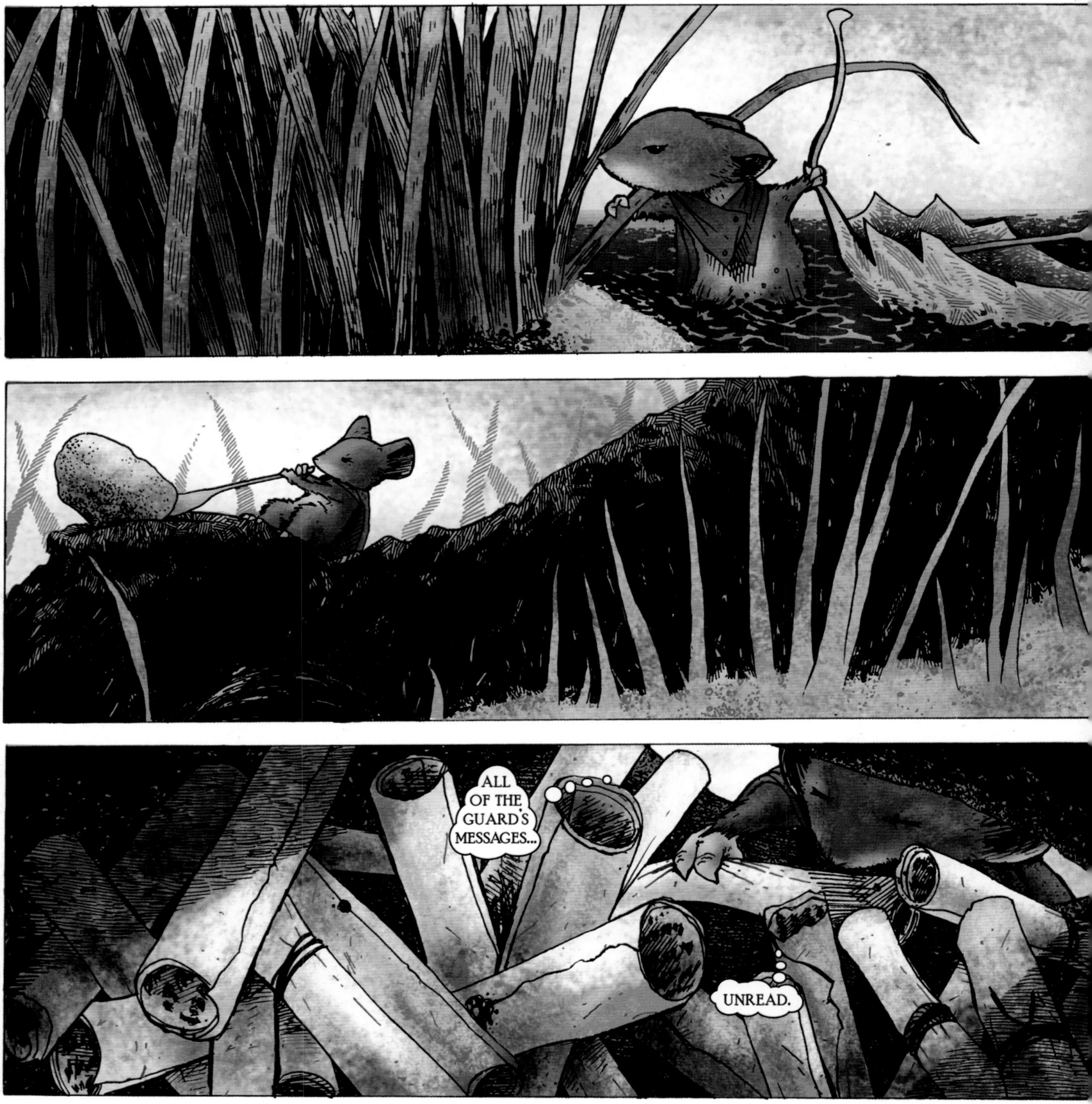
ALL OF THE GUARD'S MESSAGES...
UNREAD.

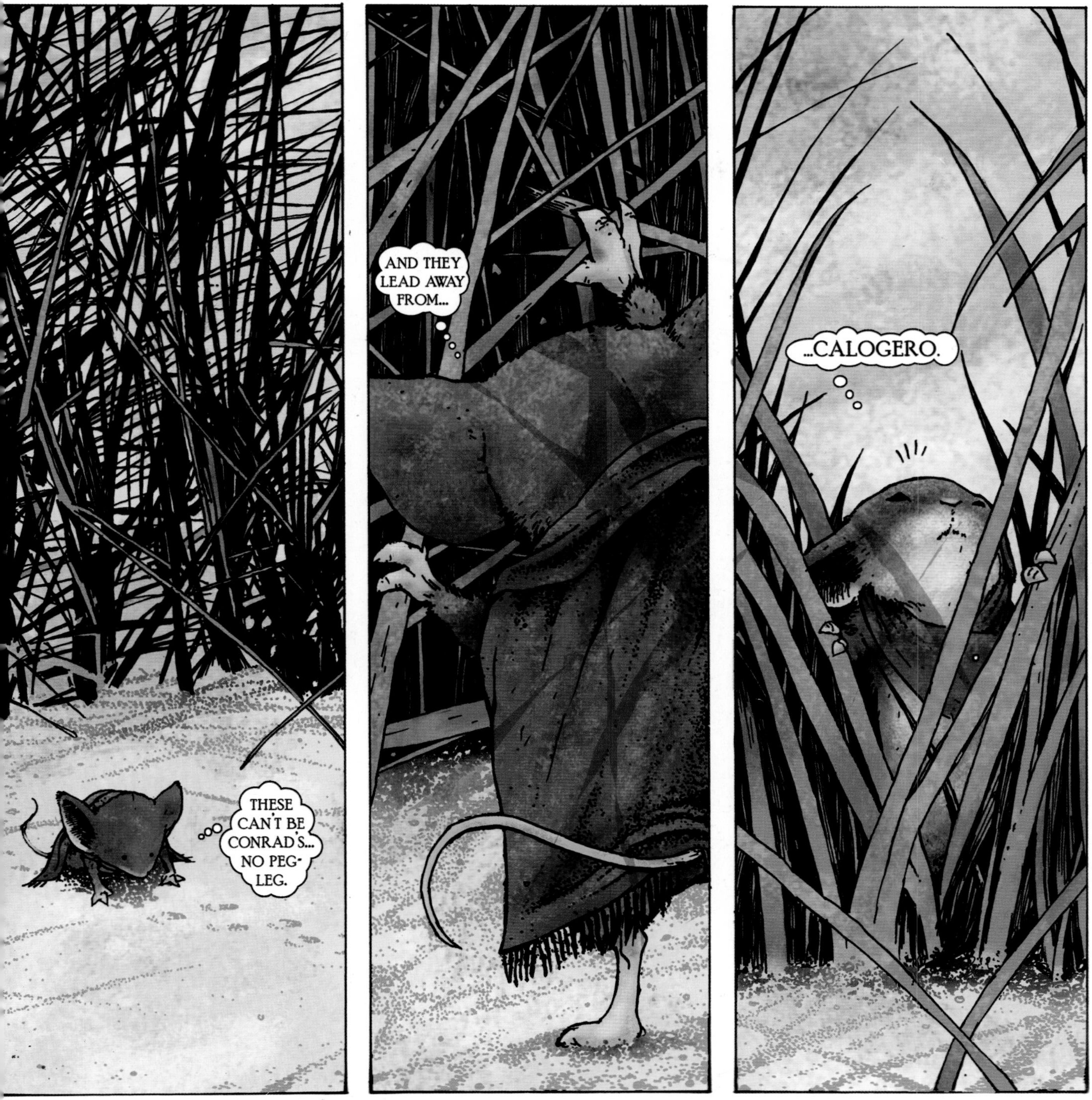
THESE CAN'T BE CONRAD'S... NO PEG-LEG.
AND THEY LEAD AWAY FROM...
...CALOGERO.

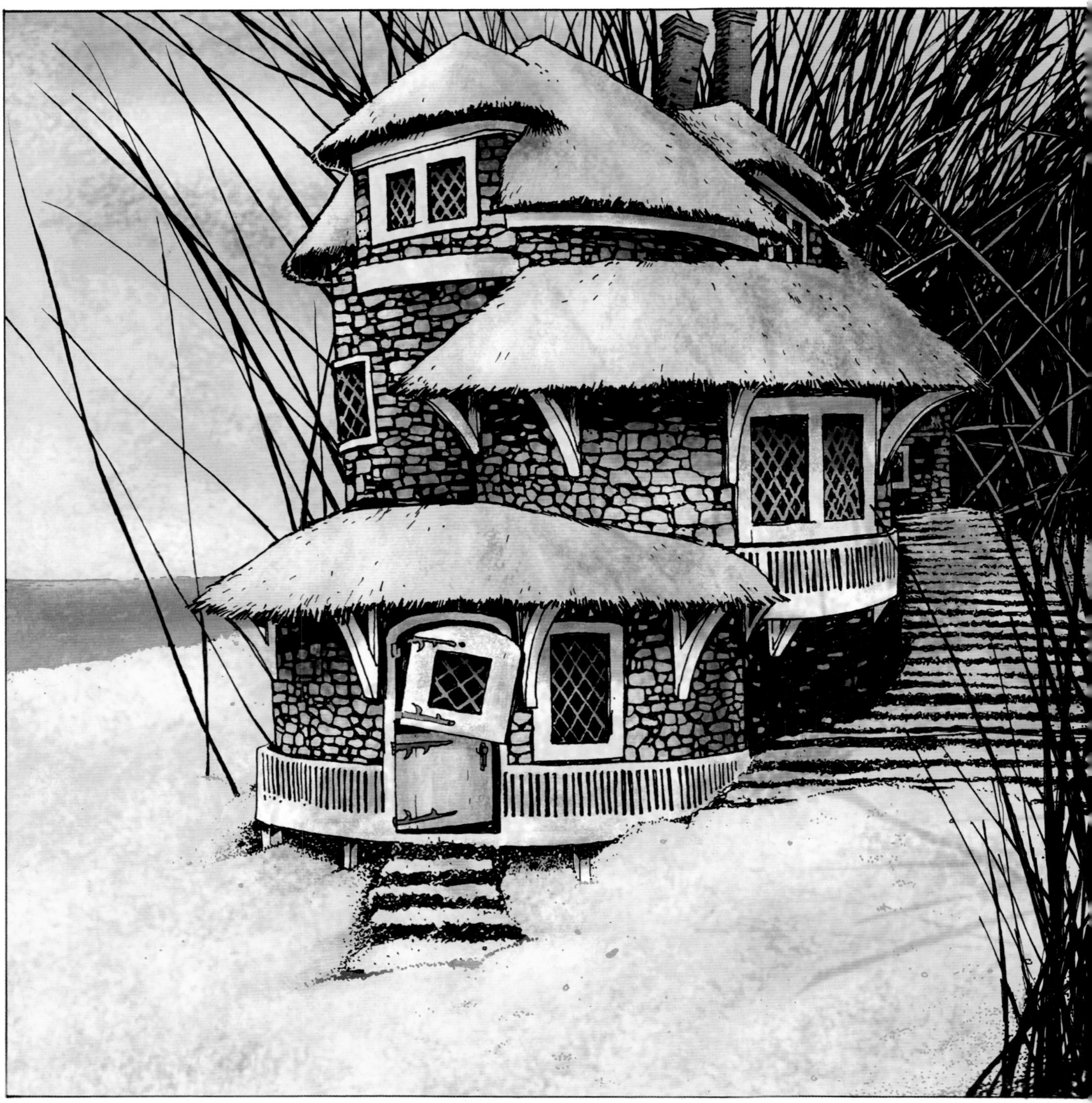

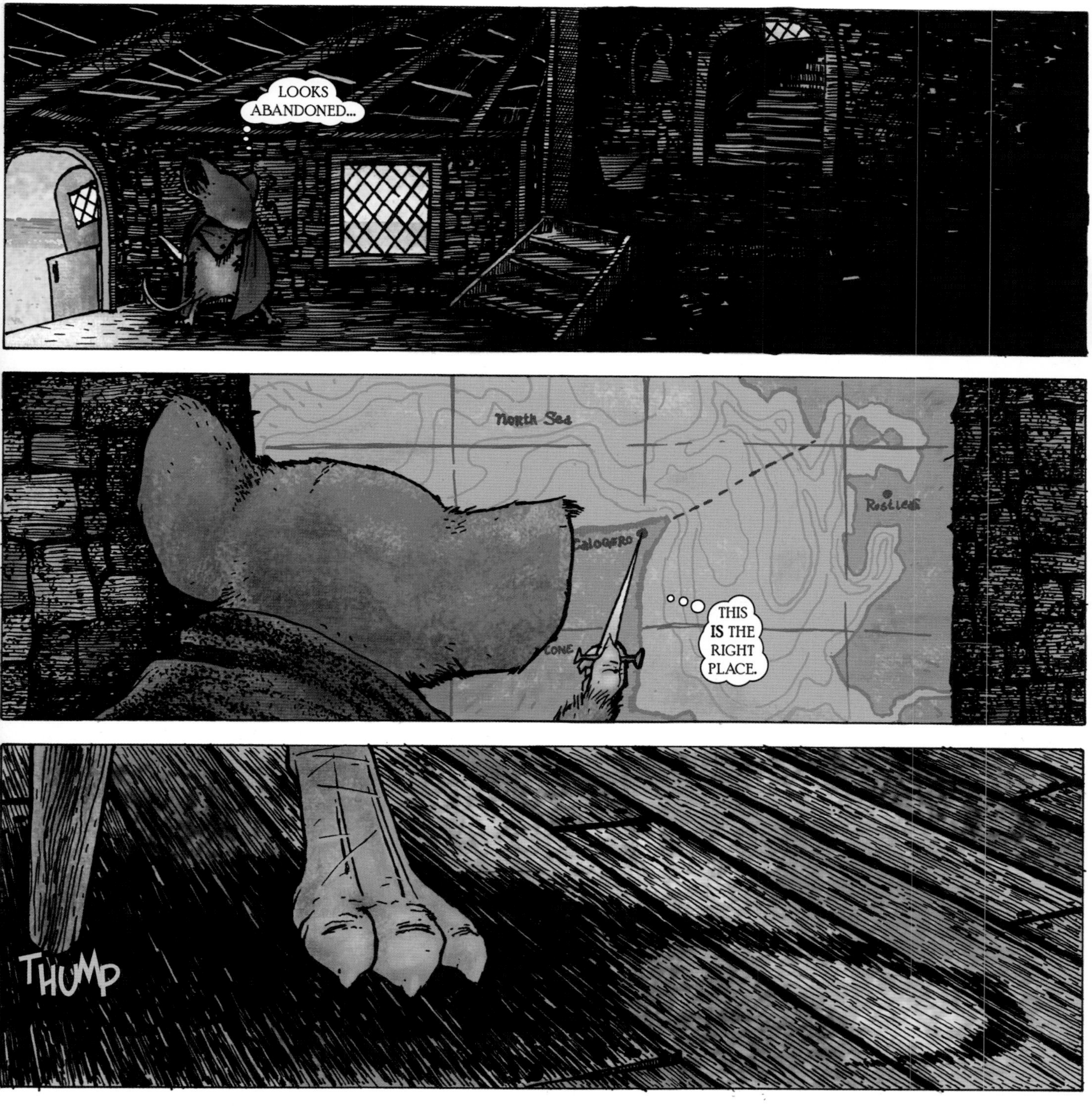
LOOKS ABANDONED...
North Sea
CALOGERO
THIS IS THE RIGHT PLACE.
THUMP

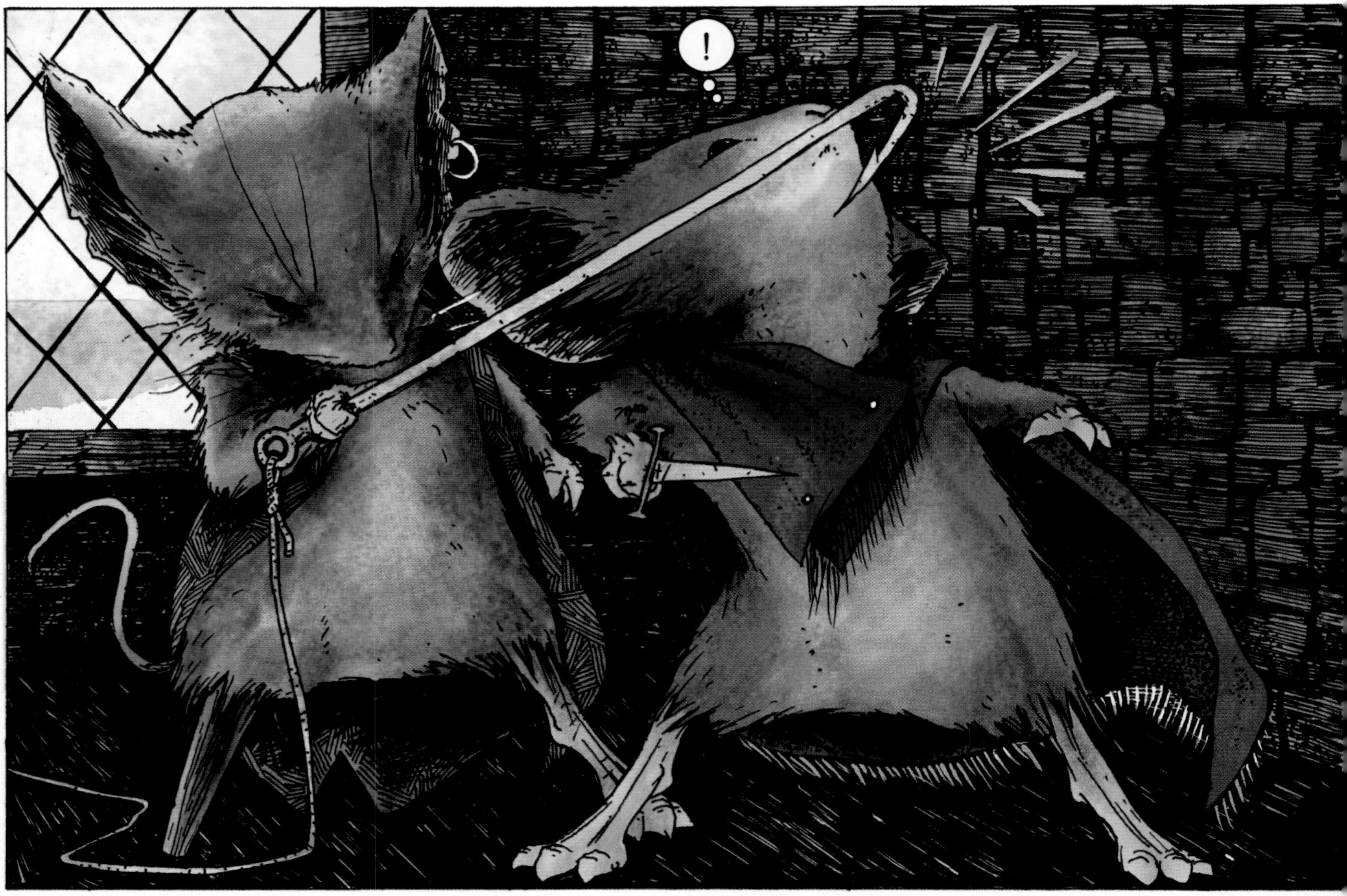
!

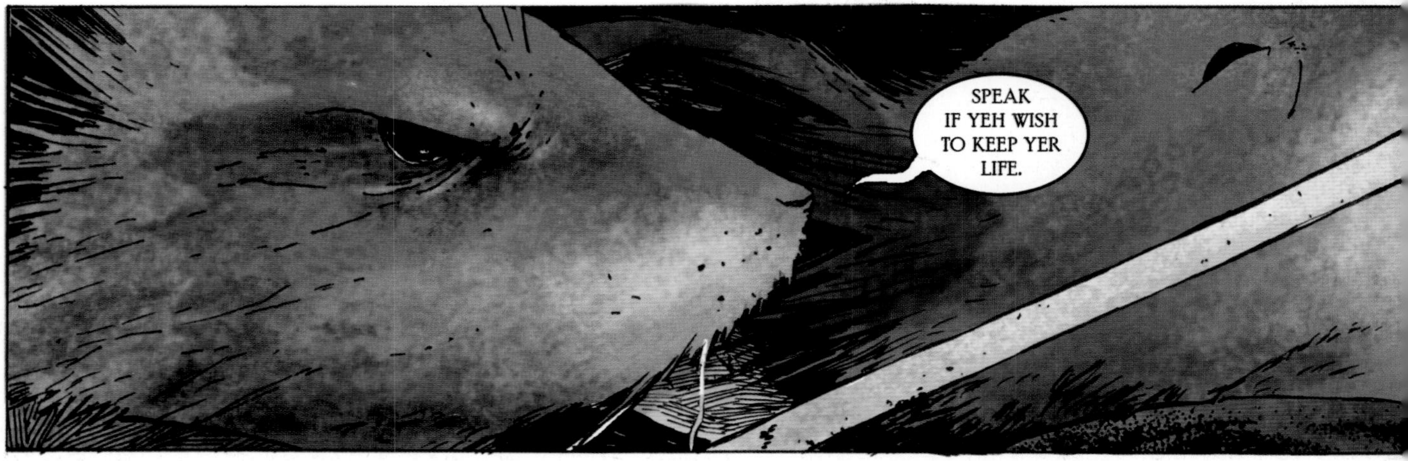
SPEAK IF YEH WISH TO KEEP YER LIFE.

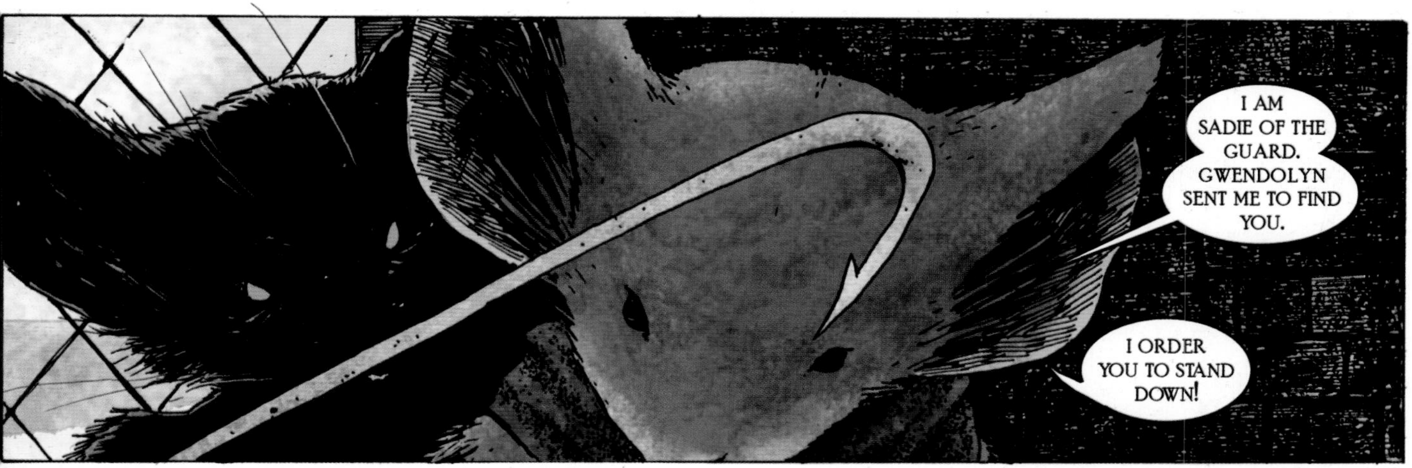
I AM SADIE OF THE GUARD. GWENDOLYN SENT ME TO FIND YOU.
I ORDER YOU TO STAND DOWN!

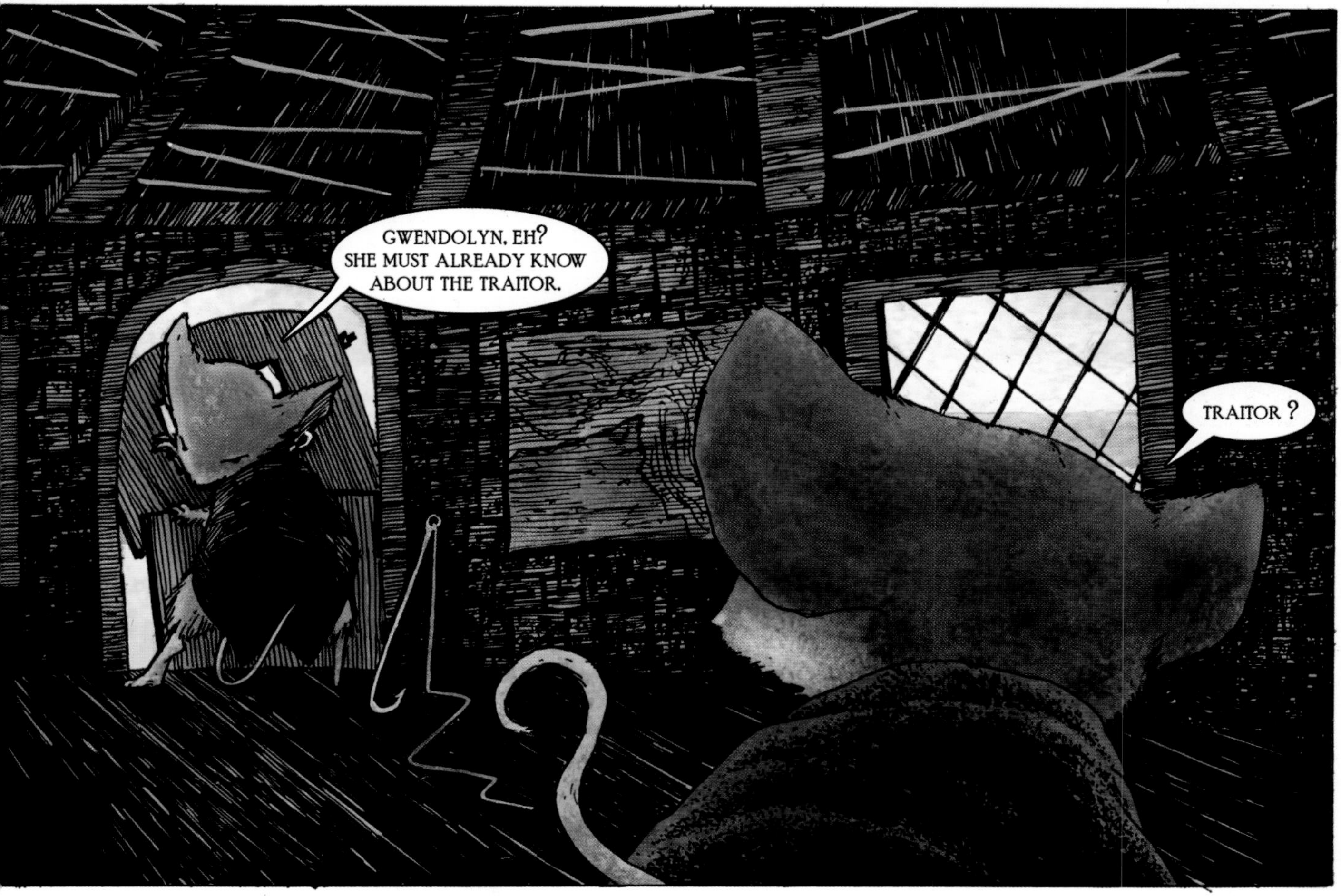
GWENDOLYN, EH? SHE MUST ALREADY KNOW ABOUT THE TRAITOR.
TRAITOR ?

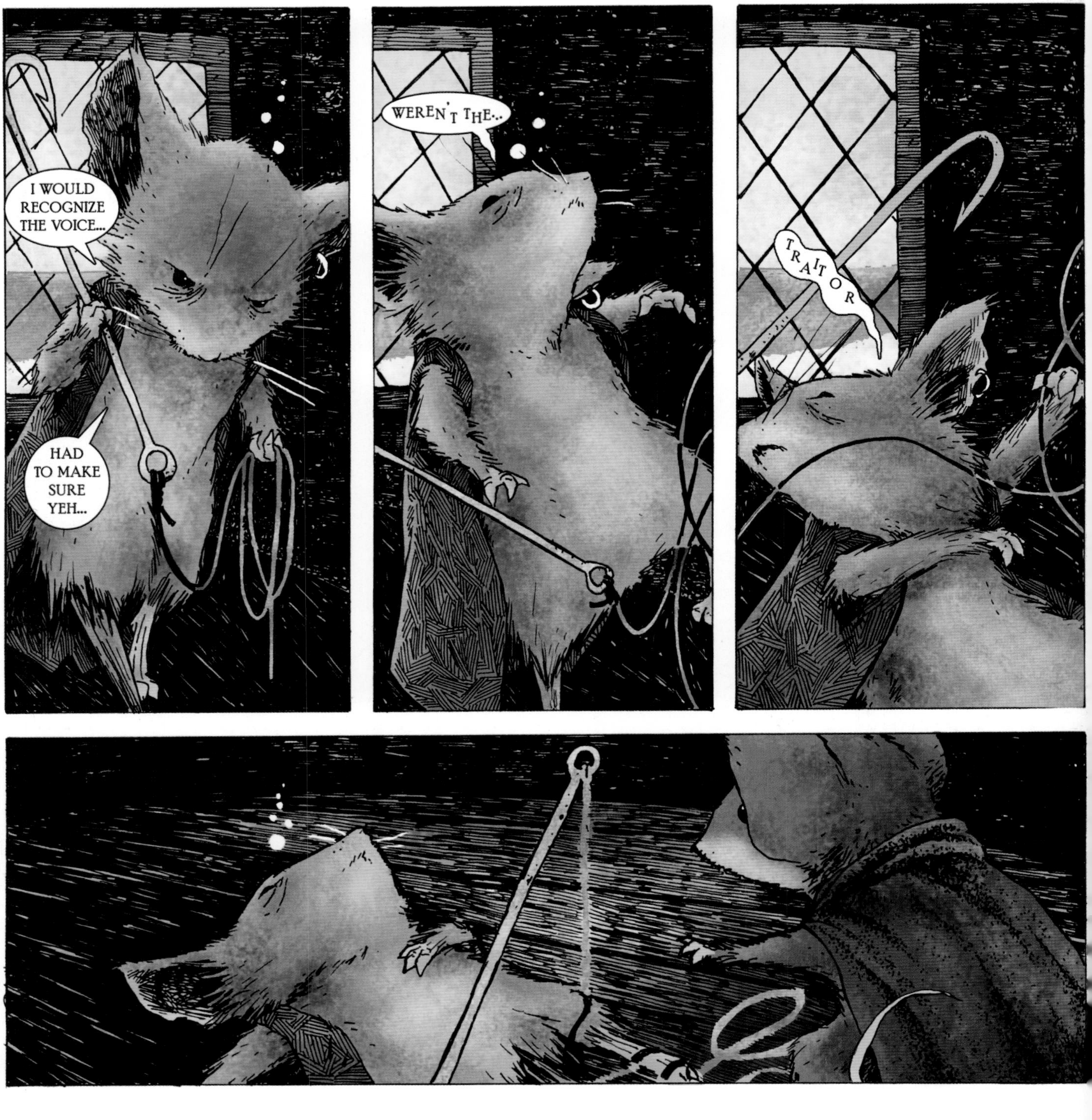
I WOULD RECOGNIZE THE VOICE...
HAD TO MAKE SURE YEH...
WEREN'T THE...
TRAITOR

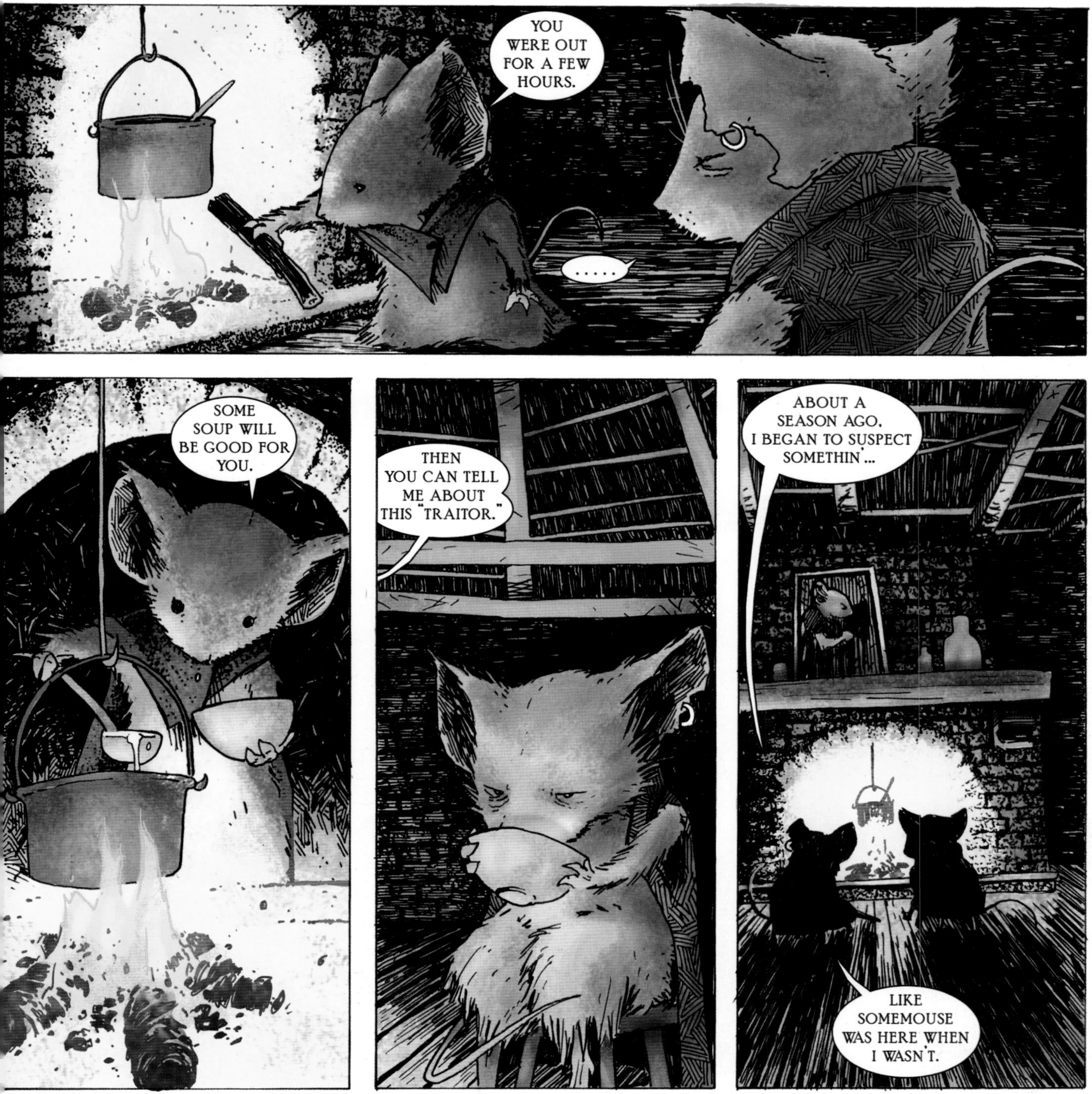
YOU WERE OUT FOR A FEW HOURS.
......
SOME SOUP WILL BE GOOD FOR YOU.
THEN YOU CAN TELL ME ABOUT THIS "TRAITOR."
ABOUT A SEASON AGO, I BEGAN TO SUSPECT SOMETHIN'...
LIKE SOMEMOUSE WAS HERE WHEN I WASN'T.

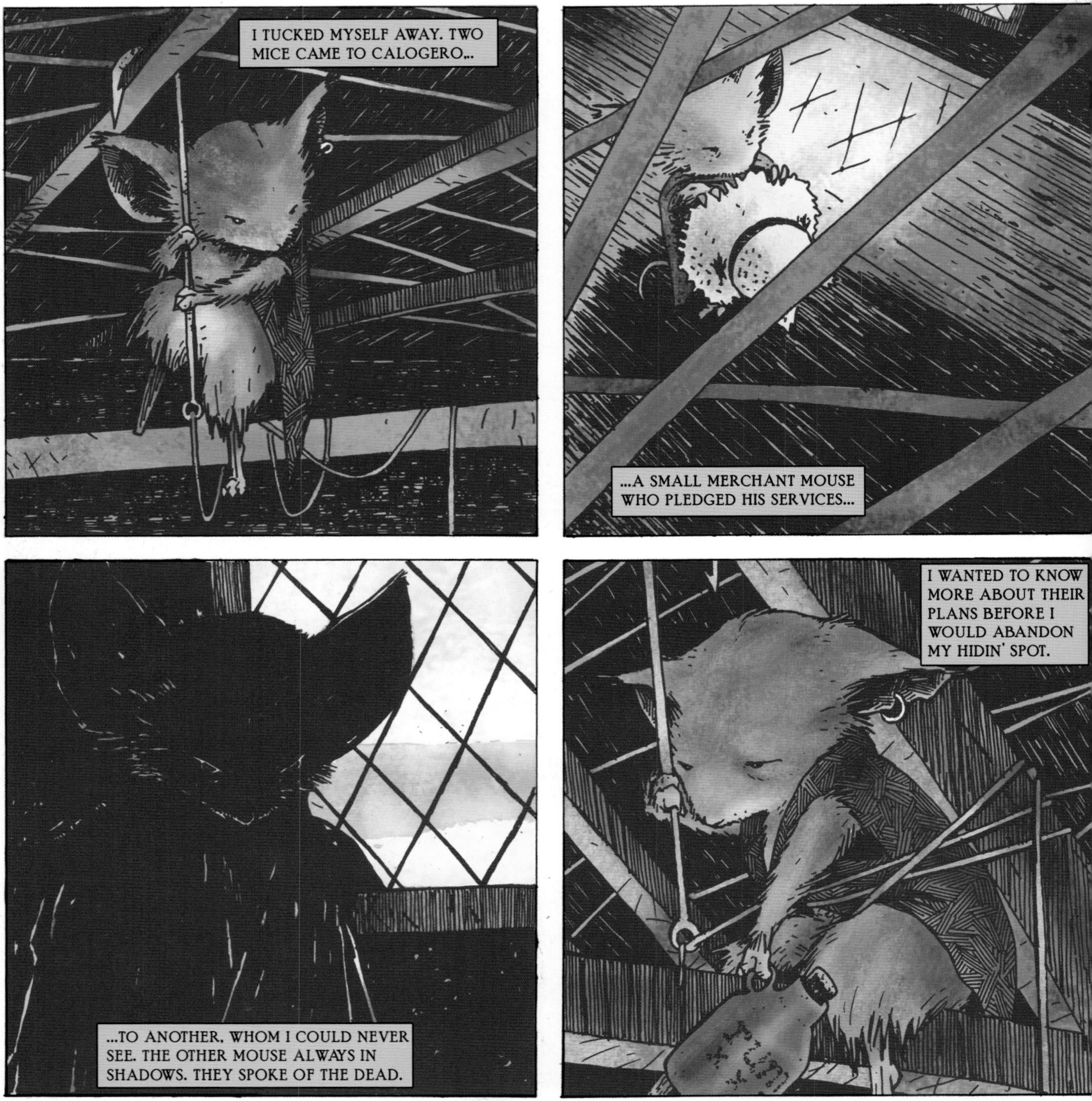
I TUCKED MYSELF AWAY. TWO MICE CAME TO CALOGERO...
...A SMALL MERCHANT MOUSE WHO PLEDGED HIS SERVICES...
...TO ANOTHER, WHOM I COULD NEVER SEE. THE OTHER MOUSE ALWAYS IN SHADOWS. THEY SPOKE OF THE DEAD.
I WANTED TO KNOW MORE ABOUT THEIR PLANS BEFORE I WOULD ABANDON MY HIDIN' SPOT.

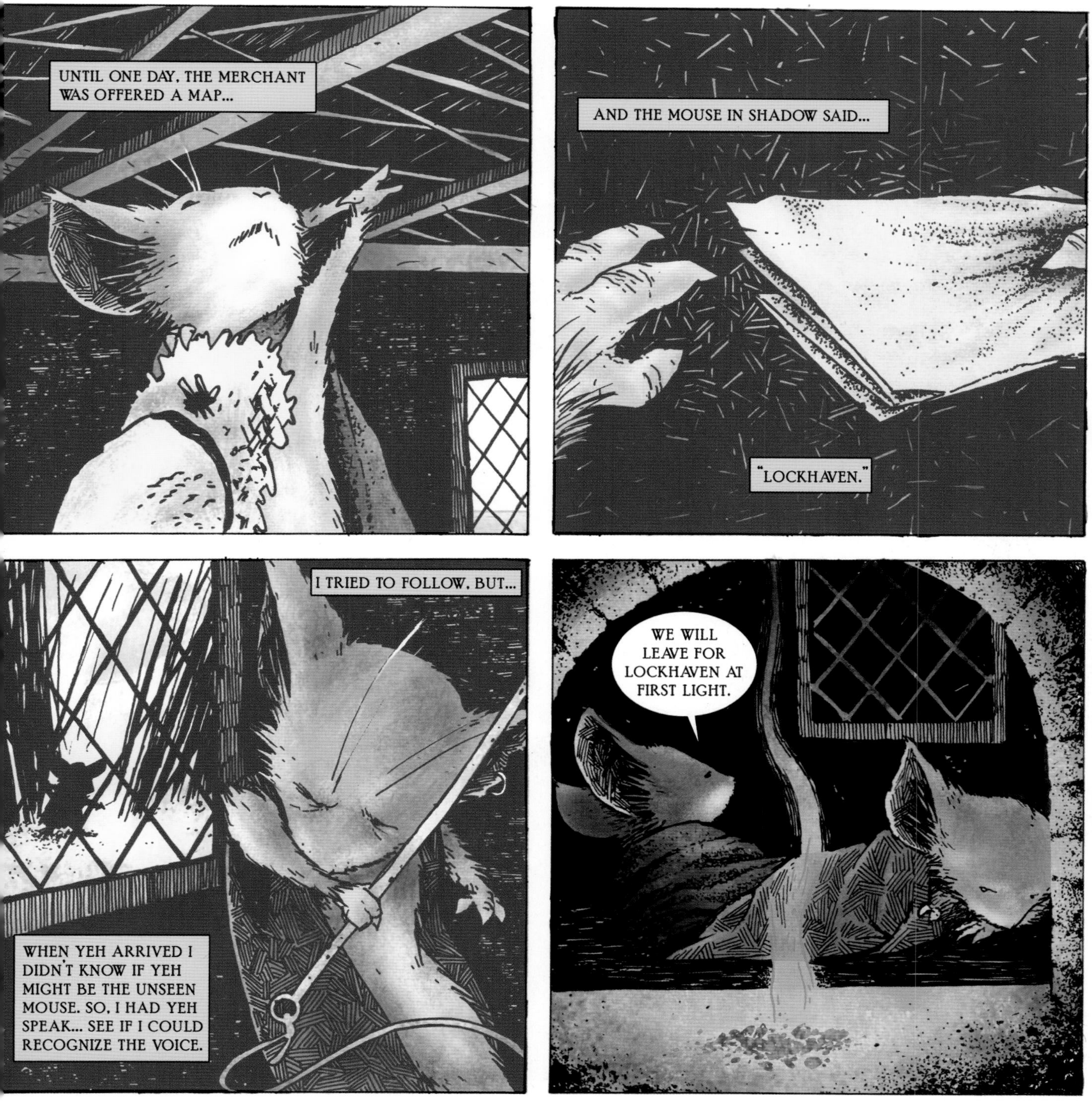
UNTIL ONE DAY, THE MERCHANT WAS OFFERED A MAP...
AND THE MOUSE IN SHADOW SAID...
"LOCKHAVEN."
I TRIED TO FOLLOW, BUT...
WHEN YEH ARRIVED I DIDN'T KNOW IF YEH MIGHT BE THE UNSEEN MOUSE. SO, I HAD YEH SPEAK... SEE IF I COULD RECOGNIZE THE VOICE.
WE WILL LEAVE FOR LOCKHAVEN AT FIRST LIGHT.

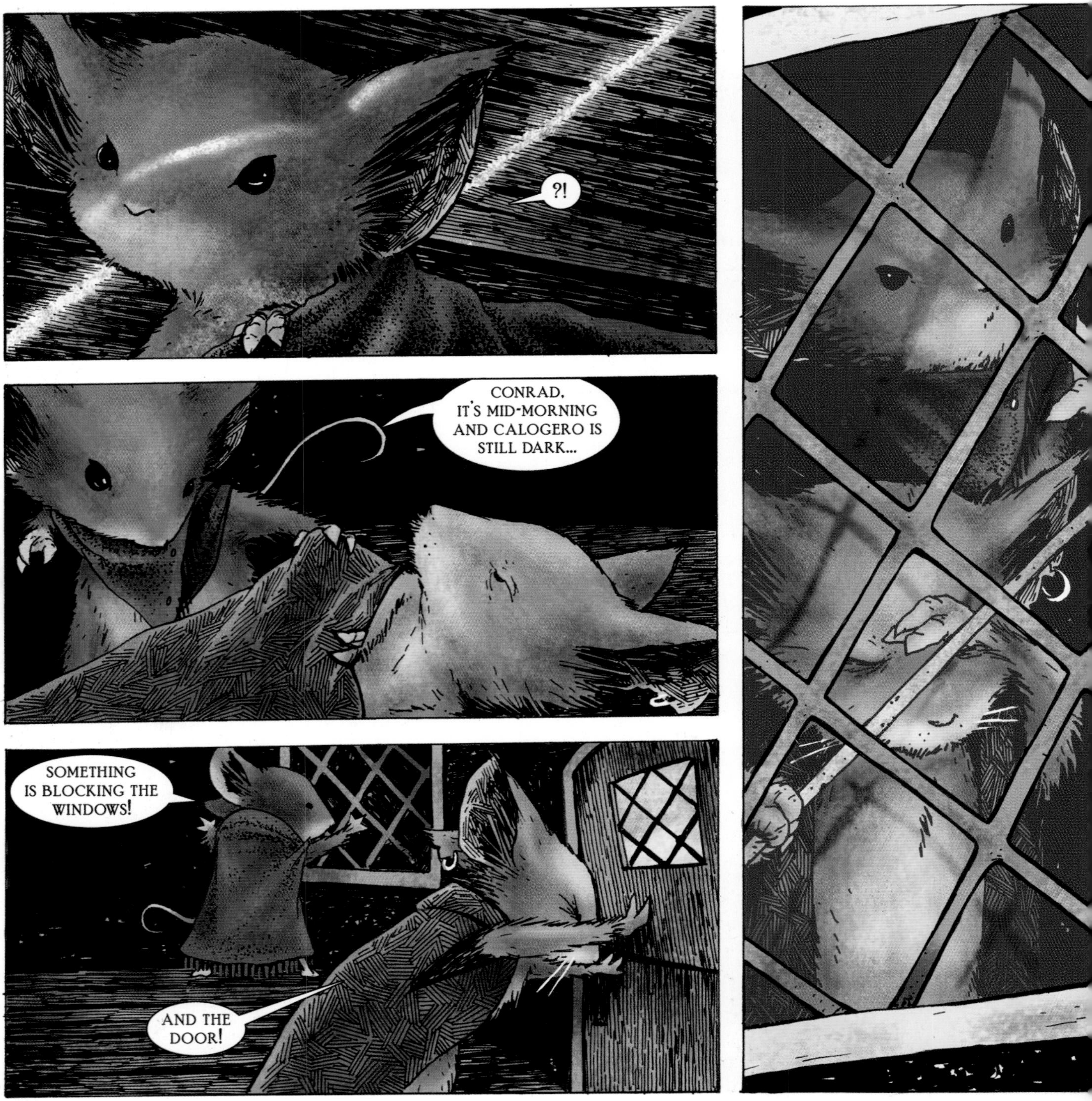
?!
CONRAD, IT'S MID-MORNING AND CALOGERO IS STILL DARK...
SOMETHING IS BLOCKING THE WINDOWS!
AND THE DOOR!

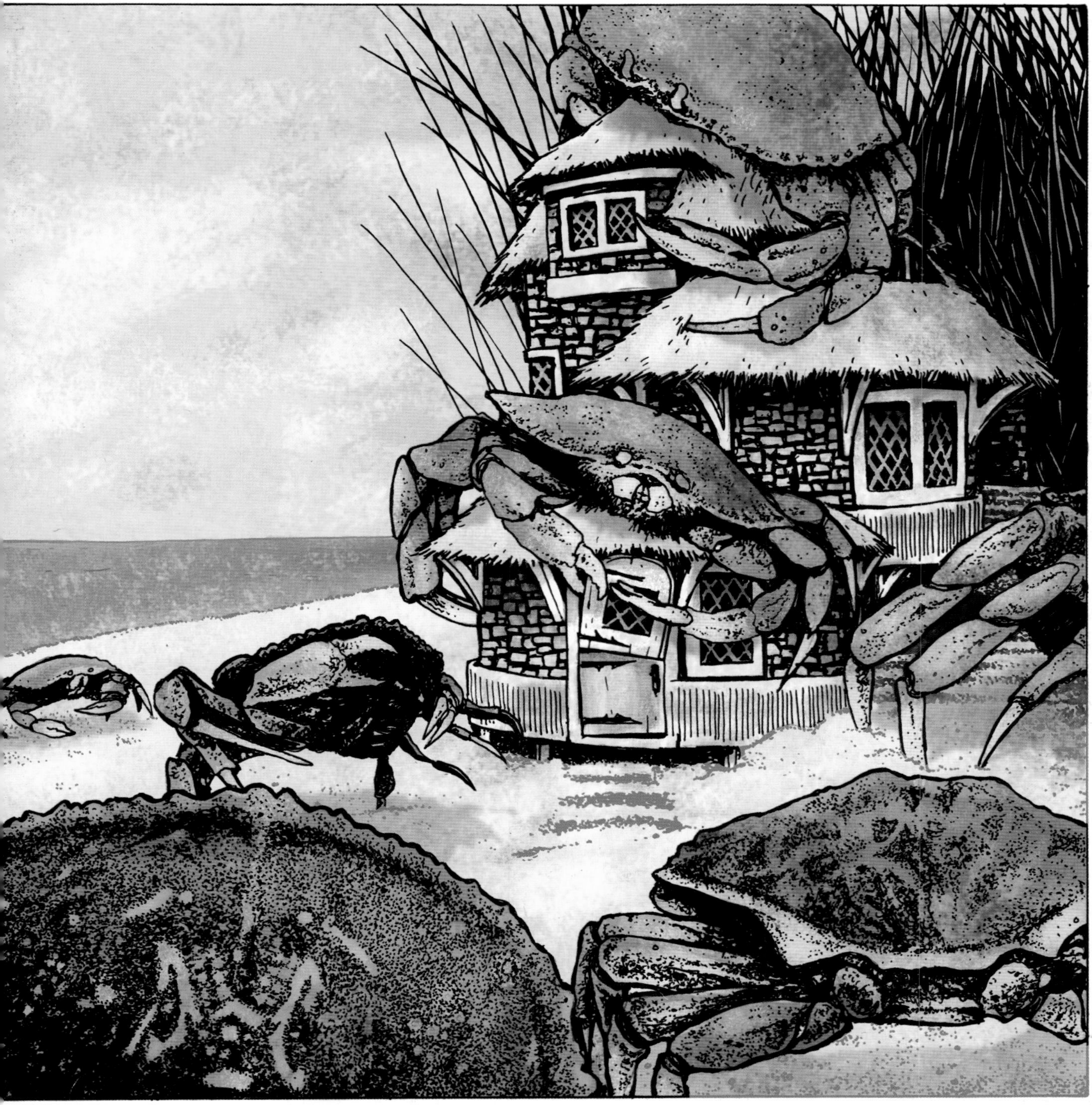

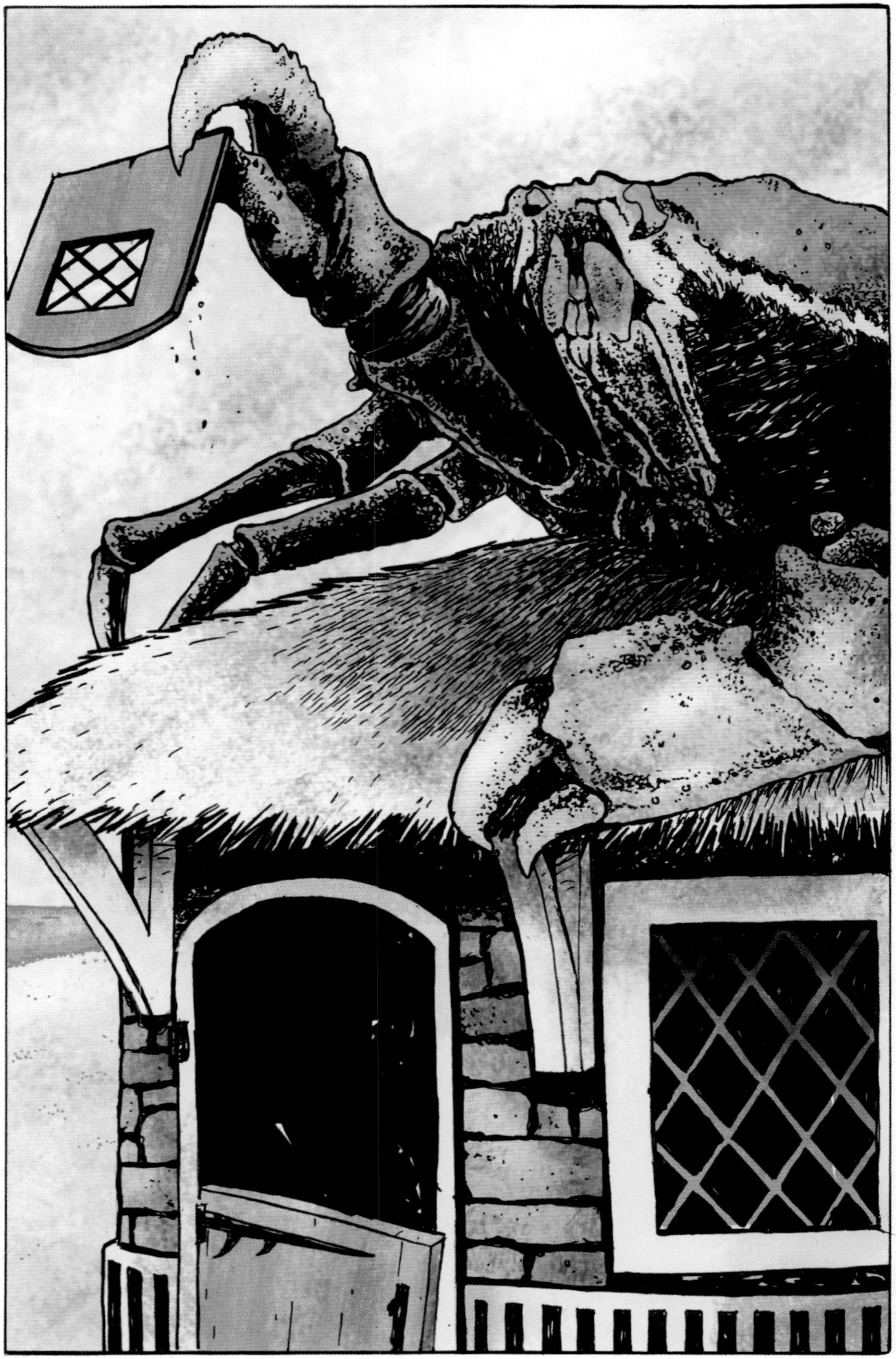

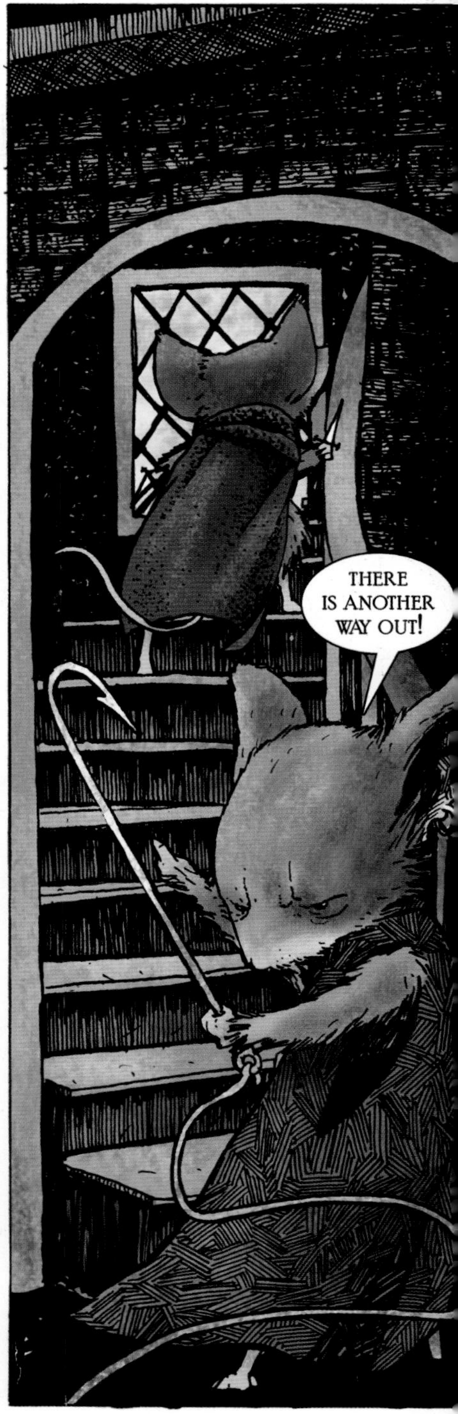
THERE IS ANOTHER WAY OUT!

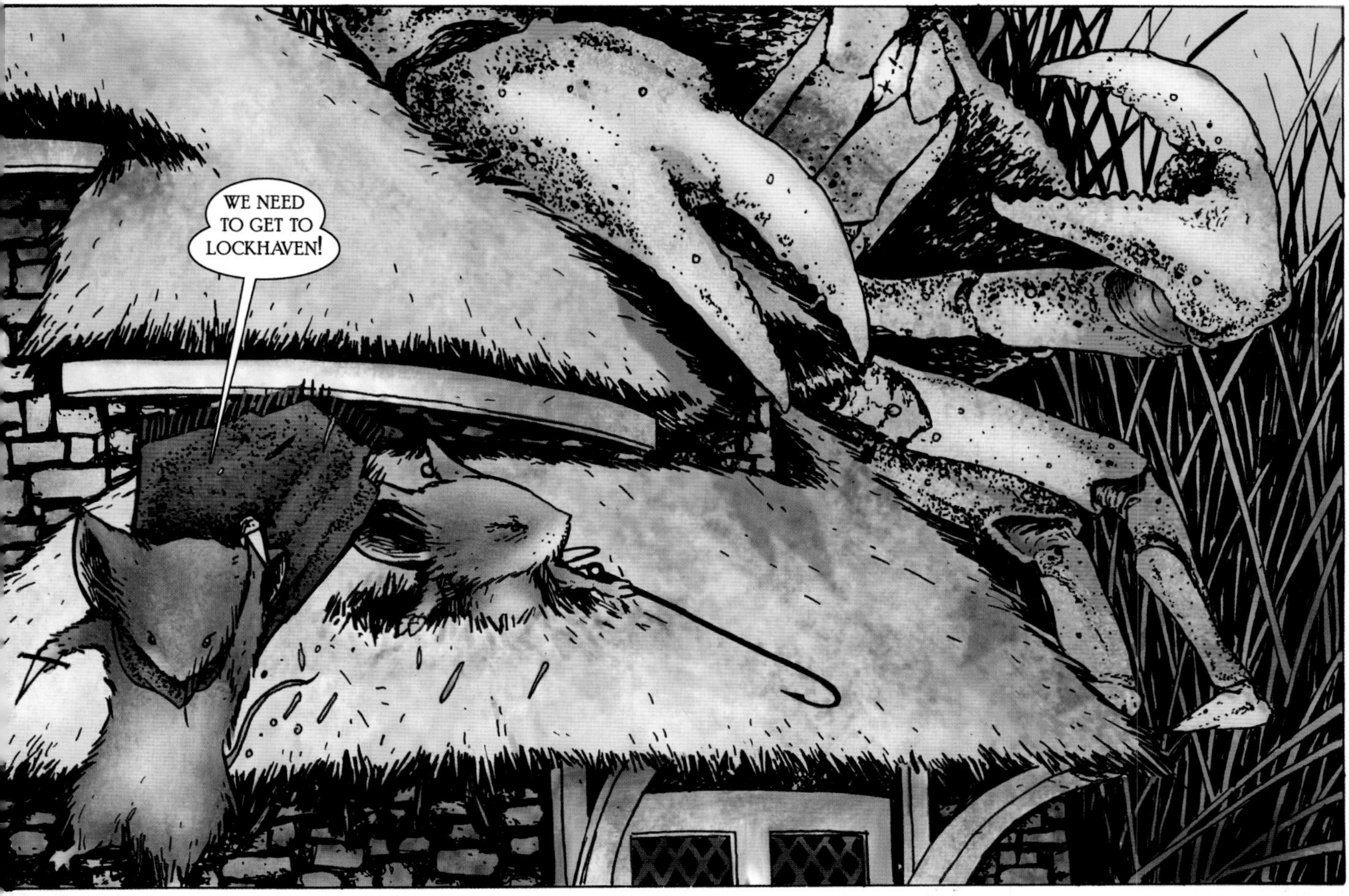
WE NEED TO GET TO LOCKHAVEN!

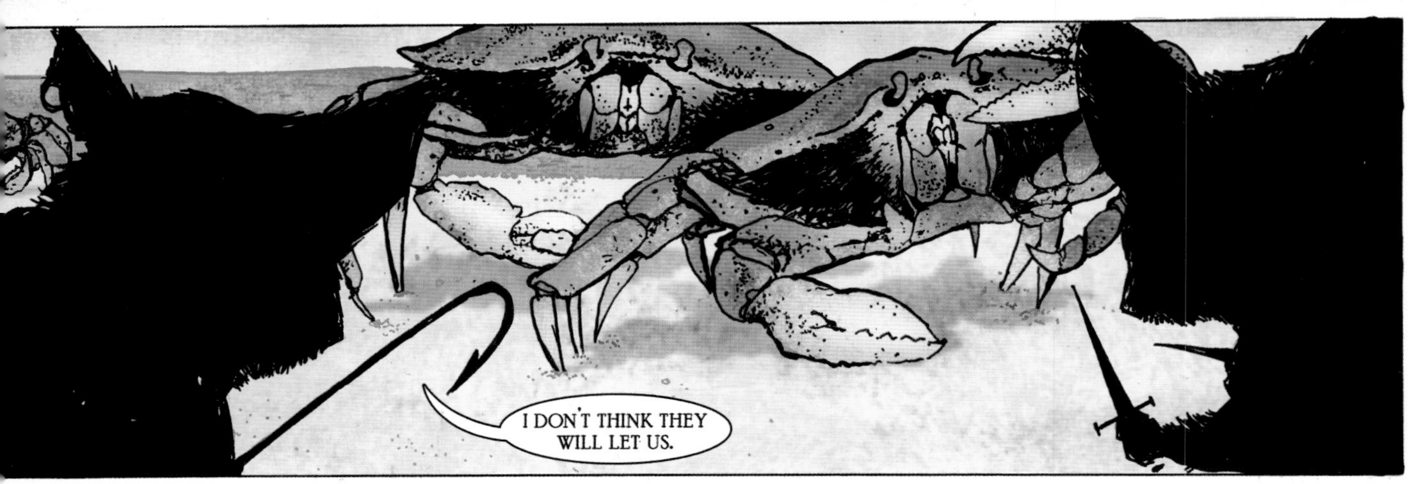
I DON'T THINK THEY WILL LET US.

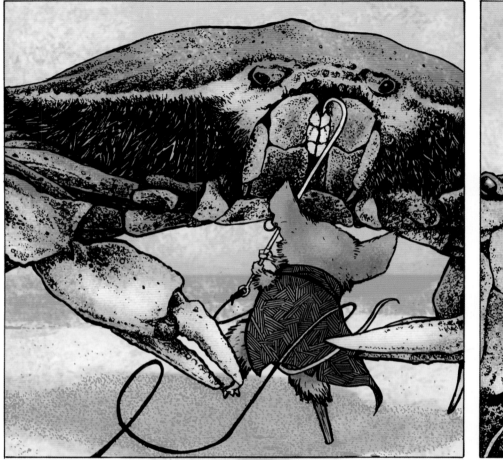

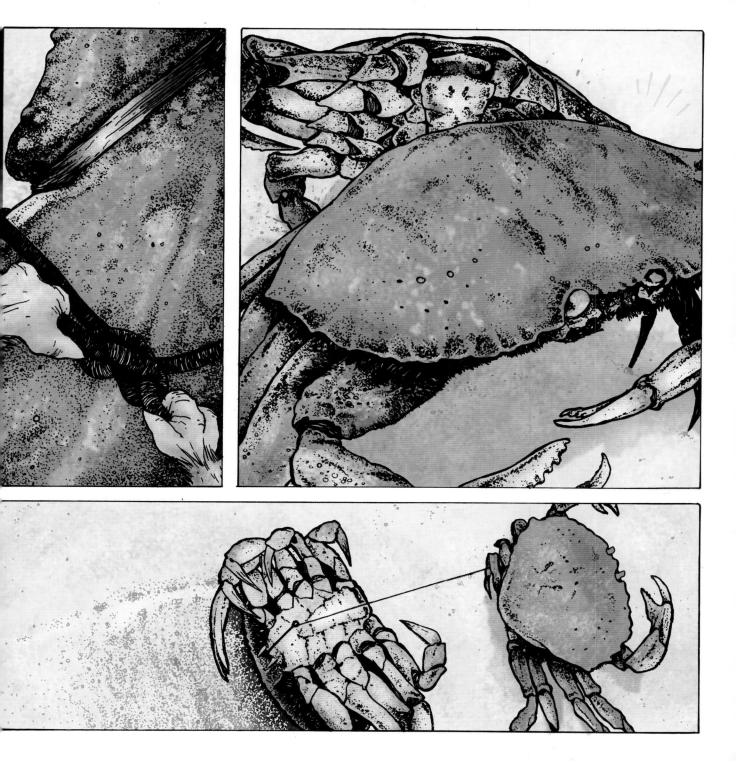

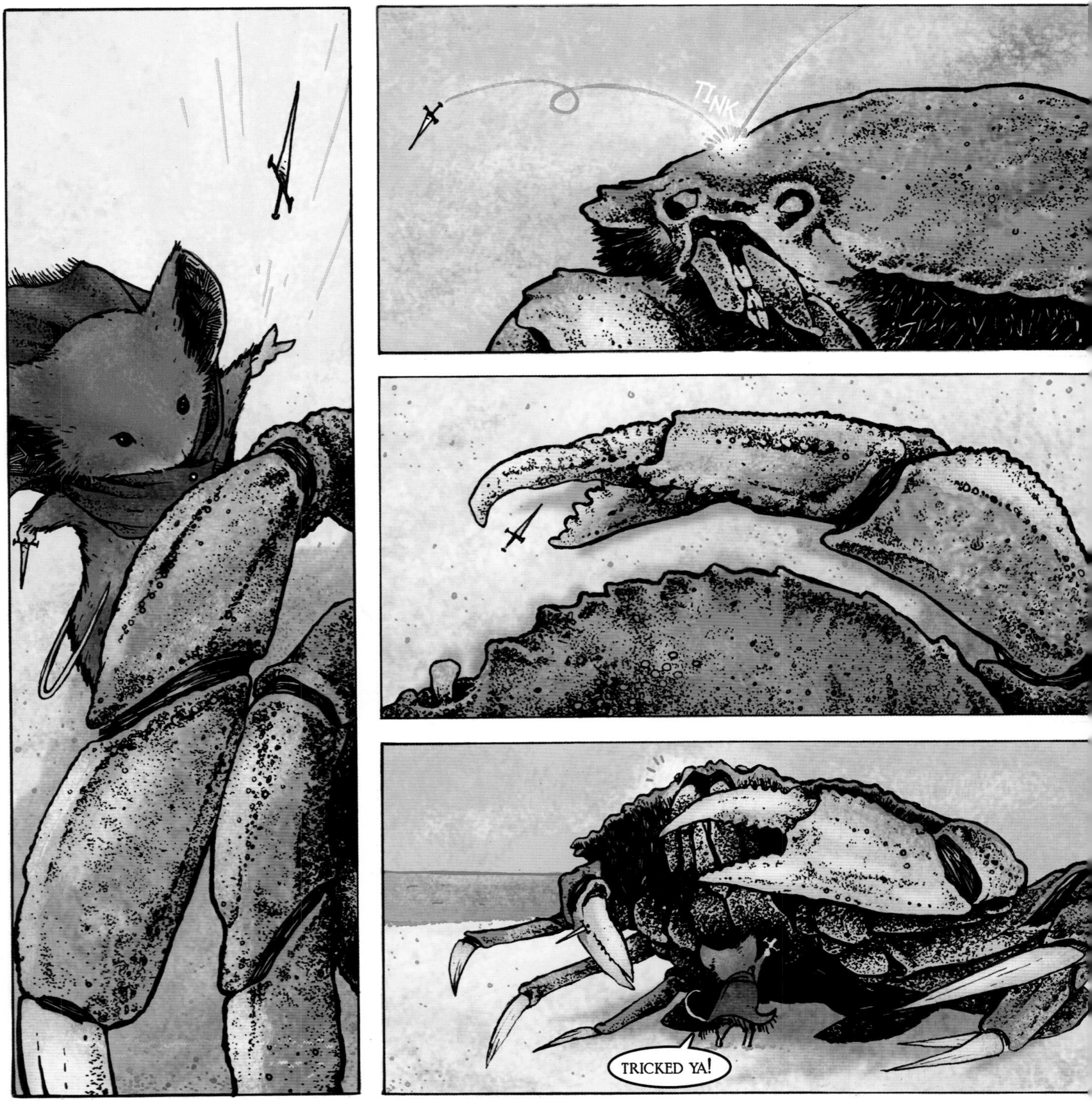
TINK
TRICKED YA!

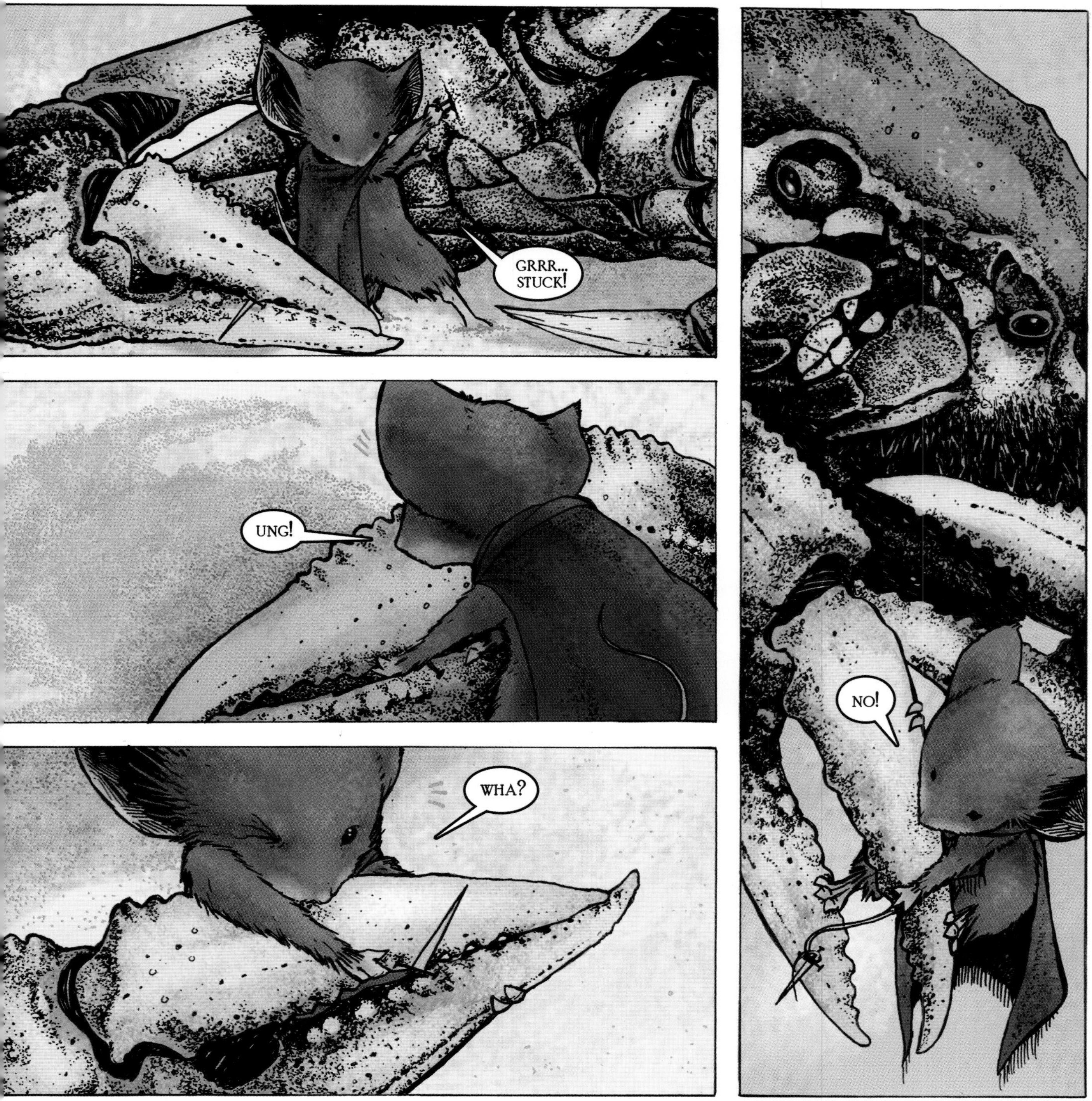
GRRR... STUCK!
UNG!
WHA?
NO!

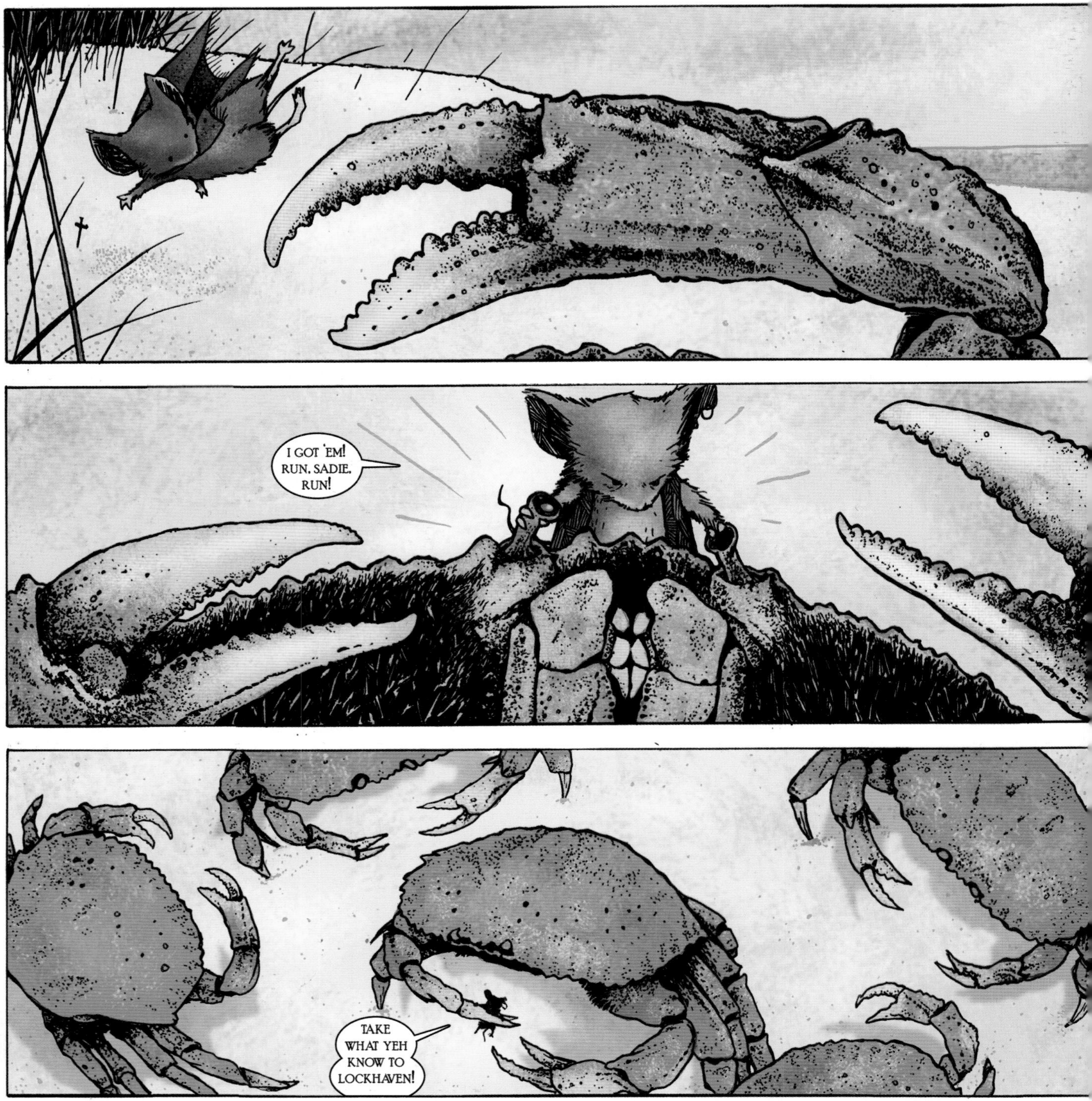
I GOT 'EM! RUN, SADIE, RUN!
TAKE WHAT YEH KNOW TO LOCKHAVEN!

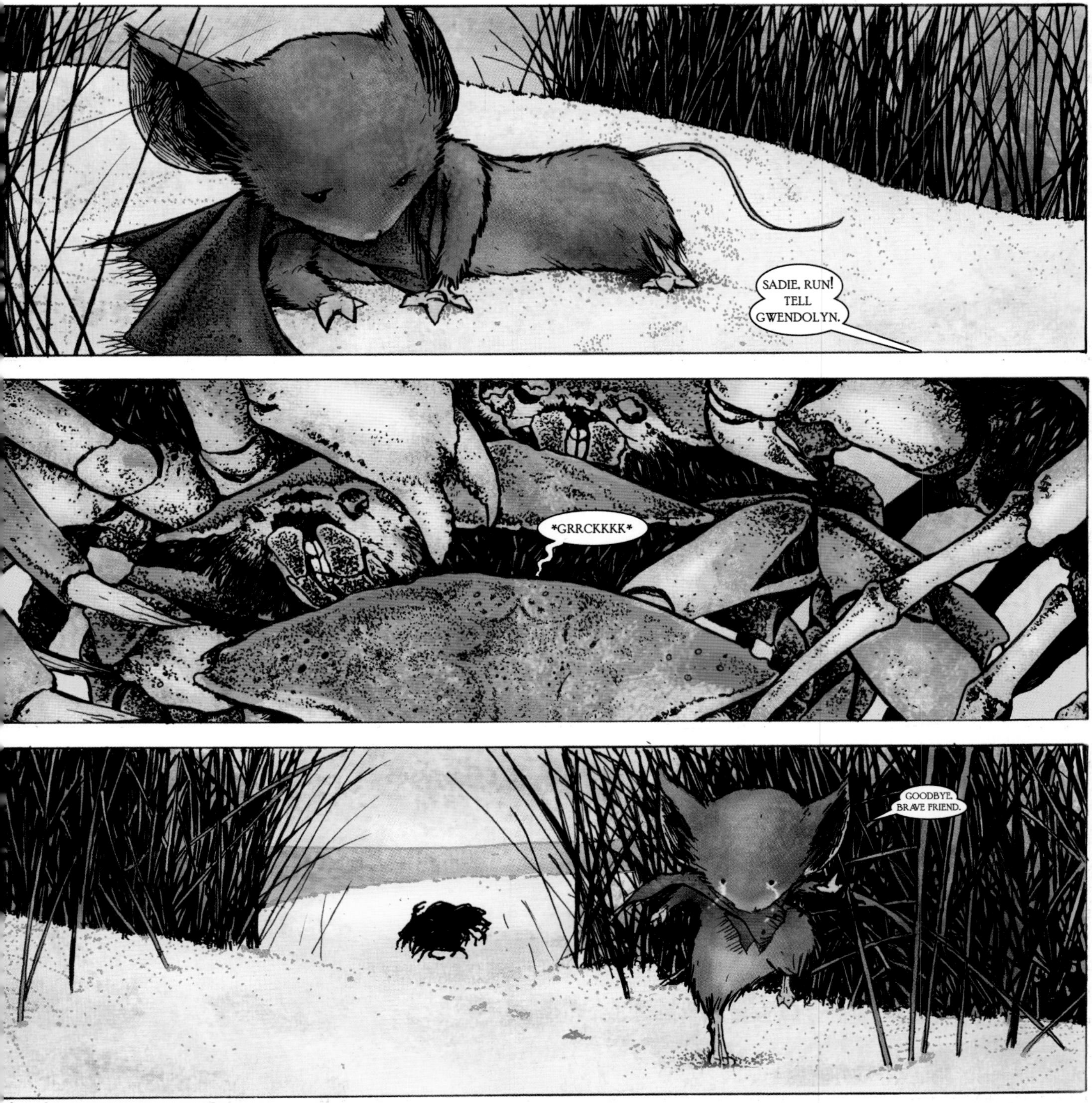
SADIE, RUN! TELL GWENDOLYN.
GRRCKKKK
GOODBYE, BRAVE FRIEND.

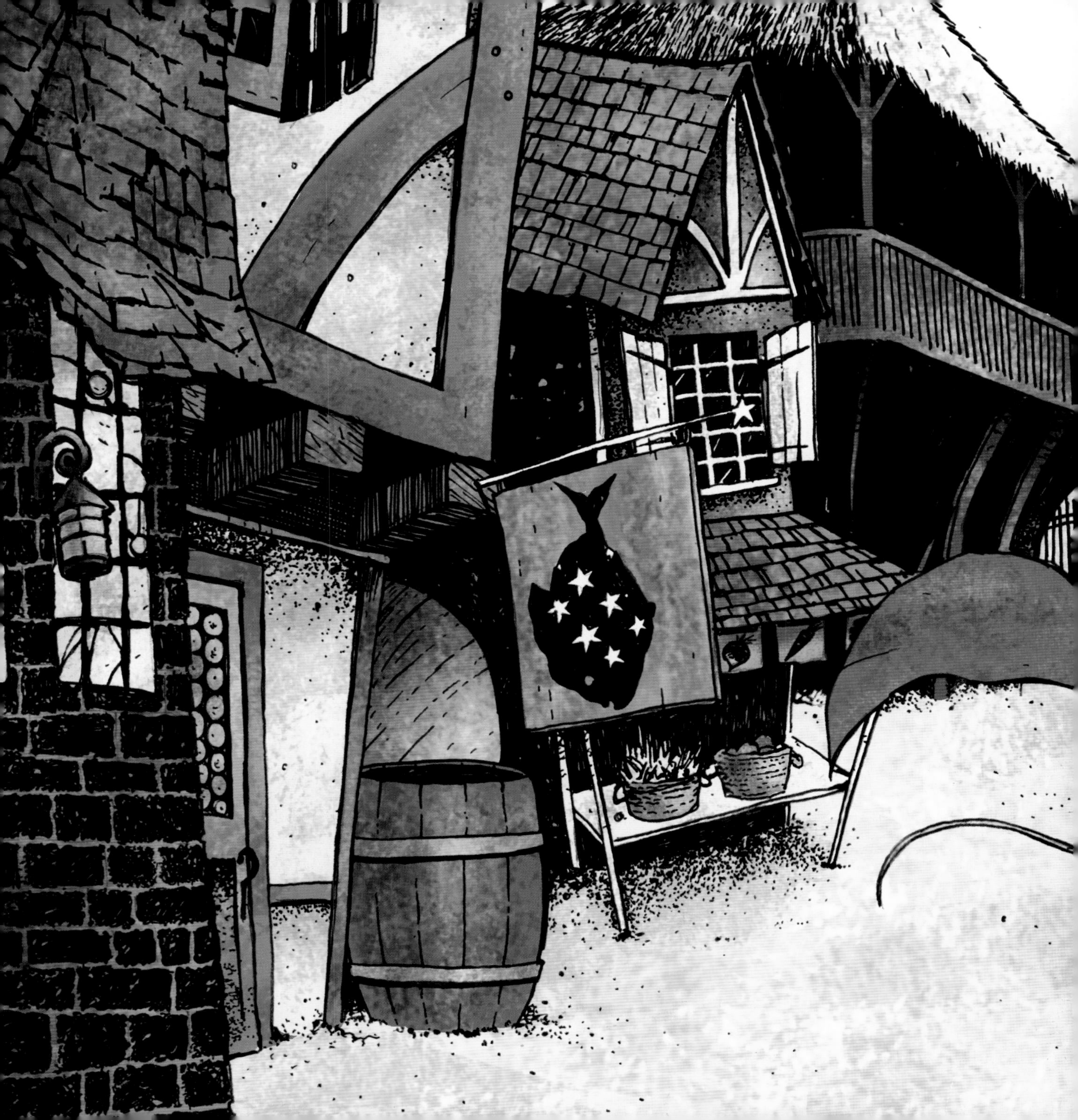

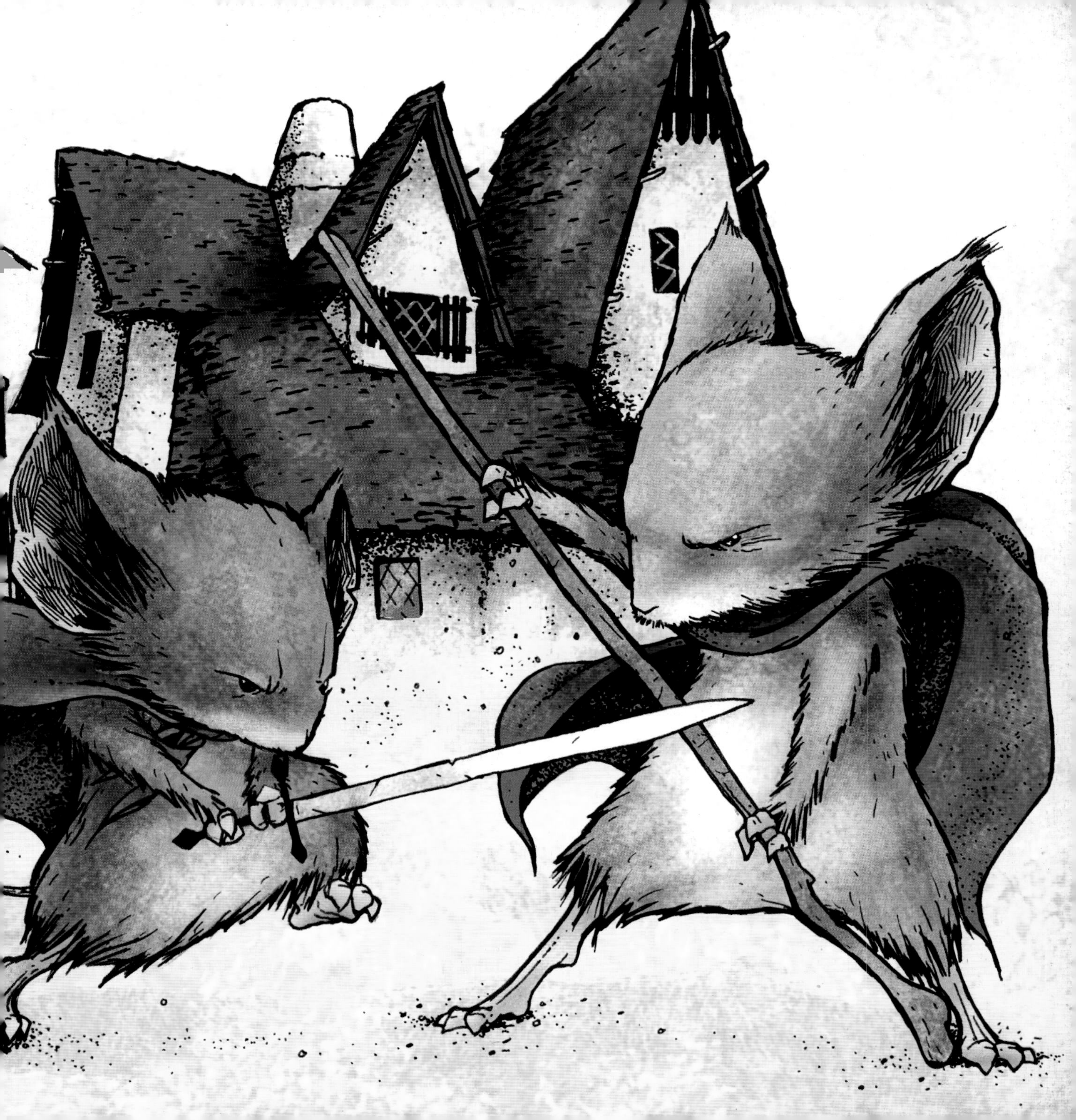

Chapter Three

Rise of the Axe

Saxon, Kenzie, and Lieam, having abandoned the grain cart, have opted to take a lesser known path to the city of Barkstone, hoping to keep as low a profile as possible. What worries them more than knowing of a traitor is not knowing who the traitor is. They are unaware of the information Sadie carries with her to Lockhaven, or the fate of fellow Guard, Conrad.

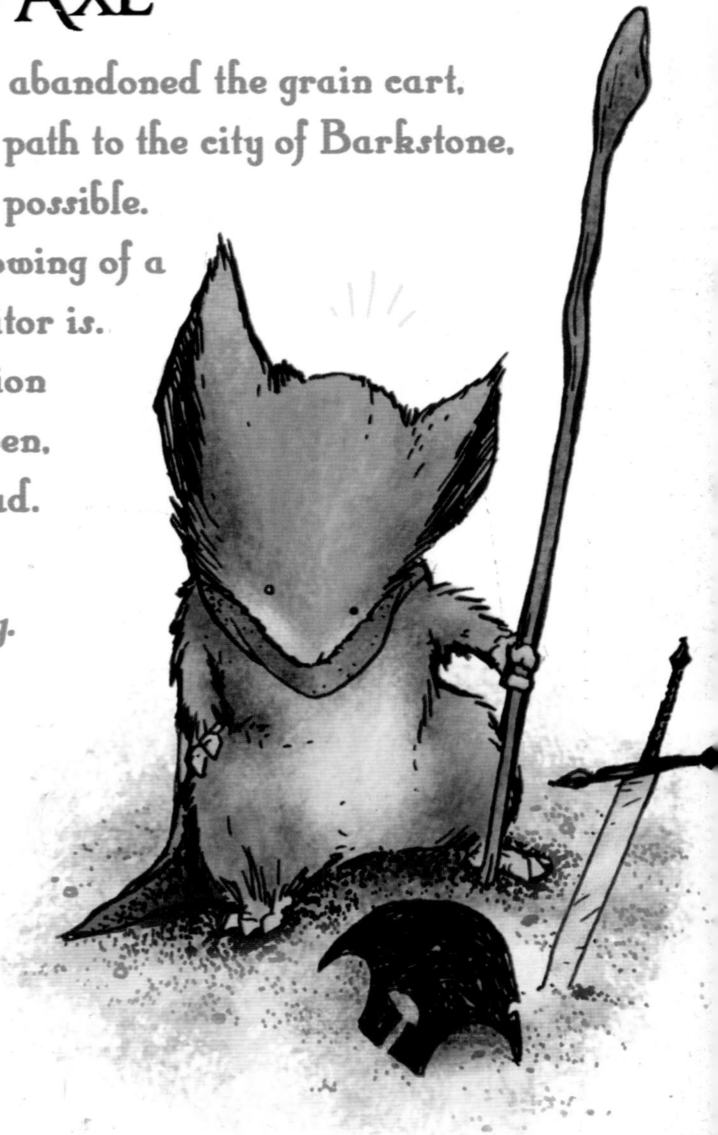

'Take not the duty of the Guard lightly.
Friends must not be enemies
Just as enemies must not be friends.
Discerning the two is a life's work.'

--From the writings of Laria
4th Lockhaven Guard Matron

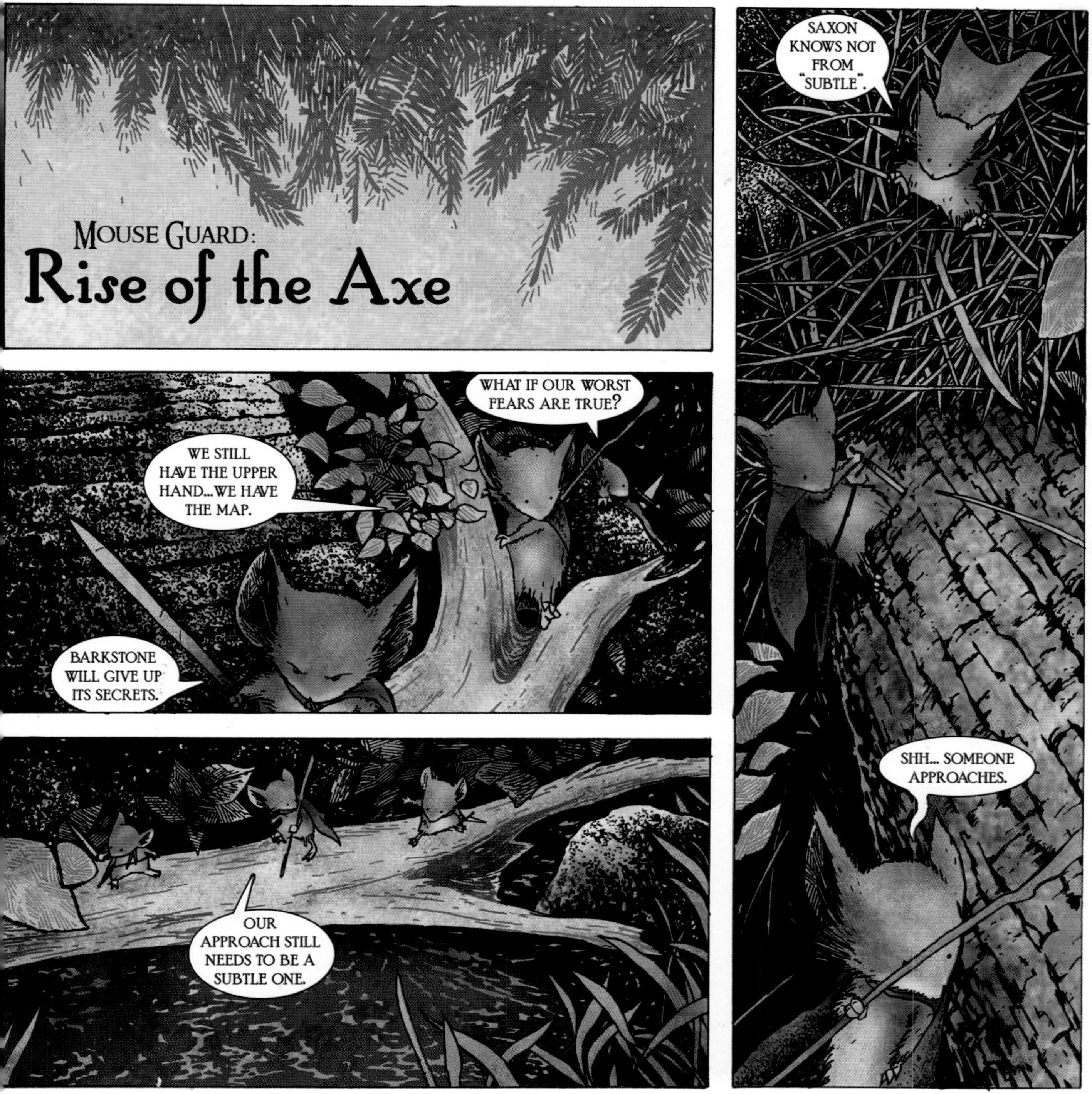
MOUSE GUARD:
Rise of the Axe
WHAT IF OUR WORST FEARS ARE TRUE?
WE STILL HAVE THE UPPER HAND...WE HAVE THE MAP.
BARKSTONE WILL GIVE UP ITS SECRETS.
OUR APPROACH STILL NEEDS TO BE A SUBTLE ONE.
SAXON KNOWS NOT FROM "SUBTLE".
SHH... SOMEONE APPROACHES.

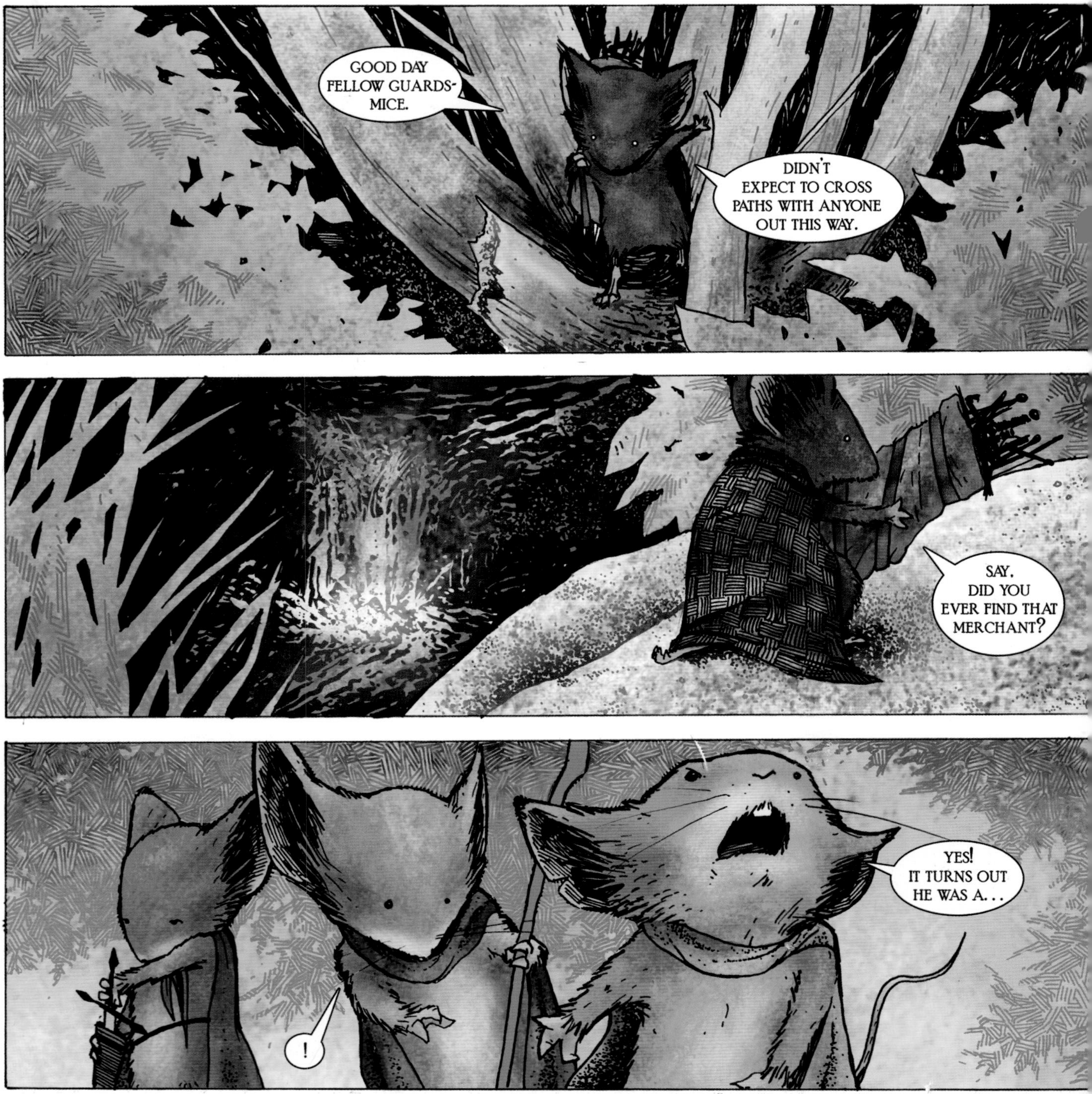
GOOD DAY FELLOW GUARDS-MICE.
DIDN'T EXPECT TO CROSS PATHS WITH ANYONE OUT THIS WAY.
SAY, DID YOU EVER FIND THAT MERCHANT?
YES! IT TURNS OUT HE WAS A...
!

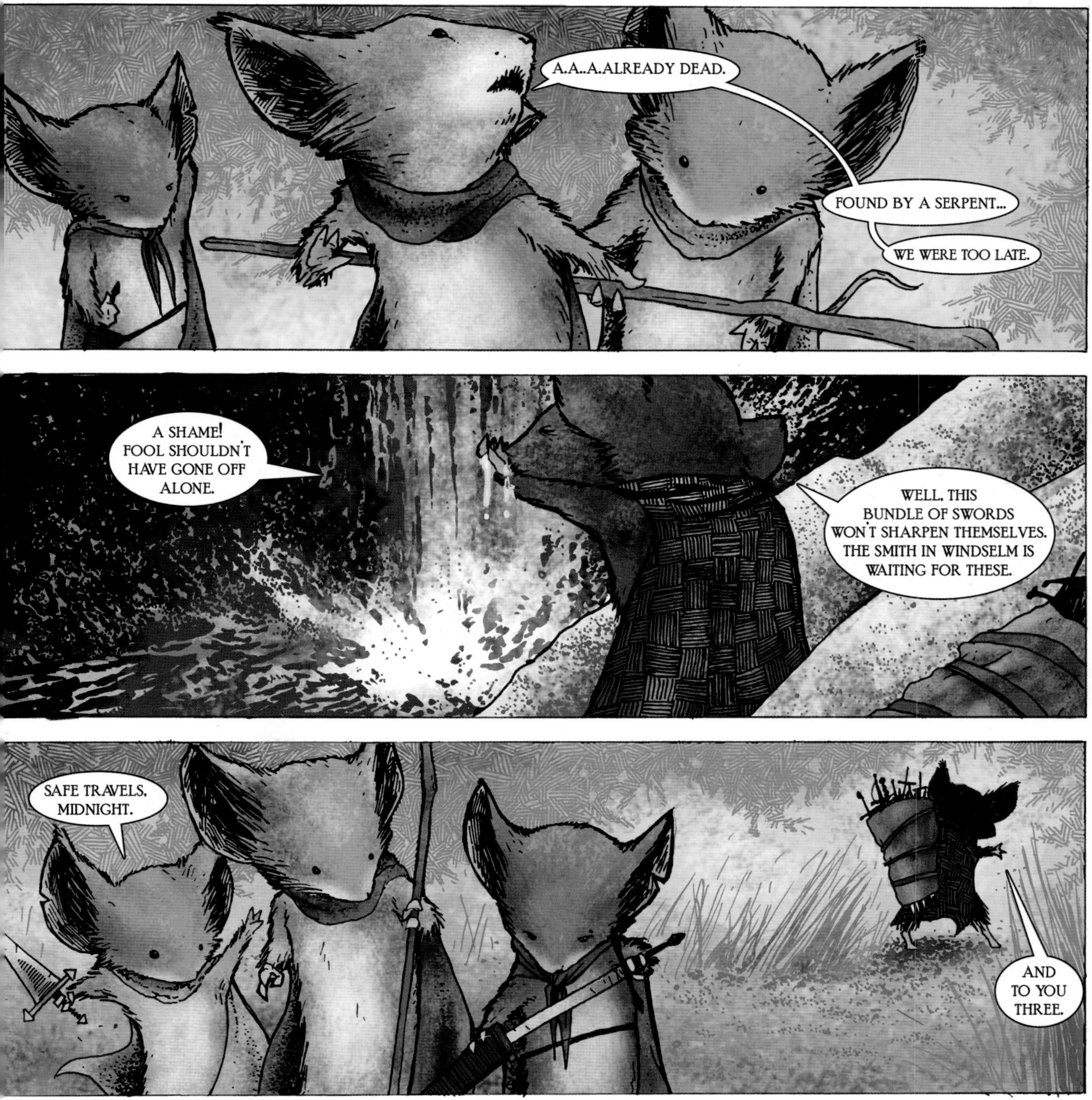
A.A..A.ALREADY DEAD.
FOUND BY A SERPENT...
WE WERE TOO LATE.
A SHAME! FOOL SHOULDN'T HAVE GONE OFF ALONE.
WELL, THIS BUNDLE OF SWORDS WON'T SHARPEN THEMSELVES. THE SMITH IN WINDSELM IS WAITING FOR THESE.
SAFE TRAVELS, MIDNIGHT.
AND TO YOU THREE.

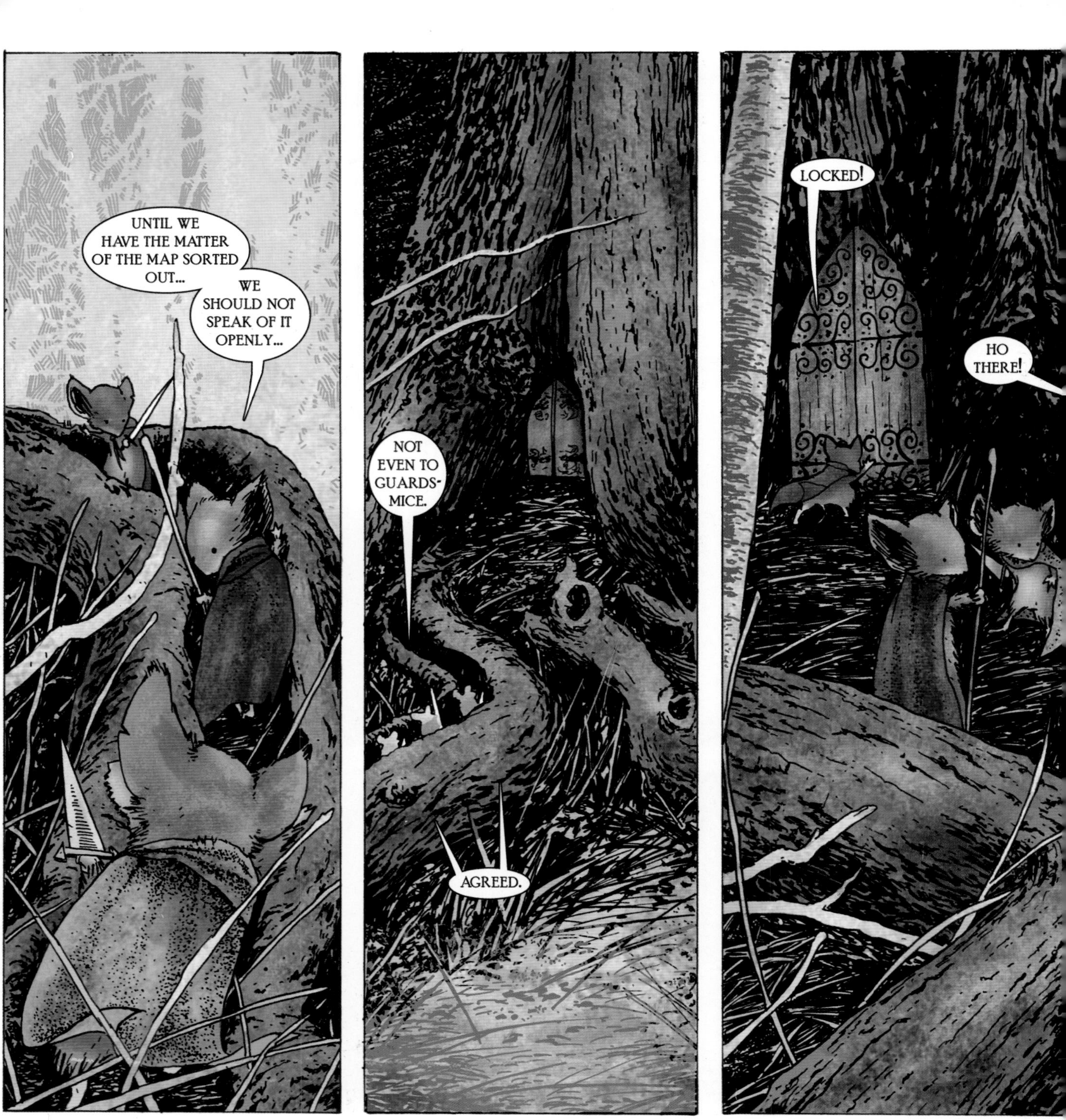
UNTIL WE HAVE THE MATTER OF THE MAP SORTED OUT...
WE SHOULD NOT SPEAK OF IT OPENLY...
NOT EVEN TO GUARDS-MICE.
AGREED.
LOCKED!
HO THERE!

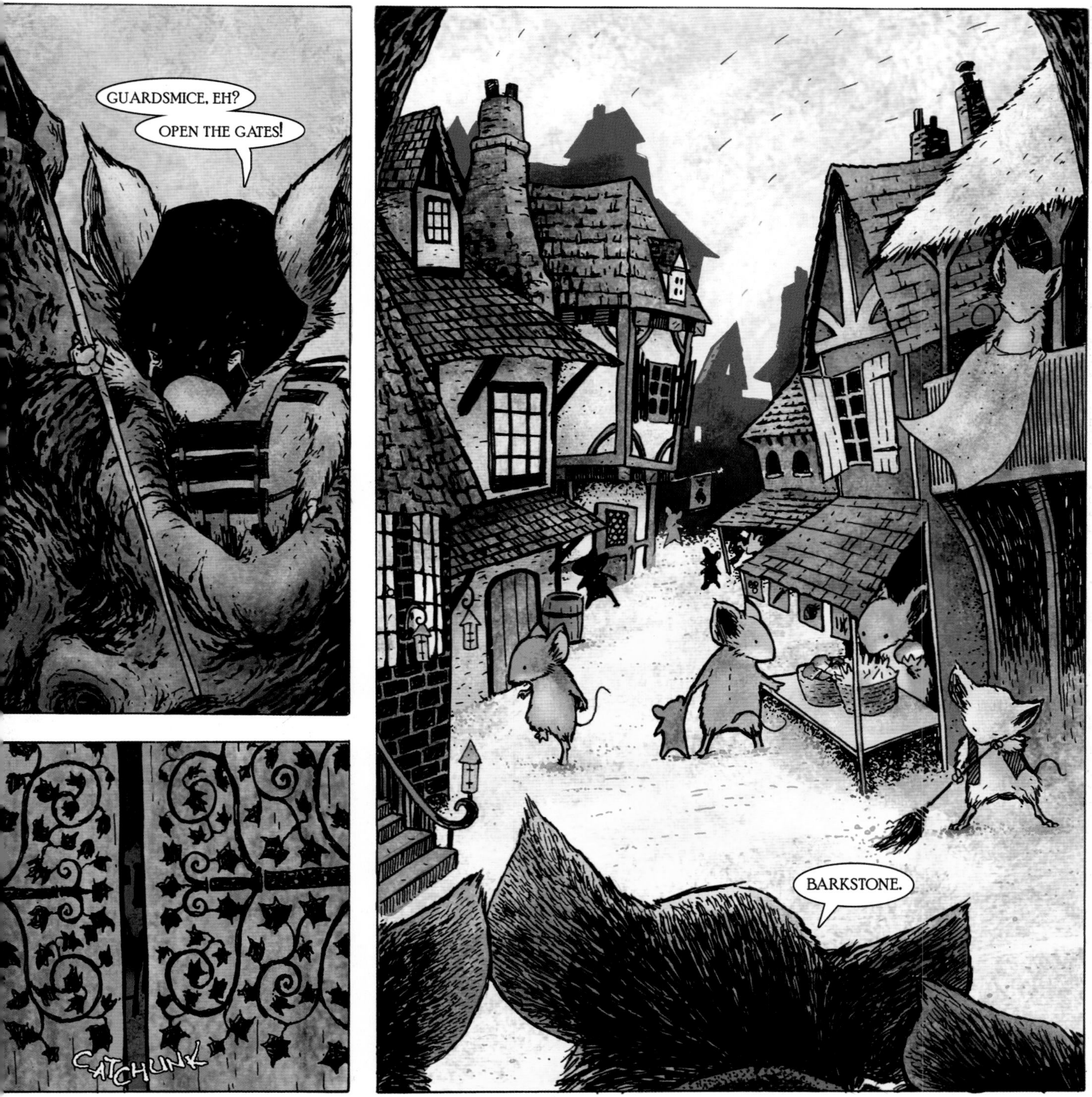
GUARDSMICE, EH?
OPEN THE GATES!
CATCHUNK
BARKSTONE.

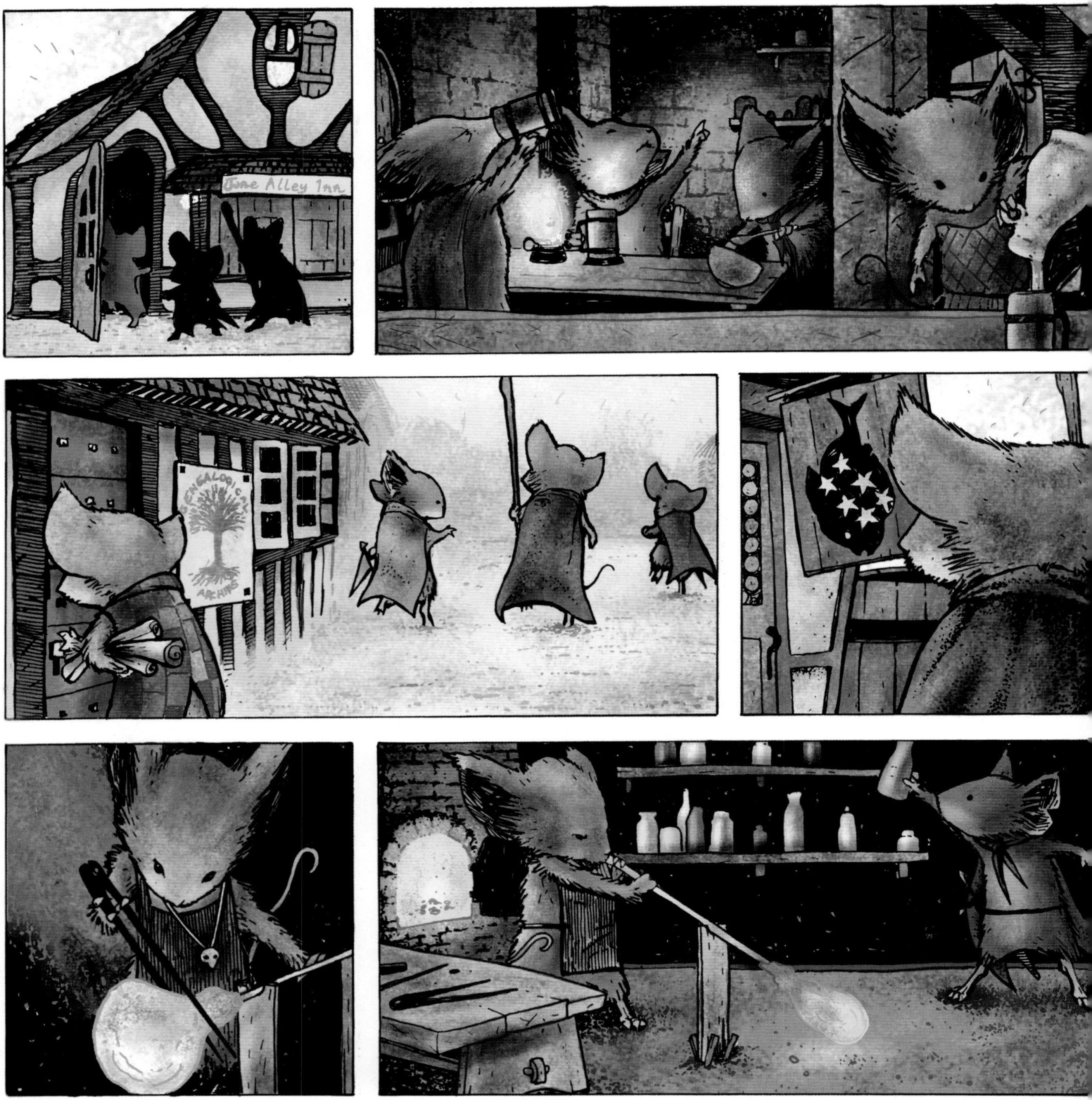
June Alley Inn
GENEALOGICAL ARCHIVE

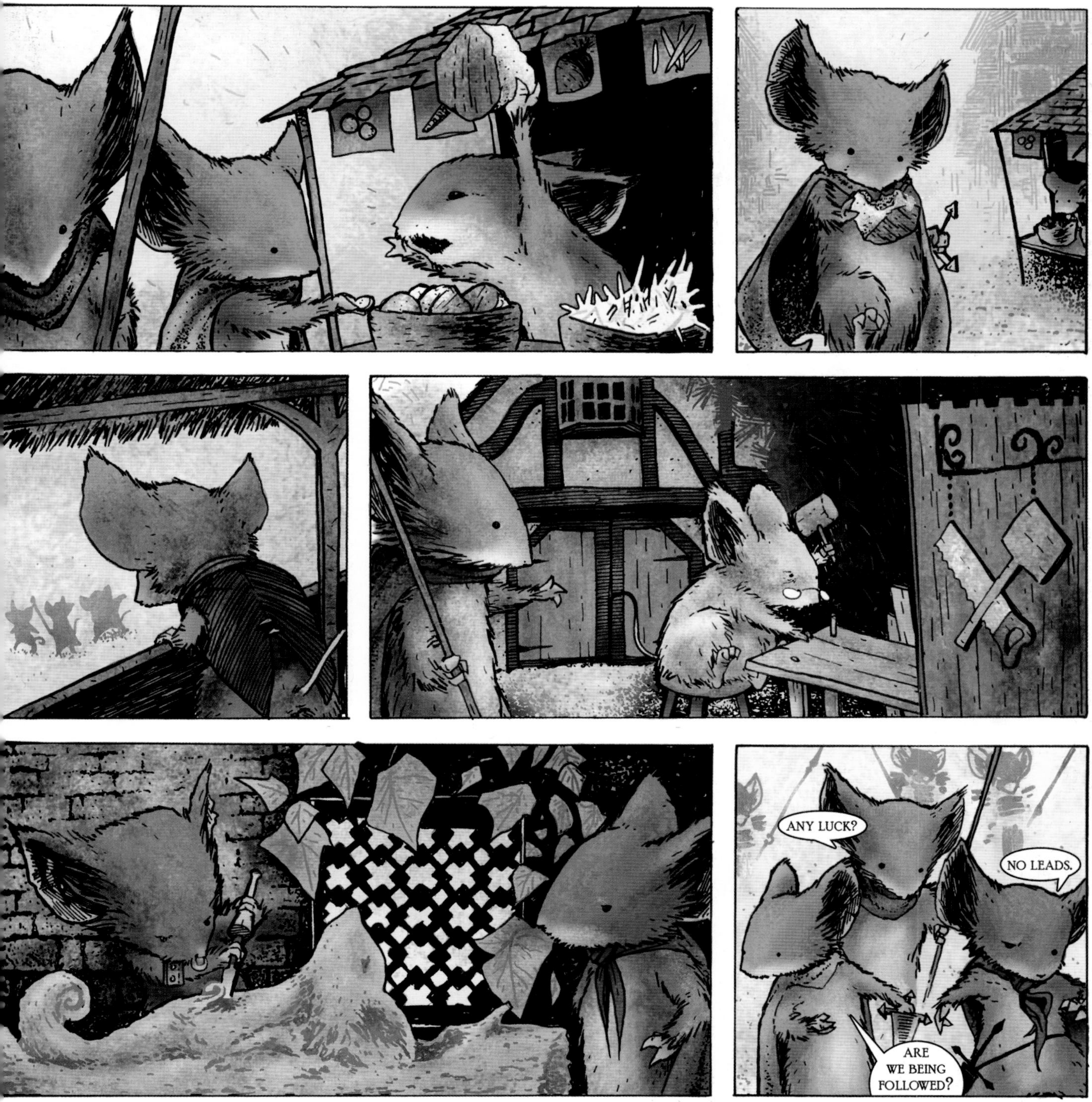
ANY LUCK?
NO LEADS.
ARE
WE BEING
FOLLOWED?

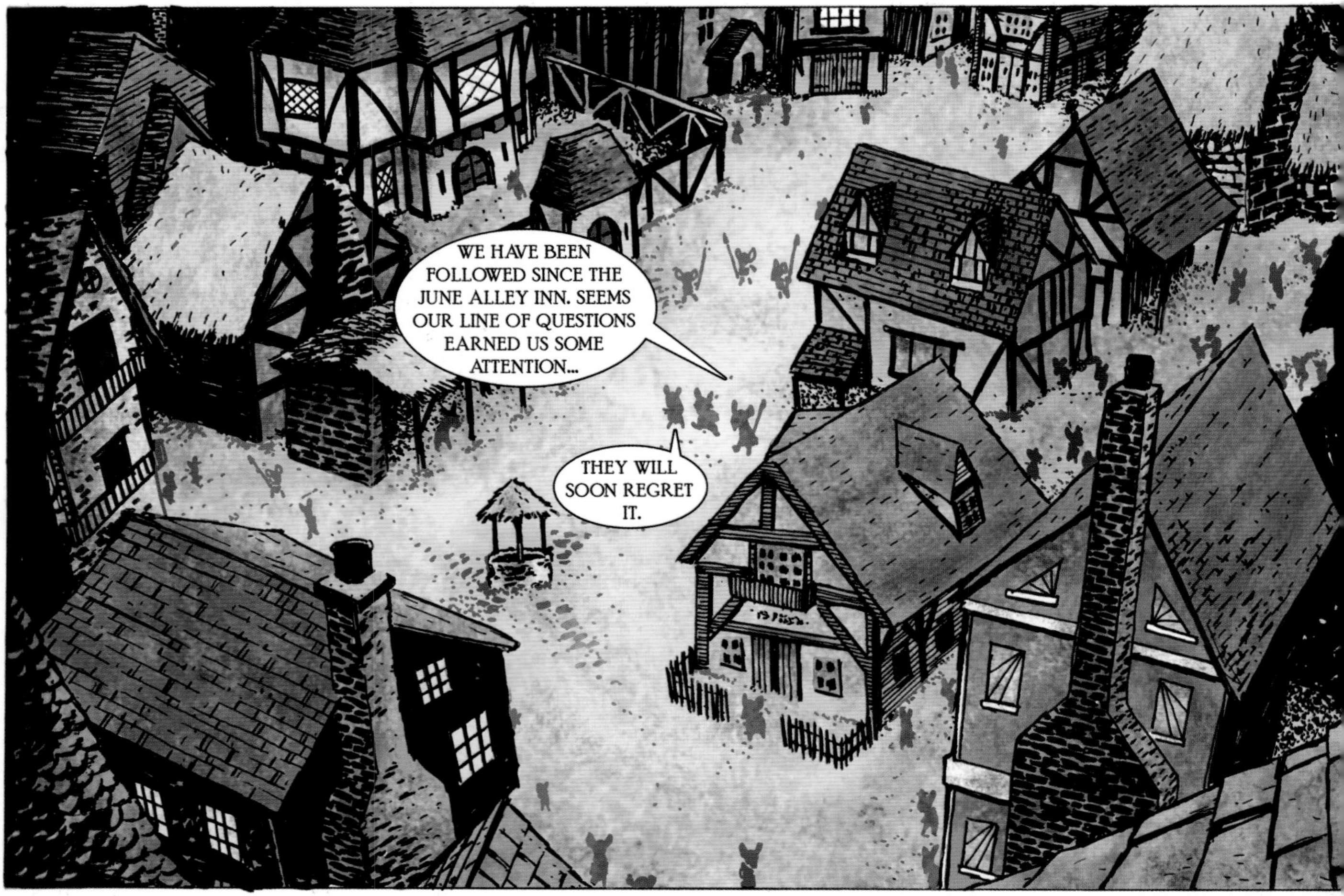
WE HAVE BEEN FOLLOWED SINCE THE JUNE ALLEY INN. SEEMS OUR LINE OF QUESTIONS EARNED US SOME ATTENTION...
THEY WILL SOON REGRET IT.

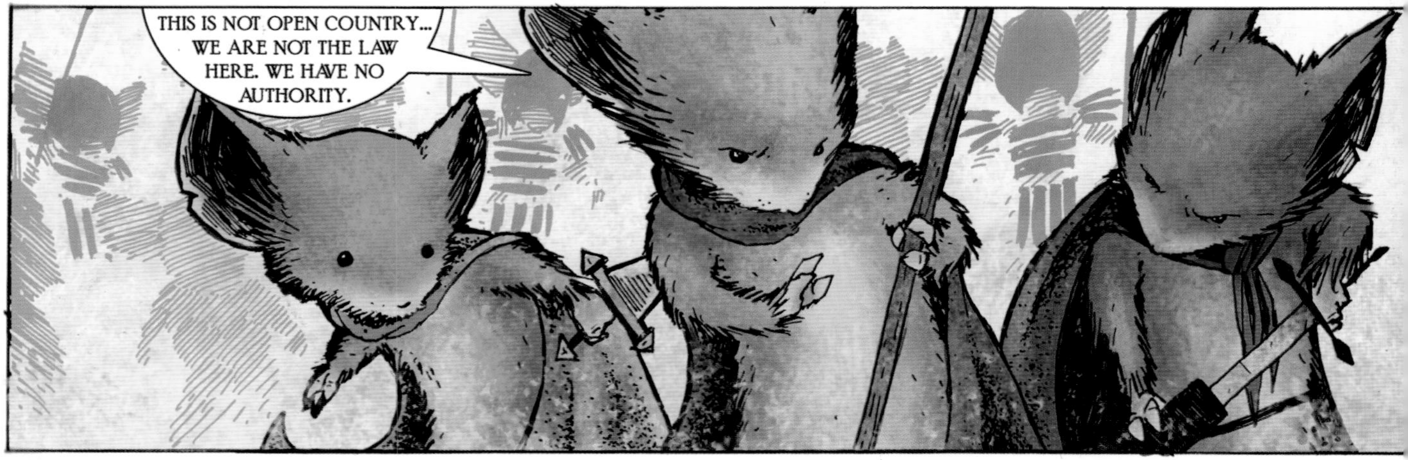
THIS IS NOT OPEN COUNTRY... WE ARE NOT THE LAW HERE. WE HAVE NO AUTHORITY.

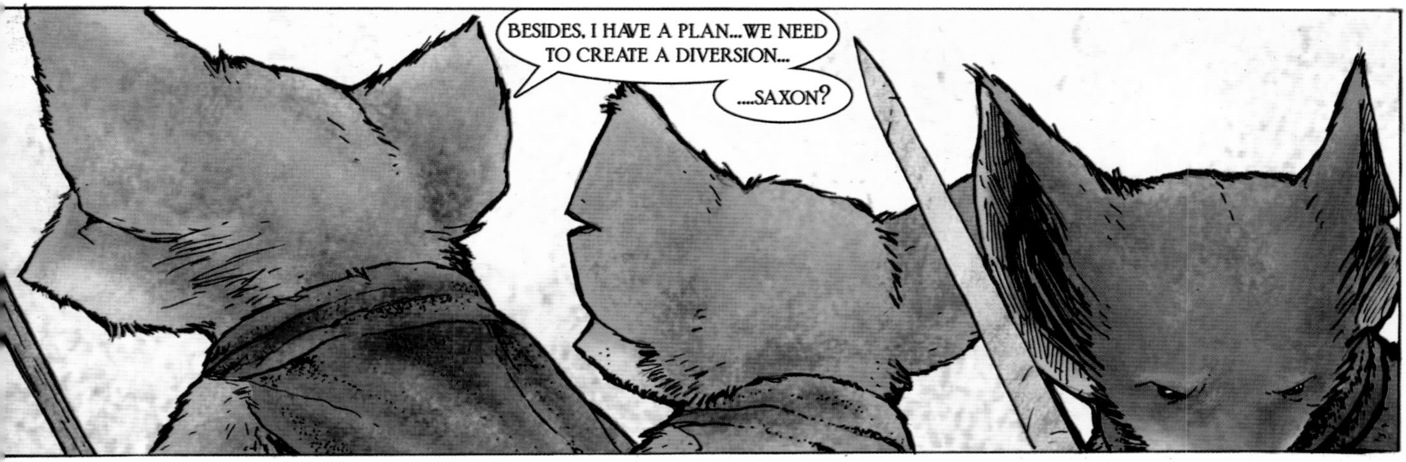
BESIDES, I HAVE A PLAN...WE NEED TO CREATE A DIVERSION...
....SAXON?

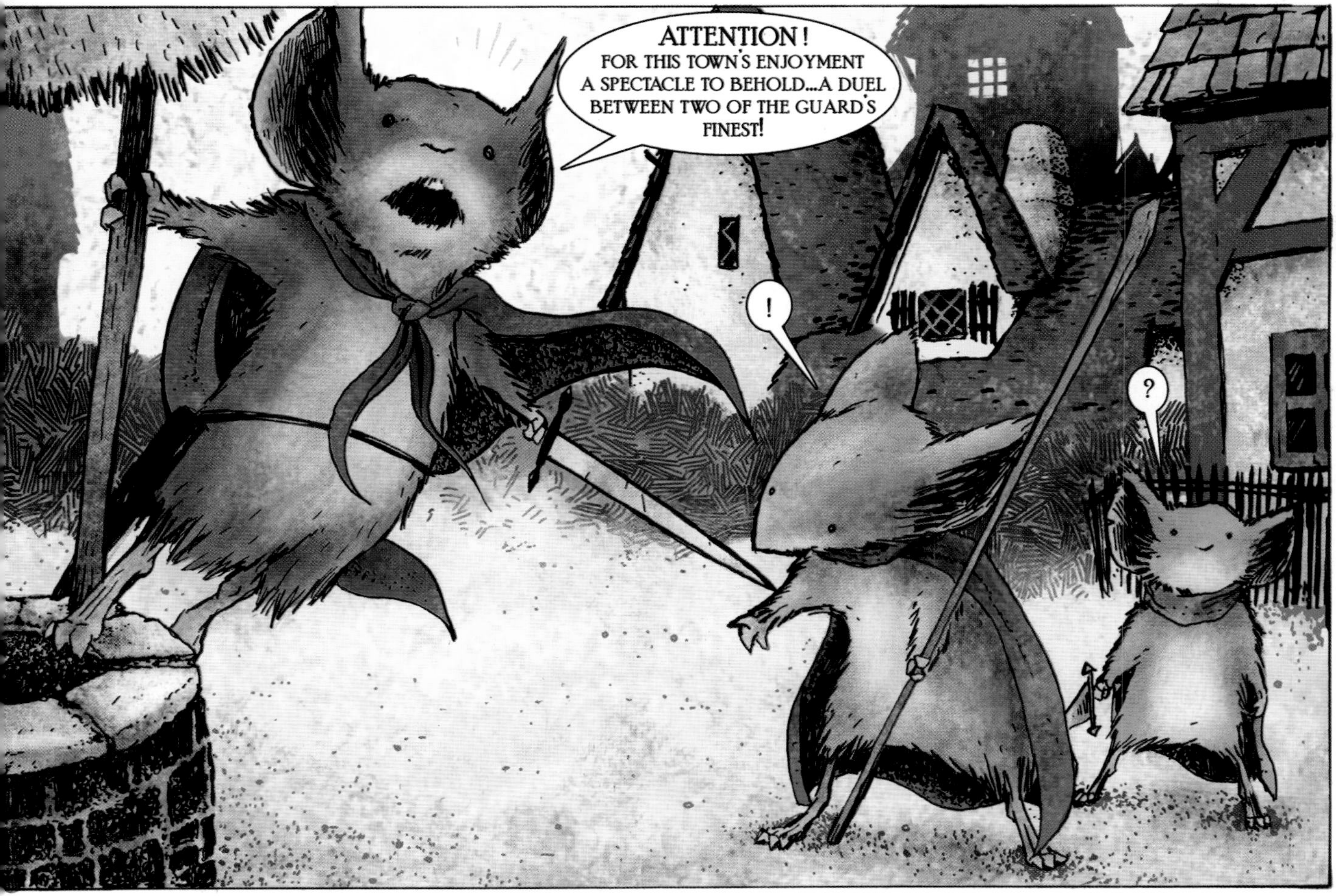
ATTENTION! FOR THIS TOWN'S ENJOYMENT A SPECTACLE TO BEHOLD...A DUEL BETWEEN TWO OF THE GUARD'S FINEST!
!
?

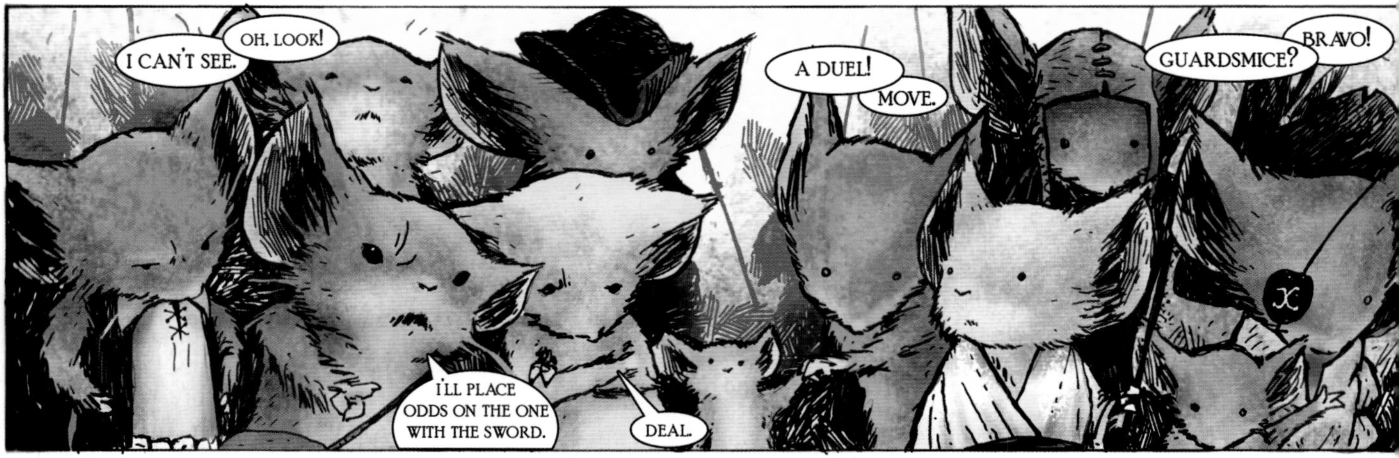
I CAN'T SEE.
OH, LOOK!
I'LL PLACE ODDS ON THE ONE WITH THE SWORD.
DEAL.
A DUEL!
MOVE.
GUARDSMICE?
BRAVO!

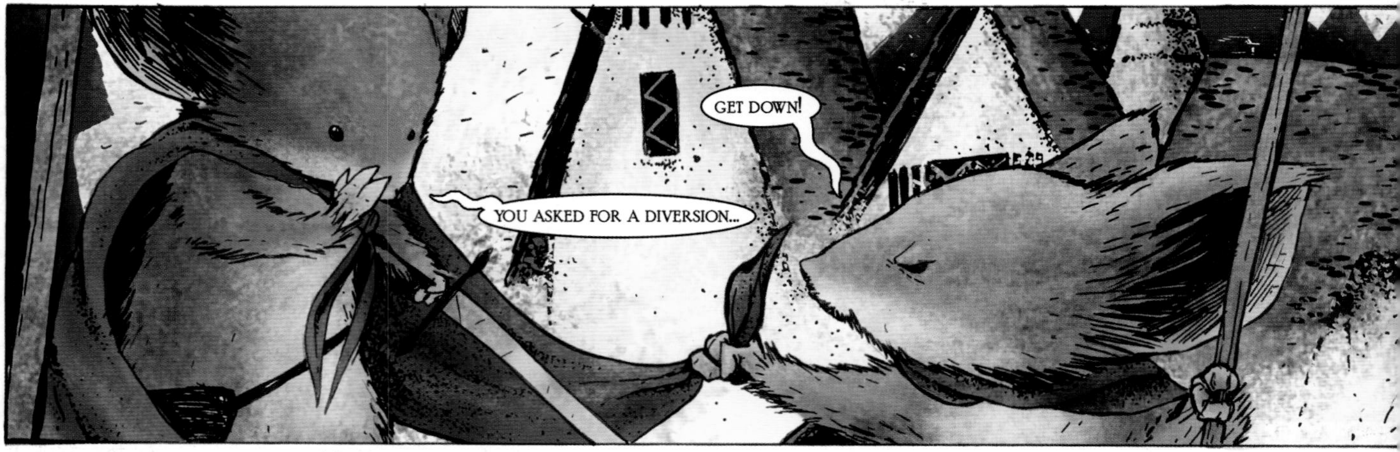
YOU ASKED FOR A DIVERSION...
GET DOWN!

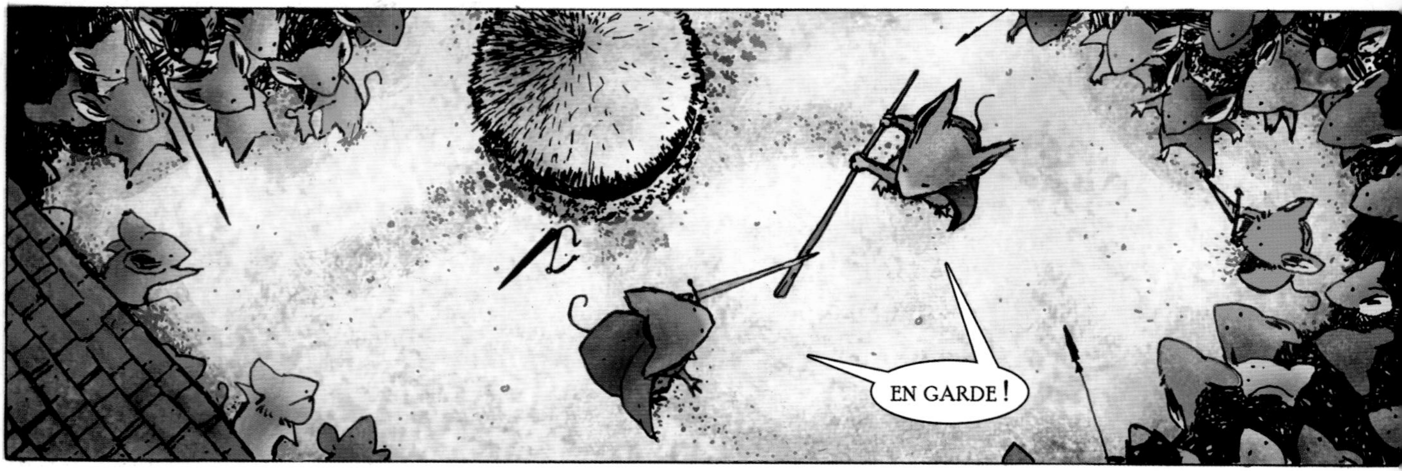
EN GARDE!

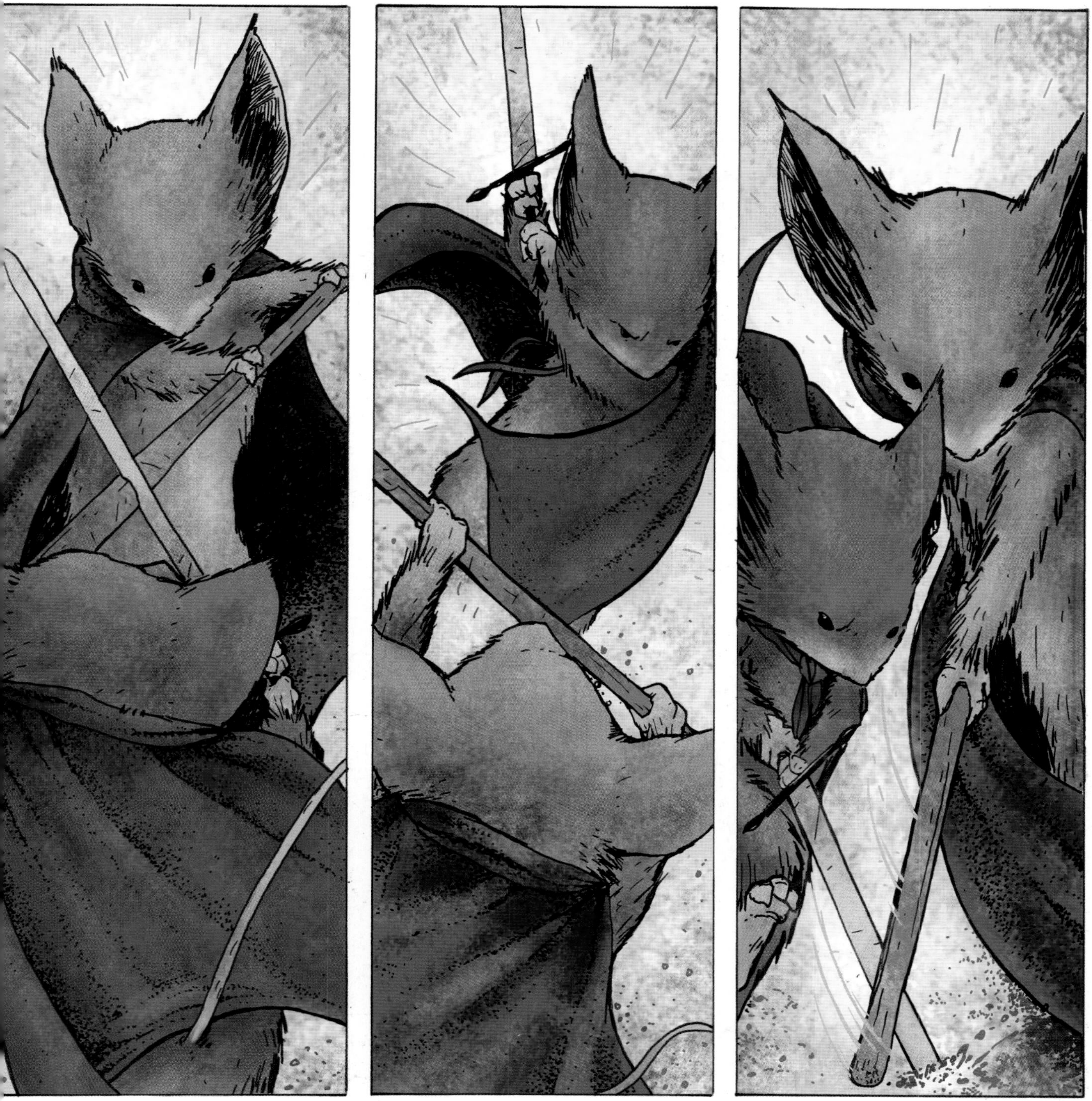

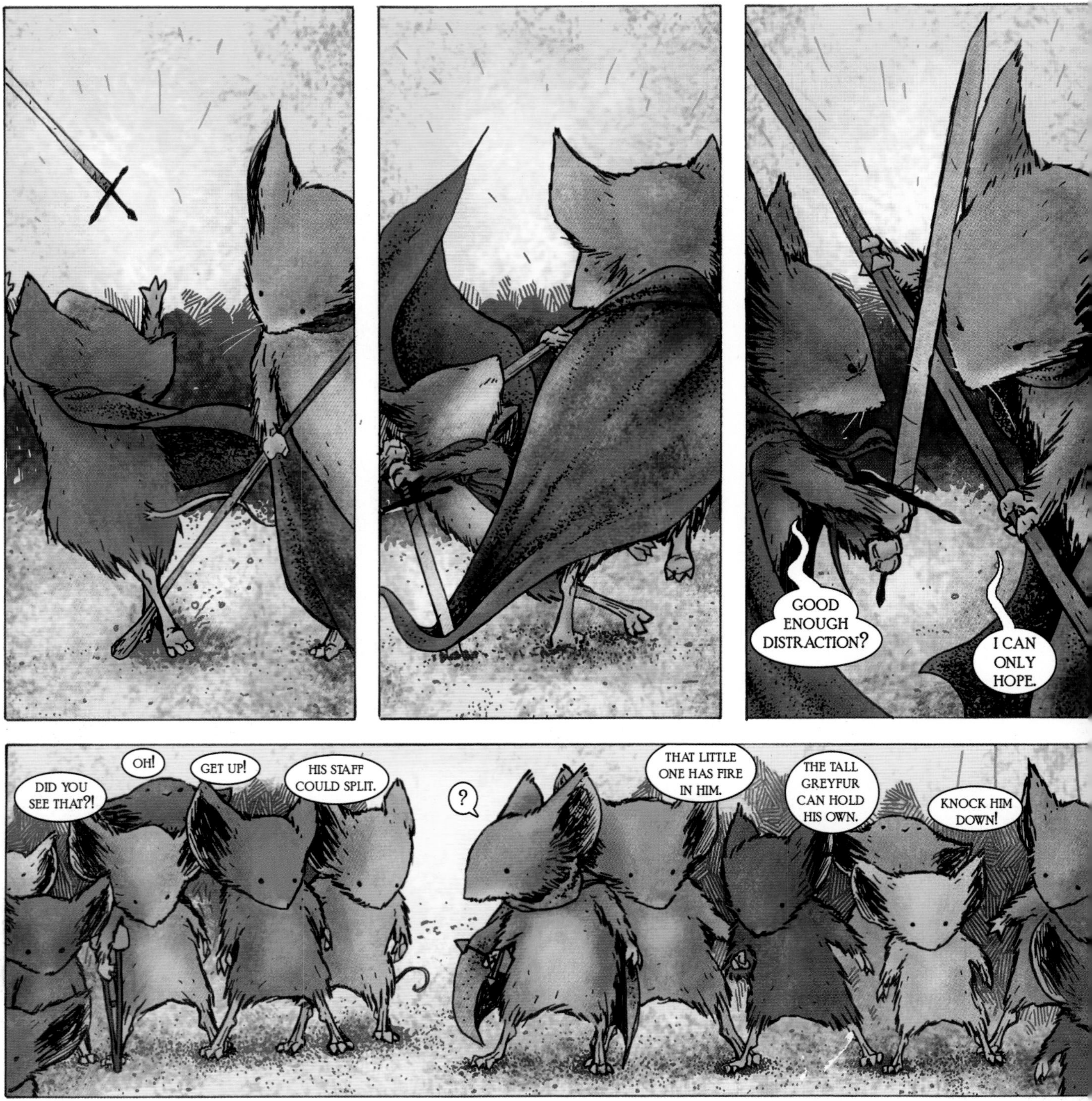
GOOD ENOUGH DISTRACTION?
I CAN ONLY HOPE.
DID YOU SEE THAT?!
OH!
GET UP!
HIS STAFF COULD SPLIT.
?
THAT LITTLE ONE HAS FIRE IN HIM.
THE TALL GREYFUR CAN HOLD HIS OWN.
KNOCK HIM DOWN!

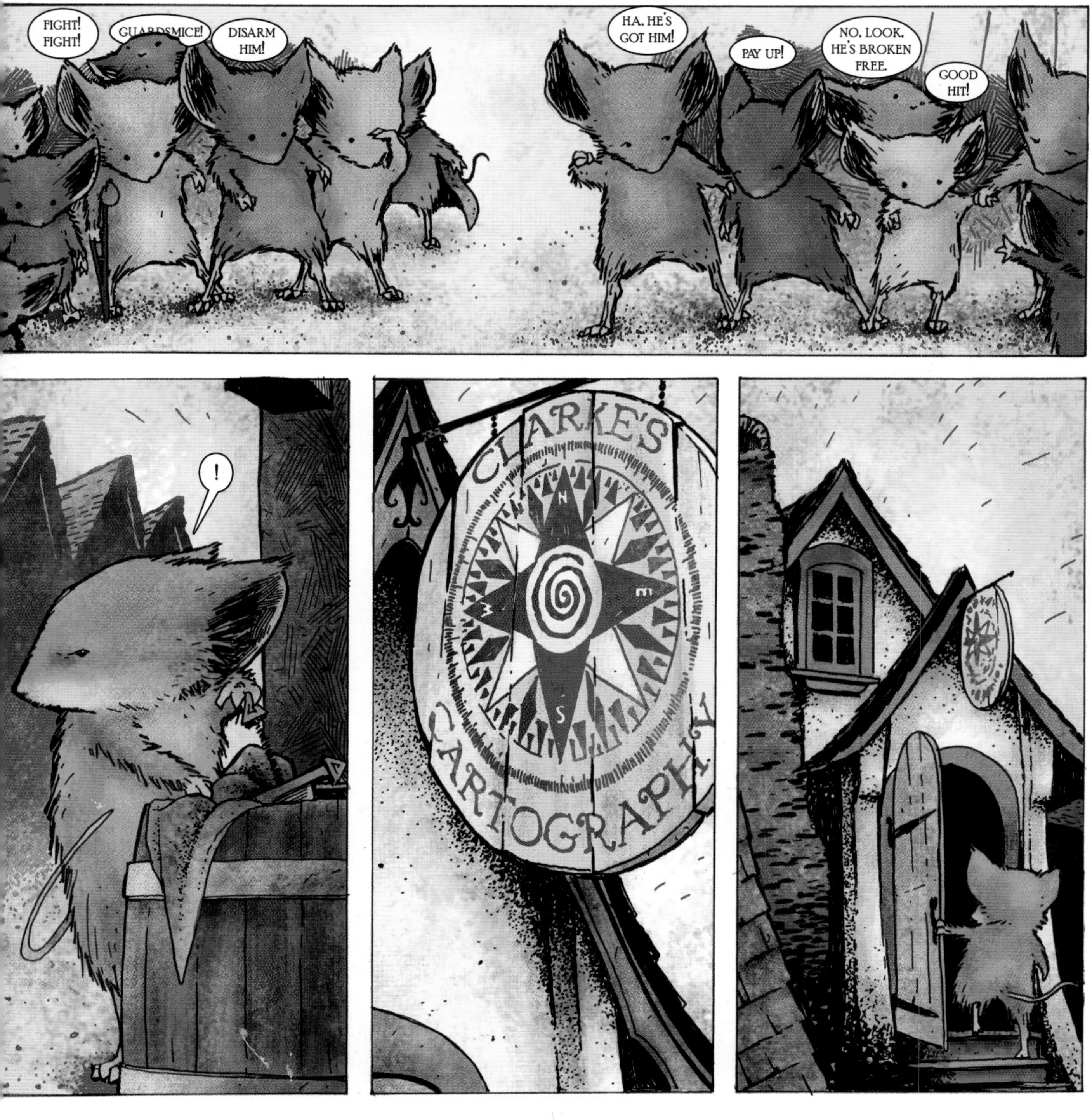
FIGHT! FIGHT!
GUARDSMICE!
DISARM HIM!
HA, HE'S GOT HIM!
PAY UP!
NO, LOOK, HE'S BROKEN FREE.
GOOD HIT!
!
CLARKE'S CARTOGRAPHY

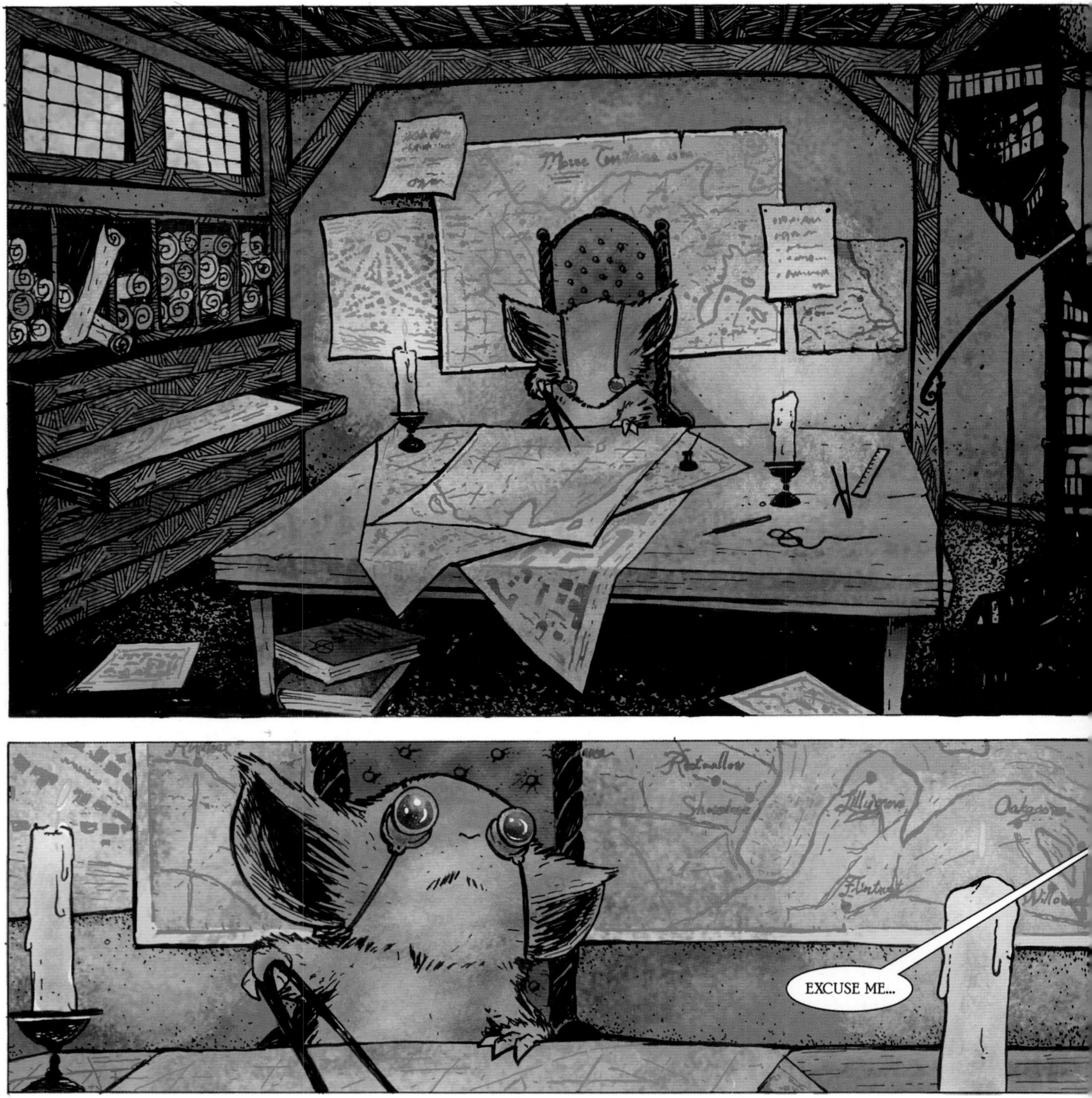
EXCUSE ME...

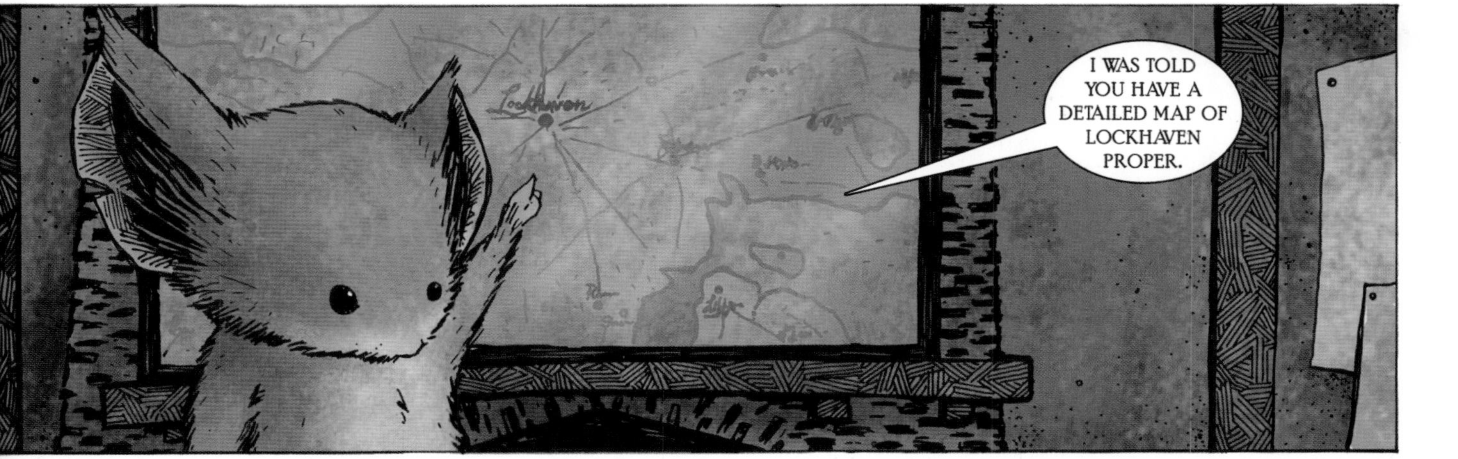
Lockhaven
I WAS TOLD YOU HAVE A DETAILED MAP OF LOCKHAVEN PROPER.

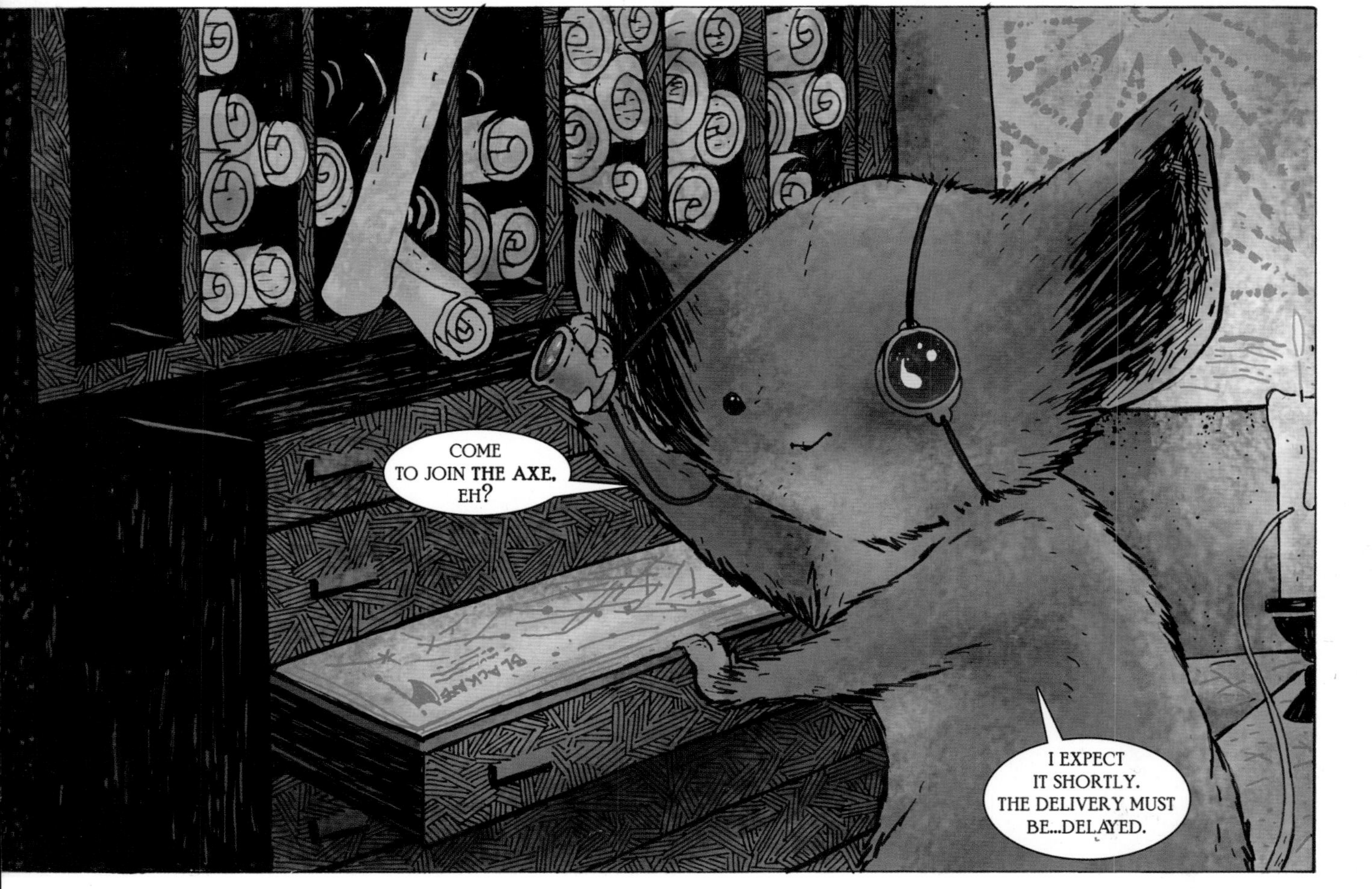
COME TO JOIN THE AXE, EH?
I EXPECT IT SHORTLY. THE DELIVERY MUST BE...DELAYED.

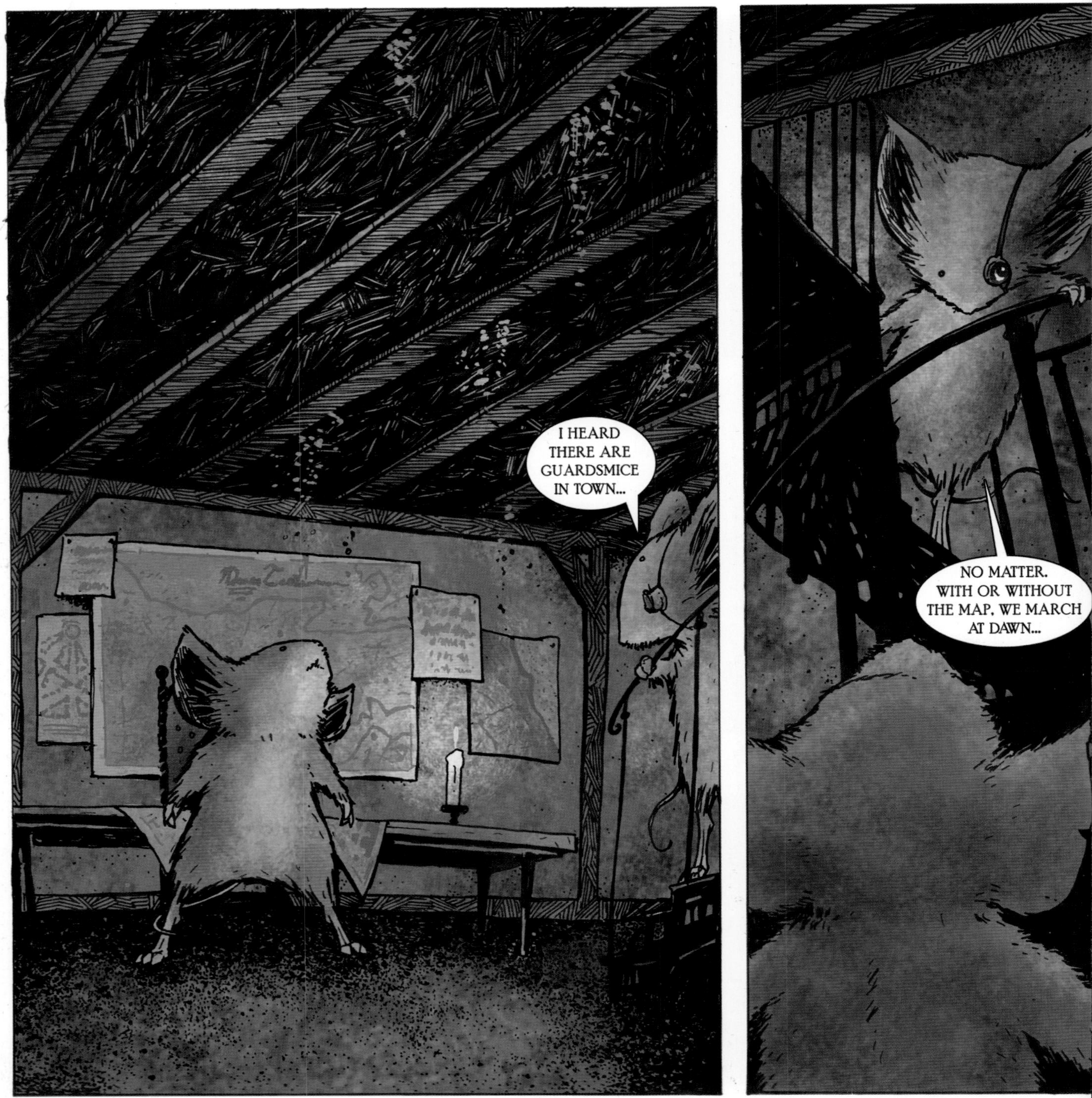
I HEARD THERE ARE GUARDSMICE IN TOWN...
NO MATTER. WITH OR WITHOUT THE MAP, WE MARCH AT DAWN...

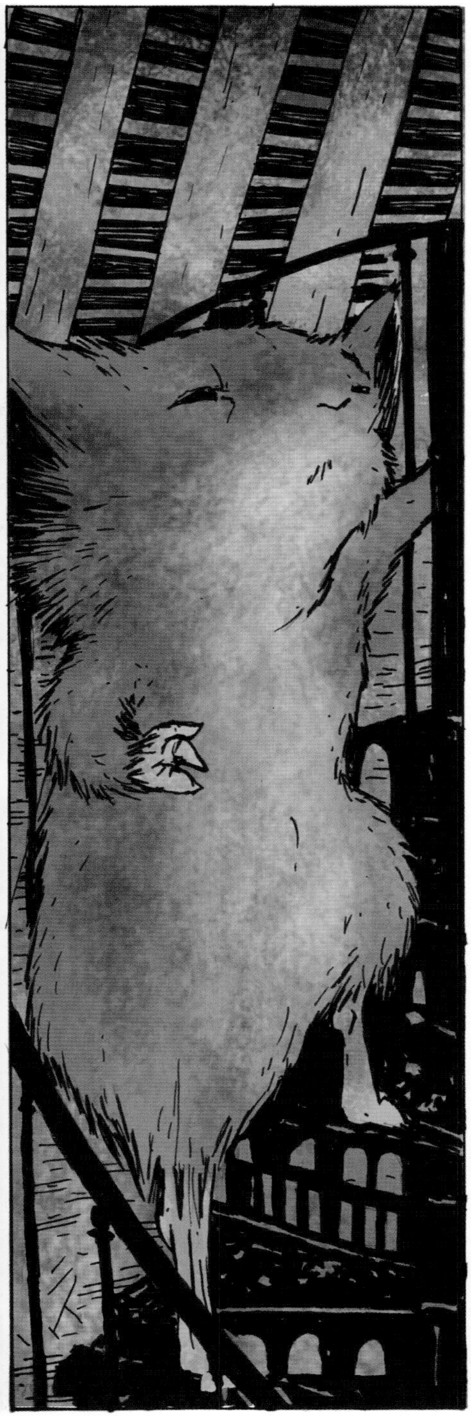

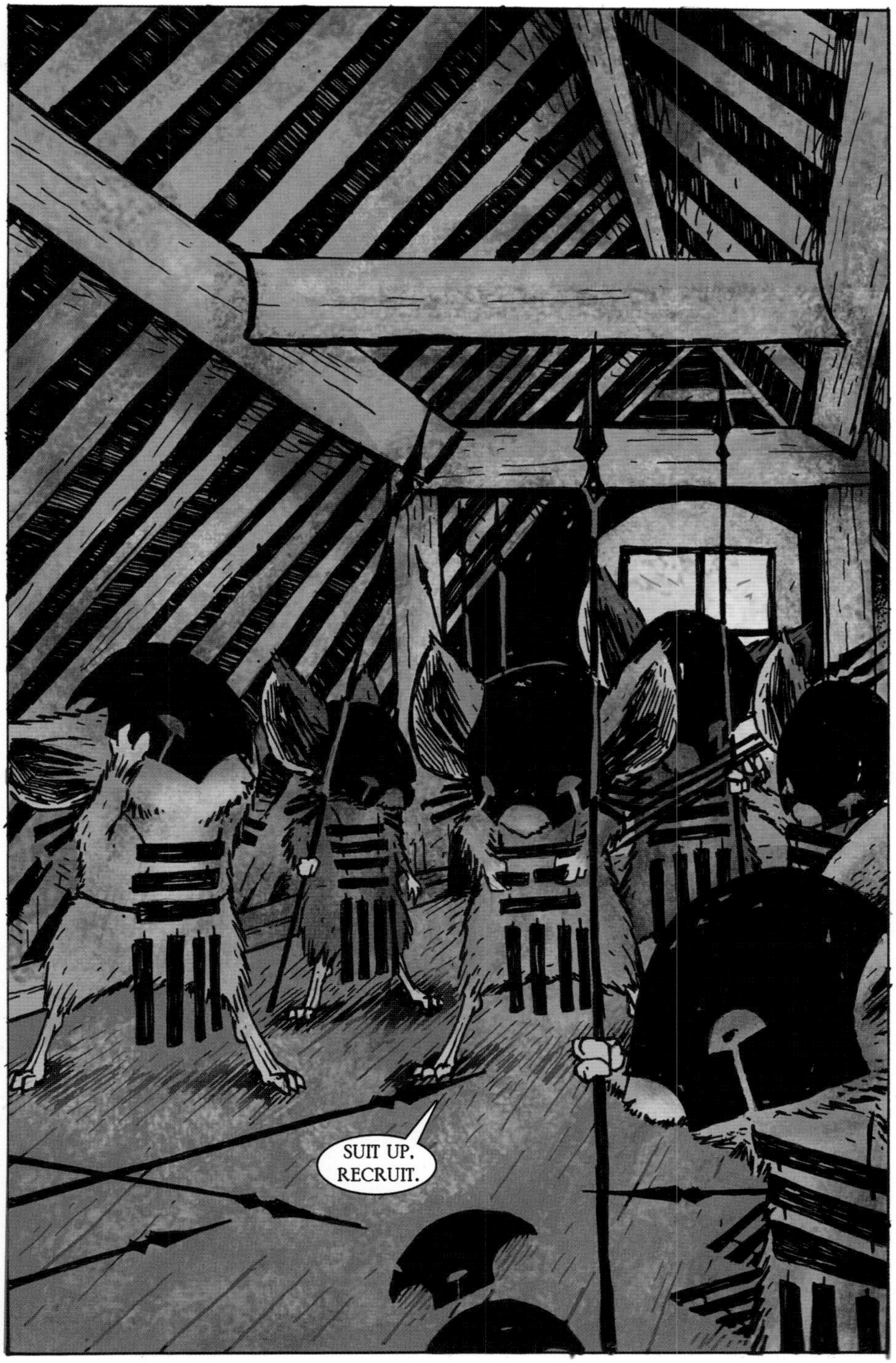
SUIT UP,
RECRUIT.

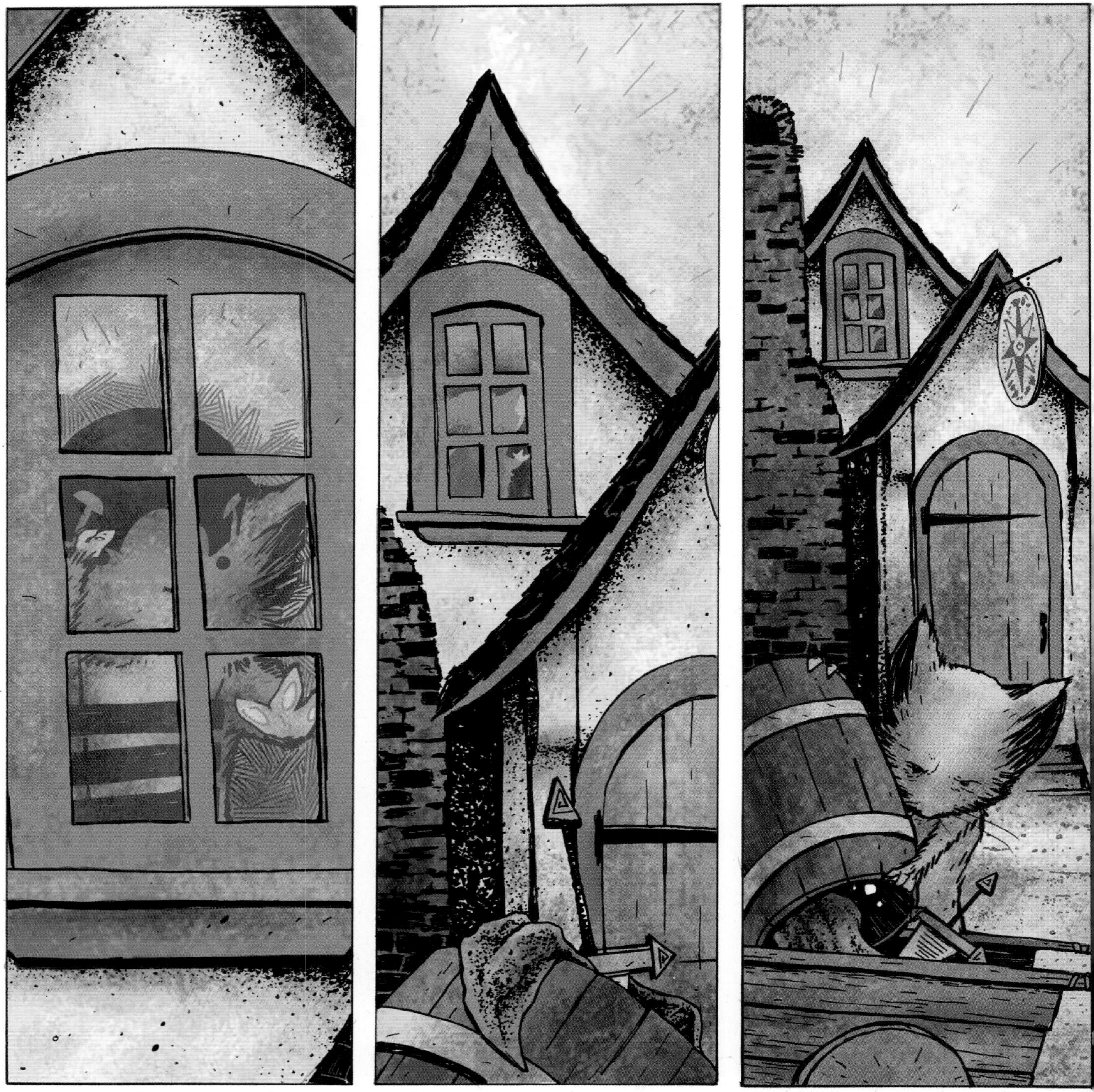

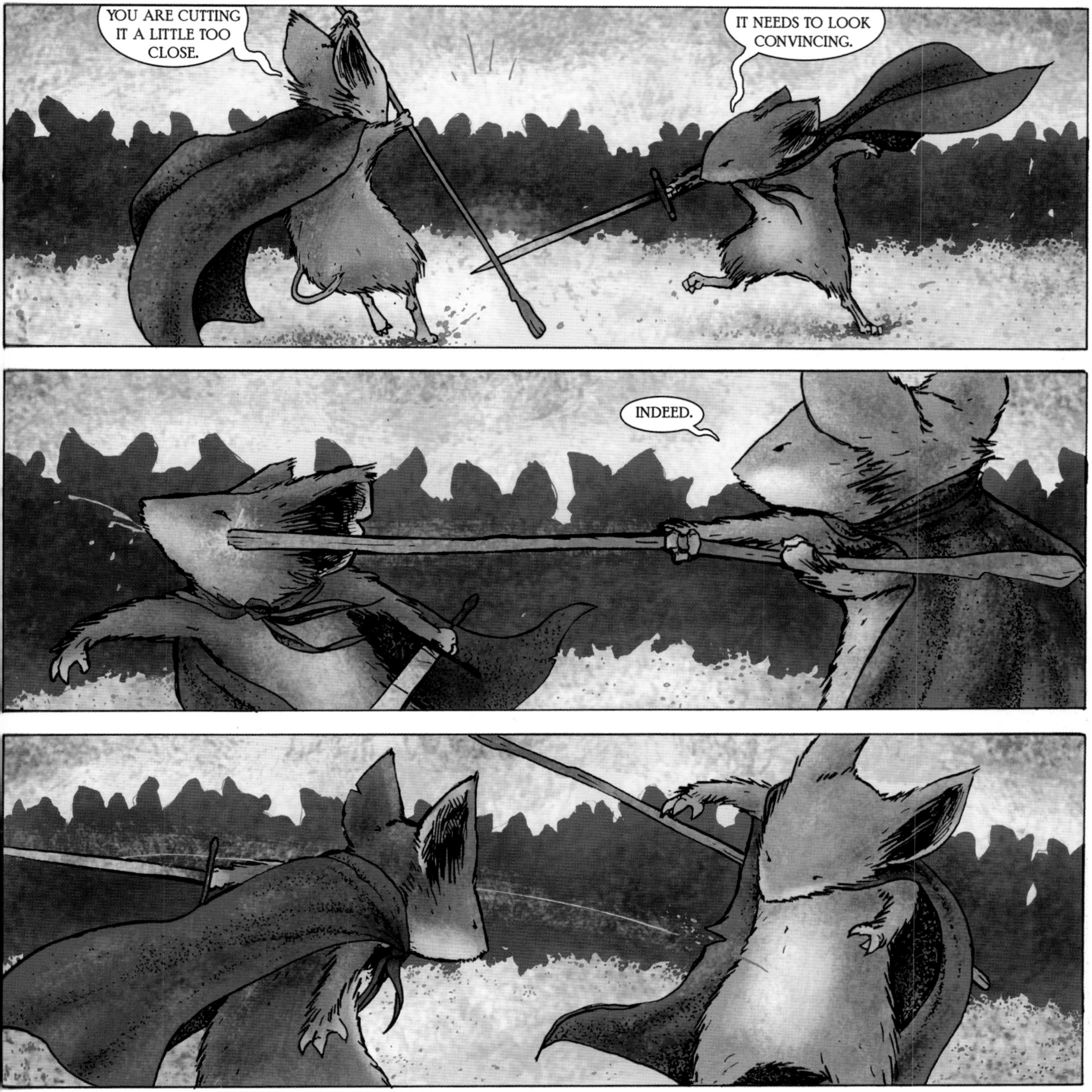
YOU ARE CUTTING IT A LITTLE TOO CLOSE.
IT NEEDS TO LOOK CONVINCING.
INDEED.

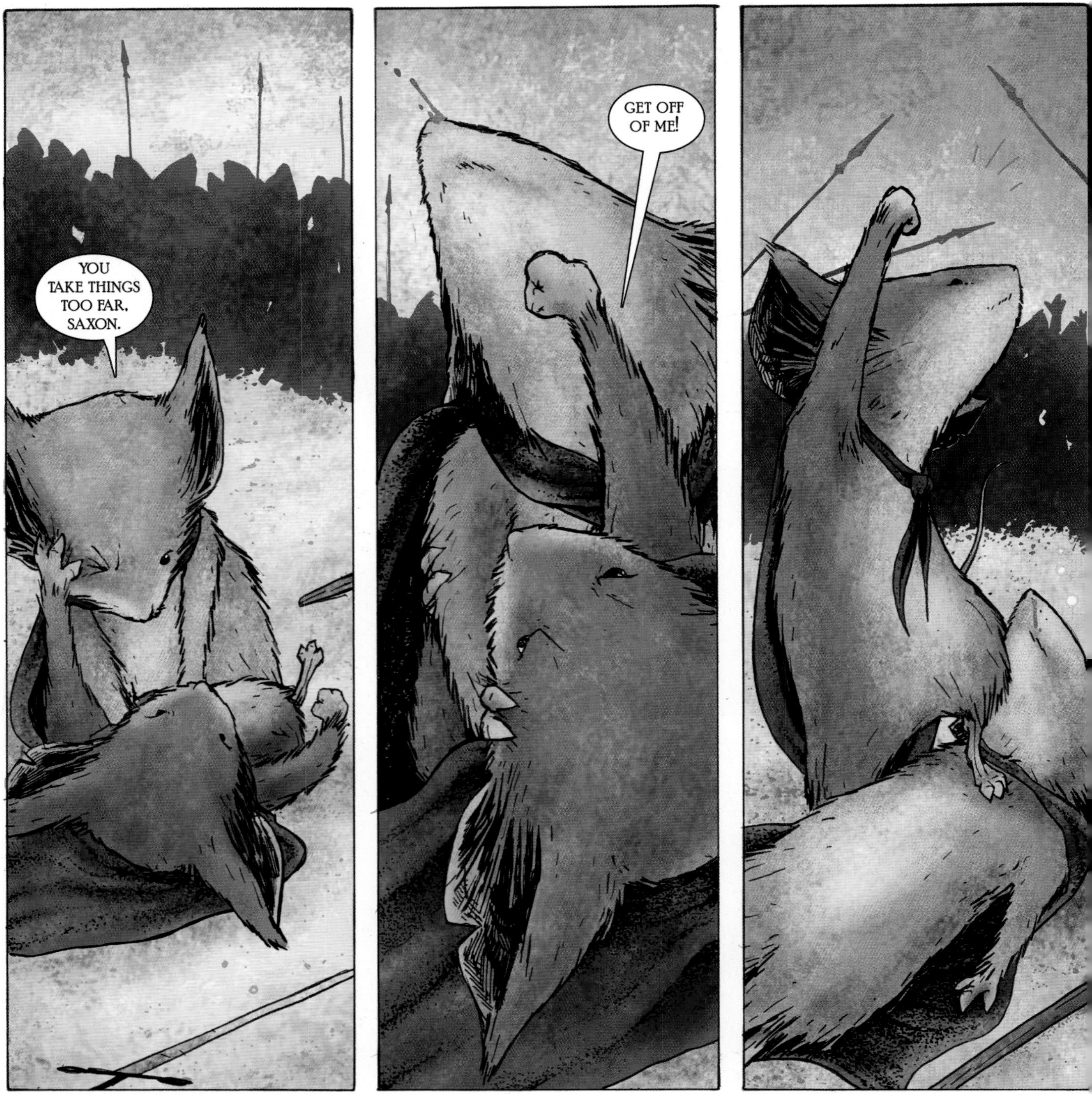
YOU TAKE THINGS TOO FAR, SAXON.
GET OFF OF ME!

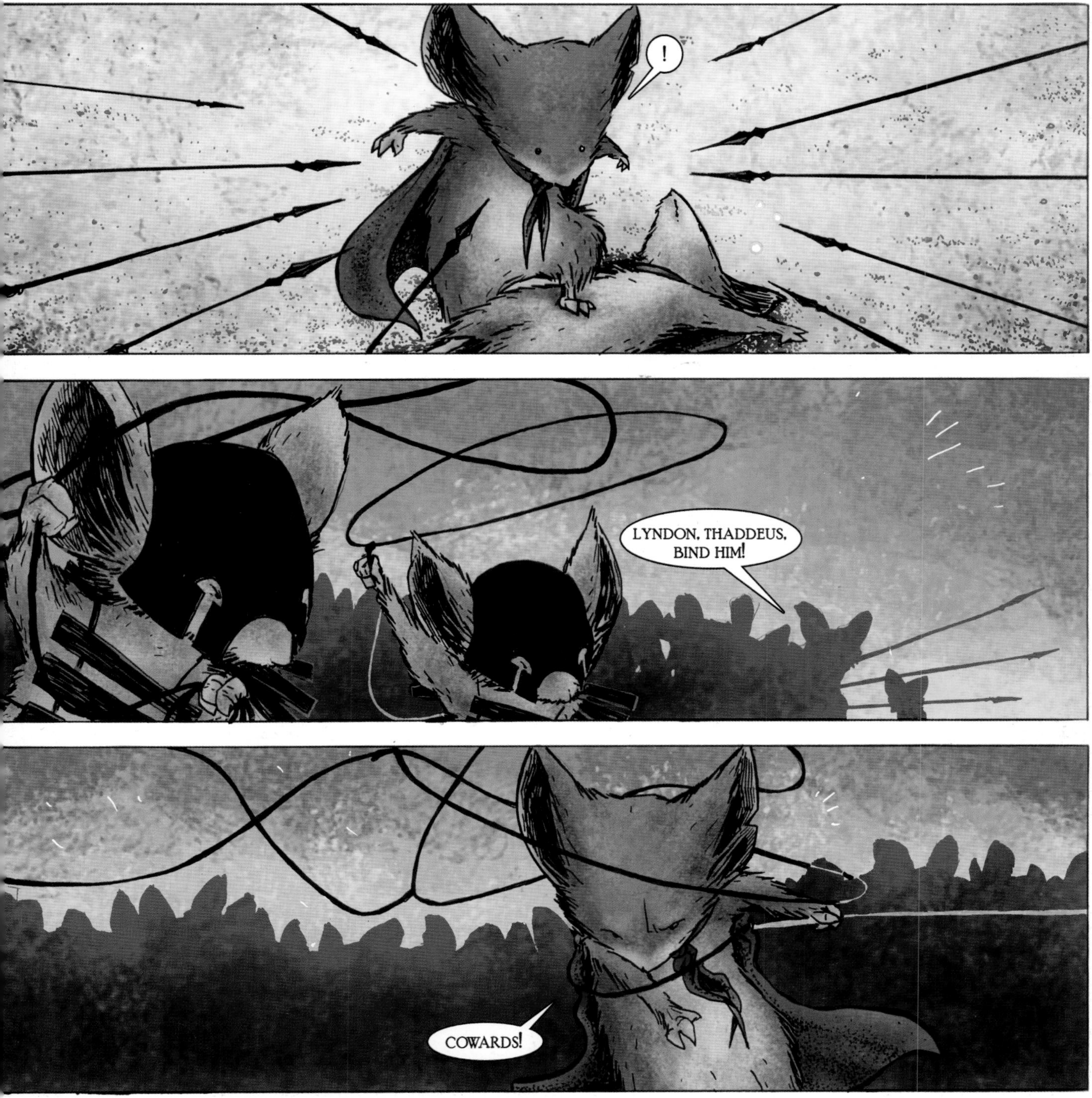
!
LYNDON, THADDEUS, BIND HIM!
COWARDS!

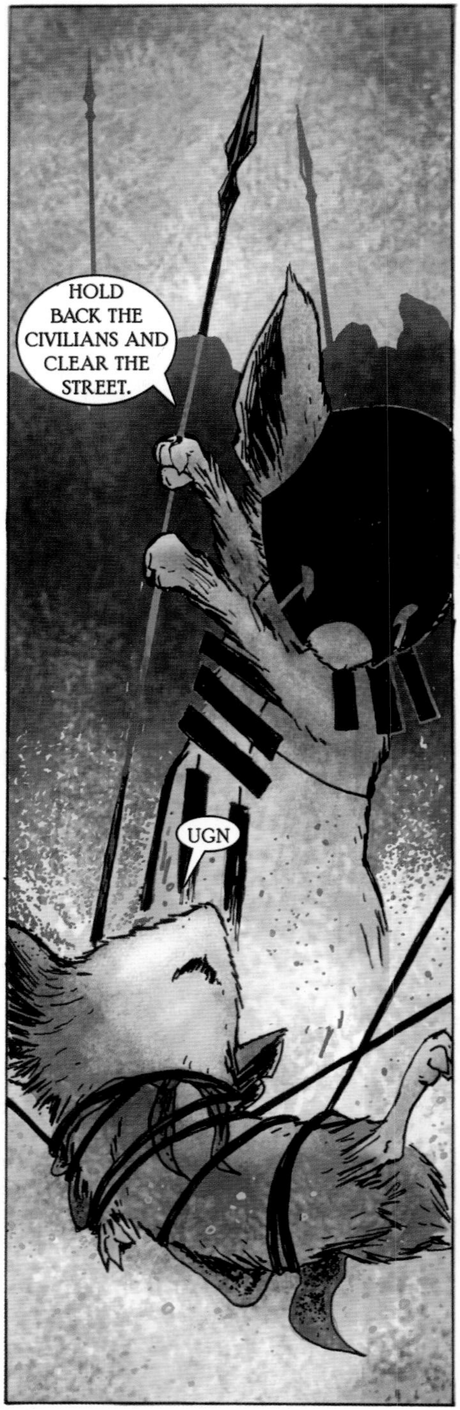
HOLD BACK THE CIVILIANS AND CLEAR THE STREET.
UGN

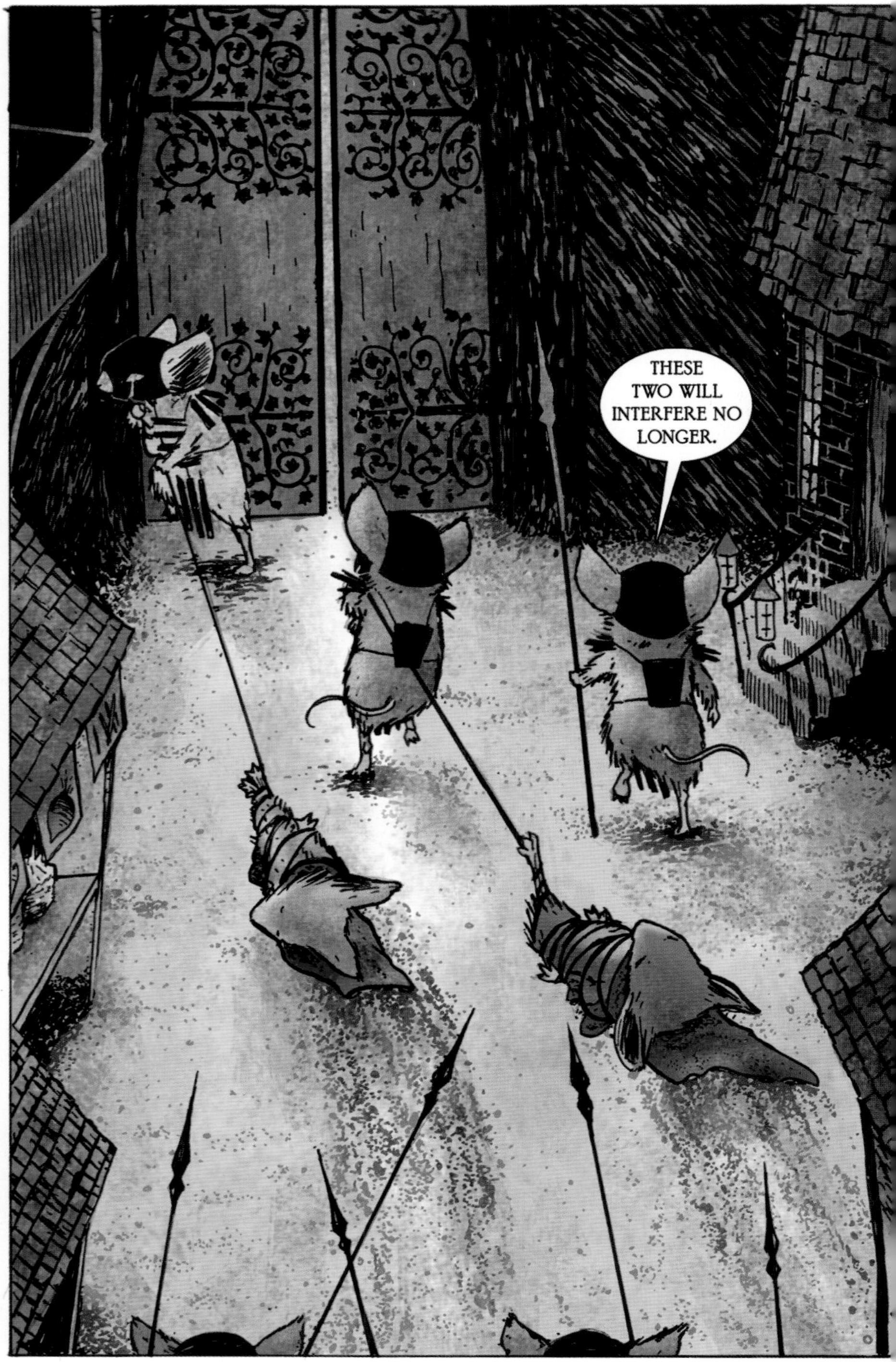
THESE TWO WILL INTERFERE NO LONGER.

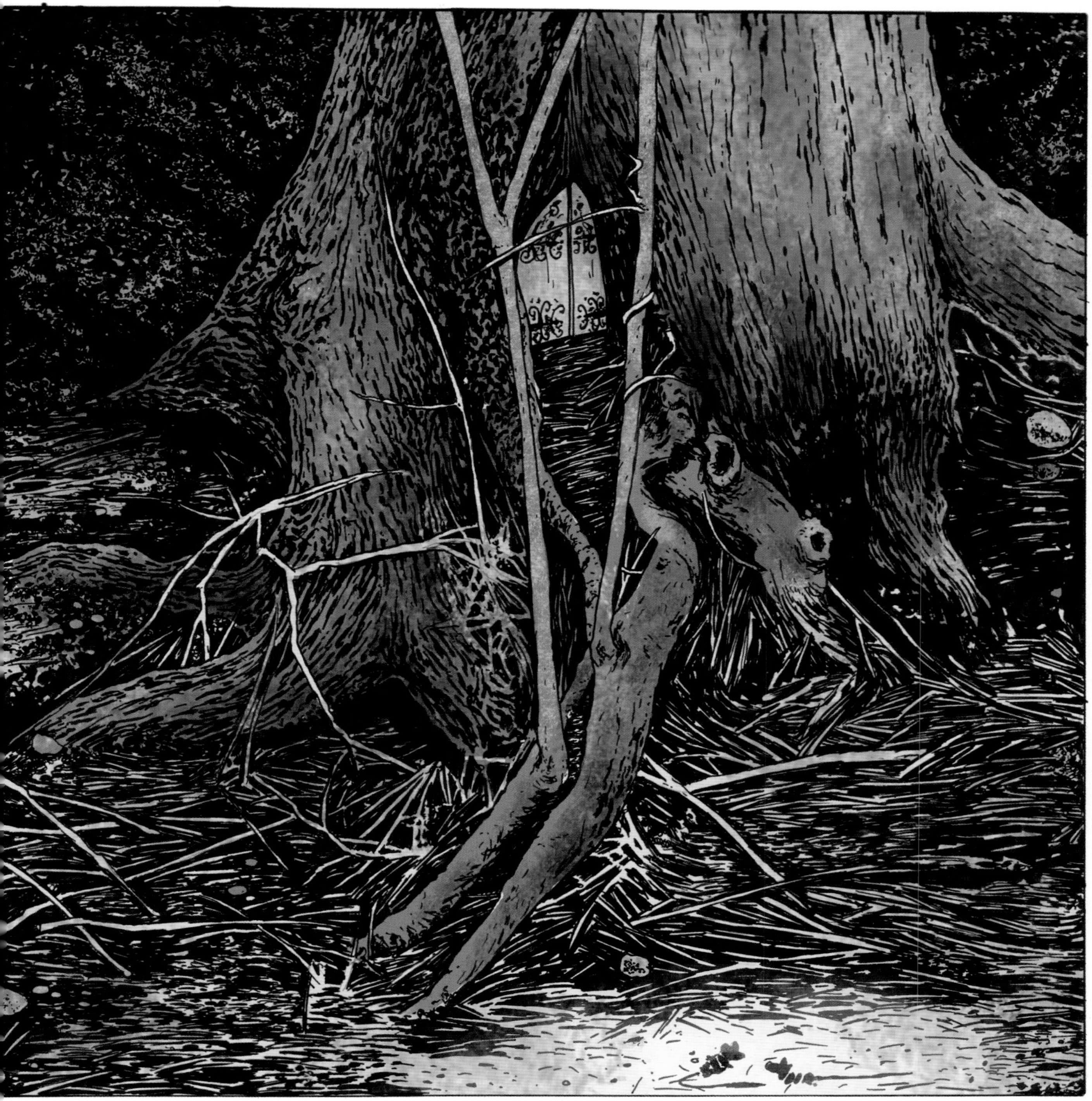

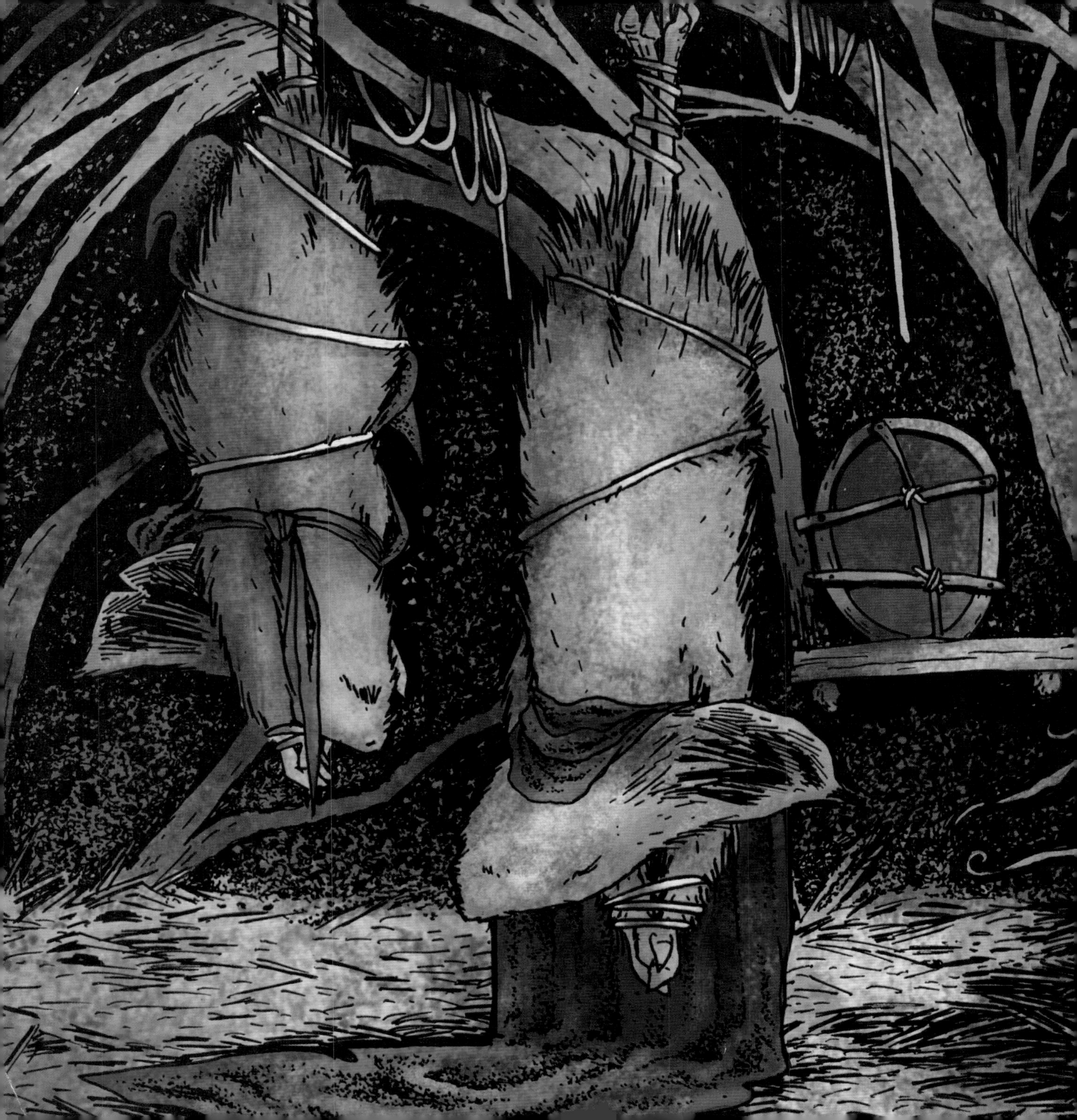

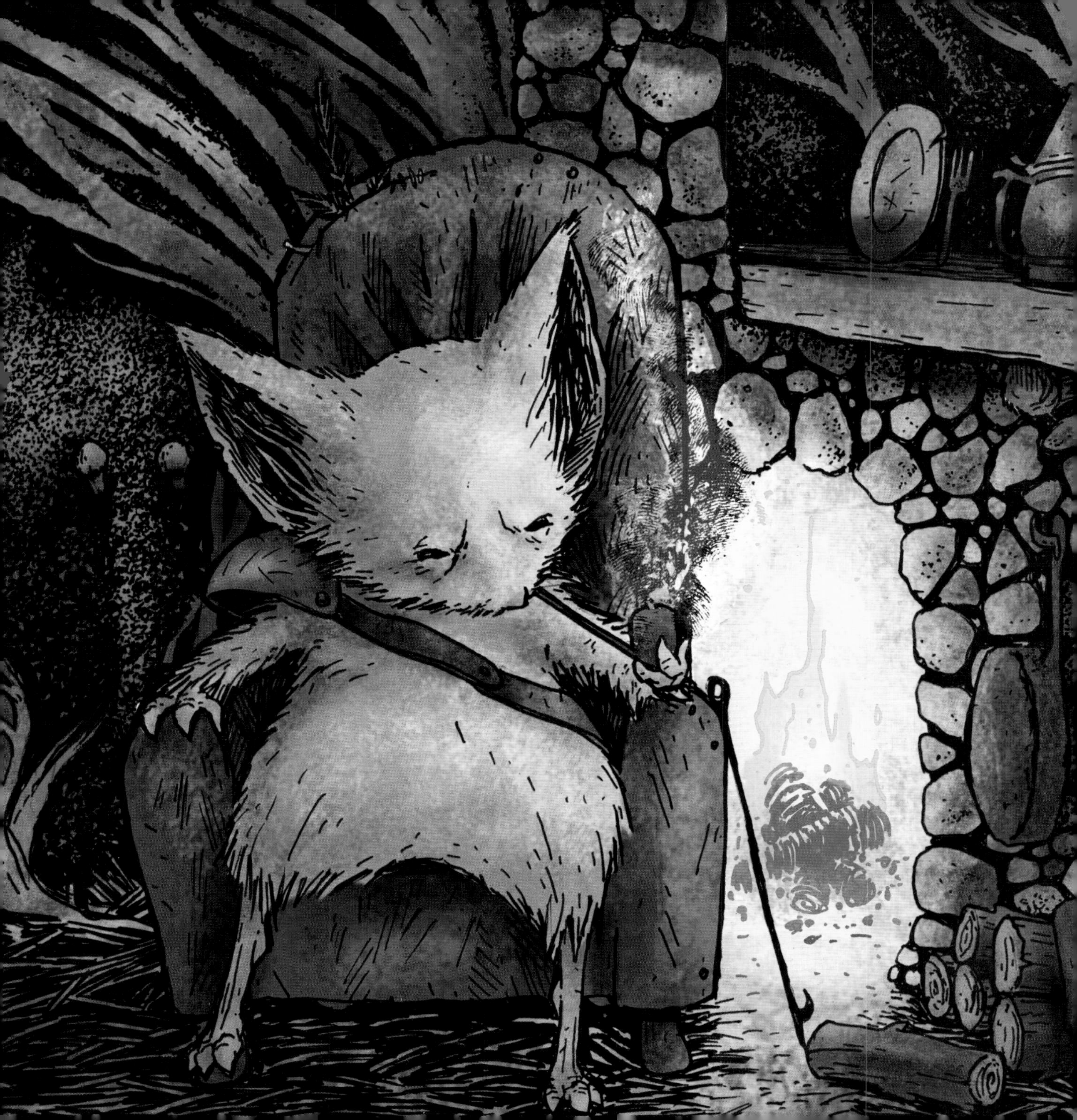

CHAPTER FOUR

THE DARK GHOST

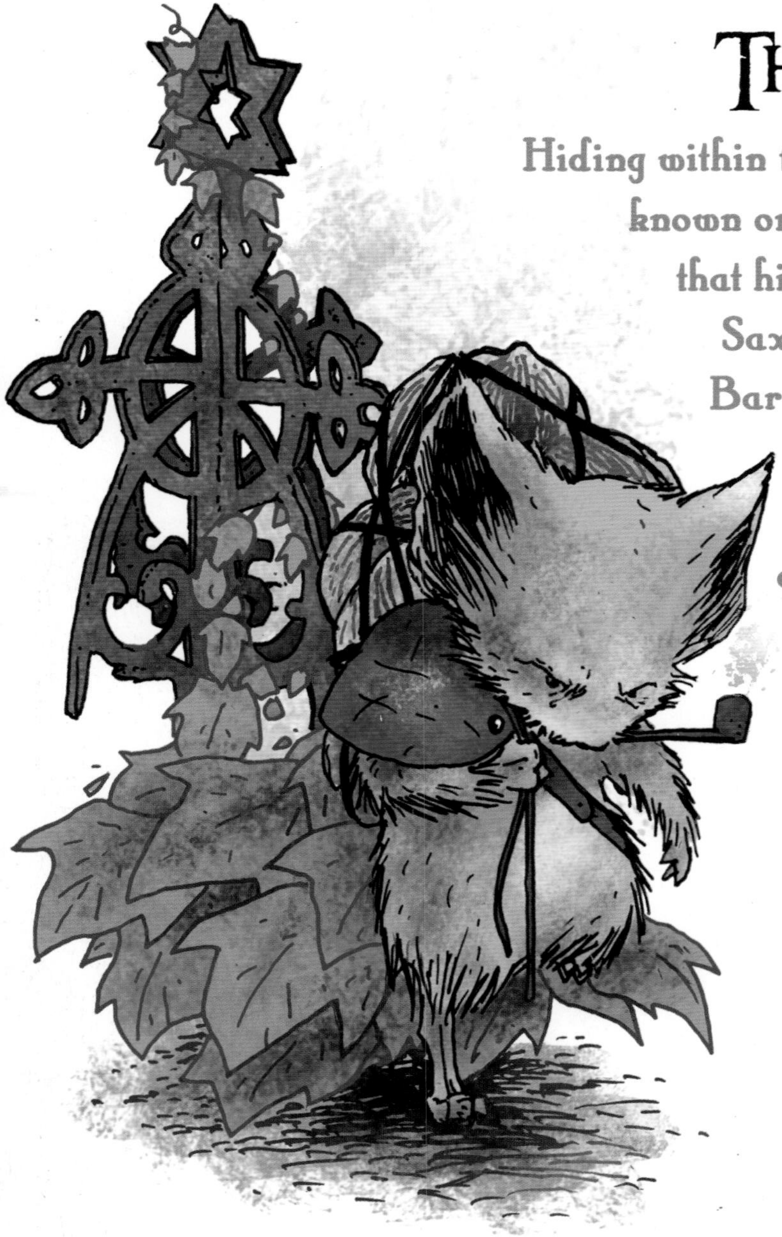

Hiding within the ranks of the mysterious militia known only as 'the Axe', Lieam is unaware that his Guard companions, Kenzie and Saxon, have been left for dead outside Barkstone's gates. Celanawe, a hermit and stranger to the mouse cities, has retrieved the red and blue cloaked mice and dragged them to his secluded home...and a dark plot quietly grows.

'Death is as powerful a weapon
as it is an easy escape.
Heroes can pass in to legend,
Legends into myths,
Myths fuel new heroes.'

-the last recorded words of the Black Axe:
Champion of the Mouse Guard

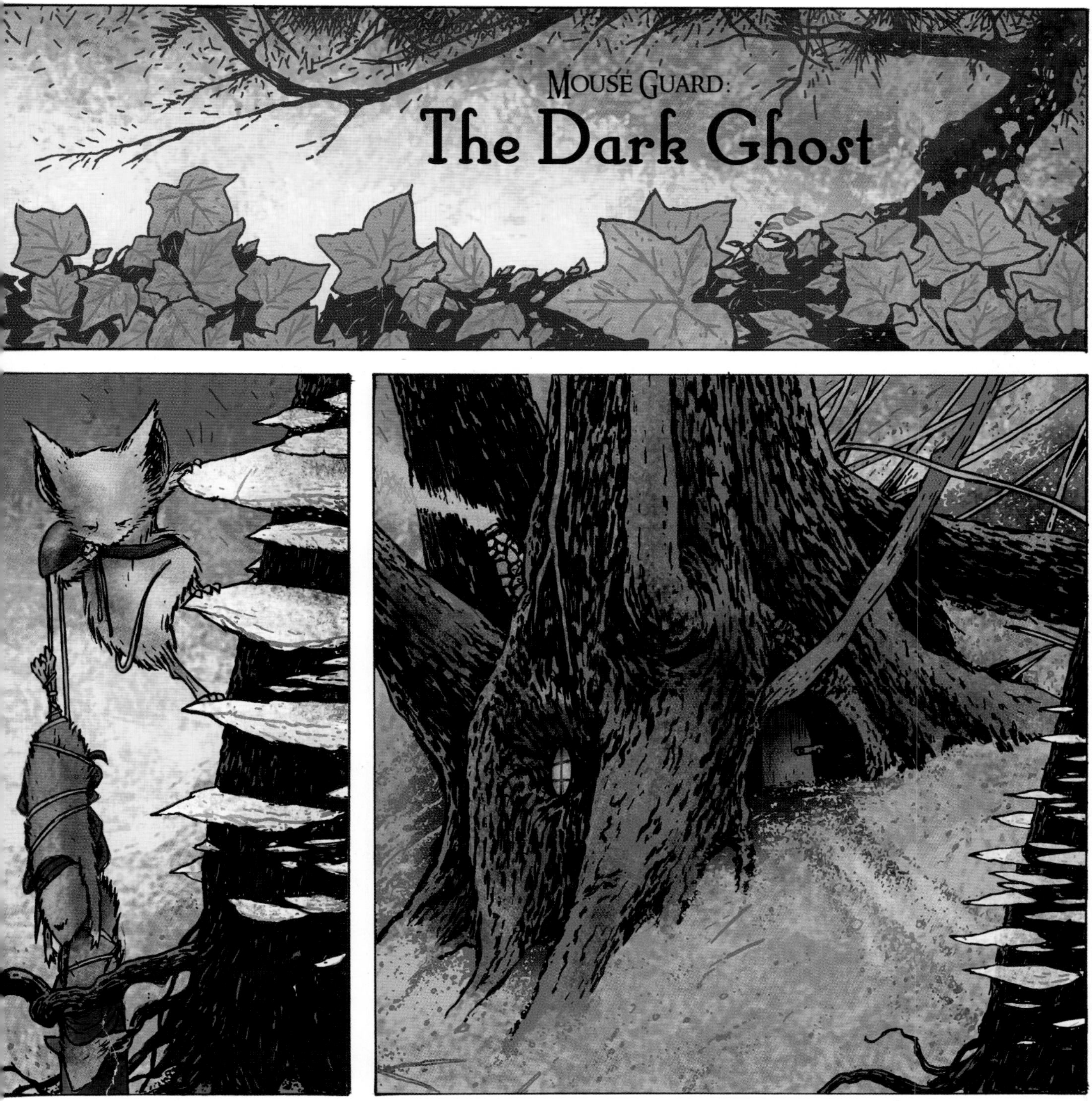
MOUSE GUARD:
The Dark Ghost

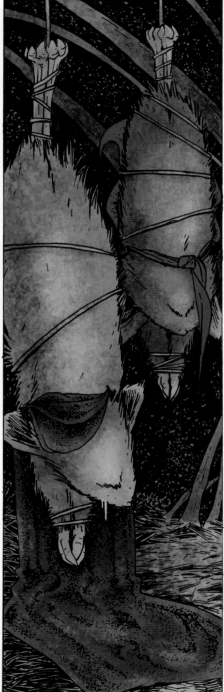

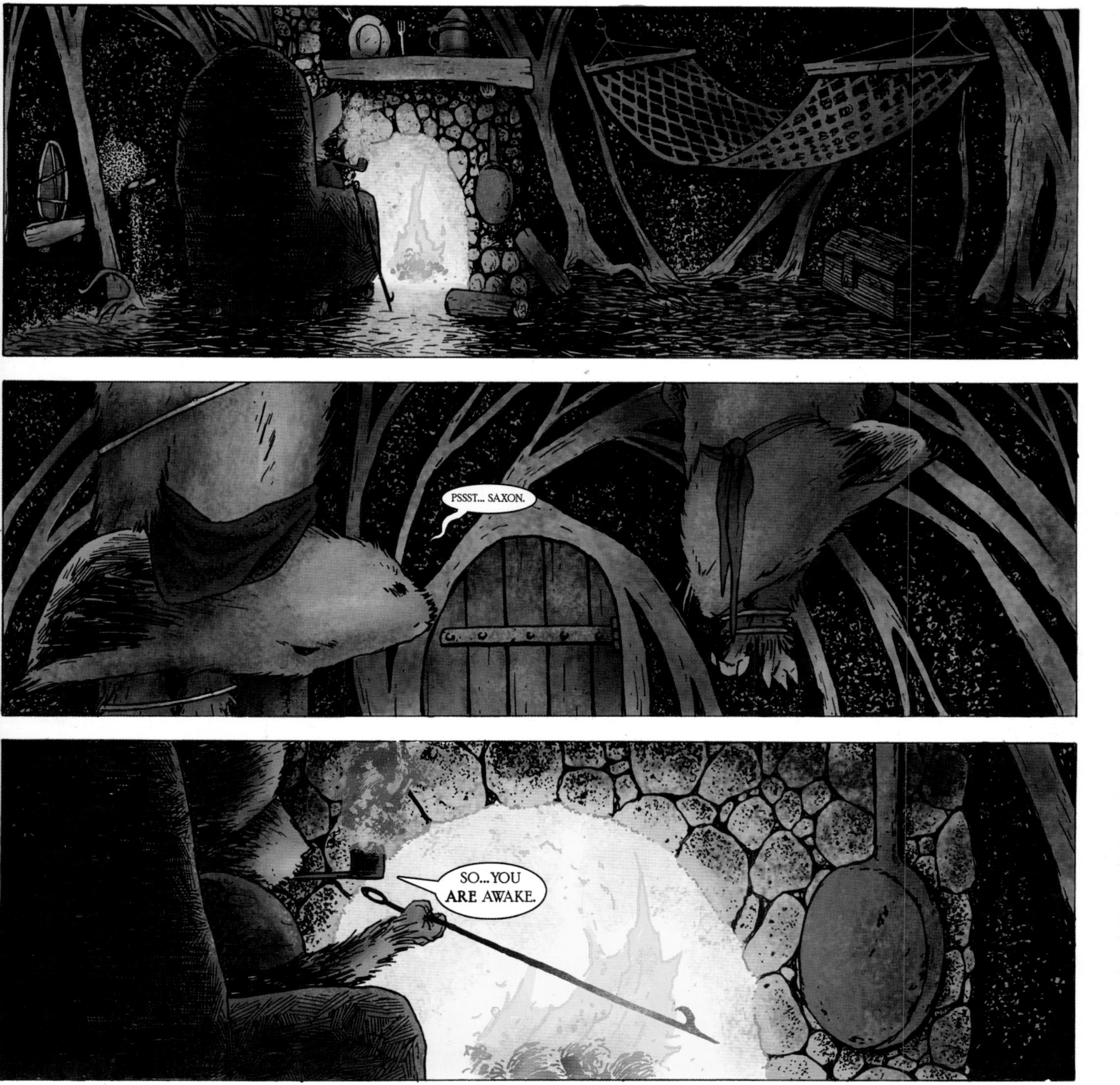
PSSST... SAXON.
SO...YOU ARE AWAKE.

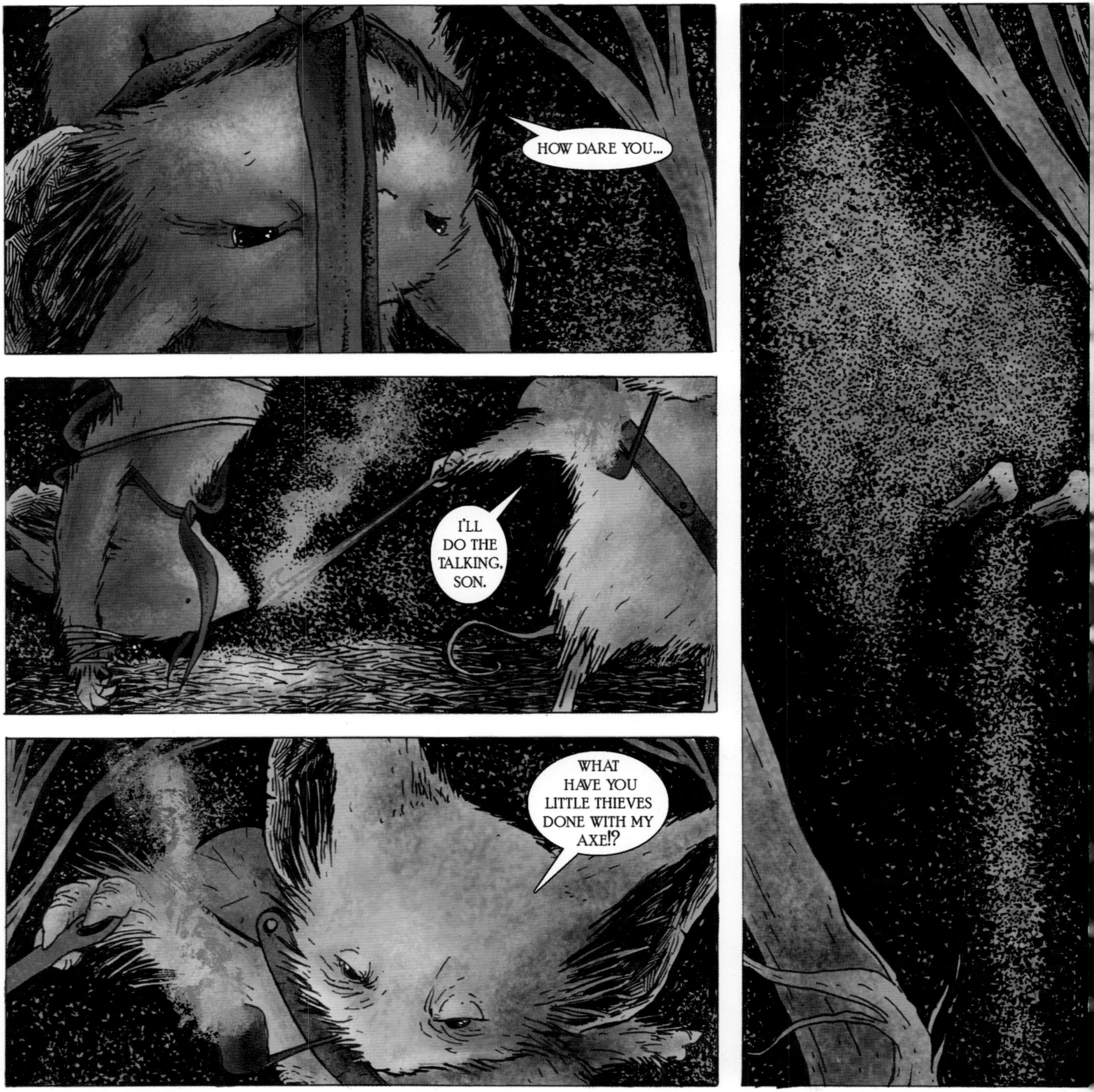
HOW DARE YOU...
I'LL DO THE TALKING, SON.
WHAT HAVE YOU LITTLE THIEVES DONE WITH MY AXE!?

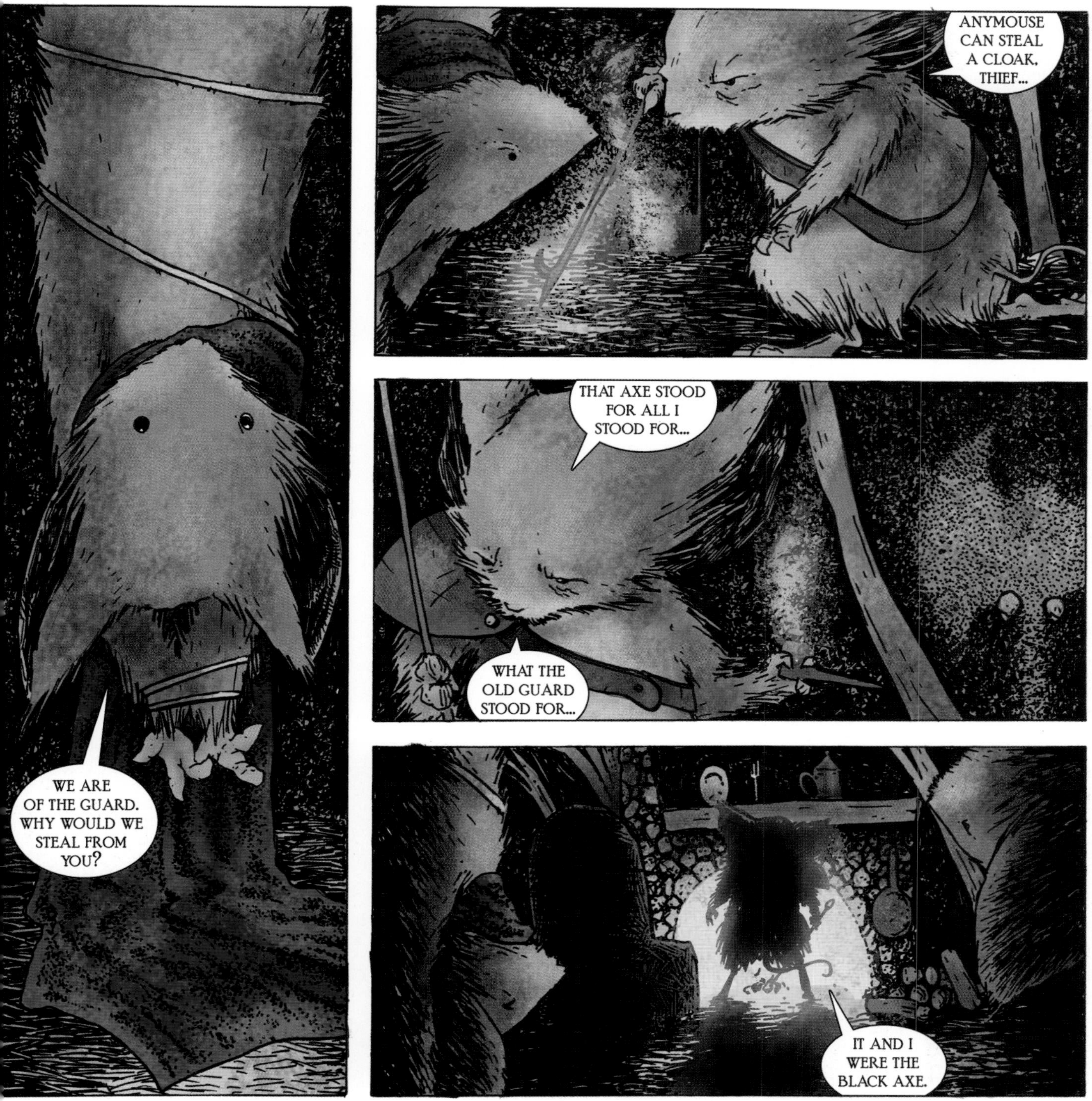
WE ARE OF THE GUARD. WHY WOULD WE STEAL FROM YOU?
ANYMOUSE CAN STEAL A CLOAK, THIEF...
THAT AXE STOOD FOR ALL I STOOD FOR...
WHAT THE OLD GUARD STOOD FOR...
IT AND I WERE THE BLACK AXE.

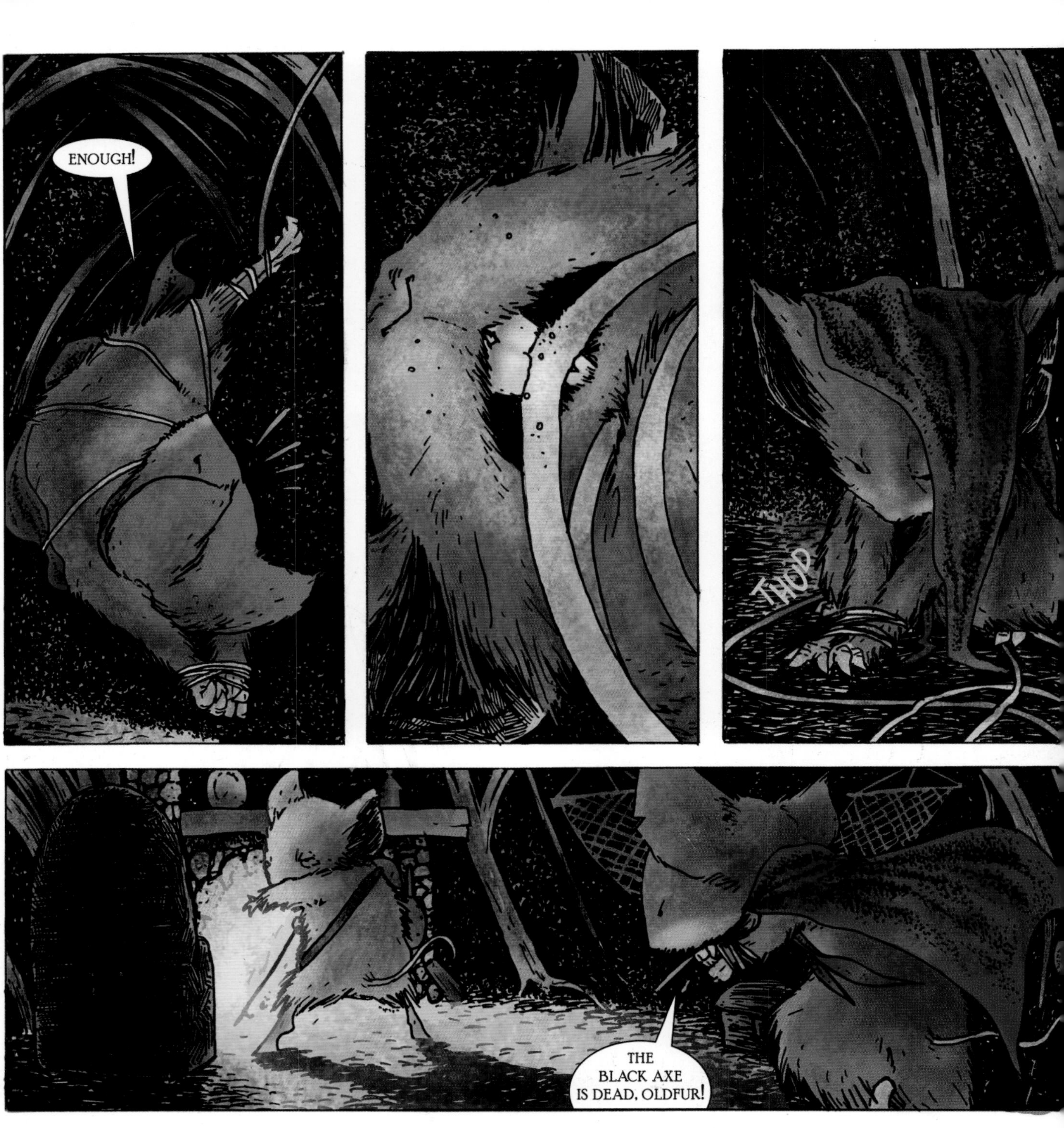
ENOUGH!
THUP
THE BLACK AXE IS DEAD, OLDFUR!

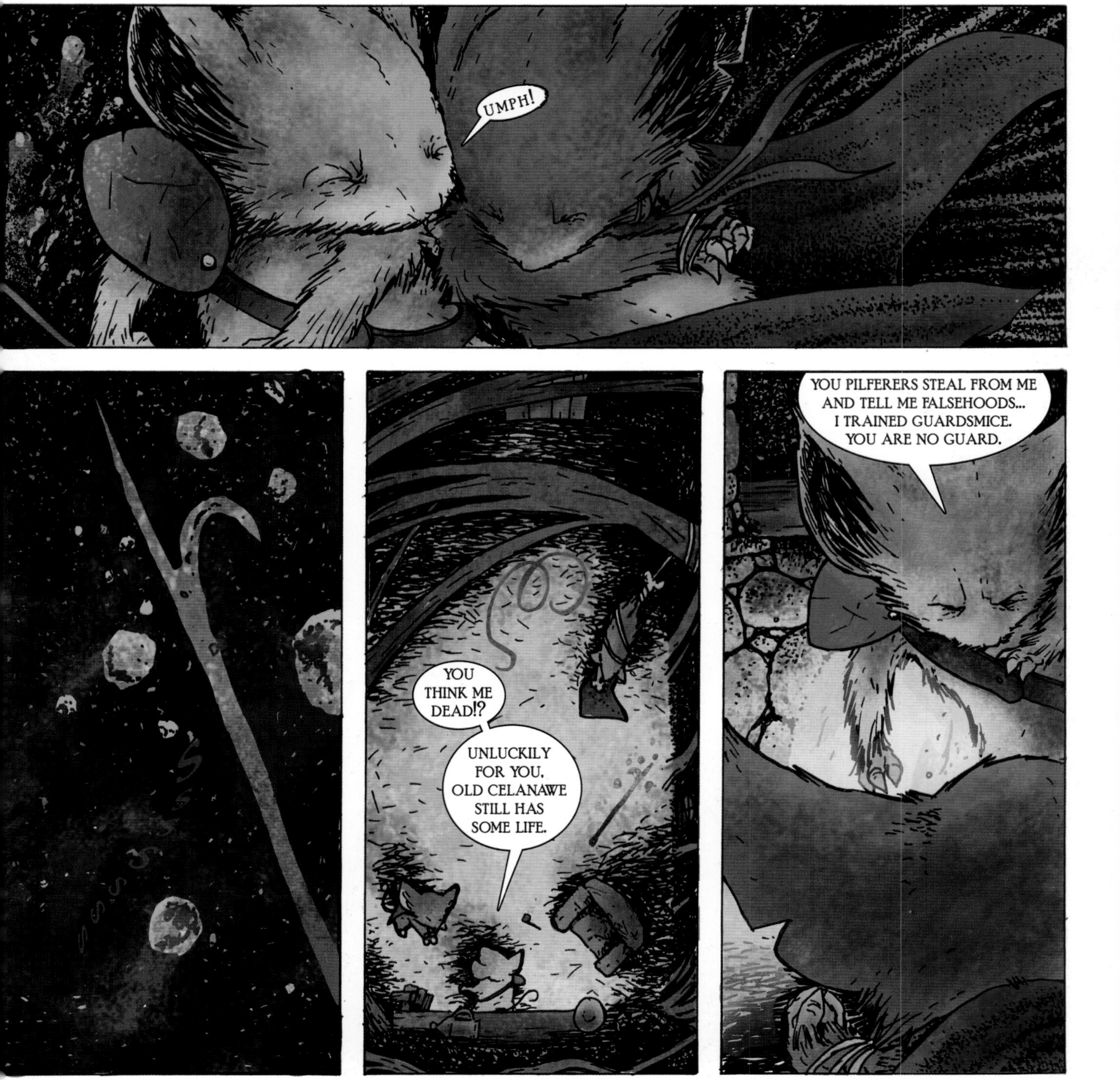
UMPH!
YOU THINK ME DEAD!?
UNLUCKILY FOR YOU, OLD CELANAWE STILL HAS SOME LIFE.
YOU PILFERERS STEAL FROM ME AND TELL ME FALSEHOODS... I TRAINED GUARDSMICE. YOU ARE NO GUARD.

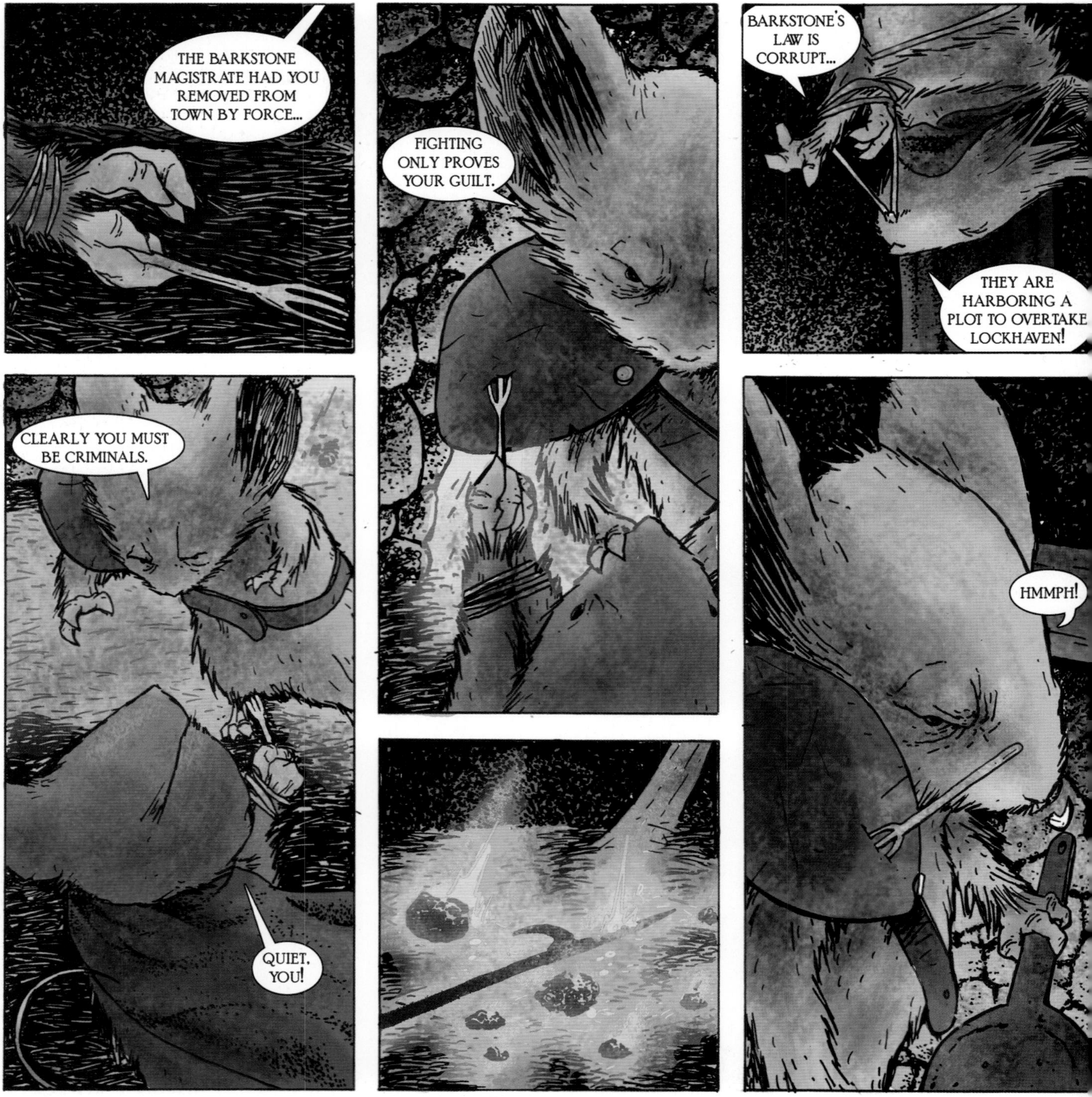
THE BARKSTONE MAGISTRATE HAD YOU REMOVED FROM TOWN BY FORCE...
FIGHTING ONLY PROVES YOUR GUILT.
BARKSTONE'S LAW IS CORRUPT...
THEY ARE HARBORING A PLOT TO OVERTAKE LOCKHAVEN!
CLEARLY YOU MUST BE CRIMINALS.
QUIET, YOU!
HMMPH!

LIES!
UNG!
KENZIE?
WE HAVE PROOF...
THUD
MAPS OF LOCKHAVEN ARE NOT TO LEAVE ITS WALLS...
WE FOUND THIS IN A MERCHANT'S GOODS...
HEADED TO BARKSTONE.
Lockhaven

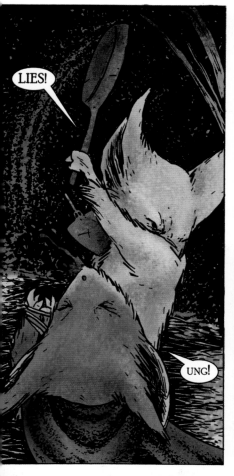

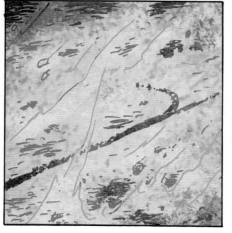

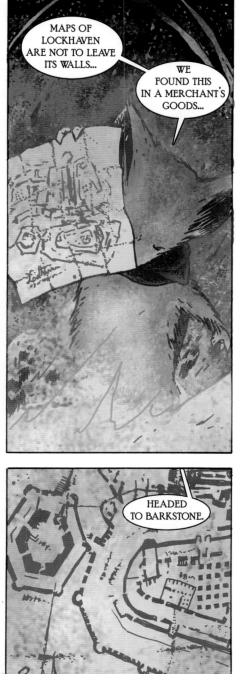

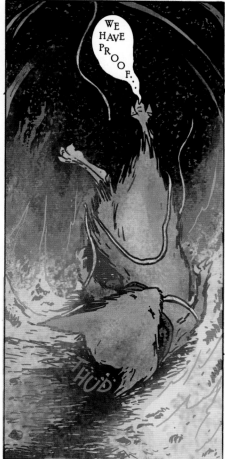

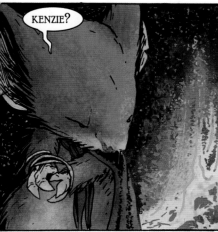

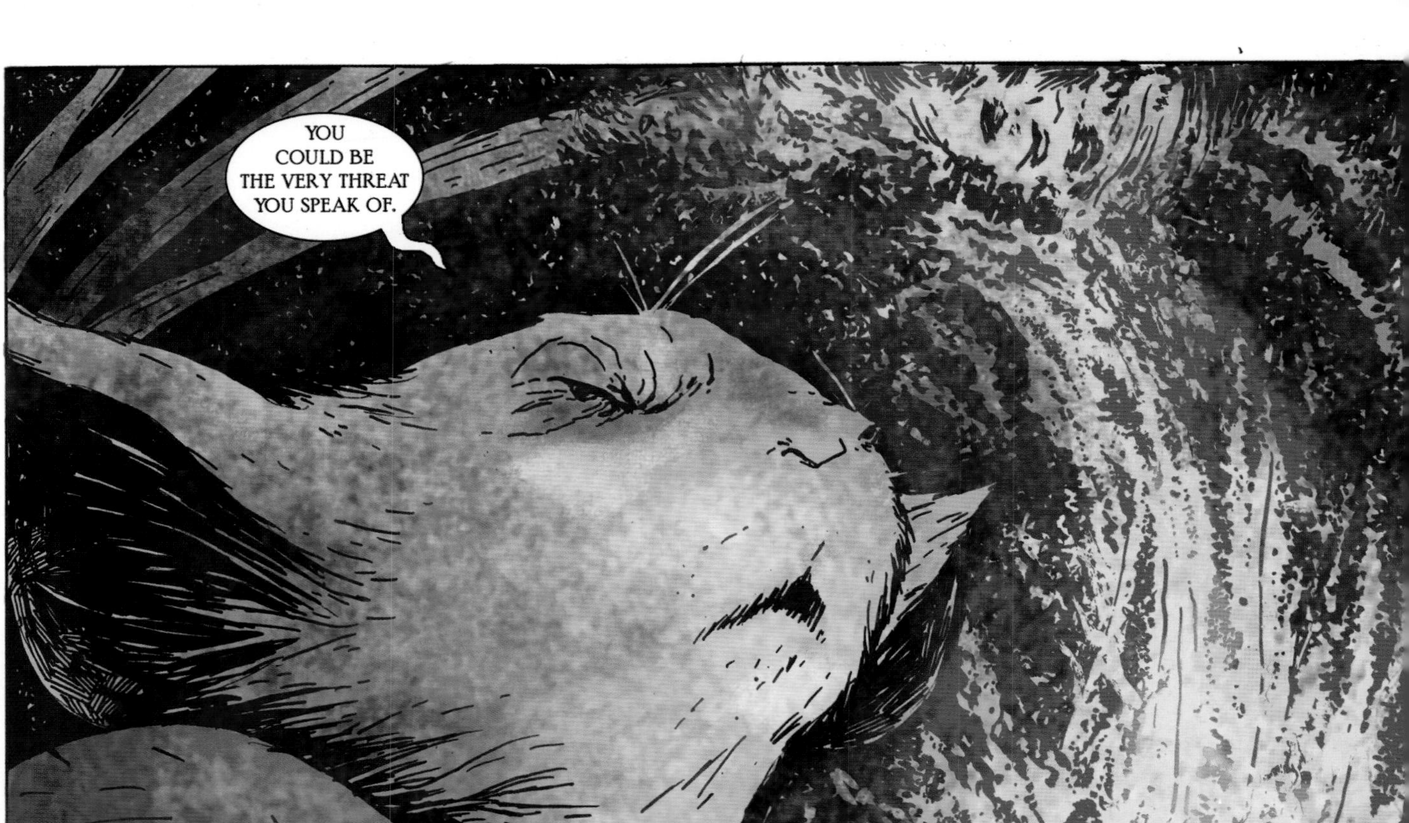
YOU COULD BE THE VERY THREAT YOU SPEAK OF.

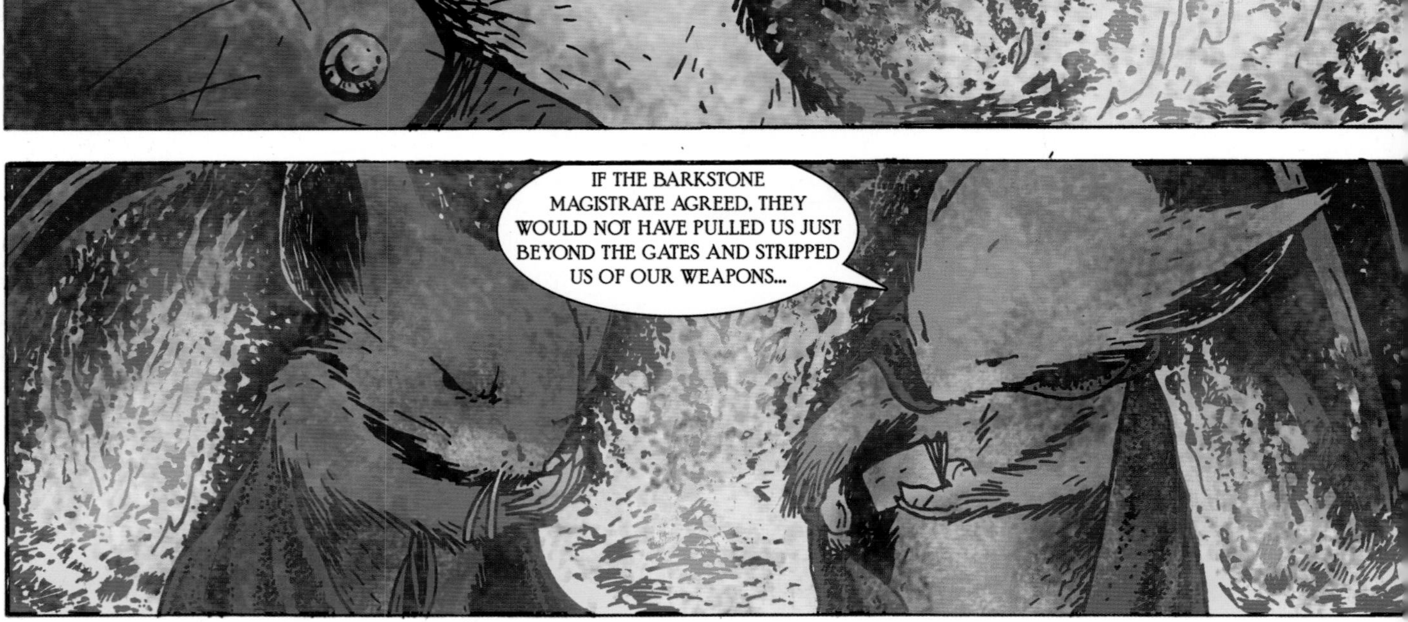
IF THE BARKSTONE MAGISTRATE AGREED, THEY WOULD NOT HAVE PULLED US JUST BEYOND THE GATES AND STRIPPED US OF OUR WEAPONS...

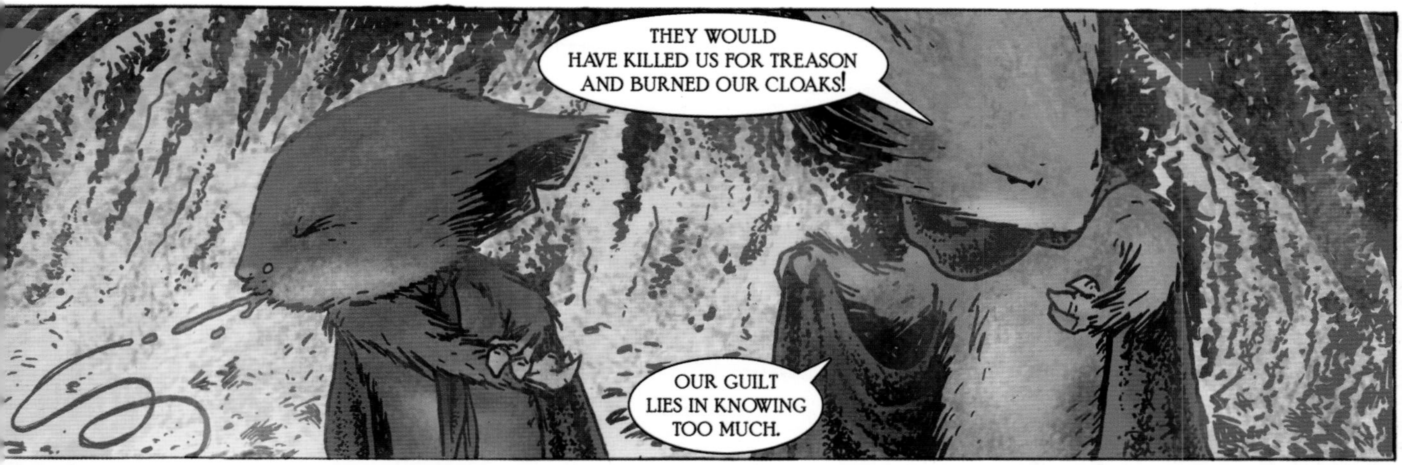
THEY WOULD HAVE KILLED US FOR TREASON AND BURNED OUR CLOAKS!
OUR GUILT LIES IN KNOWING TOO MUCH.

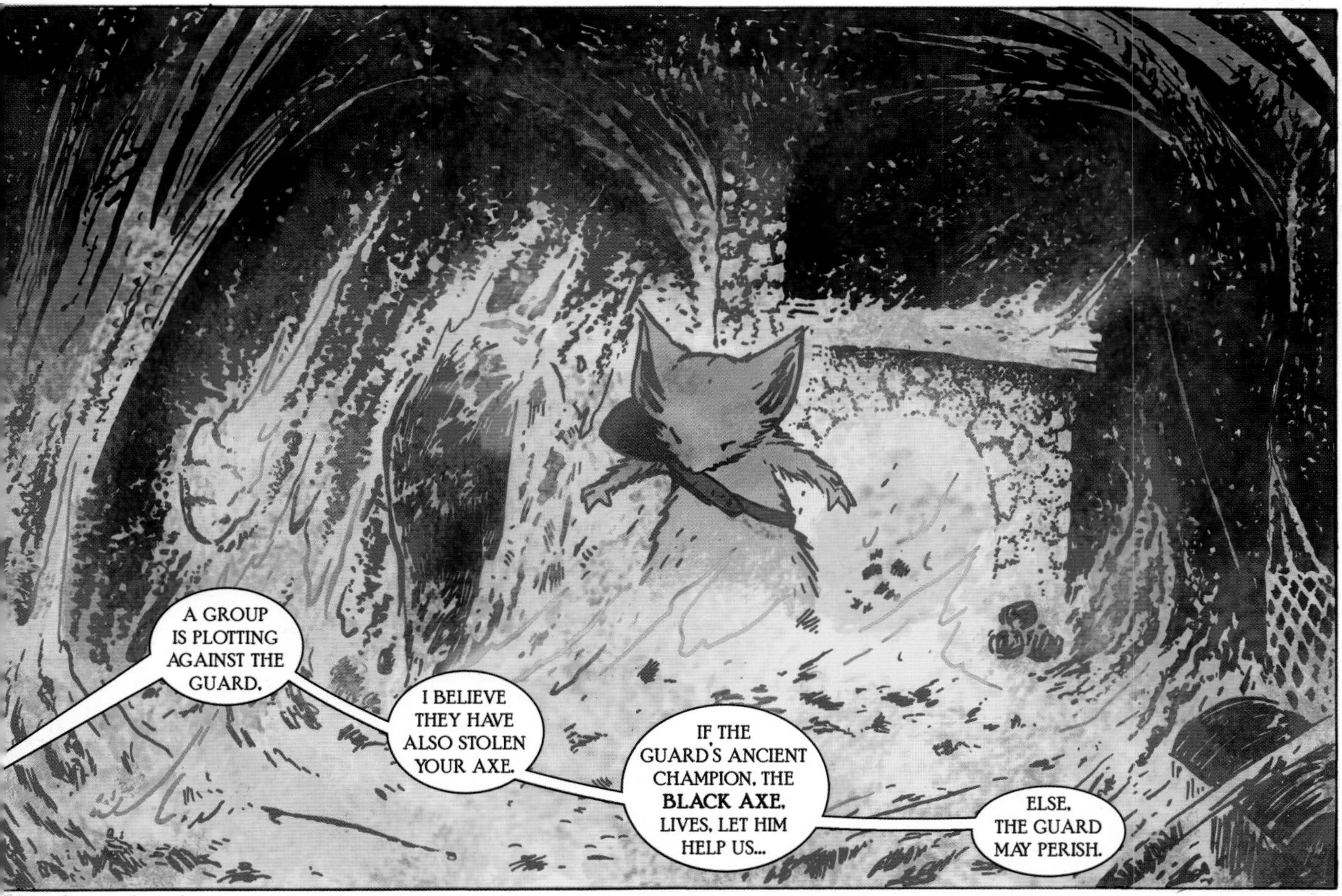
A GROUP IS PLOTTING AGAINST THE GUARD.
I BELIEVE THEY HAVE ALSO STOLEN YOUR AXE.
IF THE GUARD'S ANCIENT CHAMPION, THE **BLACK AXE**, LIVES, LET HIM HELP US...
ELSE, THE GUARD MAY PERISH.

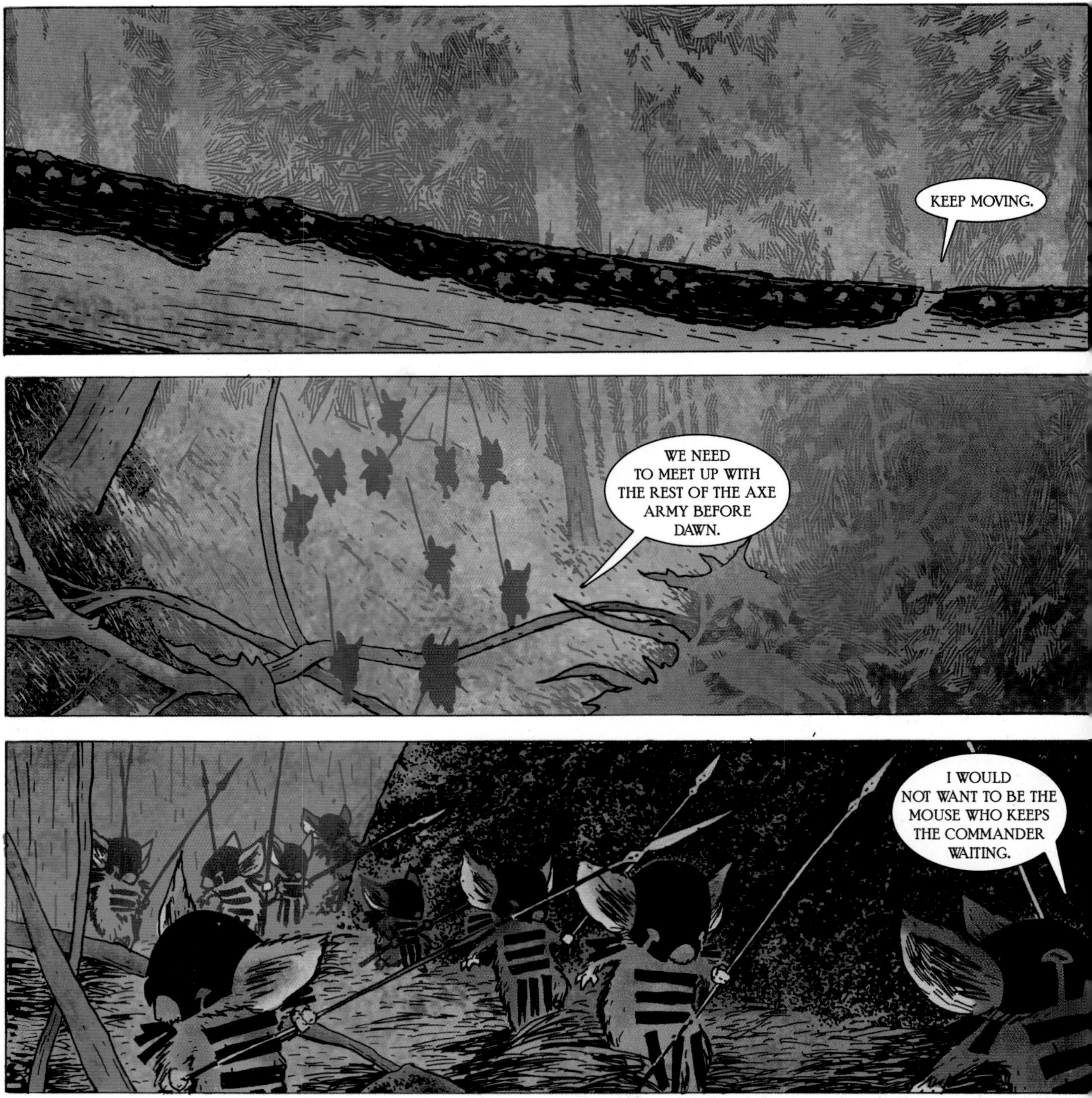
KEEP MOVING.
WE NEED TO MEET UP WITH THE REST OF THE AXE ARMY BEFORE DAWN.
I WOULD NOT WANT TO BE THE MOUSE WHO KEEPS THE COMMANDER WAITING.

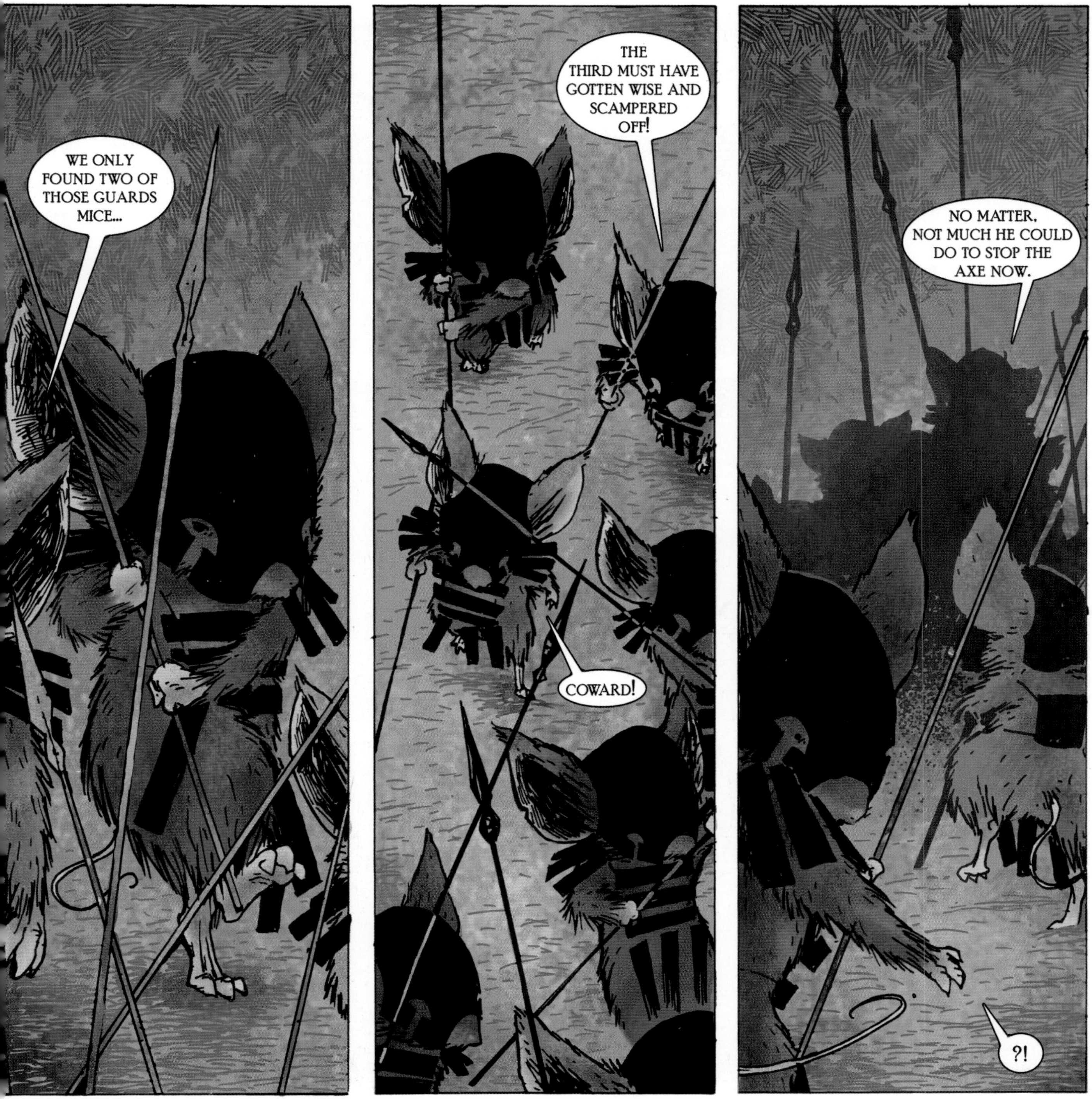
WE ONLY FOUND TWO OF THOSE GUARDS MICE...
THE THIRD MUST HAVE GOTTEN WISE AND SCAMPERED OFF!
COWARD!
NO MATTER, NOT MUCH HE COULD DO TO STOP THE AXE NOW.
?!

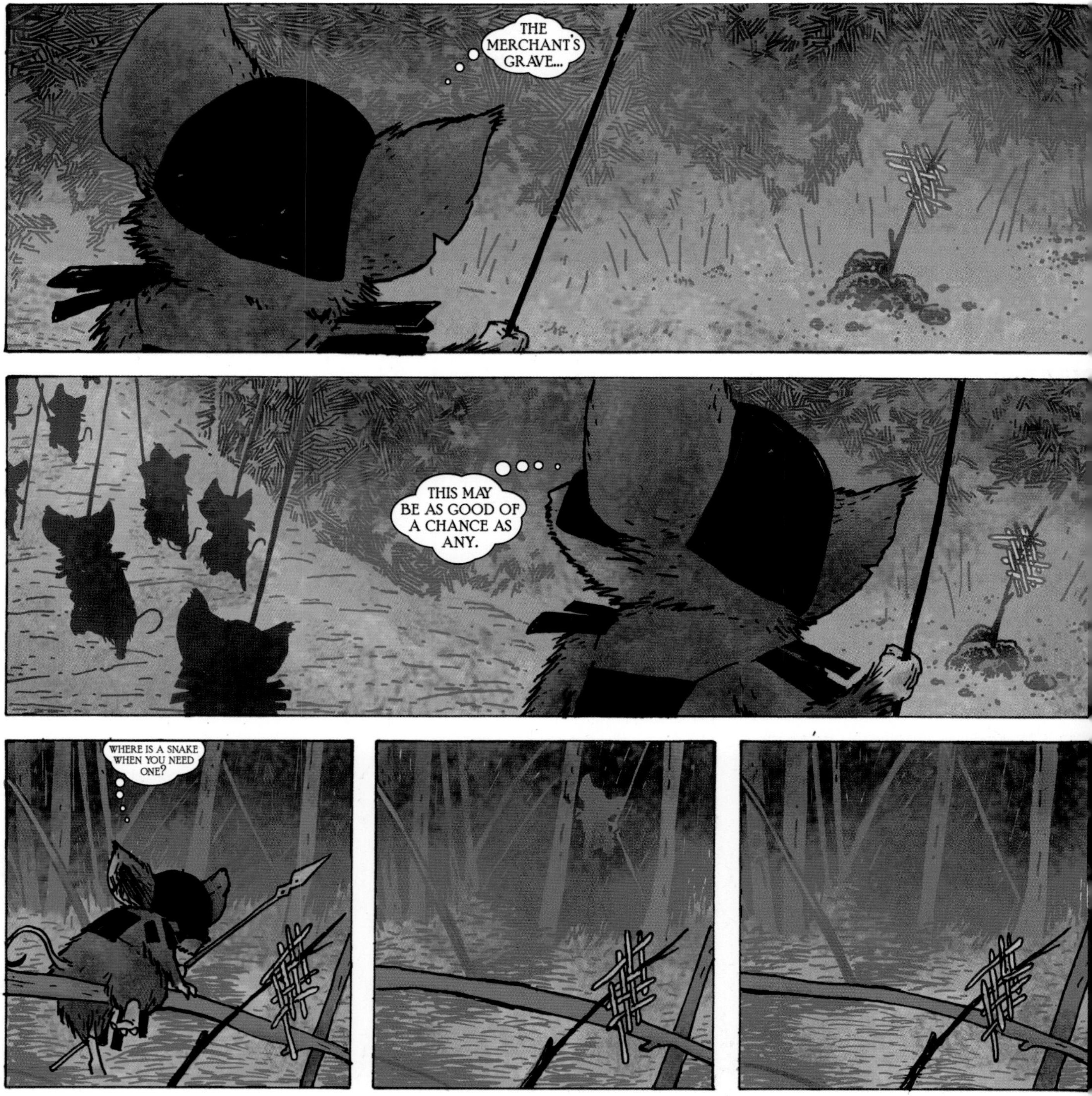
THE MERCHANT'S GRAVE...
THIS MAY BE AS GOOD OF A CHANCE AS ANY.
WHERE IS A SNAKE WHEN YOU NEED ONE?

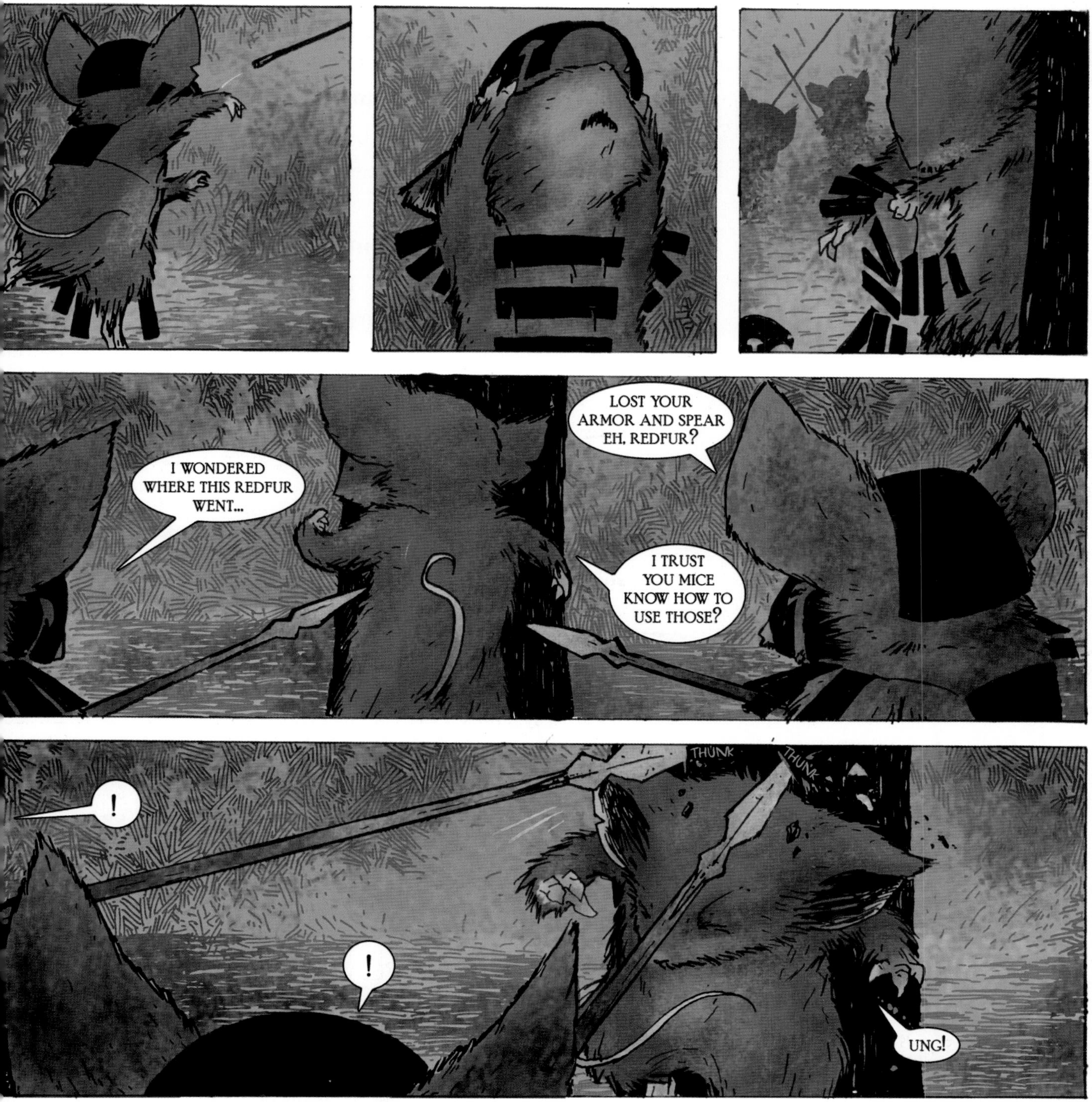
I WONDERED WHERE THIS REDFUR WENT...
LOST YOUR ARMOR AND SPEAR EH, REDFUR?
I TRUST YOU MICE KNOW HOW TO USE THOSE?
!
THUNK
THUNK
!
UNG!

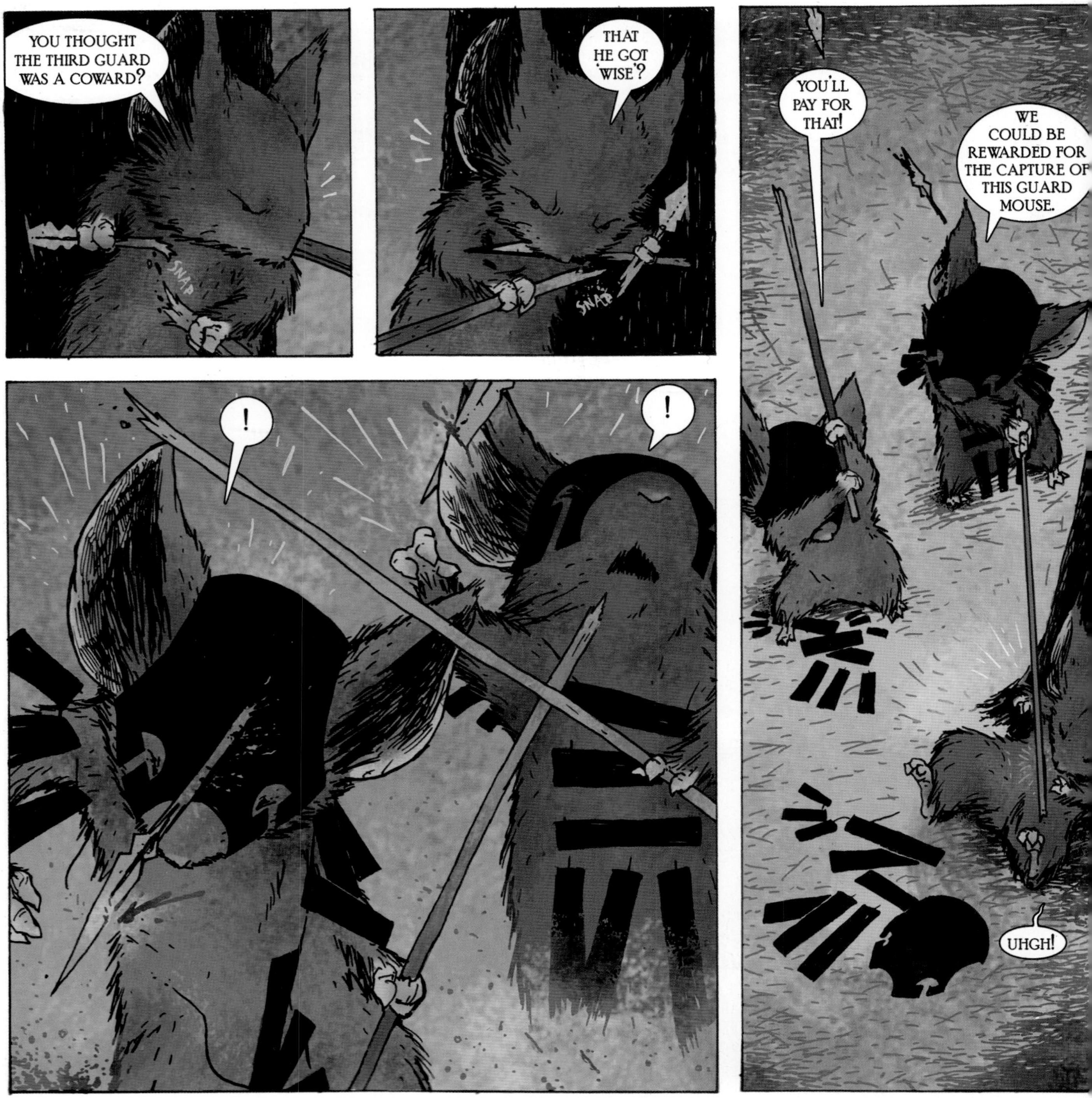
YOU THOUGHT THE THIRD GUARD WAS A COWARD?
SNAP
THAT HE GOT 'WISE'?
SNAP
!
!
YOU'LL PAY FOR THAT!
WE COULD BE REWARDED FOR THE CAPTURE OF THIS GUARD MOUSE.
UHGH!

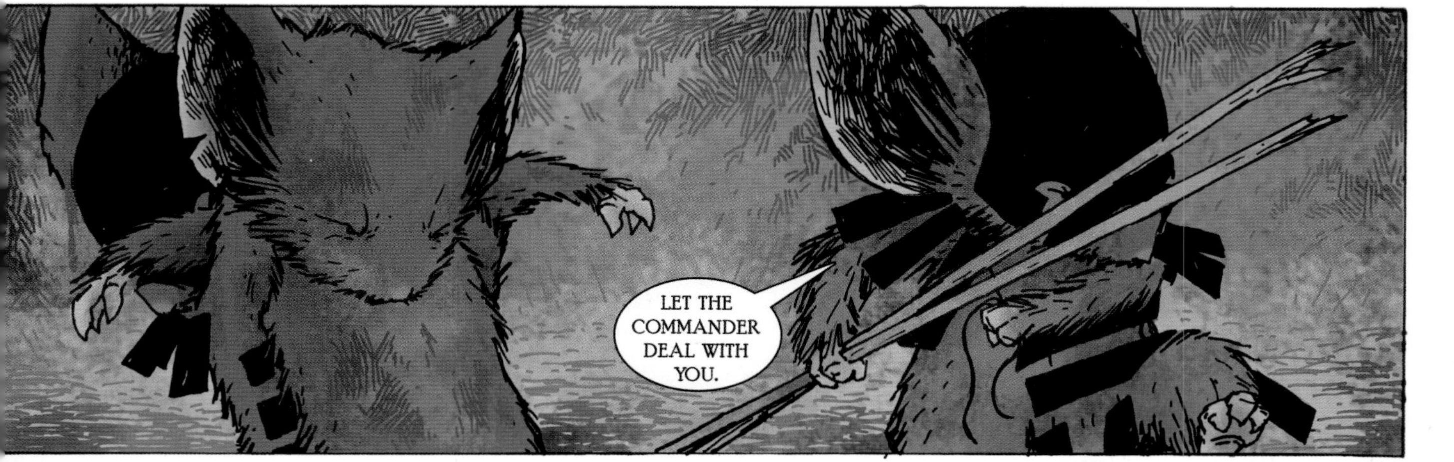
LET THE COMMANDER DEAL WITH YOU.

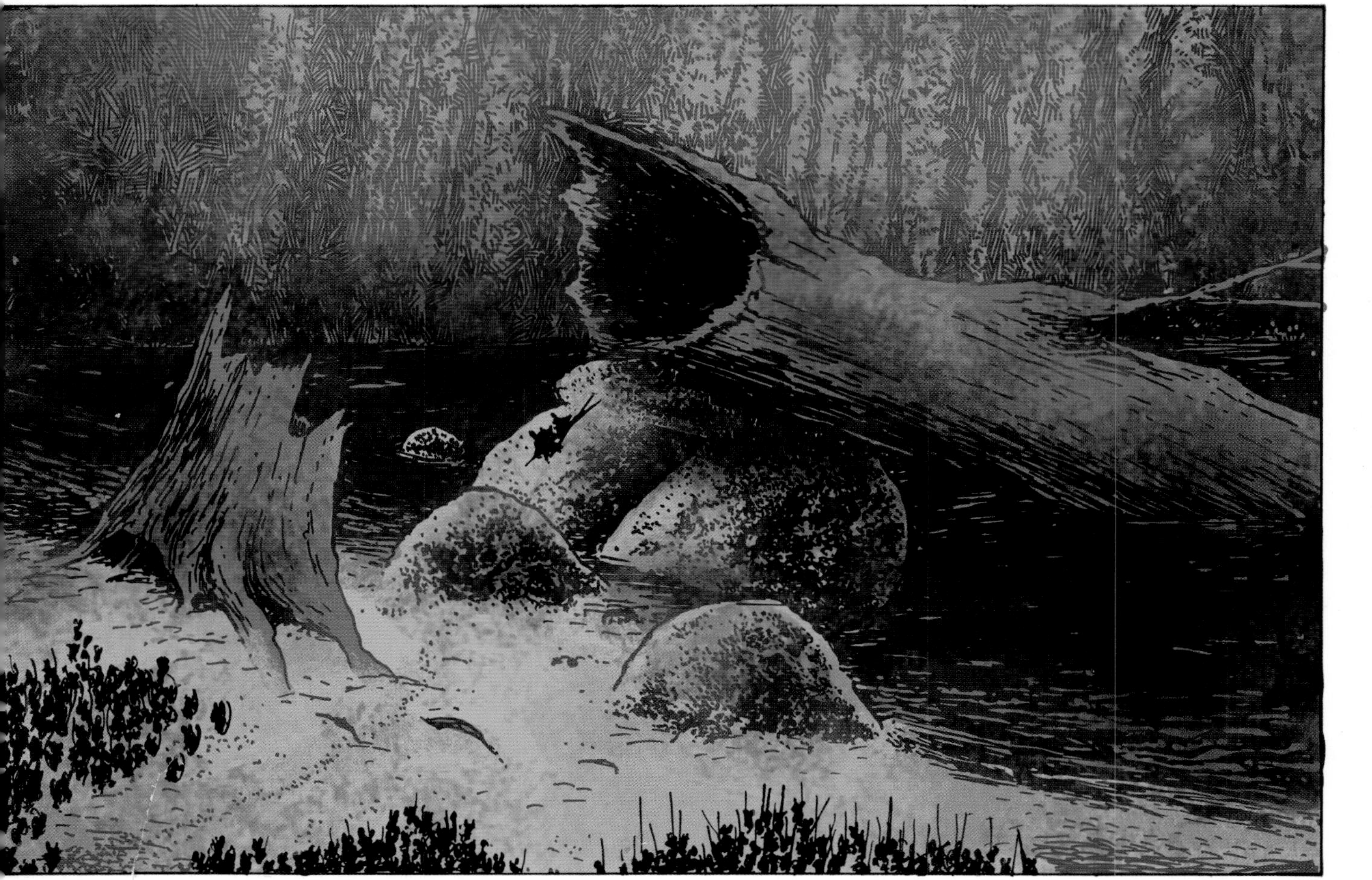

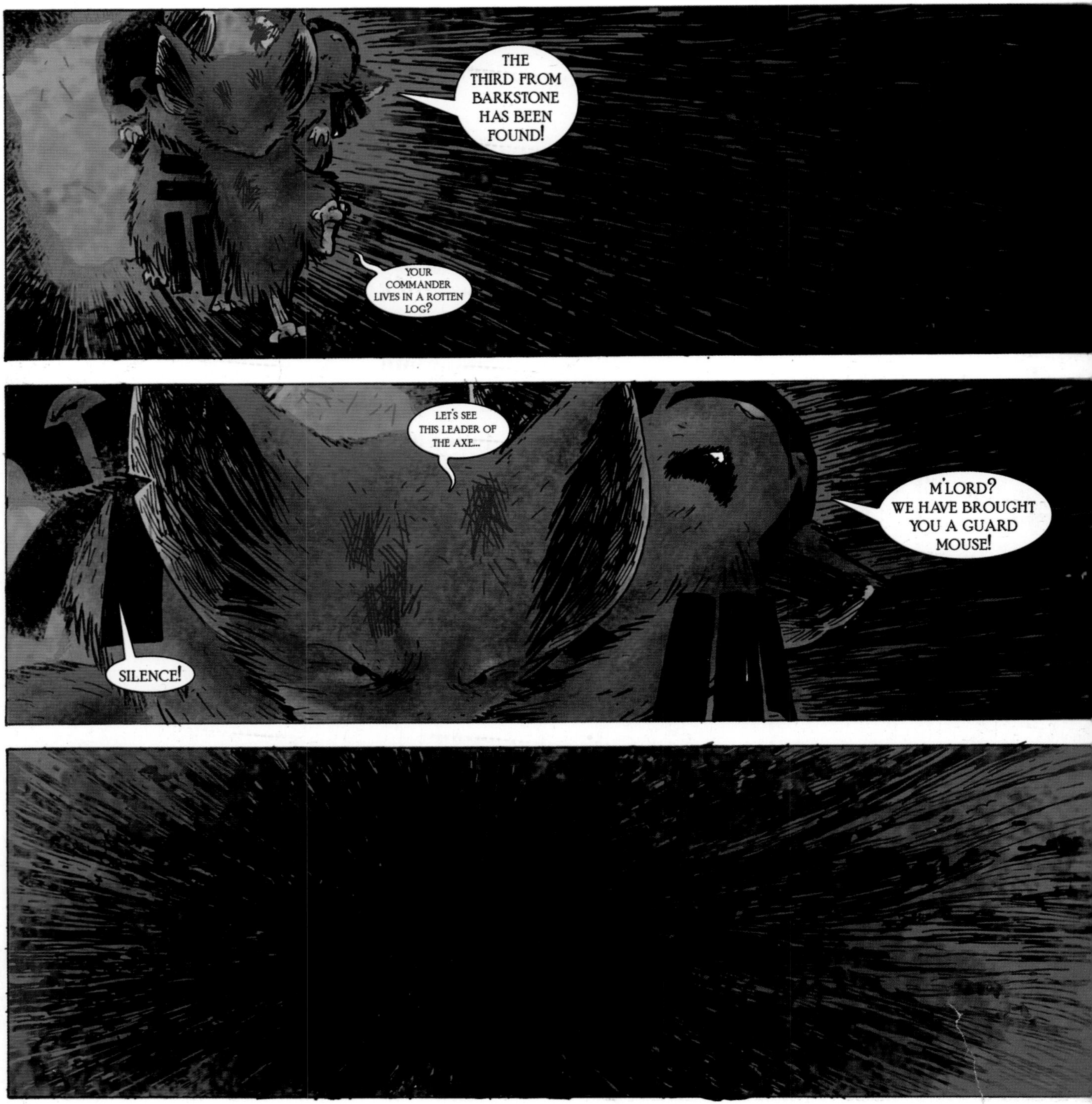
THE THIRD FROM BARKSTONE HAS BEEN FOUND!
YOUR COMMANDER LIVES IN A ROTTEN LOG?
LET'S SEE THIS LEADER OF THE AXE...
M'LORD? WE HAVE BROUGHT YOU A GUARD MOUSE!
SILENCE!

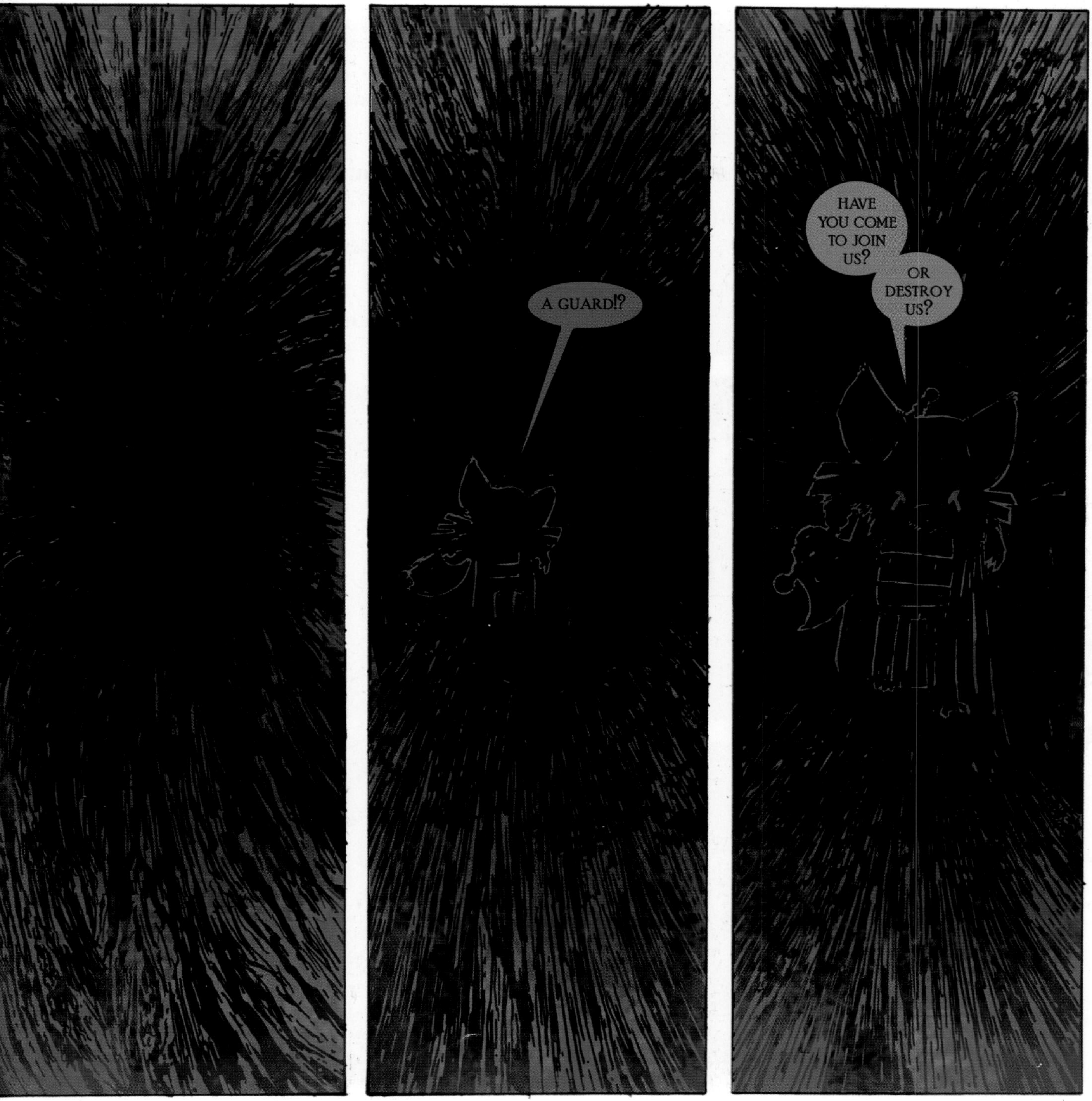
A GUARD!?
HAVE YOU COME TO JOIN US?
OR DESTROY US?

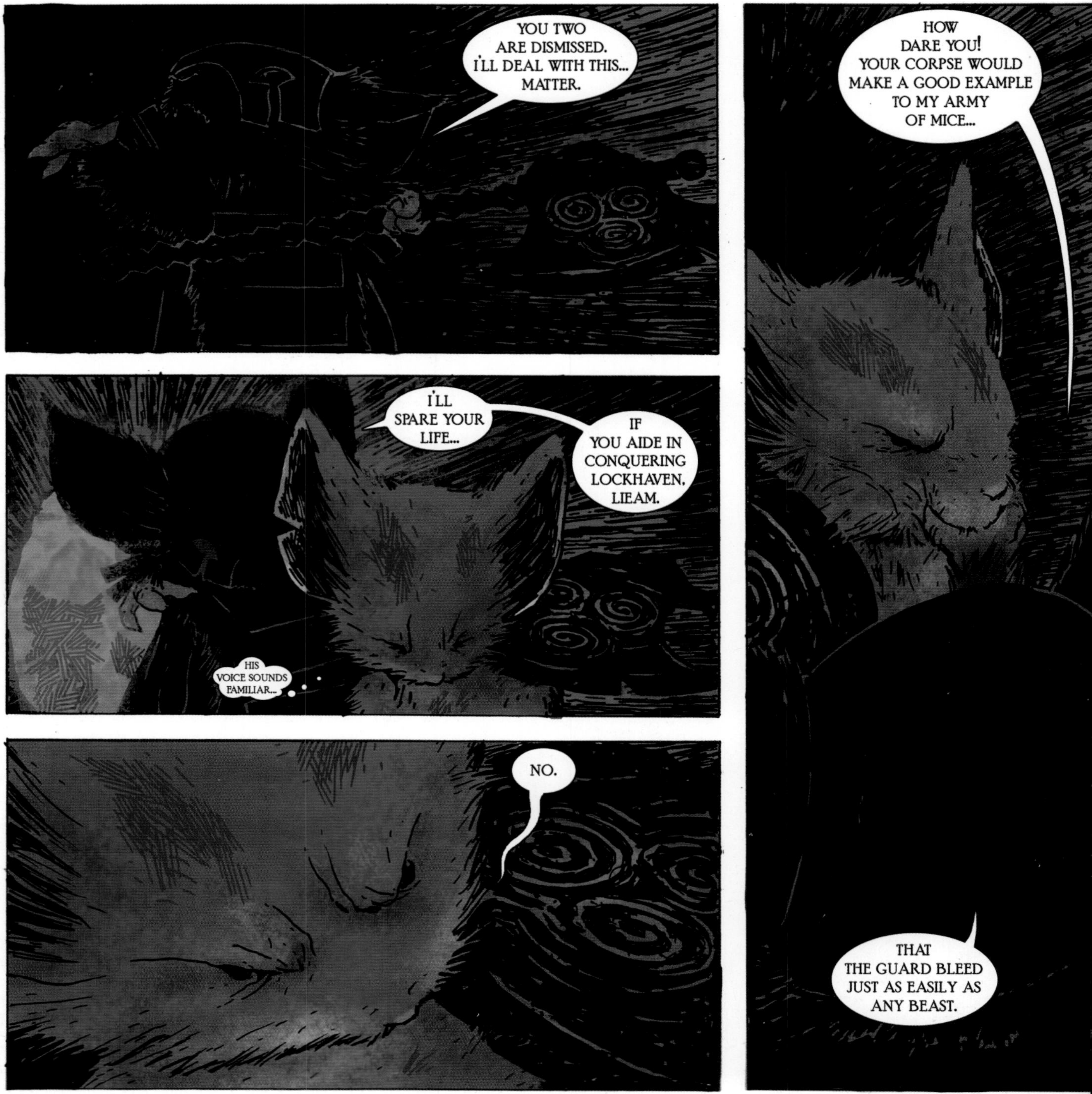
YOU TWO ARE DISMISSED. I'LL DEAL WITH THIS... MATTER.
I'LL SPARE YOUR LIFE...
IF YOU AIDE IN CONQUERING LOCKHAVEN, LIEAM.
HIS VOICE SOUNDS FAMILIAR...
NO.
HOW DARE YOU! YOUR CORPSE WOULD MAKE A GOOD EXAMPLE TO MY ARMY OF MICE...
THAT THE GUARD BLEED JUST AS EASILY AS ANY BEAST.

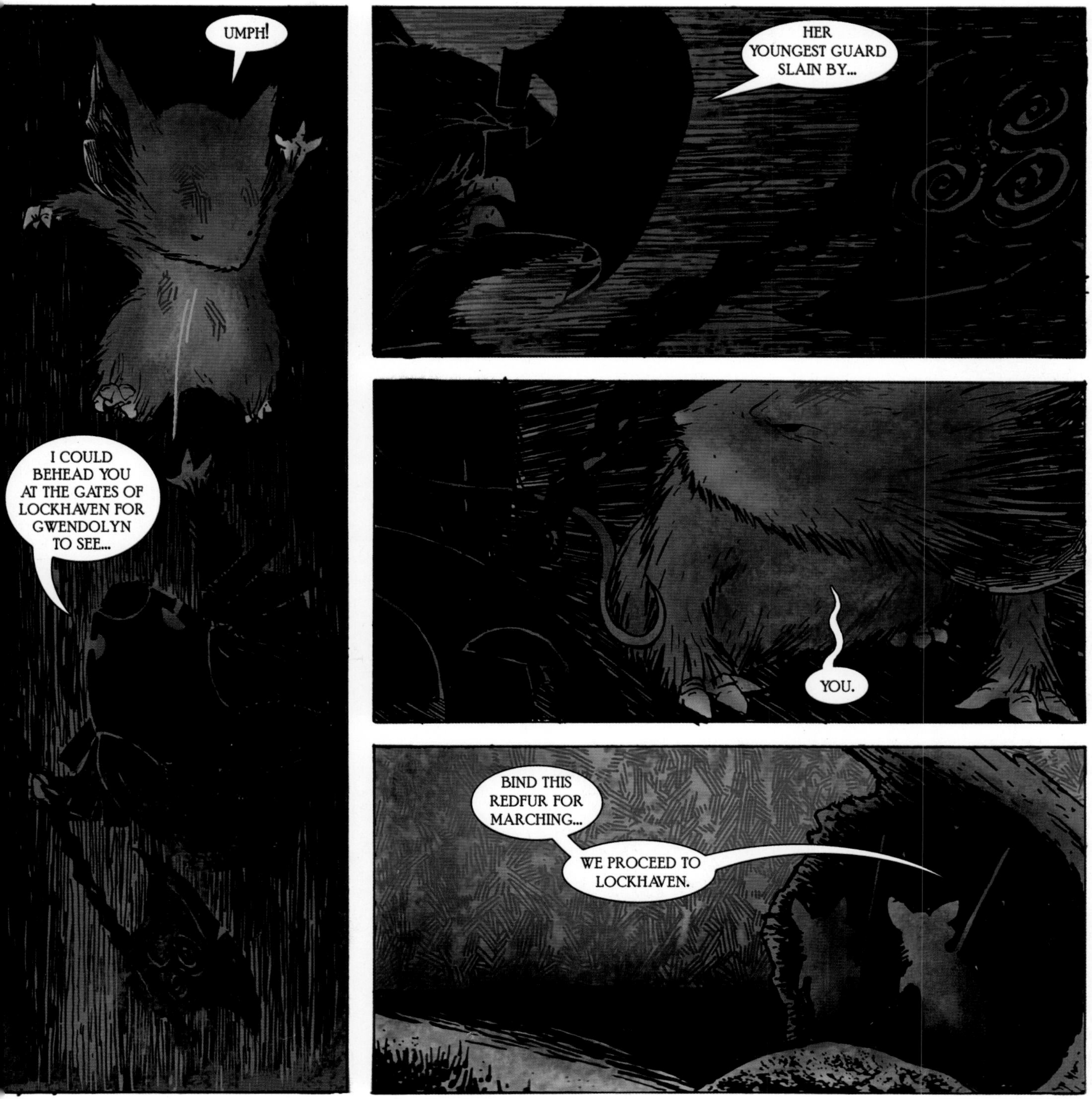
UMPH!
I COULD BEHEAD YOU AT THE GATES OF LOCKHAVEN FOR GWENDOLYN TO SEE...
HER YOUNGEST GUARD SLAIN BY...
YOU.
BIND THIS REDFUR FOR MARCHING...
WE PROCEED TO LOCKHAVEN.

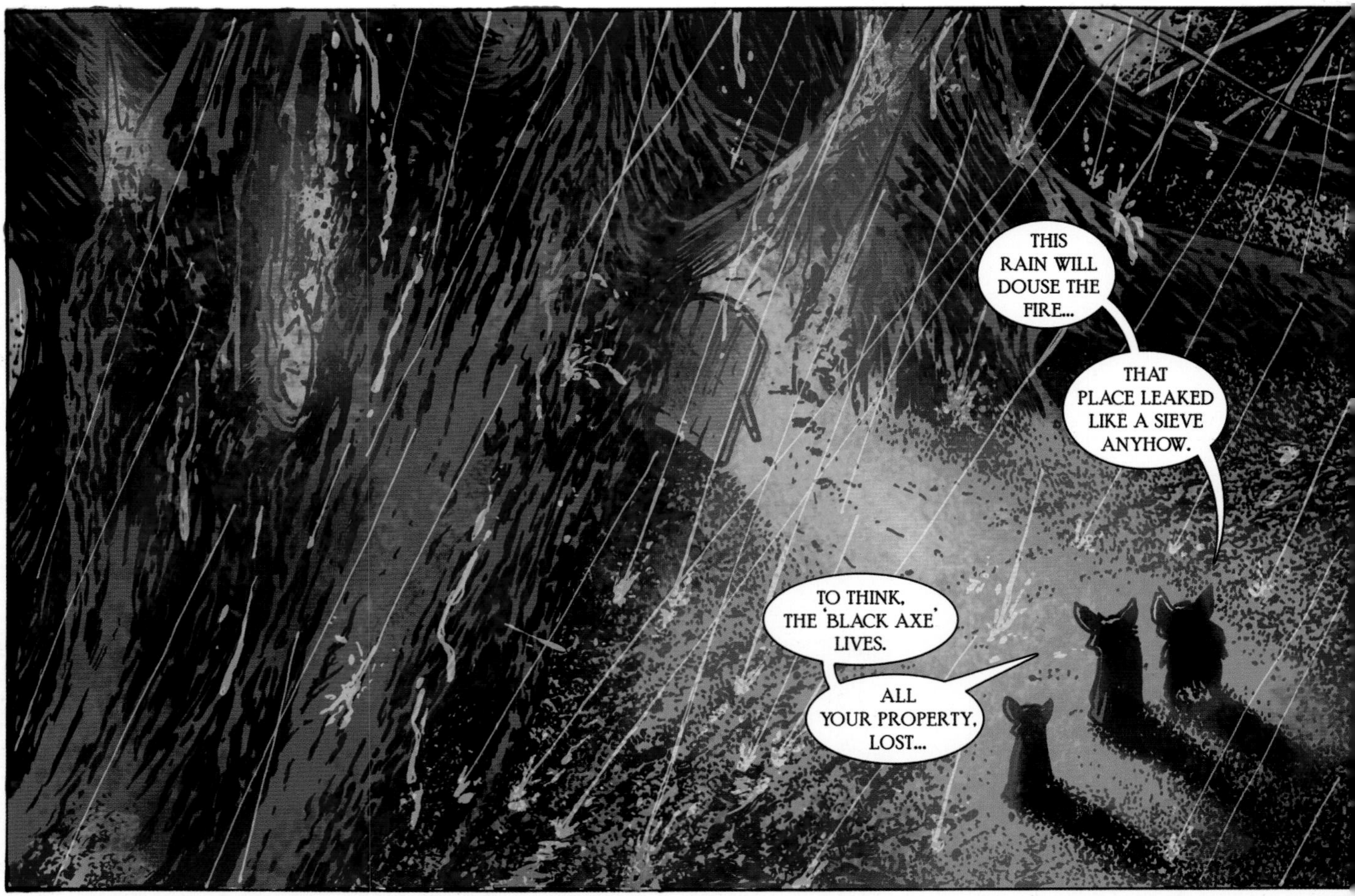
THIS RAIN WILL DOUSE THE FIRE...
THAT PLACE LEAKED LIKE A SIEVE ANYHOW.
TO THINK, THE 'BLACK AXE' LIVES.
ALL YOUR PROPERTY, LOST...

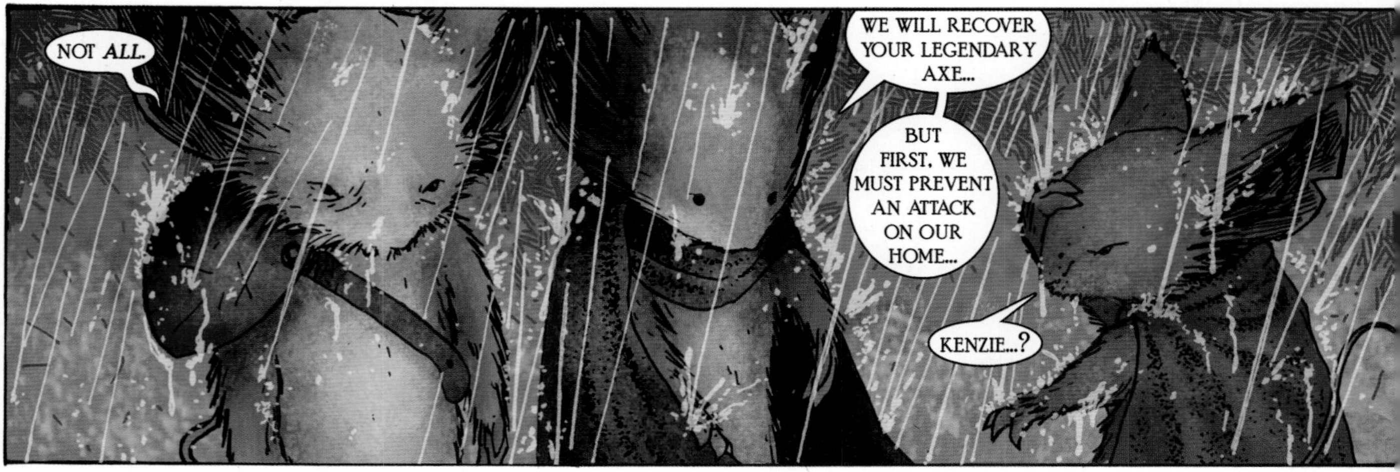
NOT *ALL*.
WE WILL RECOVER YOUR LEGENDARY AXE...
BUT FIRST, WE MUST PREVENT AN ATTACK ON OUR HOME...
KENZIE...?

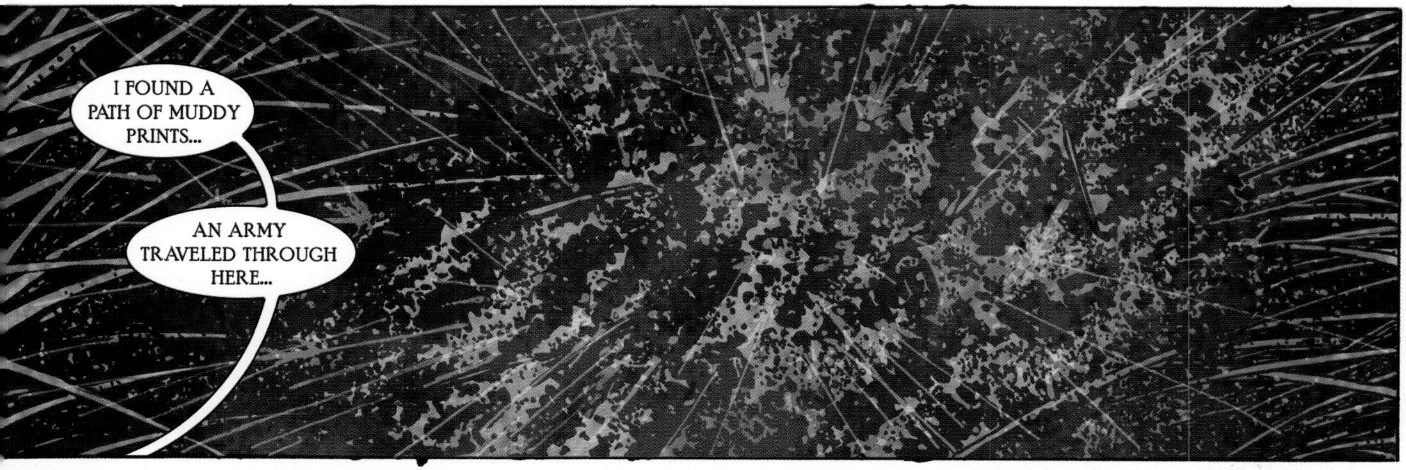
I FOUND A PATH OF MUDDY PRINTS...
AN ARMY TRAVELED THROUGH HERE...

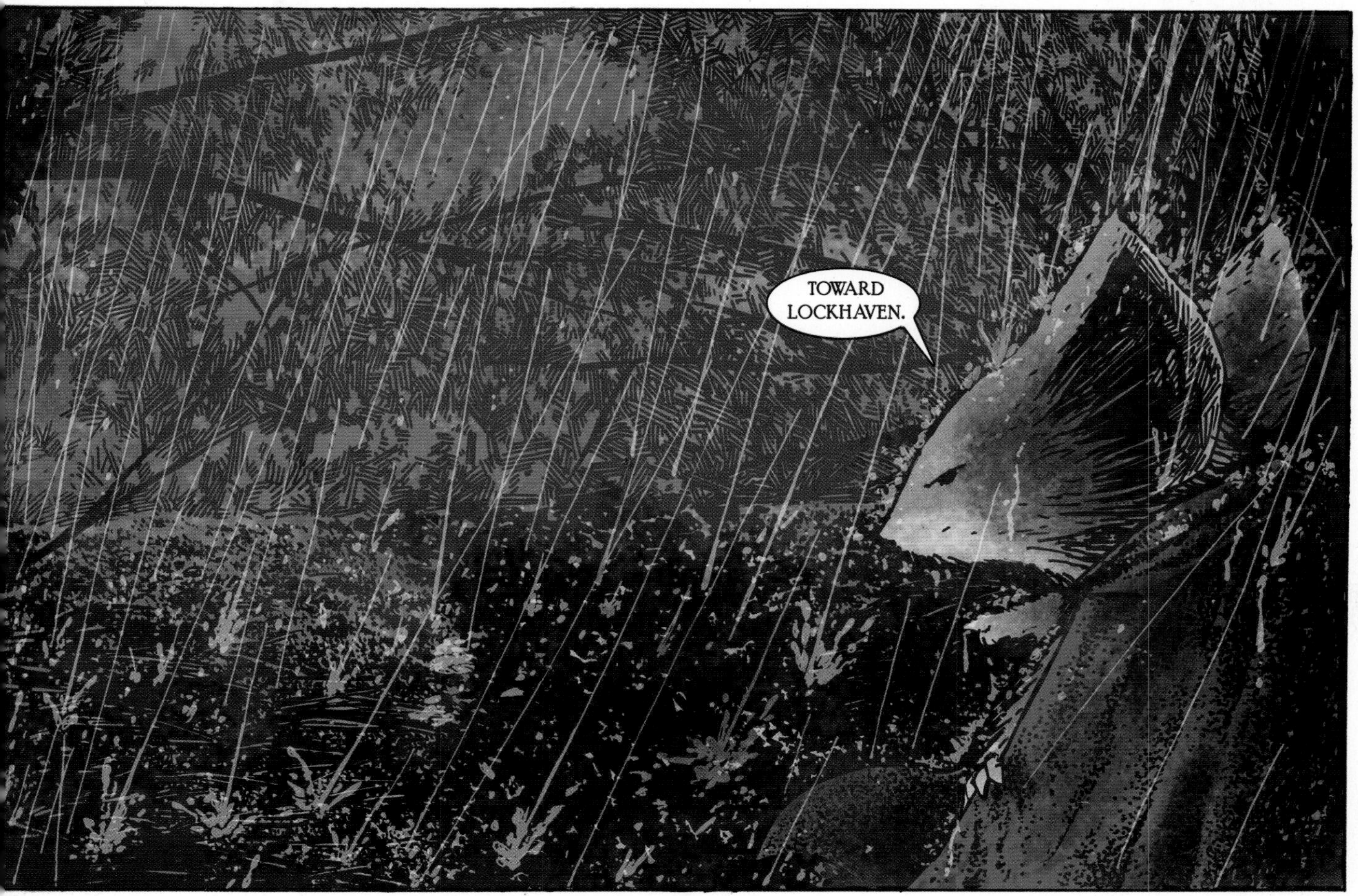
TOWARD LOCKHAVEN.

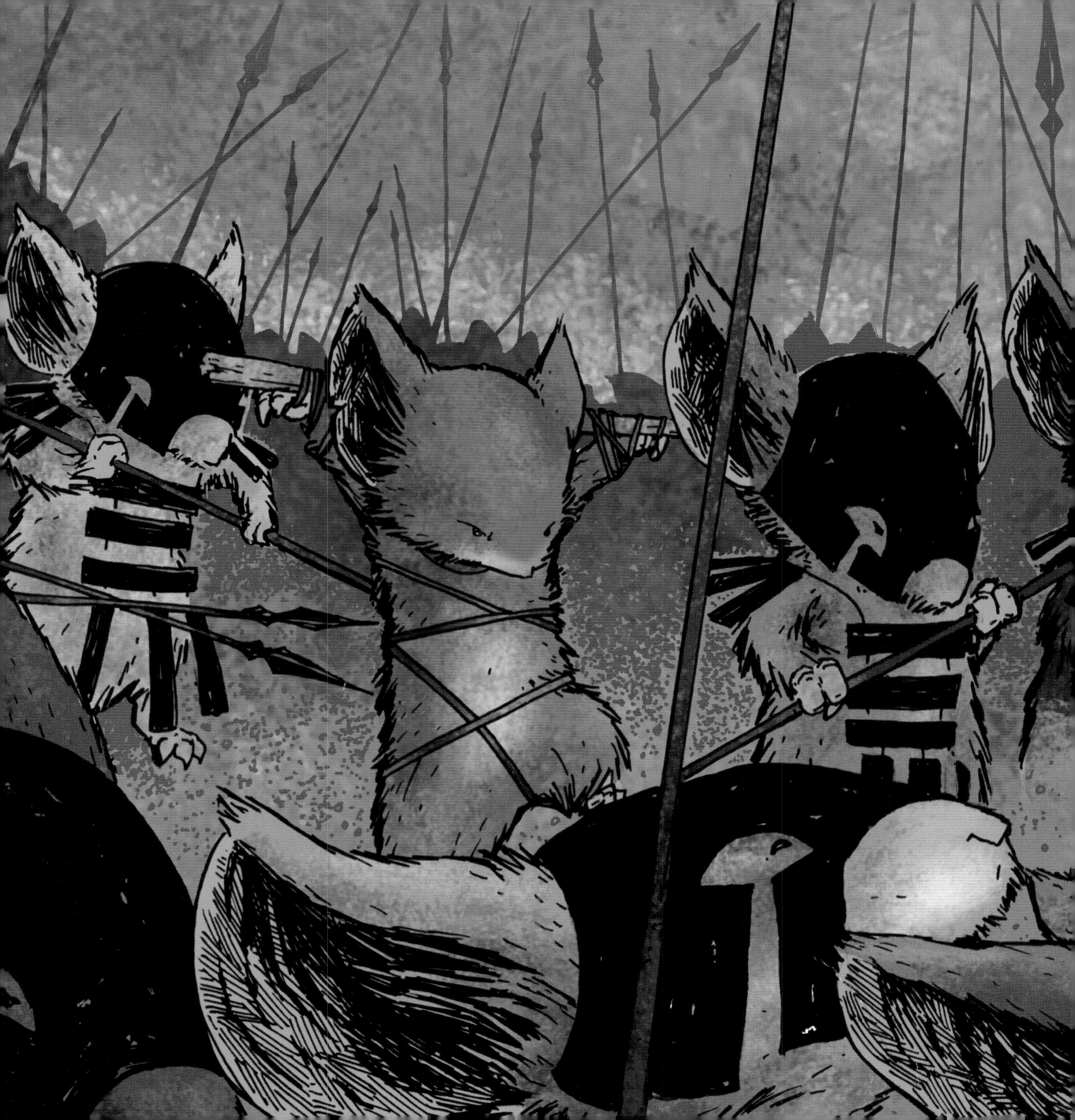

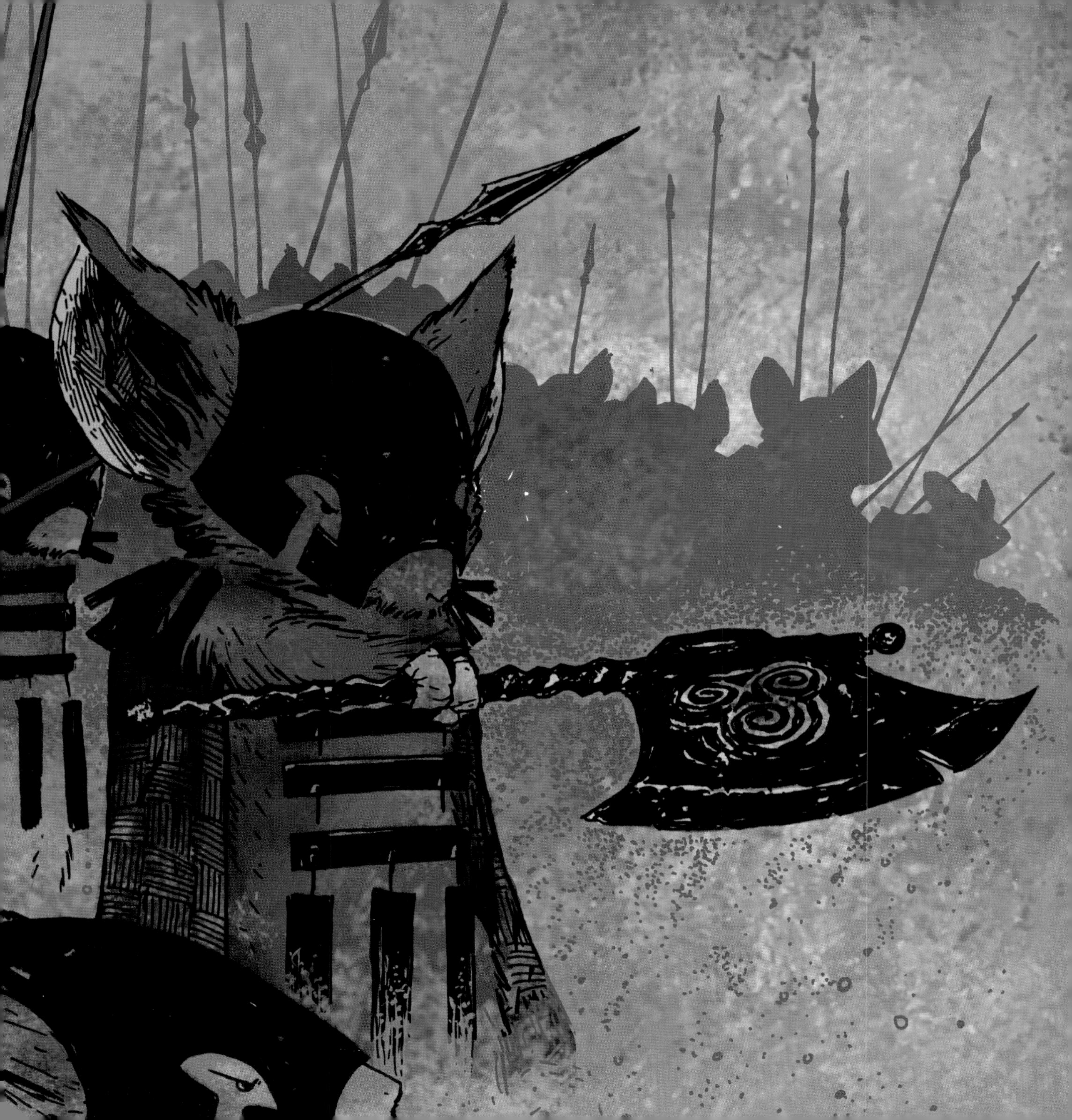

Chapter Five

Midnight's Dawn

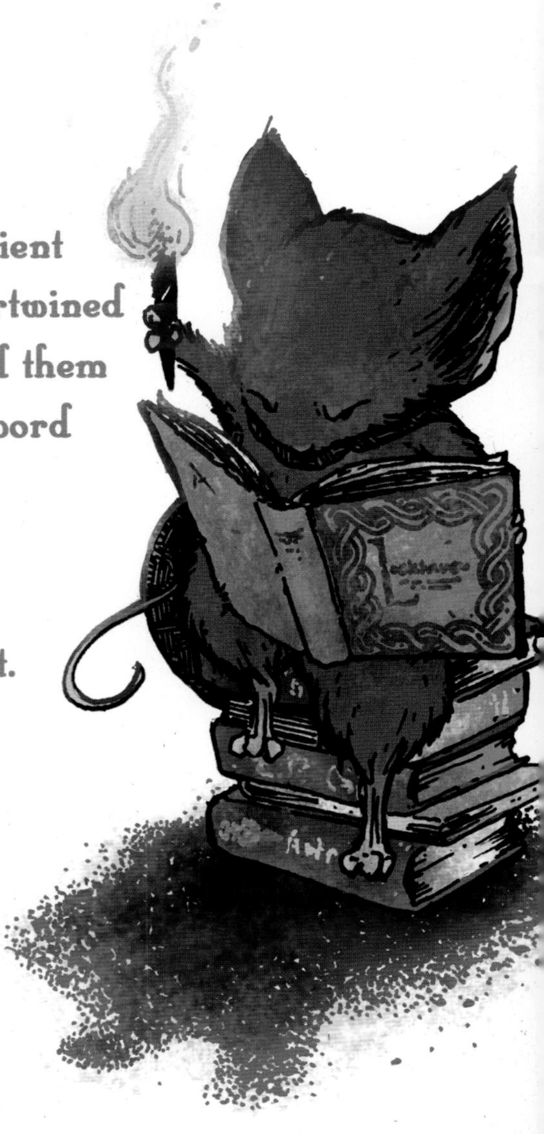

In tracking the treacherous Axe army, Saxon and Kenzie found a new ally in an old hermit mouse named Celanawe claiming to be the ancient hero of the mice: The Black Axe. His fate intertwined with two of the Guard's finest, he offered to aid them in their pursuit in hopes to hold them to their word of retrieving his missing axe.

All the while, Lieam's captors march him to Lockhaven with only one purpose: to conquer it.

'Clouds, leaves, soil, and wind
all offer themselves as signals
of changes in the weather.
However, not all the storms of life
can be predicted.

-Excerpt from 'Weather Watcher's Field Guide'
distributed to all Guard Mice

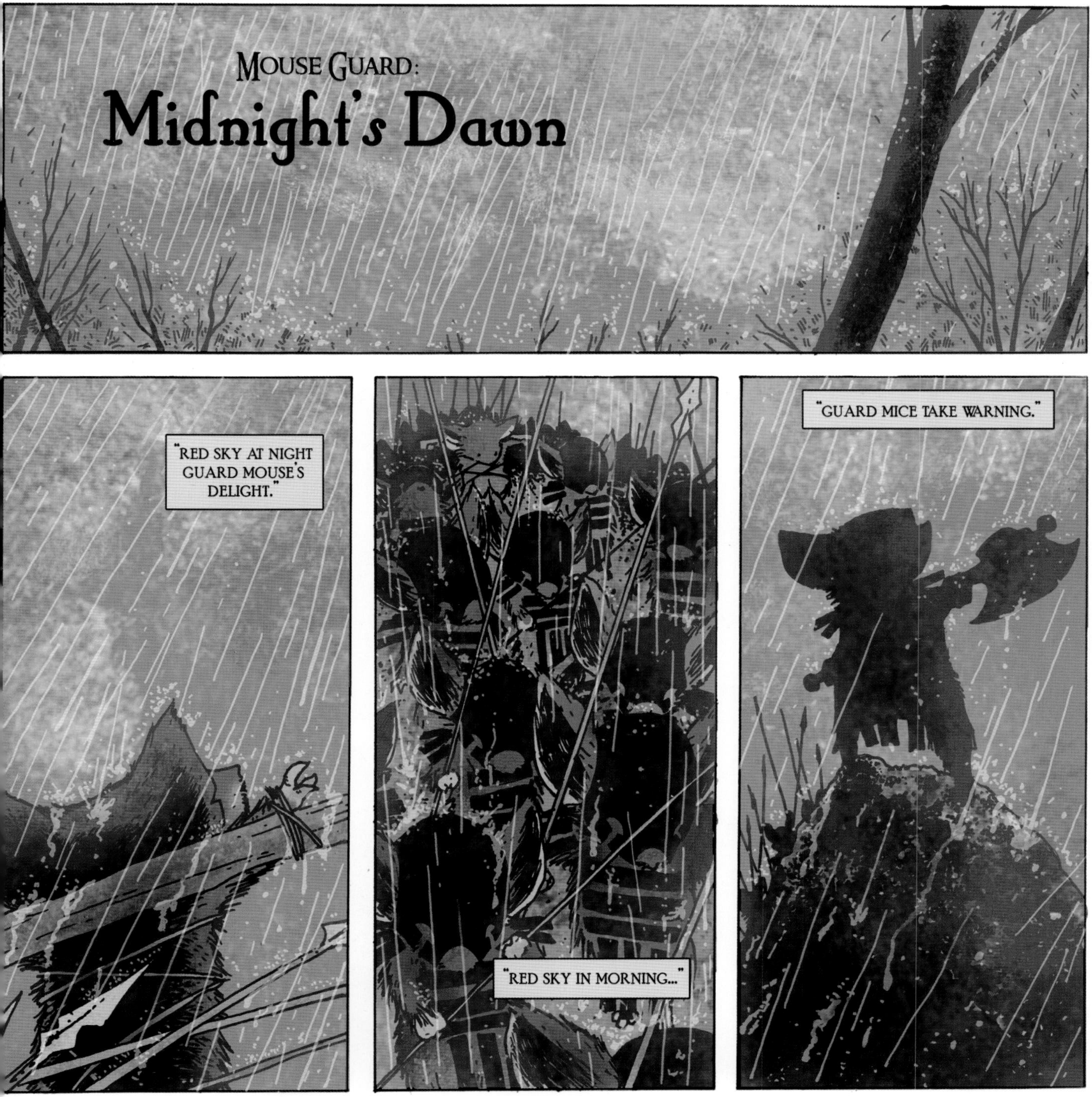
MOUSE GUARD:
Midnight's Dawn
"RED SKY AT NIGHT GUARD MOUSE'S DELIGHT."
"RED SKY IN MORNING..."
"GUARD MICE TAKE WARNING."

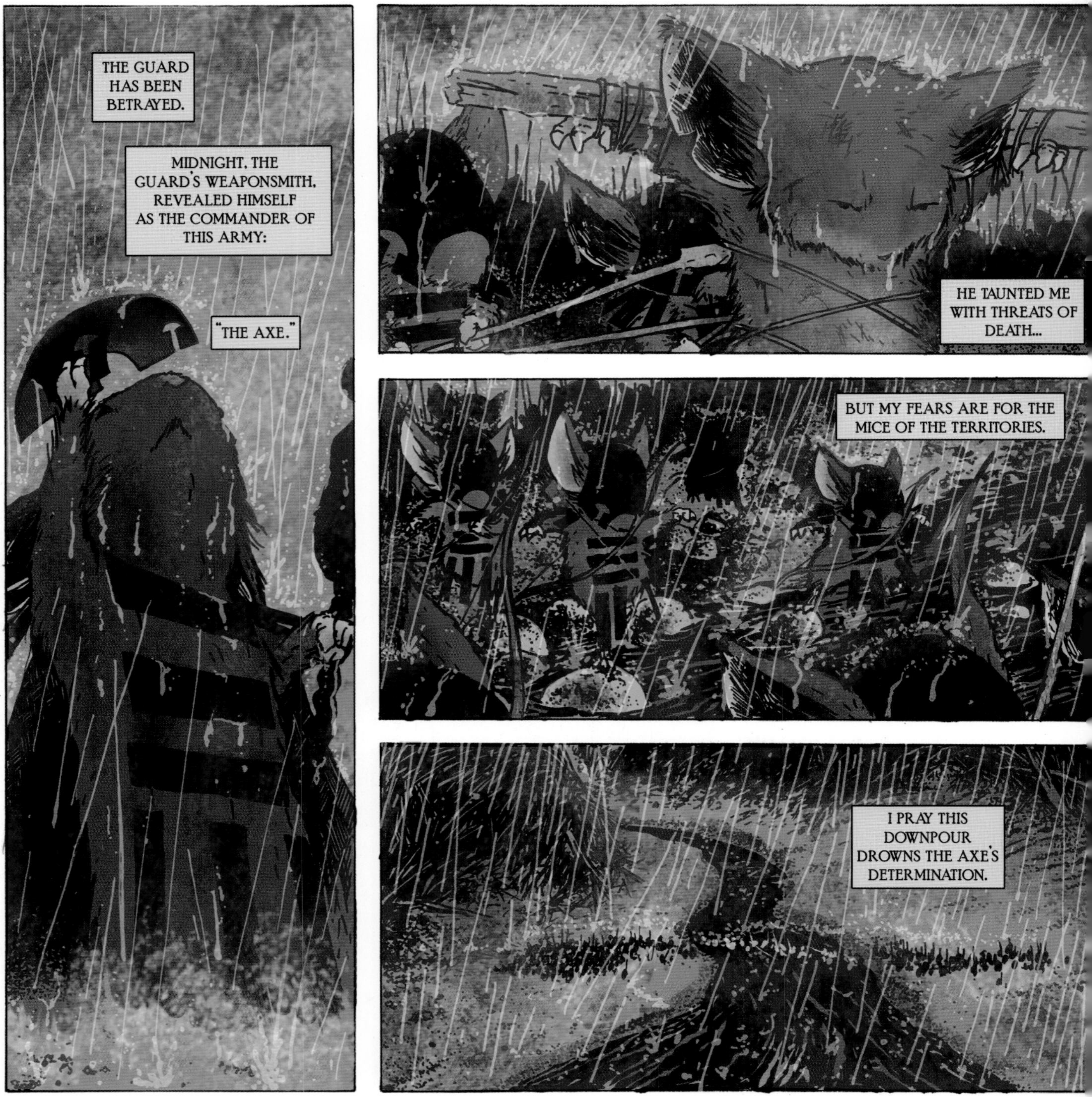
THE GUARD HAS BEEN BETRAYED.
MIDNIGHT, THE GUARD'S WEAPONSMITH, REVEALED HIMSELF AS THE COMMANDER OF THIS ARMY:
"THE AXE."
HE TAUNTED ME WITH THREATS OF DEATH...
BUT MY FEARS ARE FOR THE MICE OF THE TERRITORIES.
I PRAY THIS DOWNPOUR DROWNS THE AXE'S DETERMINATION.

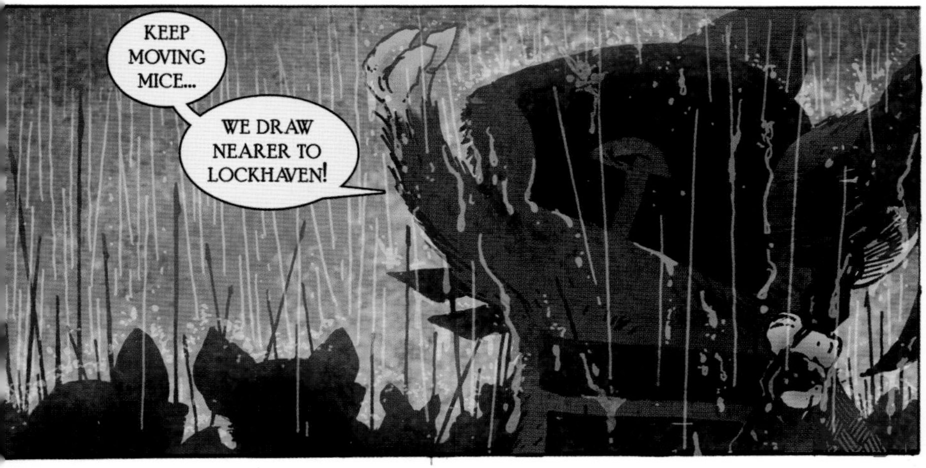
KEEP MOVING MICE...
WE DRAW NEARER TO LOCKHAVEN!

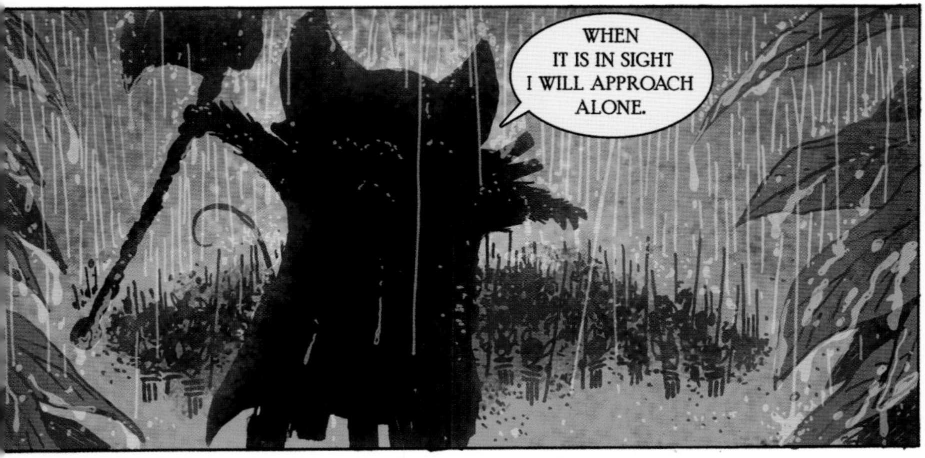
WHEN IT IS IN SIGHT I WILL APPROACH ALONE.

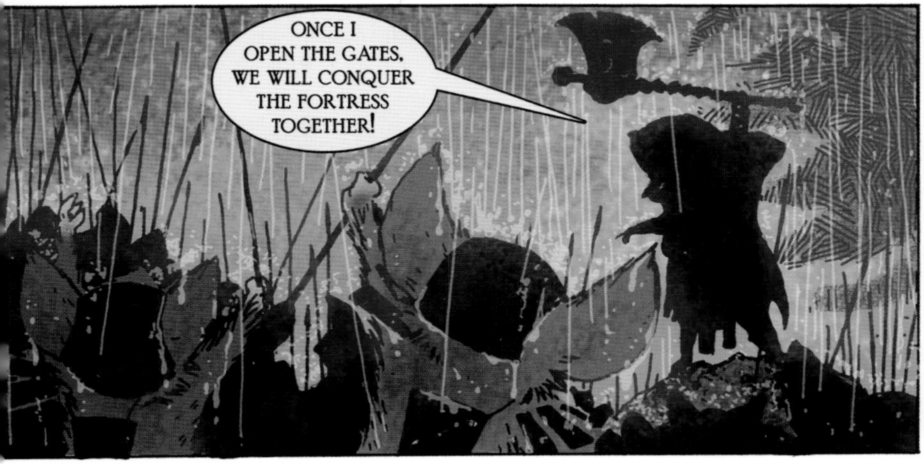
ONCE I OPEN THE GATES, WE WILL CONQUER THE FORTRESS TOGETHER!

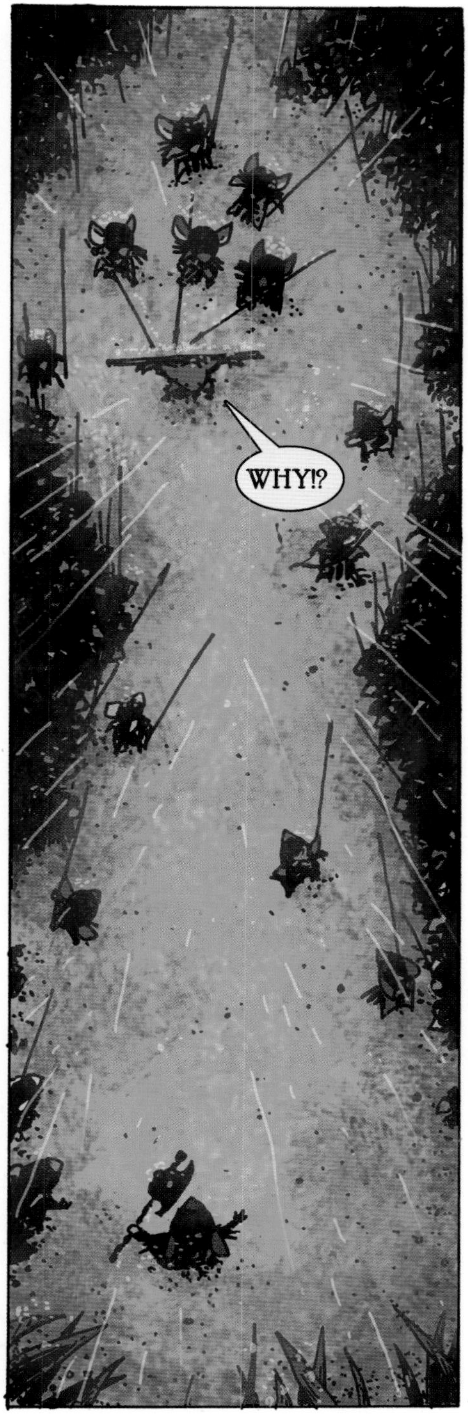
WHY!?

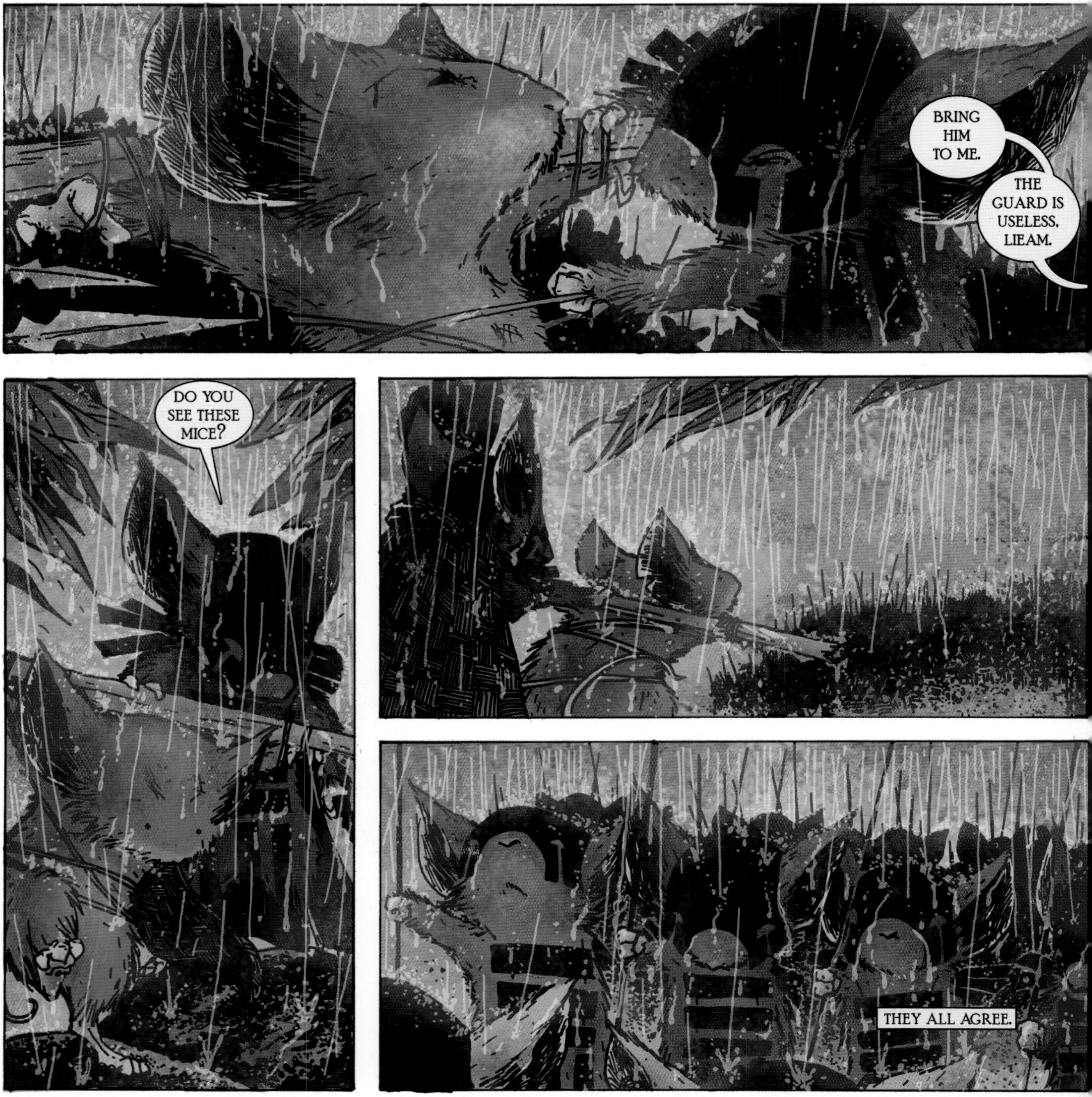
BRING HIM TO ME.
THE GUARD IS USELESS, LIEAM.
DO YOU SEE THESE MICE?
THEY ALL AGREE.

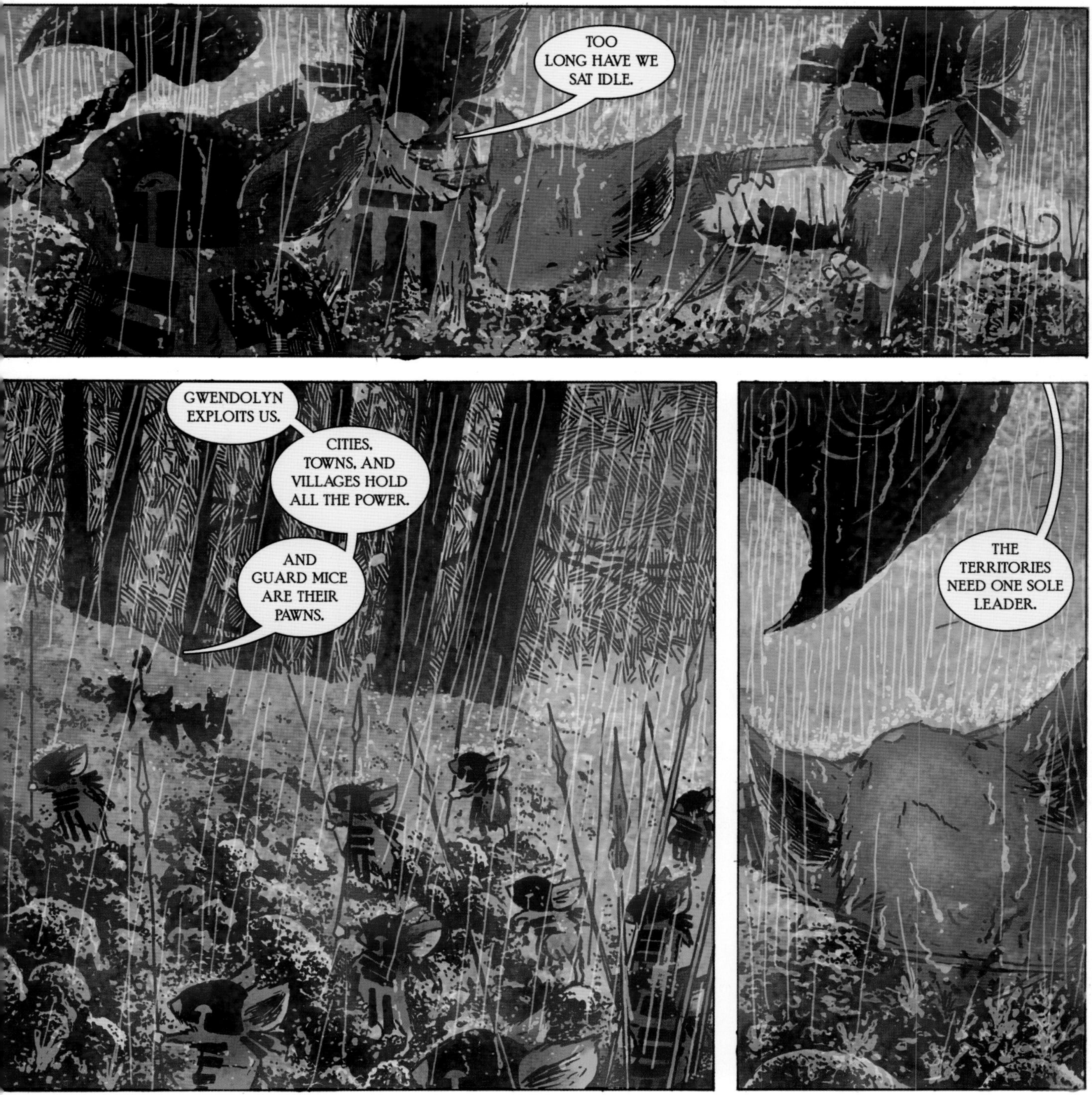
TOO LONG HAVE WE SAT IDLE.
GWENDOLYN EXPLOITS US.
CITIES, TOWNS, AND VILLAGES HOLD ALL THE POWER.
AND GUARD MICE ARE THEIR PAWNS.
THE TERRITORIES NEED ONE SOLE LEADER.

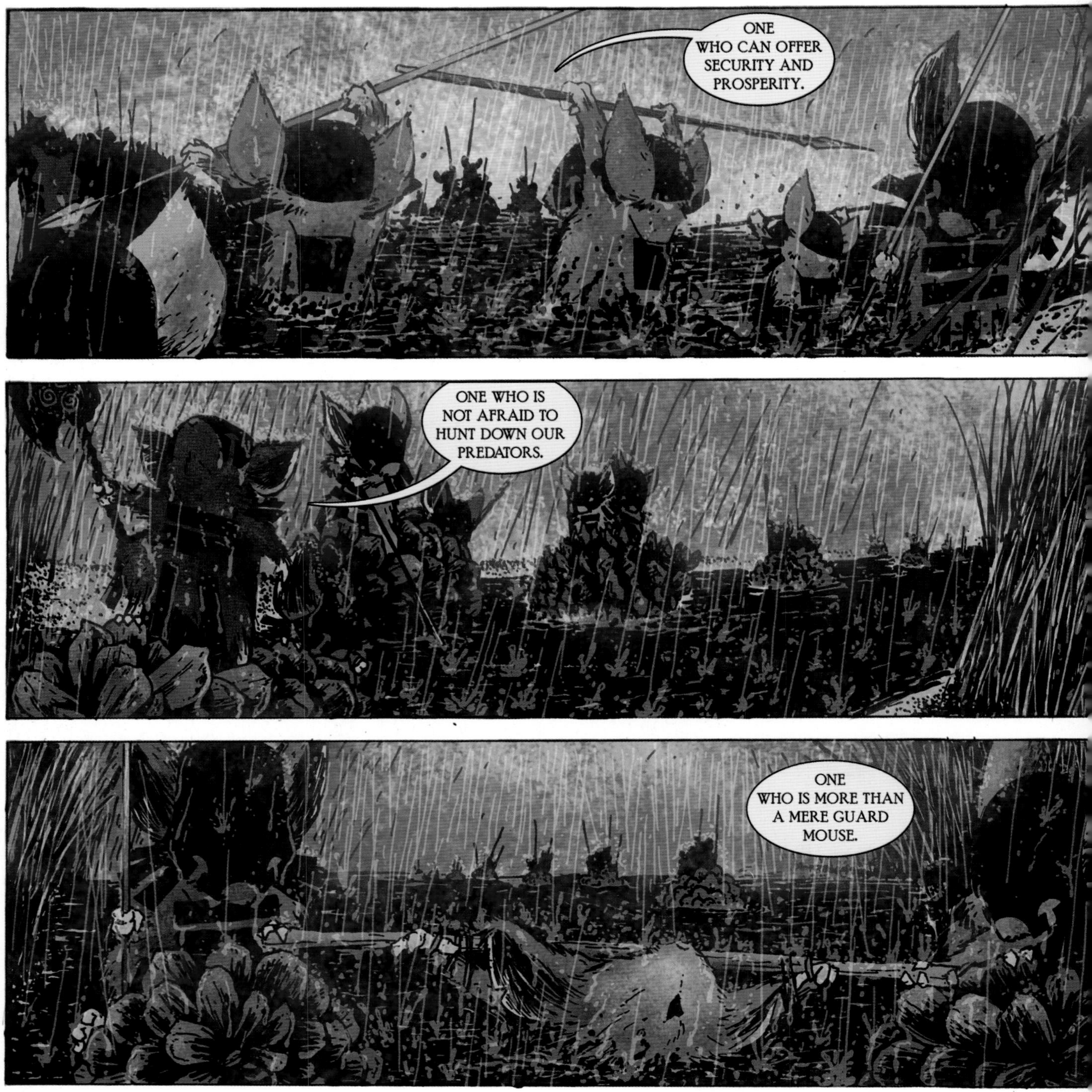
ONE WHO CAN OFFER SECURITY AND PROSPERITY.
ONE WHO IS NOT AFRAID TO HUNT DOWN OUR PREDATORS.
ONE WHO IS MORE THAN A MERE GUARD MOUSE.

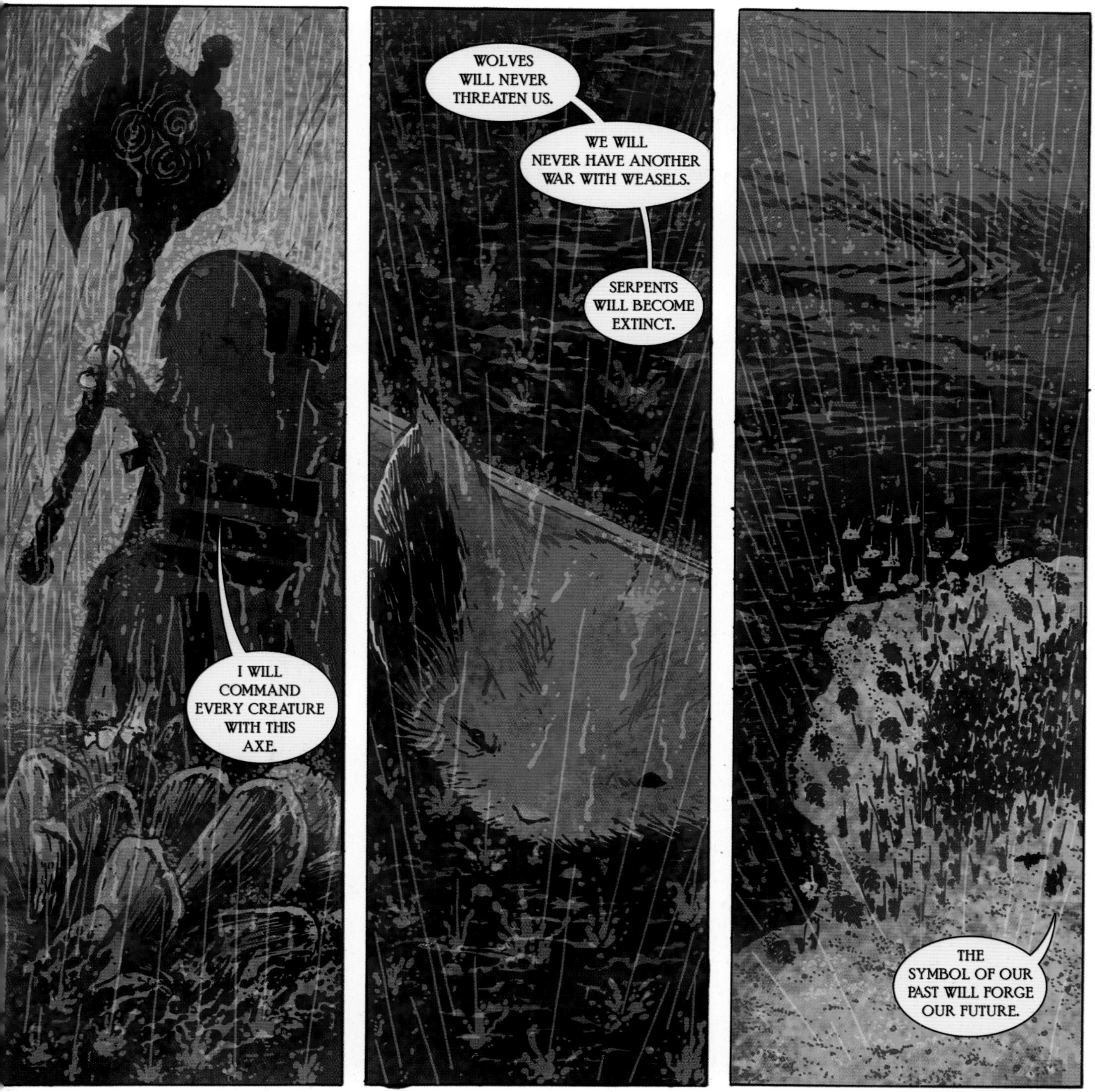
I WILL COMMAND EVERY CREATURE WITH THIS AXE.
WOLVES WILL NEVER THREATEN US.
WE WILL NEVER HAVE ANOTHER WAR WITH WEASELS.
SERPENTS WILL BECOME EXTINCT.
THE SYMBOL OF OUR PAST WILL FORGE OUR FUTURE.

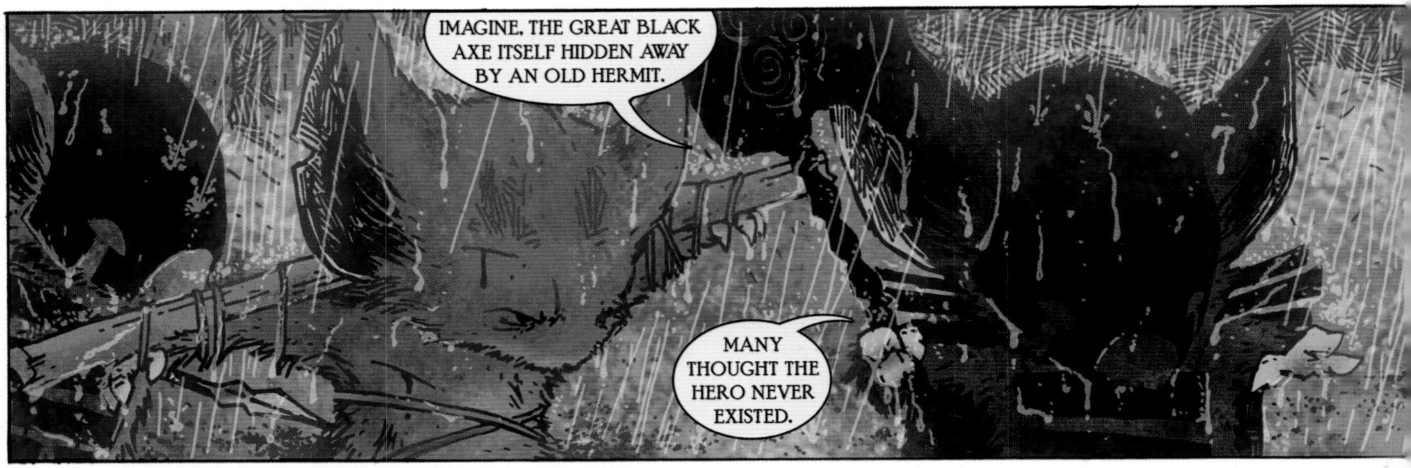
IMAGINE, THE GREAT BLACK AXE ITSELF HIDDEN AWAY BY AN OLD HERMIT.
MANY THOUGHT THE HERO NEVER EXISTED.

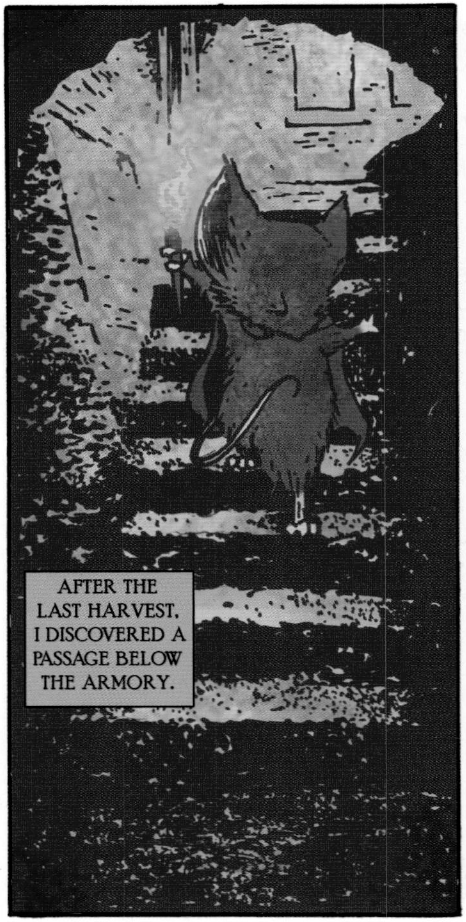
AFTER THE LAST HARVEST, I DISCOVERED A PASSAGE BELOW THE ARMORY.

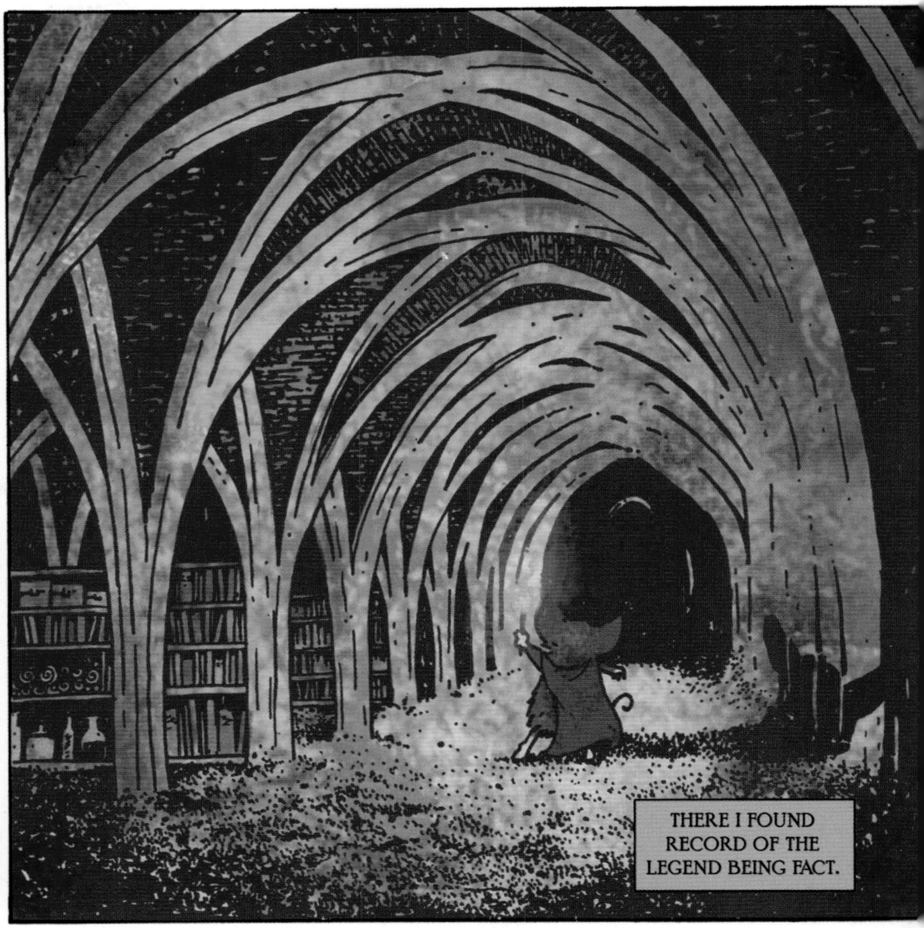
THERE I FOUND RECORD OF THE LEGEND BEING FACT.

Before the days of peace the guard needed every mouse brave enough to stand and rise above the villains of the territories. One mouse alone bore the brunt of the task. An axe of black severed the necks of the five serpents who surrounded all that is. Thus begins his tale.

The axe itself was forged into being by the blacksmith Farrer his family had been slain by predators whilst weaponless.

Hotter coals have never since been bellowed, and every strike of his hammer into the ore was a strike unto his enemies. Thus the black axe was forged.

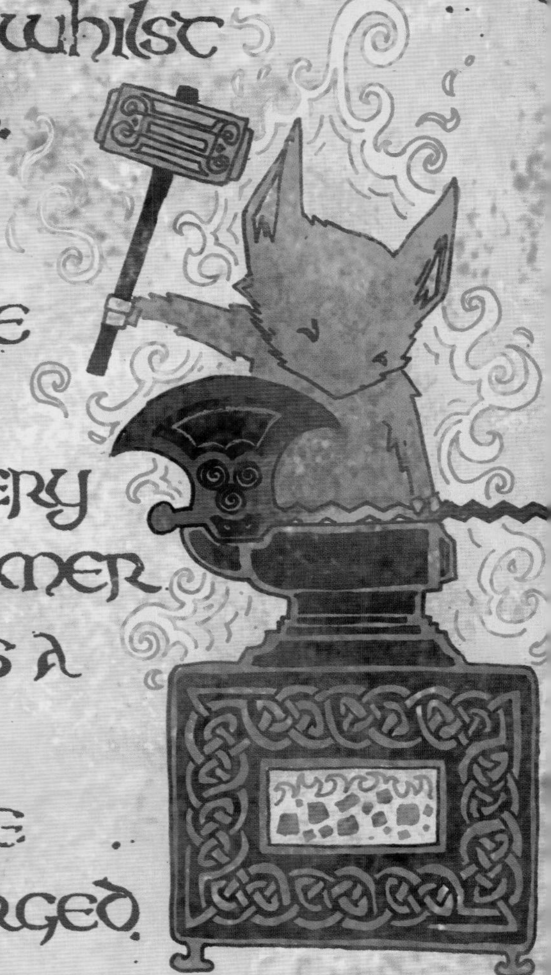

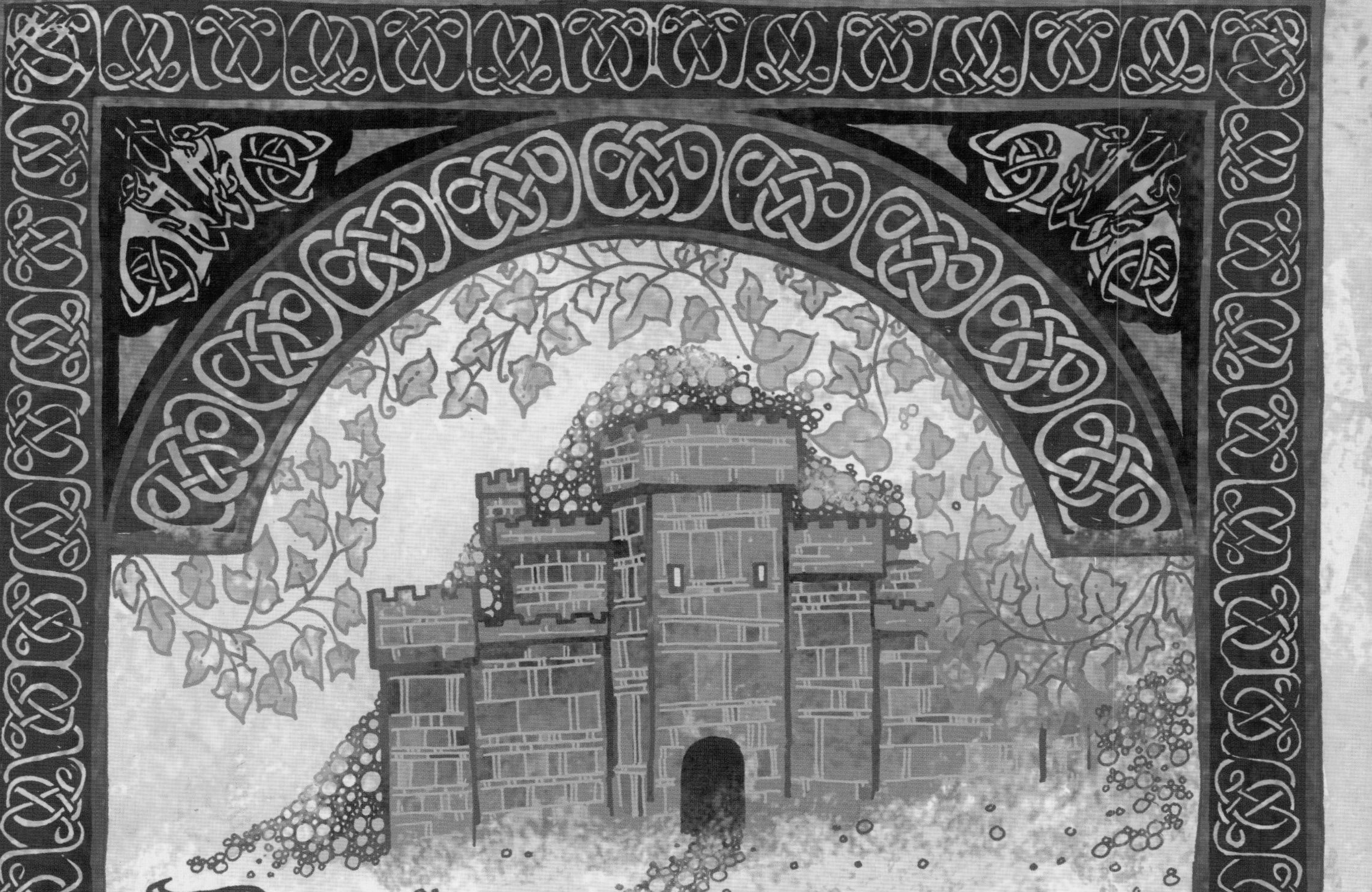

The weapon proved too heavy to wield. It held the burden of all the blacksmith's mourning. To find a true hero it was taken to Lockhaven.

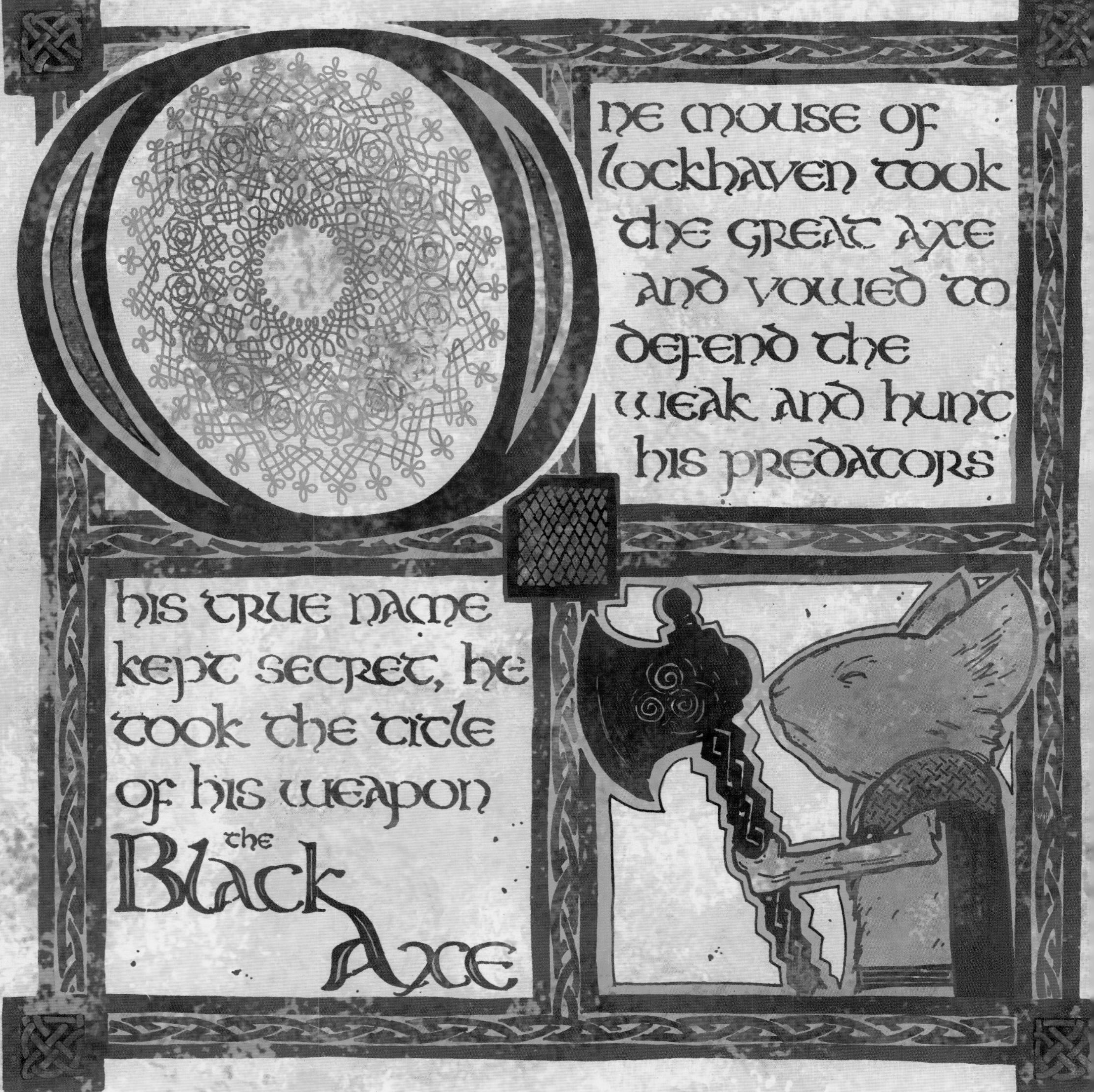
One mouse of Lockhaven took the great axe and vowed to defend the weak and hunt his predators
His true name kept secret, he took the title of his weapon
the Black Axe

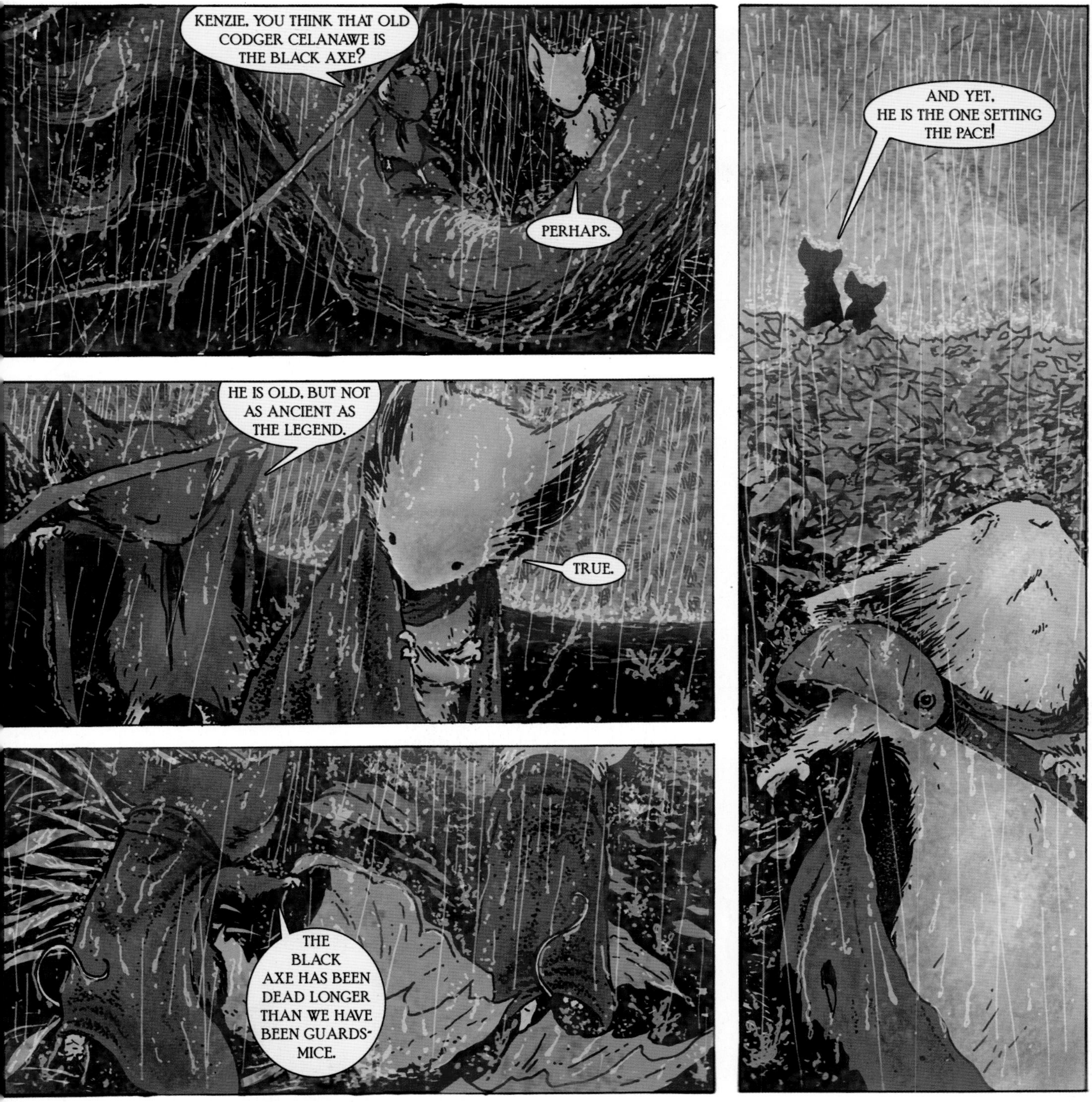
KENZIE, YOU THINK THAT OLD CODGER CELANAWE IS THE BLACK AXE?
PERHAPS.
HE IS OLD, BUT NOT AS ANCIENT AS THE LEGEND.
TRUE.
THE BLACK AXE HAS BEEN DEAD LONGER THAN WE HAVE BEEN GUARDS-MICE.
AND YET, HE IS THE ONE SETTING THE PACE!

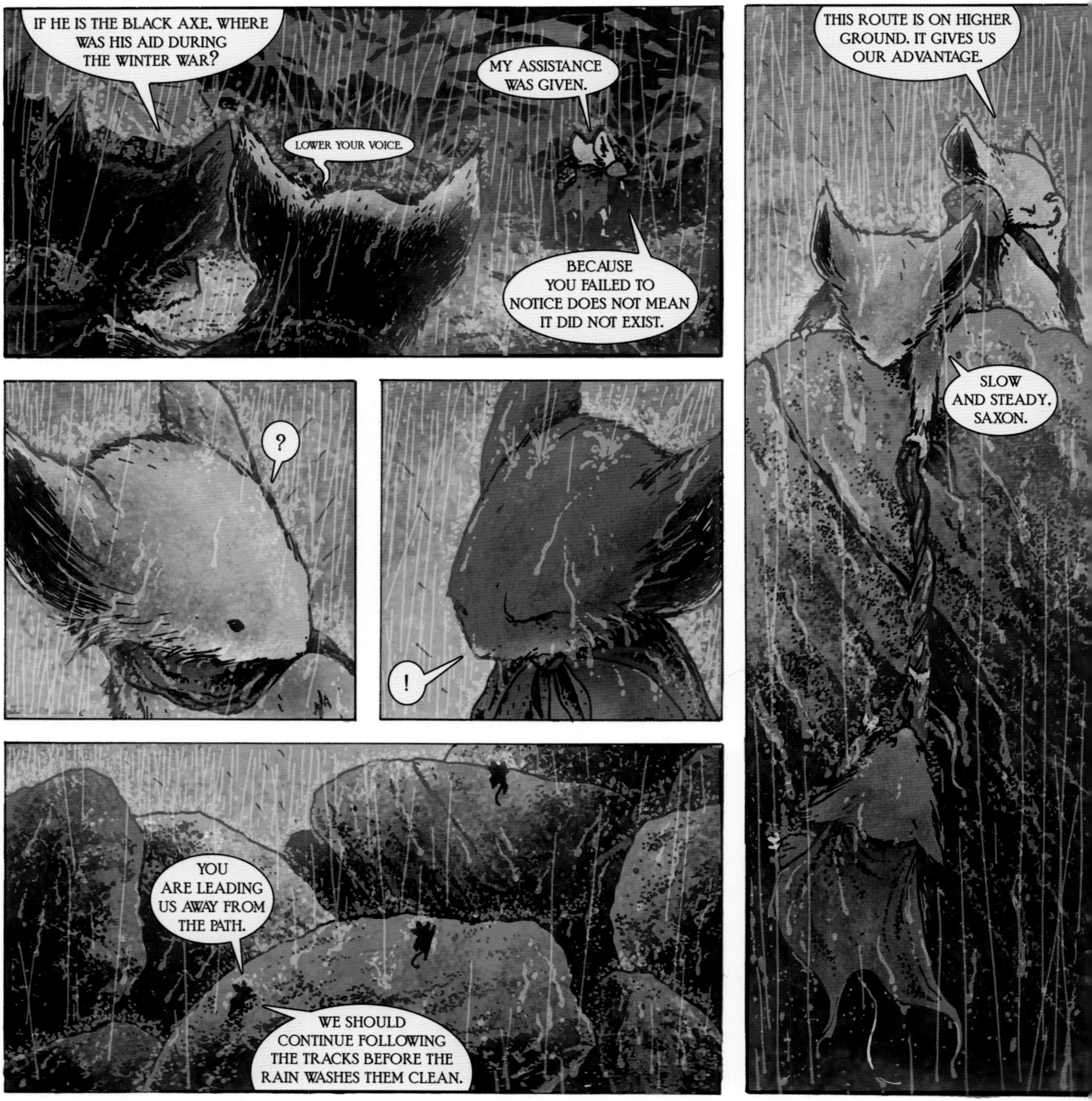
IF HE IS THE BLACK AXE, WHERE WAS HIS AID DURING THE WINTER WAR?
LOWER YOUR VOICE.
MY ASSISTANCE WAS GIVEN.
BECAUSE YOU FAILED TO NOTICE DOES NOT MEAN IT DID NOT EXIST.
?
!
YOU ARE LEADING US AWAY FROM THE PATH.
WE SHOULD CONTINUE FOLLOWING THE TRACKS BEFORE THE RAIN WASHES THEM CLEAN.
THIS ROUTE IS ON HIGHER GROUND. IT GIVES US OUR ADVANTAGE.
SLOW AND STEADY, SAXON.

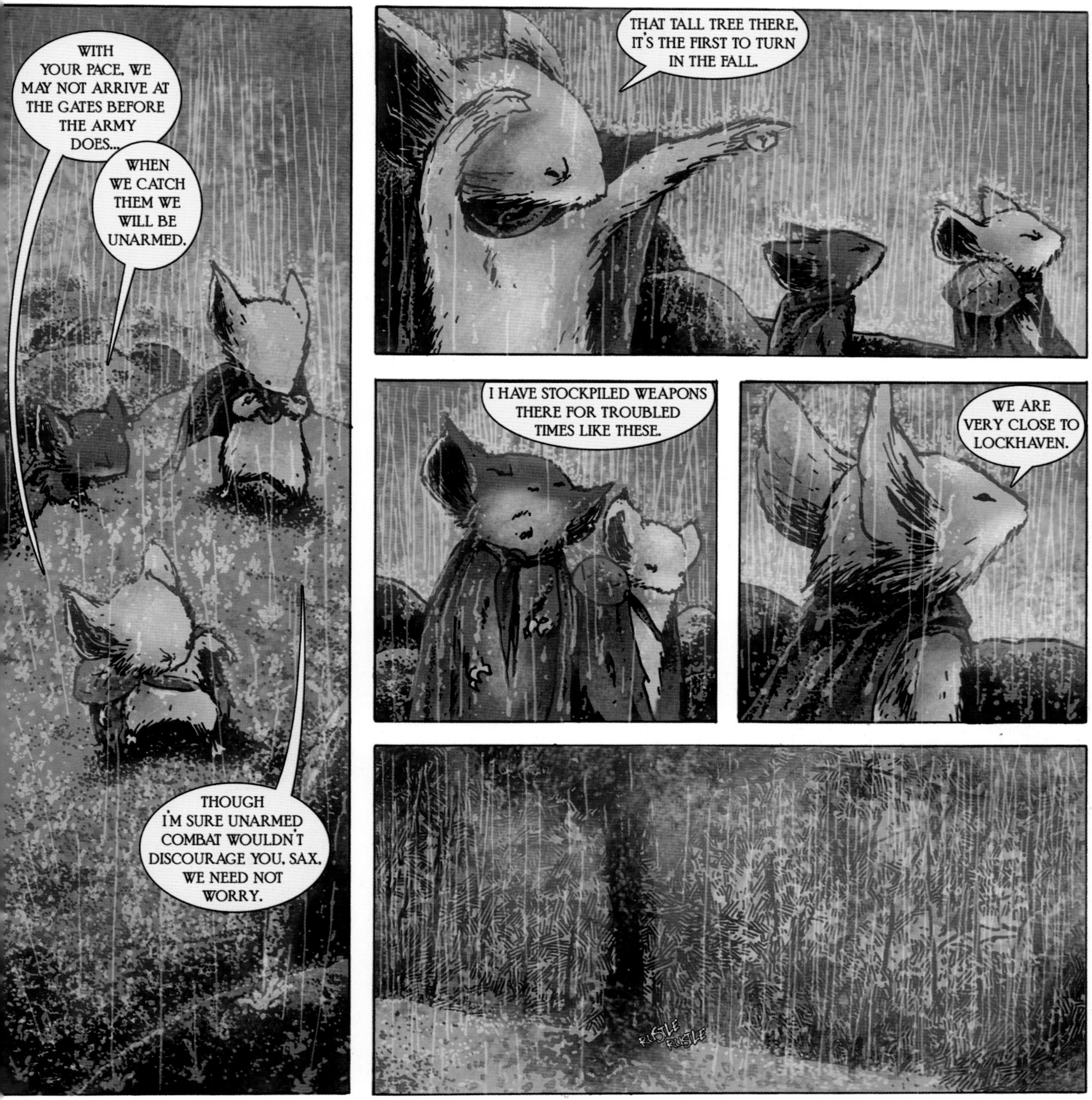
WITH YOUR PACE, WE MAY NOT ARRIVE AT THE GATES BEFORE THE ARMY DOES...
WHEN WE CATCH THEM WE WILL BE UNARMED.
THOUGH I'M SURE UNARMED COMBAT WOULDN'T DISCOURAGE YOU, SAX, WE NEED NOT WORRY.
THAT TALL TREE THERE, IT'S THE FIRST TO TURN IN THE FALL.
I HAVE STOCKPILED WEAPONS THERE FOR TROUBLED TIMES LIKE THESE.
WE ARE VERY CLOSE TO LOCKHAVEN.
RUSTLE RUSTLE

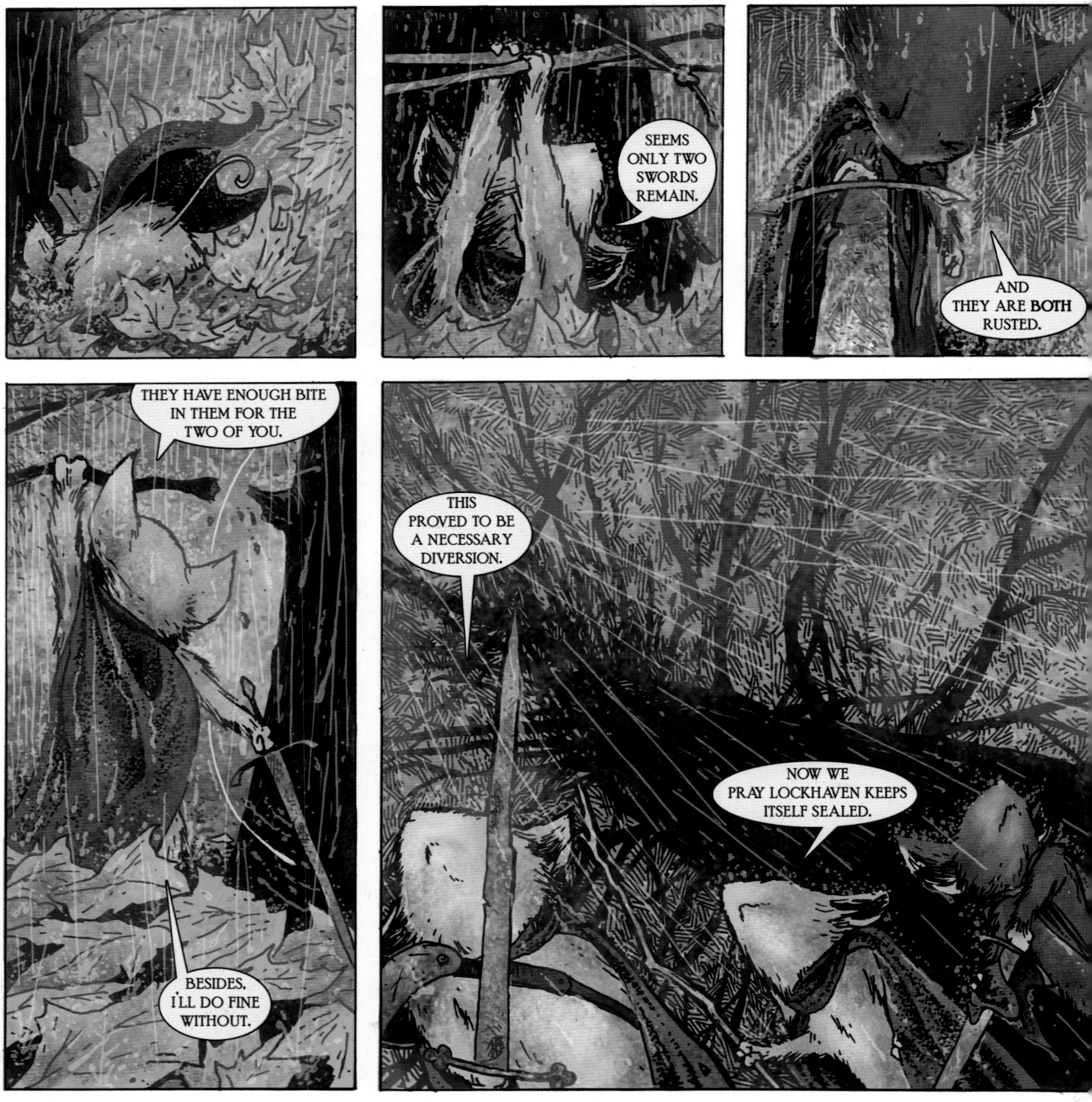

SEEMS ONLY TWO SWORDS REMAIN.
AND THEY ARE BOTH RUSTED.
THEY HAVE ENOUGH BITE IN THEM FOR THE TWO OF YOU.
BESIDES, I'LL DO FINE WITHOUT.
THIS PROVED TO BE A NECESSARY DIVERSION.
NOW WE PRAY LOCKHAVEN KEEPS ITSELF SEALED.

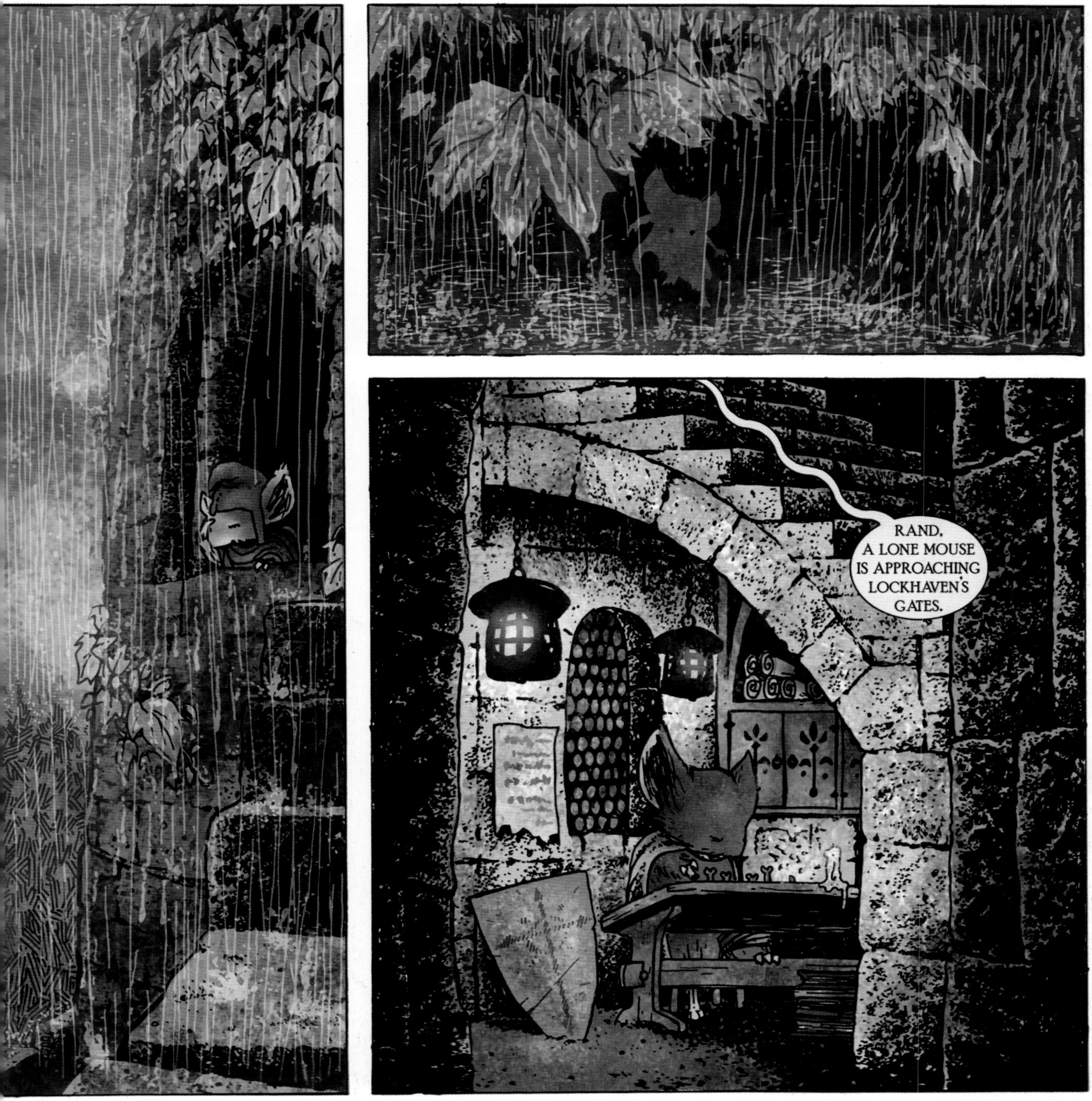
RAND, A LONE MOUSE IS APPROACHING LOCKHAVEN'S GATES.

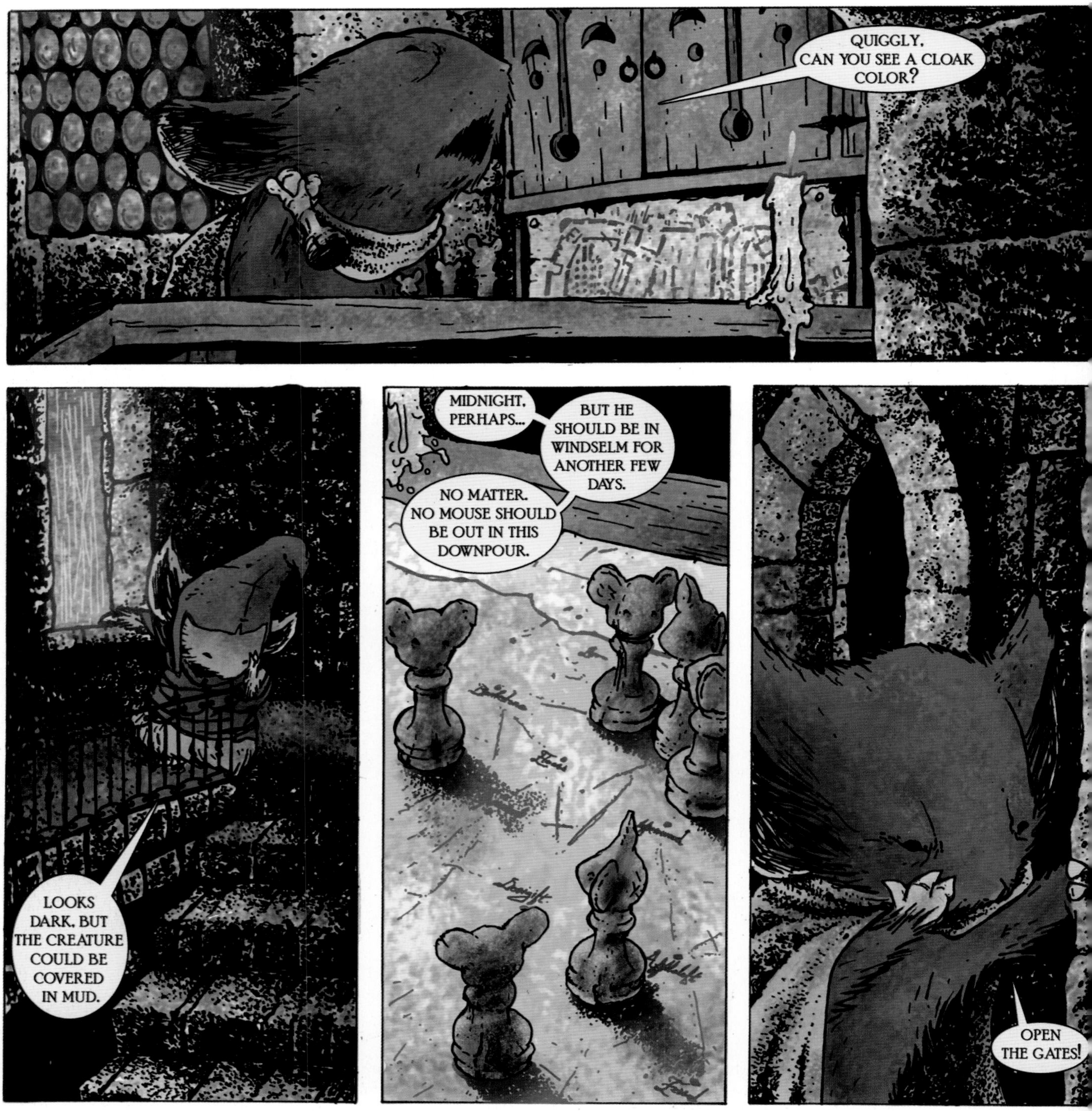
QUIGGLY, CAN YOU SEE A CLOAK COLOR?
LOOKS DARK, BUT THE CREATURE COULD BE COVERED IN MUD.
MIDNIGHT, PERHAPS...
BUT HE SHOULD BE IN WINDSELM FOR ANOTHER FEW DAYS.
NO MATTER. NO MOUSE SHOULD BE OUT IN THIS DOWNPOUR.
OPEN THE GATES!

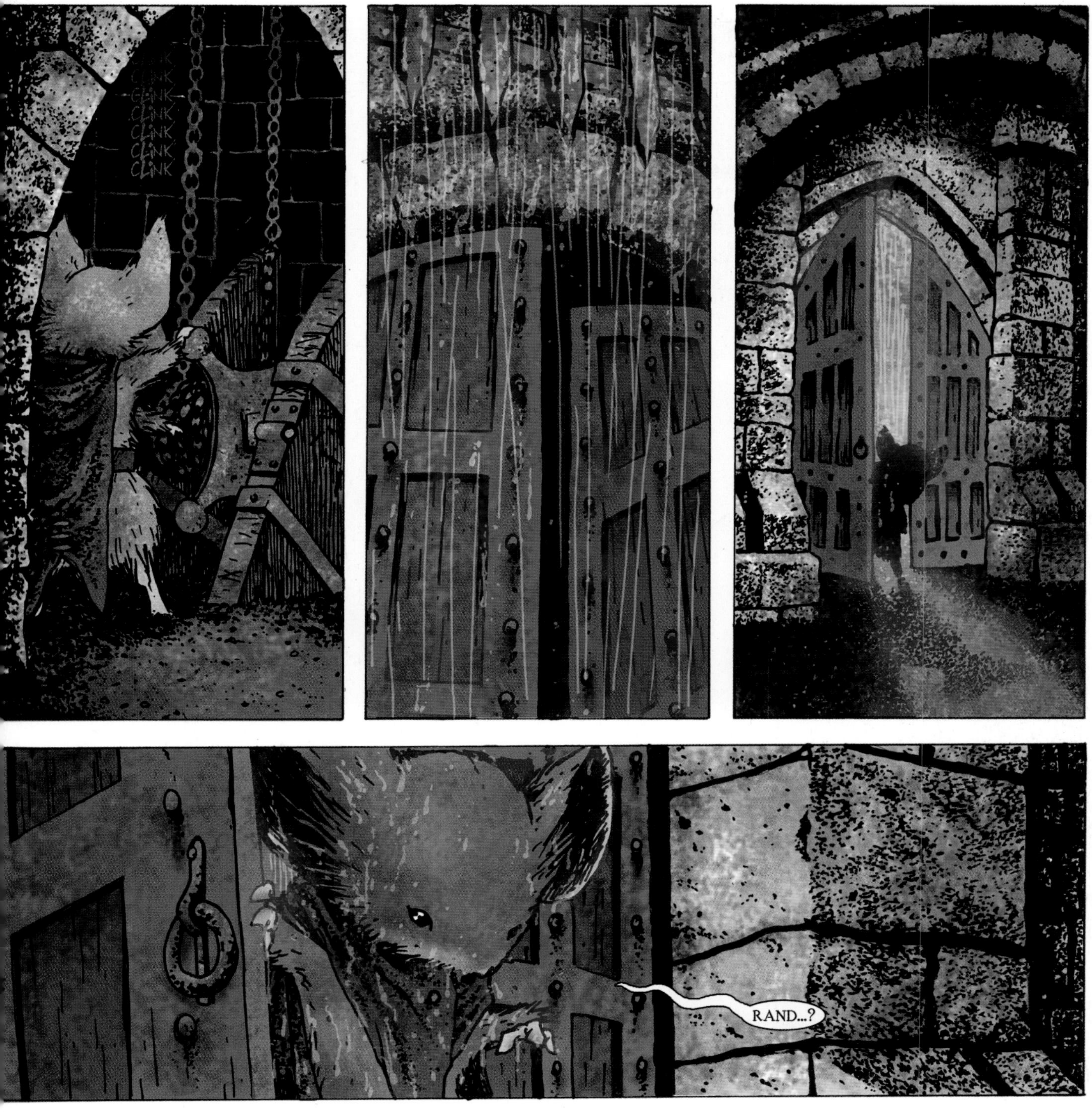
CLINK
CLINK
CLINK
CLINK
CLINK
CLINK
CLINK
RAND...?

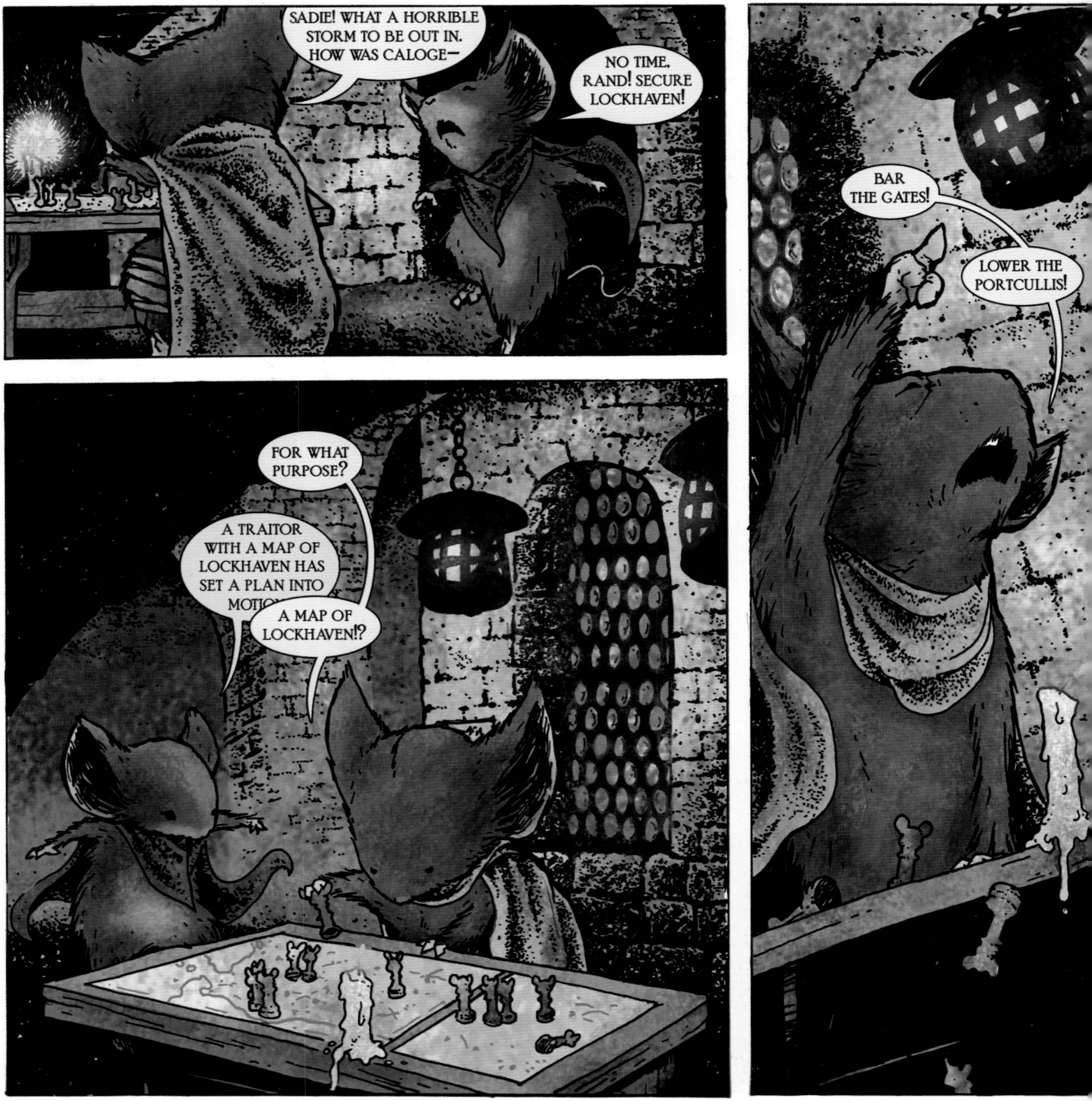
SADIE! WHAT A HORRIBLE STORM TO BE OUT IN. HOW WAS CALOGE—
NO TIME, RAND! SECURE LOCKHAVEN!
BAR THE GATES!
LOWER THE PORTCULLIS!
FOR WHAT PURPOSE?
A TRAITOR WITH A MAP OF LOCKHAVEN HAS SET A PLAN INTO MOTIO
A MAP OF LOCKHAVEN!?

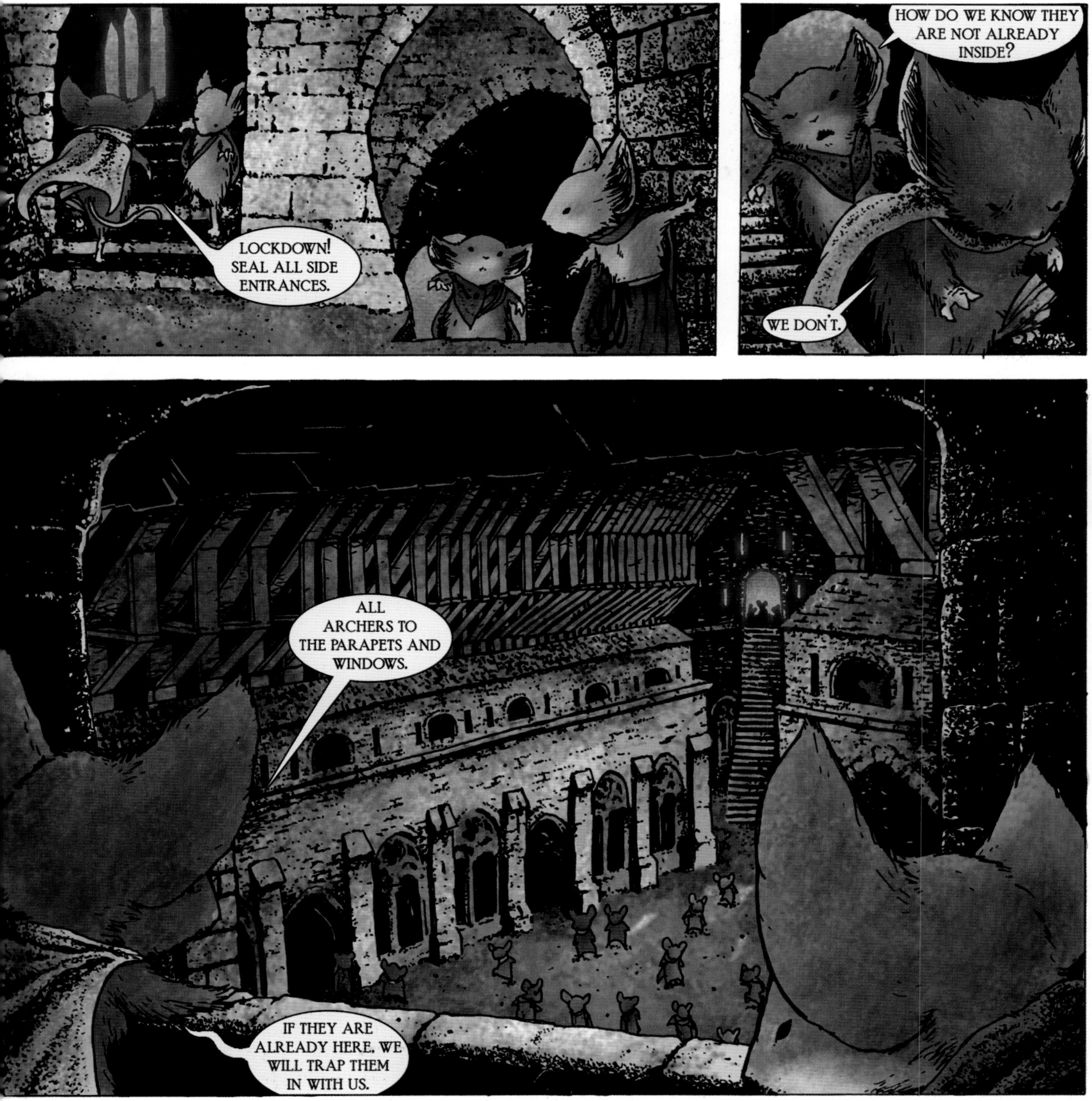
LOCKDOWN! SEAL ALL SIDE ENTRANCES.
HOW DO WE KNOW THEY ARE NOT ALREADY INSIDE?
WE DON'T.
ALL ARCHERS TO THE PARAPETS AND WINDOWS.
IF THEY ARE ALREADY HERE, WE WILL TRAP THEM IN WITH US.

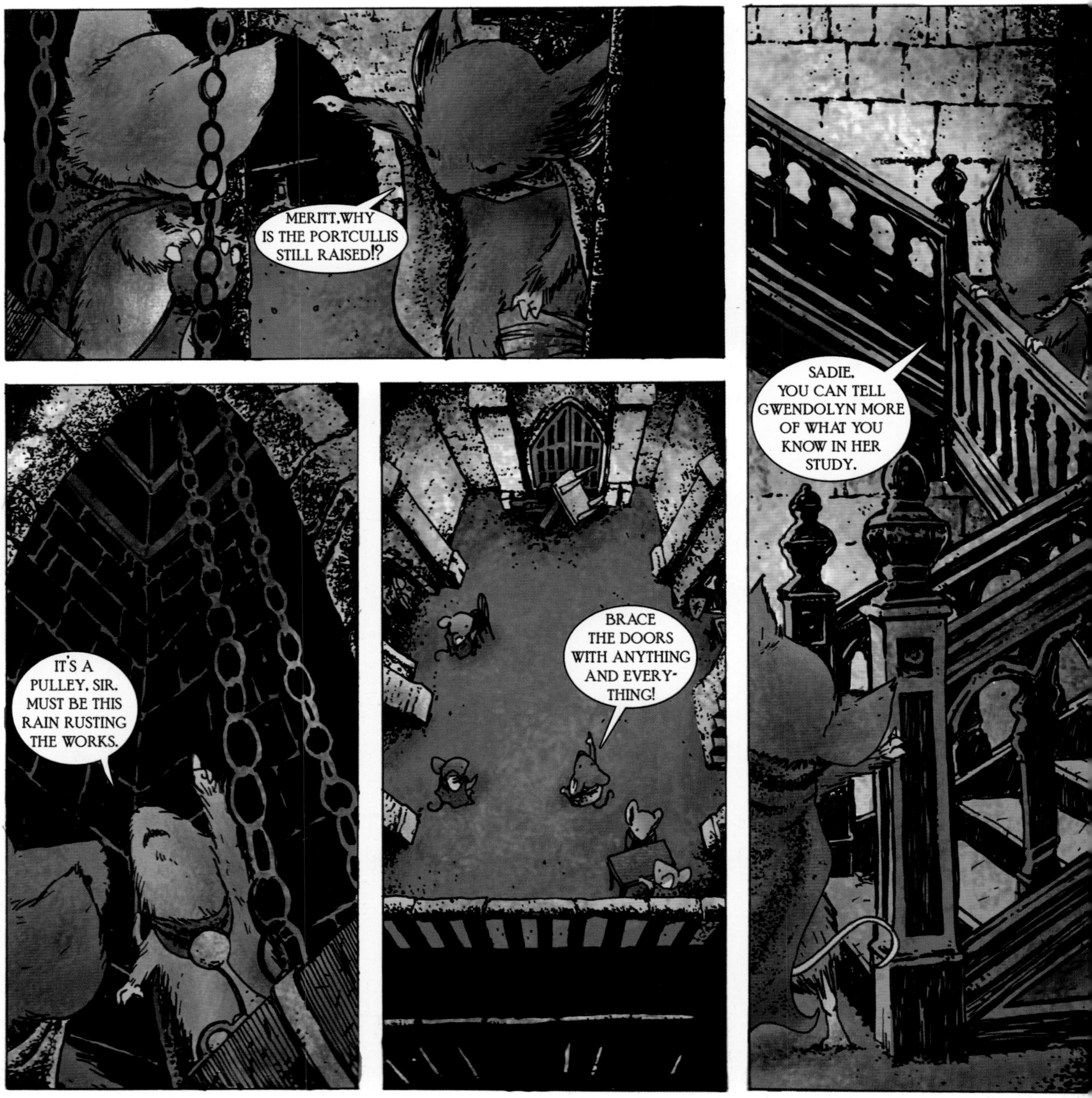
MERITT, WHY IS THE PORTCULLIS STILL RAISED!?
IT'S A PULLEY, SIR. MUST BE THIS RAIN RUSTING THE WORKS.
BRACE THE DOORS WITH ANYTHING AND EVERY-THING!
SADIE, YOU CAN TELL GWENDOLYN MORE OF WHAT YOU KNOW IN HER STUDY.

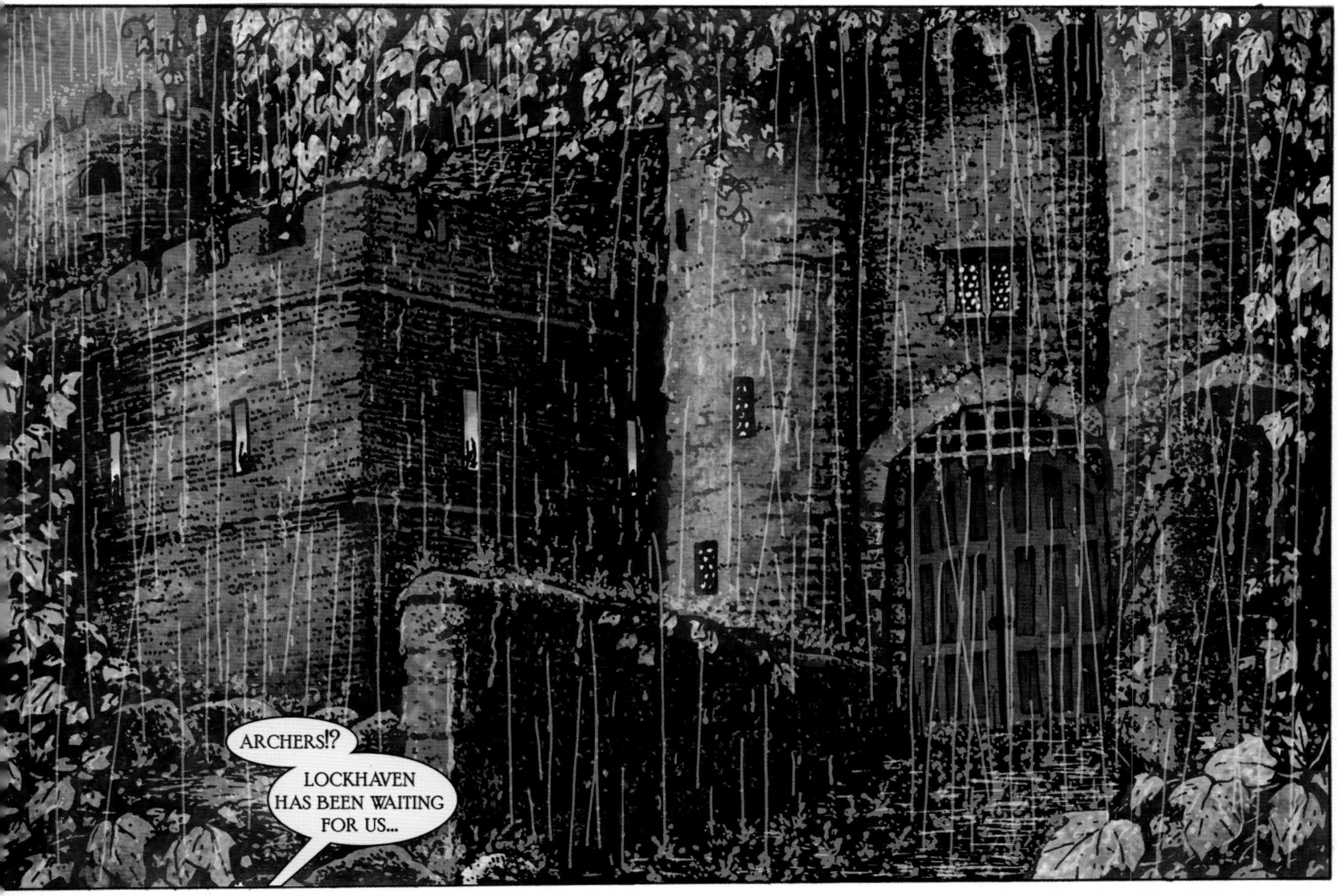
ARCHERS!?
LOCKHAVEN HAS BEEN WAITING FOR US...

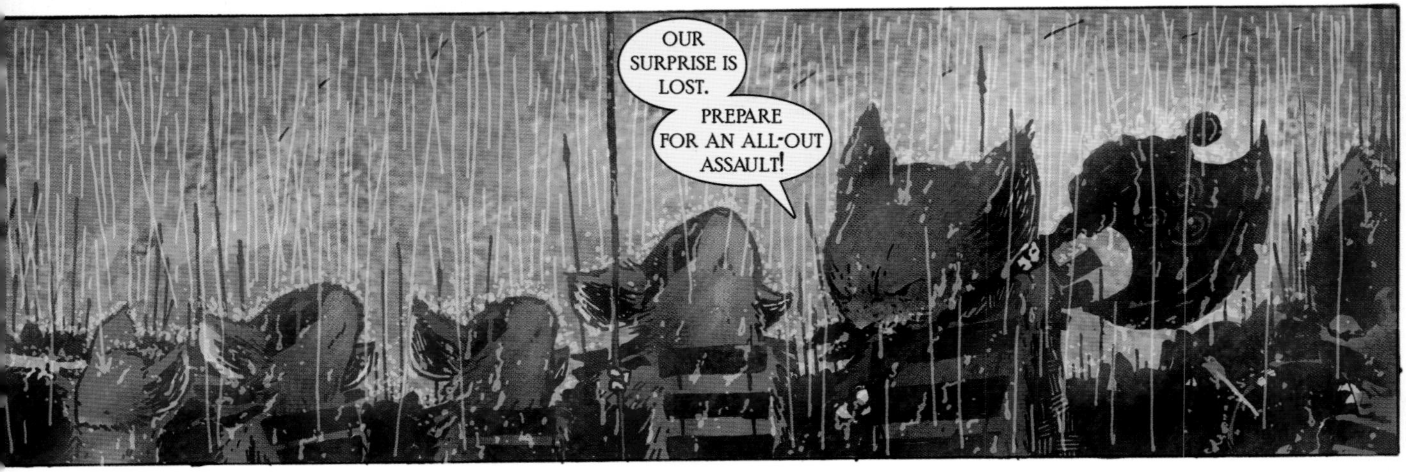
OUR SURPRISE IS LOST.
PREPARE FOR AN ALL-OUT ASSAULT!

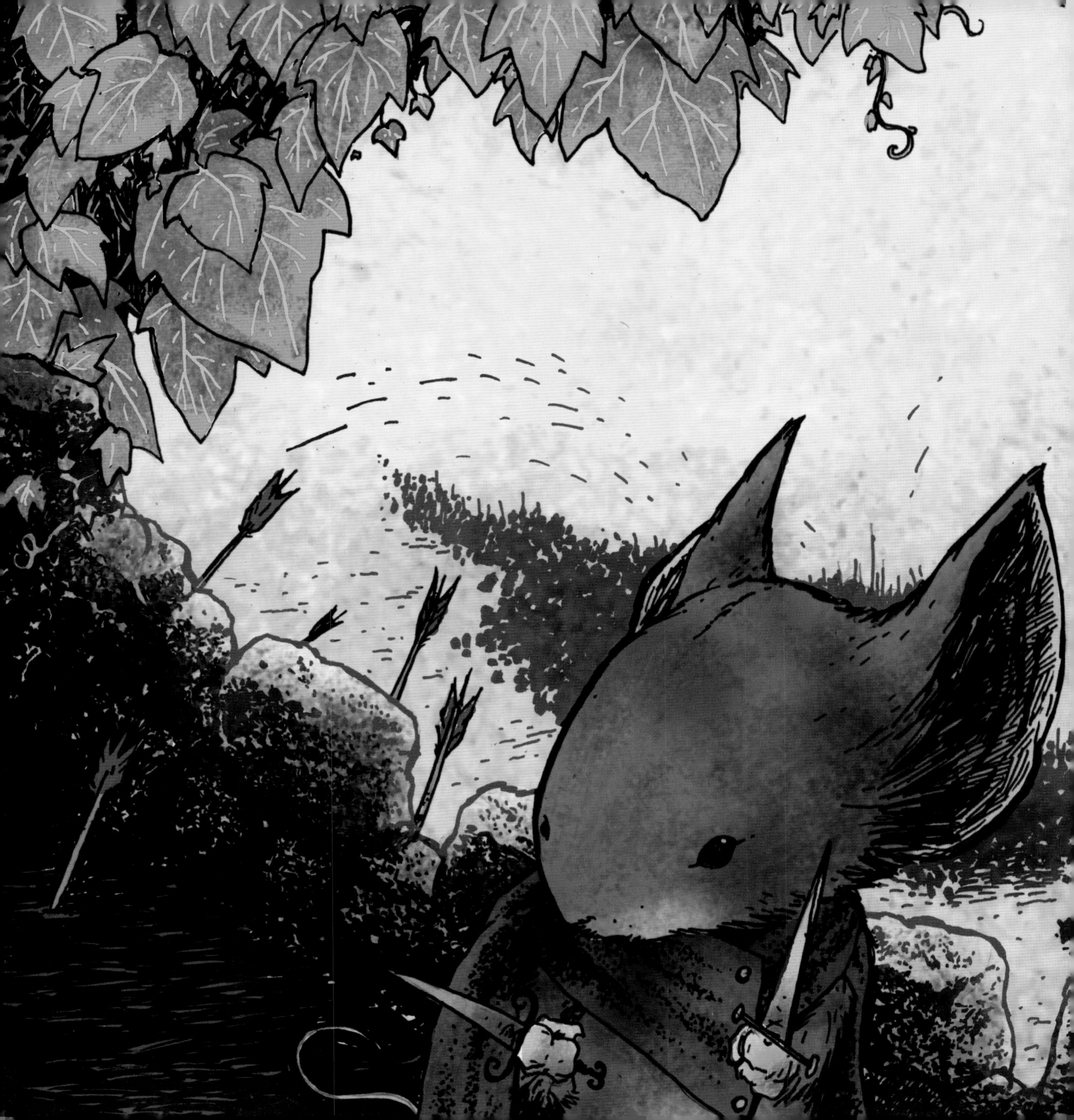

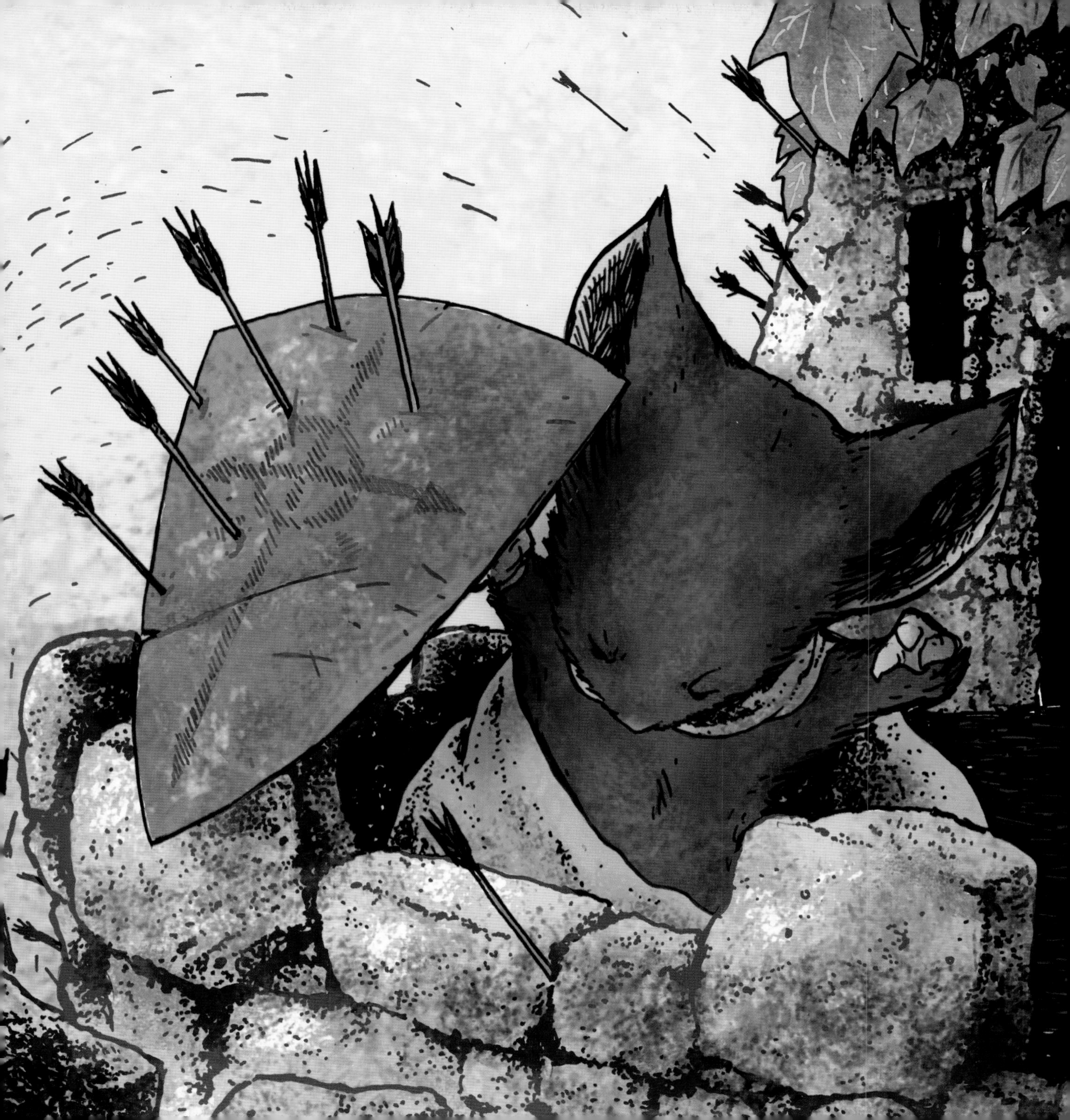

CHAPTER SIX

A RETURN TO HONOR

Lockhaven is under siege. The home of the Mouse Guard has been assaulted by many a predator, but rarely has it stood in opposition to mice. Rand, the defense expert of the Guard's home, received just enough warning from Sadie to seal the gates and secure the fortress before it came under treasonous attack.

Saxon & Kenzie, along with the oldfur Celanawe, also unable to get into Lockhaven, are forced to hide in the low maples to the east and watch their beloved home betrayed.

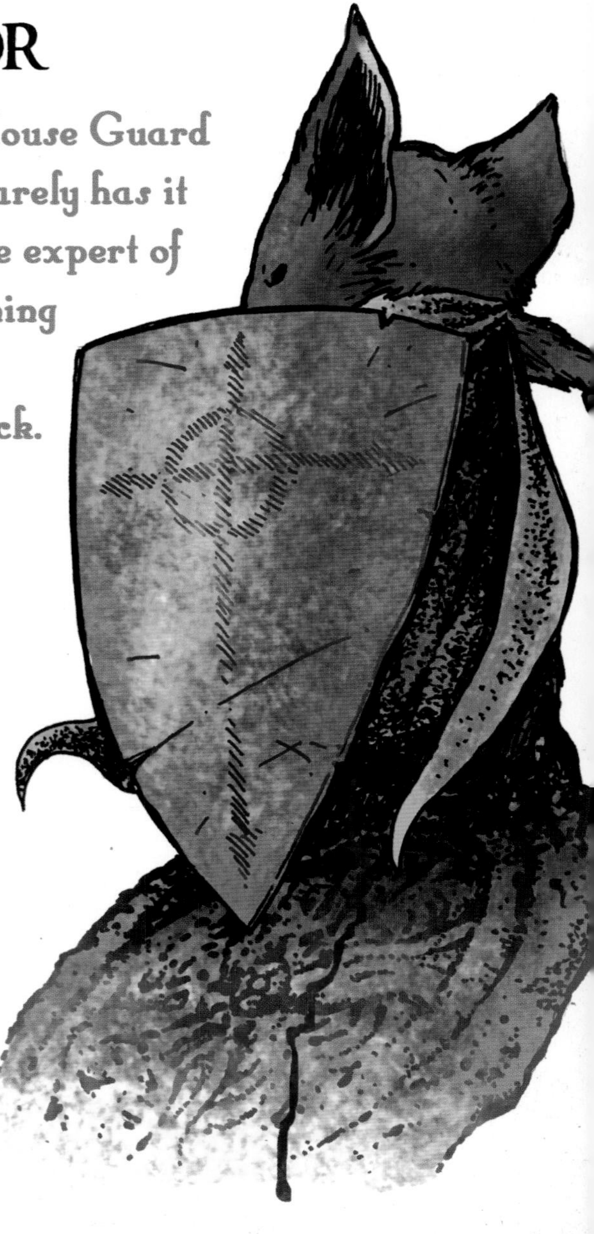

*'Let this stone always stand for safety and prosperity.
Let it be your conviction,
your pride, and your home.'*

-Dedication recited by all Mouse Guard Matriarchs to new Guard mice upon entering Lockhaven

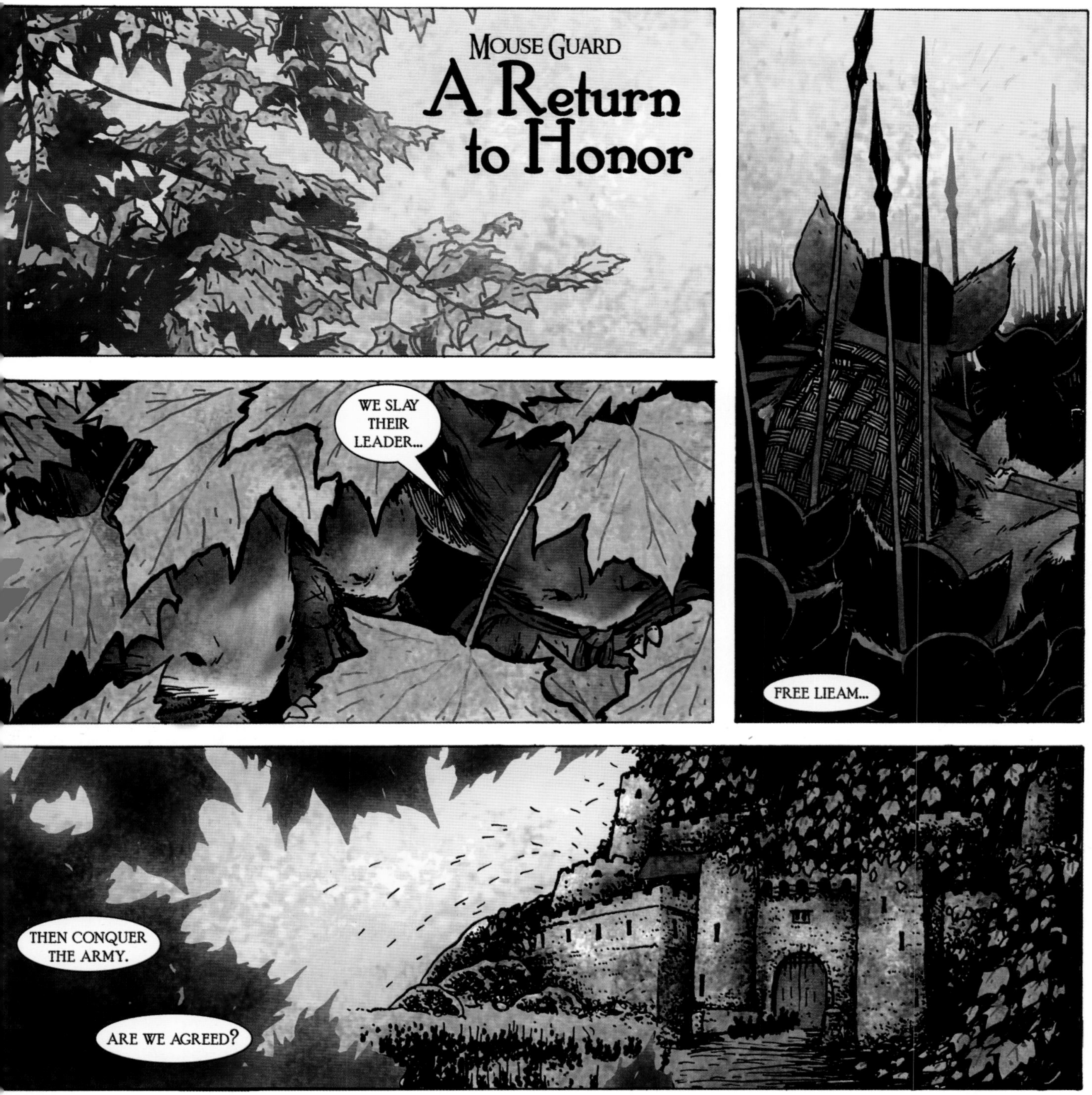

MOUSE GUARD
A Return to Honor
WE SLAY THEIR LEADER...
FREE LIEAM...
THEN CONQUER THE ARMY.
ARE WE AGREED?

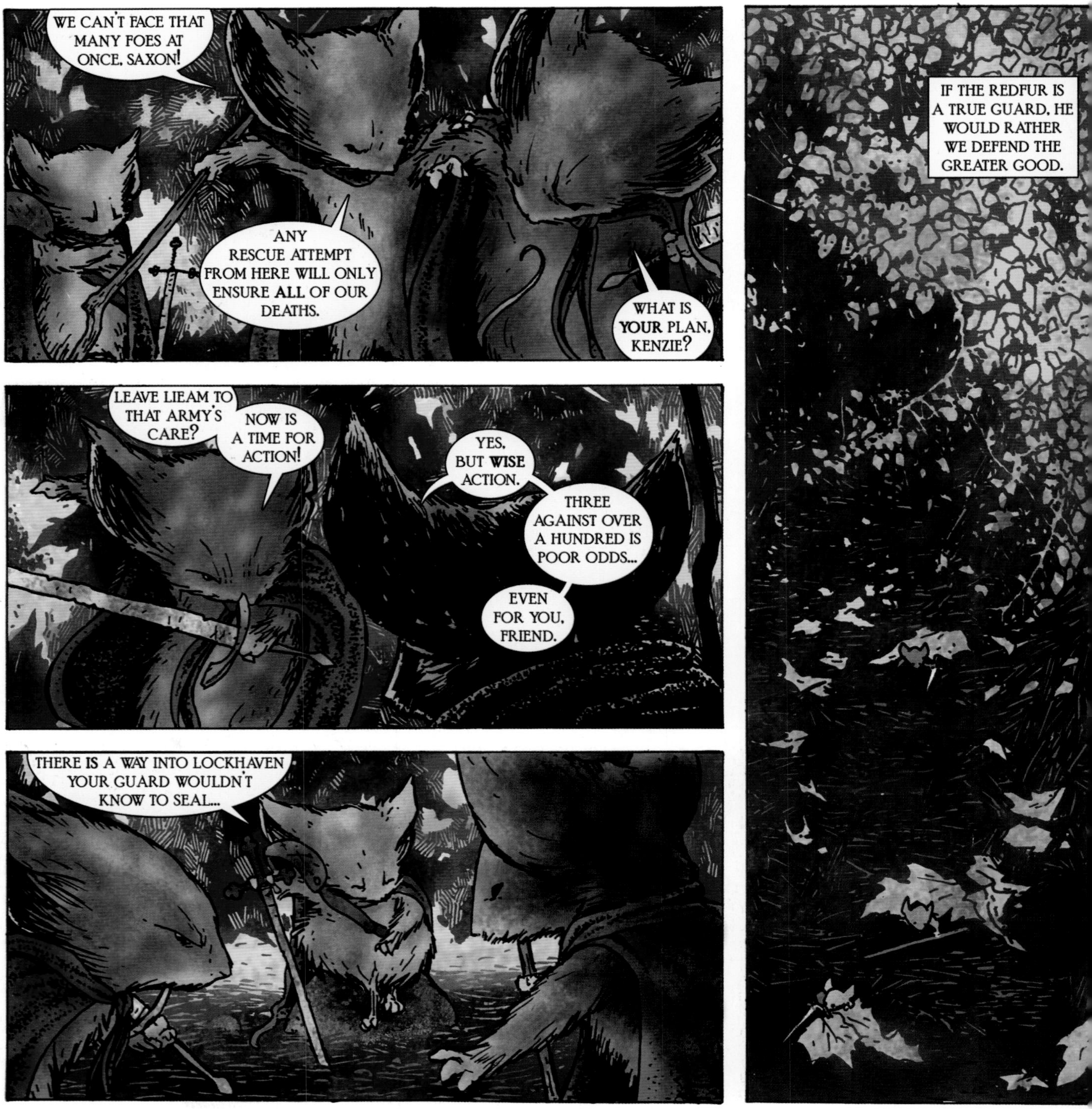
WE CAN'T FACE THAT MANY FOES AT ONCE, SAXON!
ANY RESCUE ATTEMPT FROM HERE WILL ONLY ENSURE **ALL** OF OUR DEATHS.
WHAT IS **YOUR** PLAN, KENZIE?
LEAVE LIEAM TO THAT ARMY'S CARE?
NOW IS A TIME FOR ACTION!
YES, BUT **WISE** ACTION.
THREE AGAINST OVER A HUNDRED IS POOR ODDS...
EVEN FOR YOU, FRIEND.
THERE **IS** A WAY INTO LOCKHAVEN YOUR GUARD WOULDN'T KNOW TO SEAL...
IF THE REDFUR IS A TRUE GUARD, HE WOULD RATHER WE DEFEND THE GREATER GOOD.

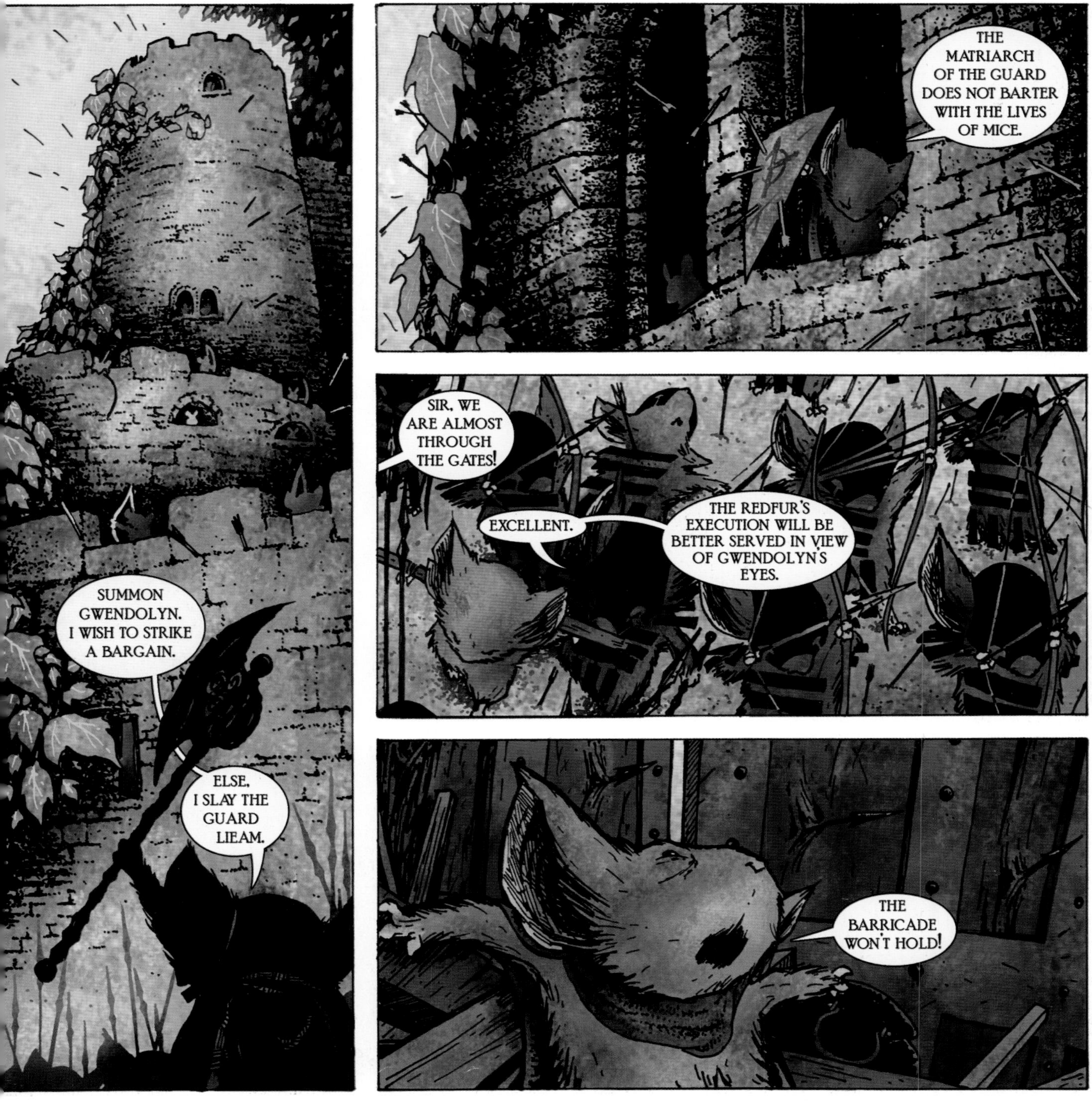
SUMMON GWENDOLYN. I WISH TO STRIKE A BARGAIN.
ELSE, I SLAY THE GUARD LIEAM.
THE MATRIARCH OF THE GUARD DOES NOT BARTER WITH THE LIVES OF MICE.
SIR, WE ARE ALMOST THROUGH THE GATES!
EXCELLENT.
THE REDFUR'S EXECUTION WILL BE BETTER SERVED IN VIEW OF GWENDOLYN'S EYES.
THE BARRICADE WON'T HOLD!

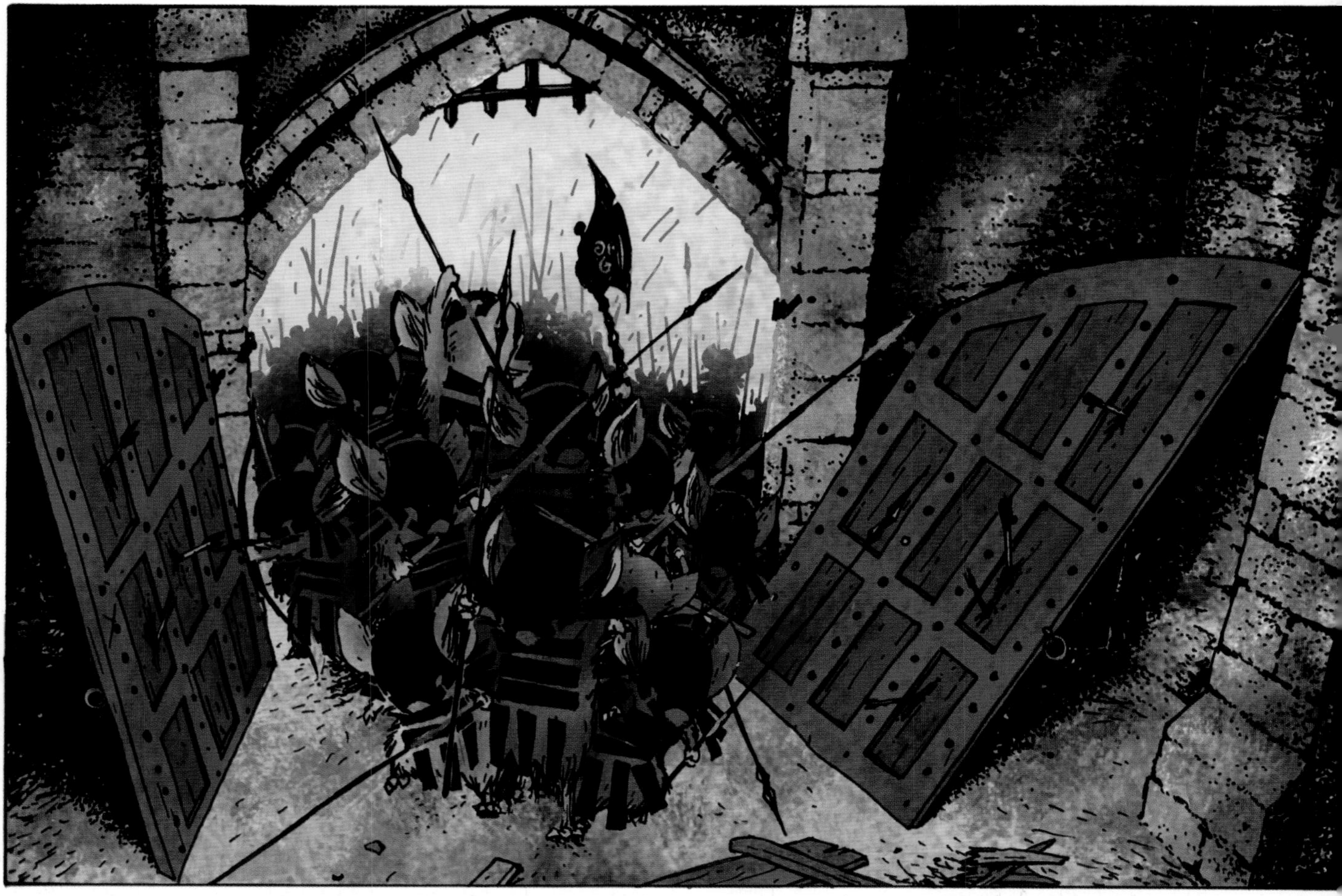

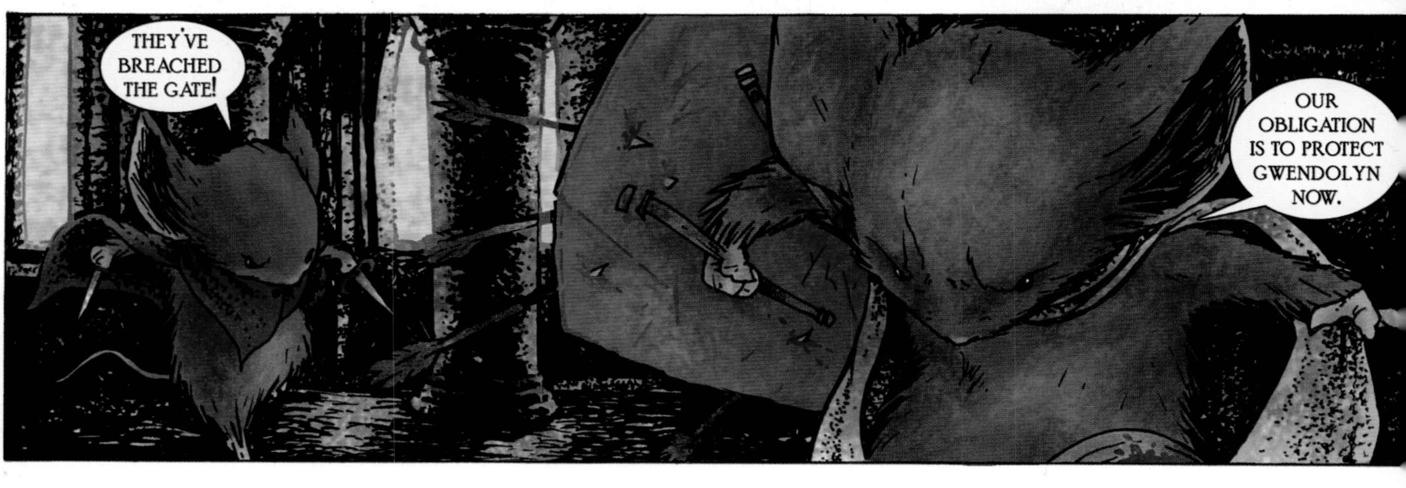
THEY'VE BREACHED THE GATE!
OUR OBLIGATION IS TO PROTECT GWENDOLYN NOW.

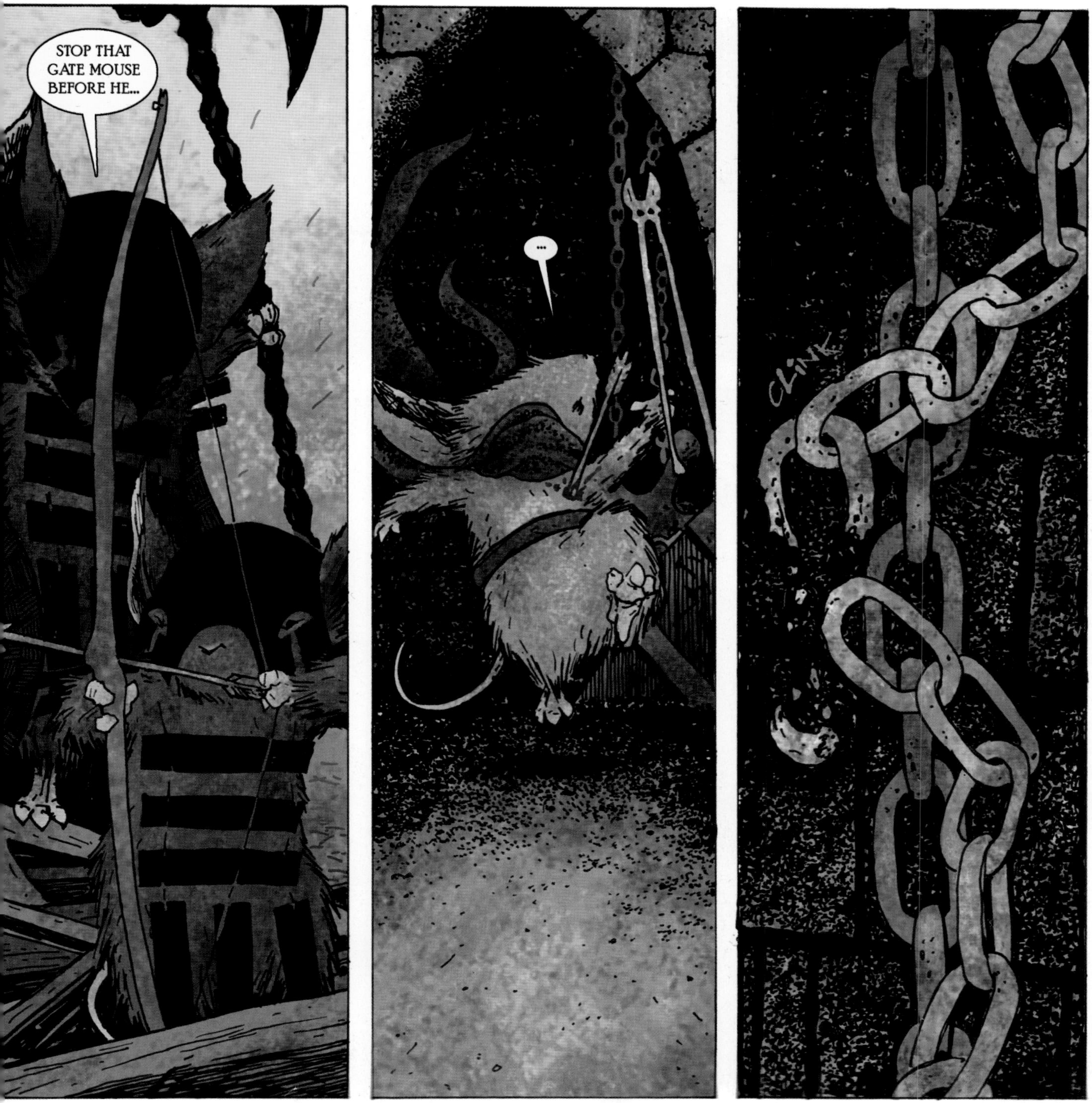
STOP THAT GATE MOUSE BEFORE HE...
...
CLINK

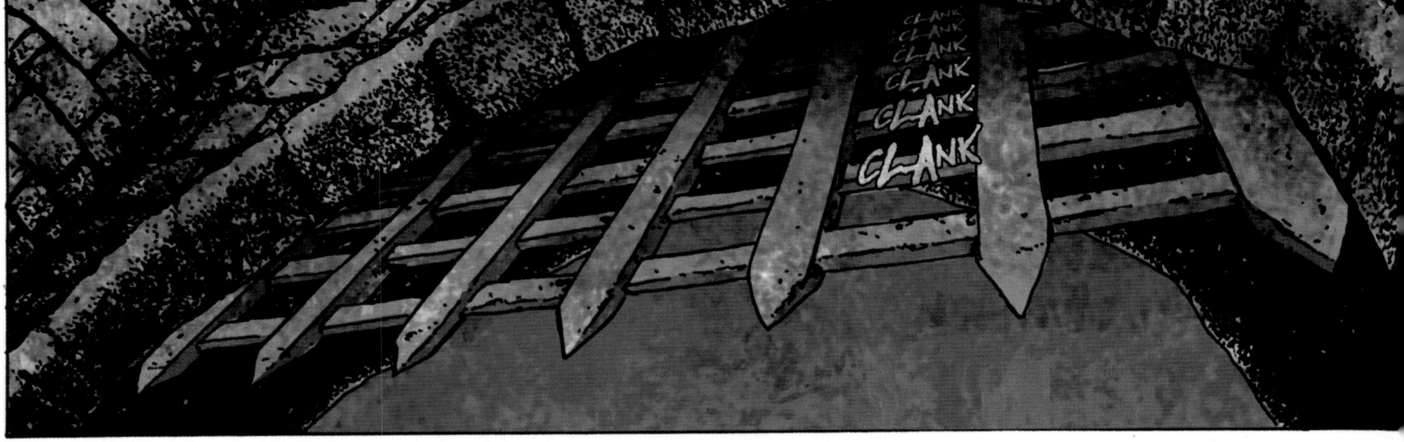
CLANK
CLANK
CLANK
CLANK
CLANK
CLANK

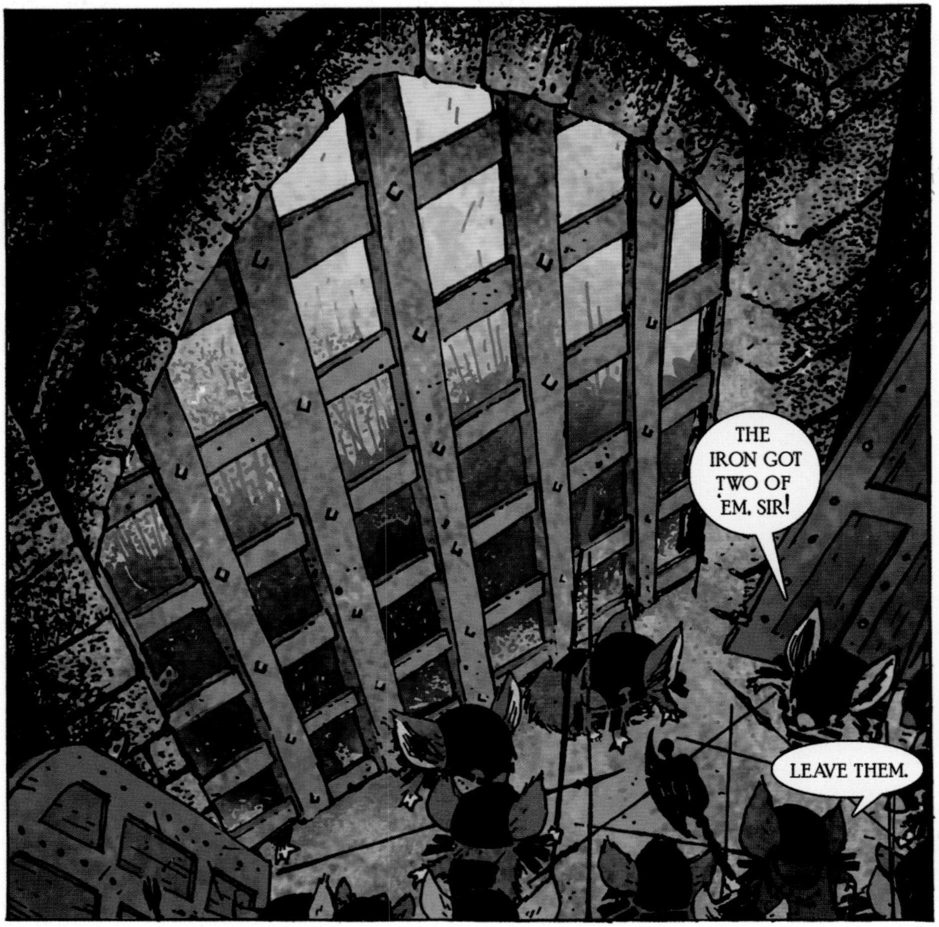
THE IRON GOT TWO OF 'EM, SIR!
LEAVE THEM.

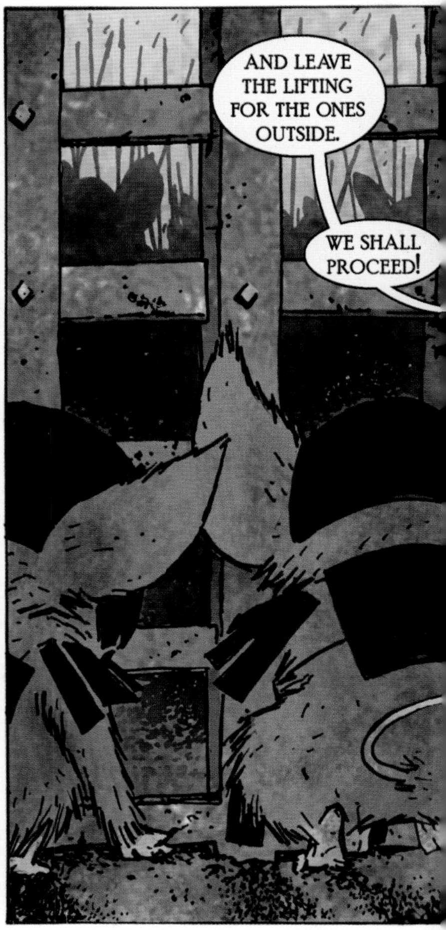
AND LEAVE THE LIFTING FOR THE ONES OUTSIDE.
WE SHALL PROCEED!

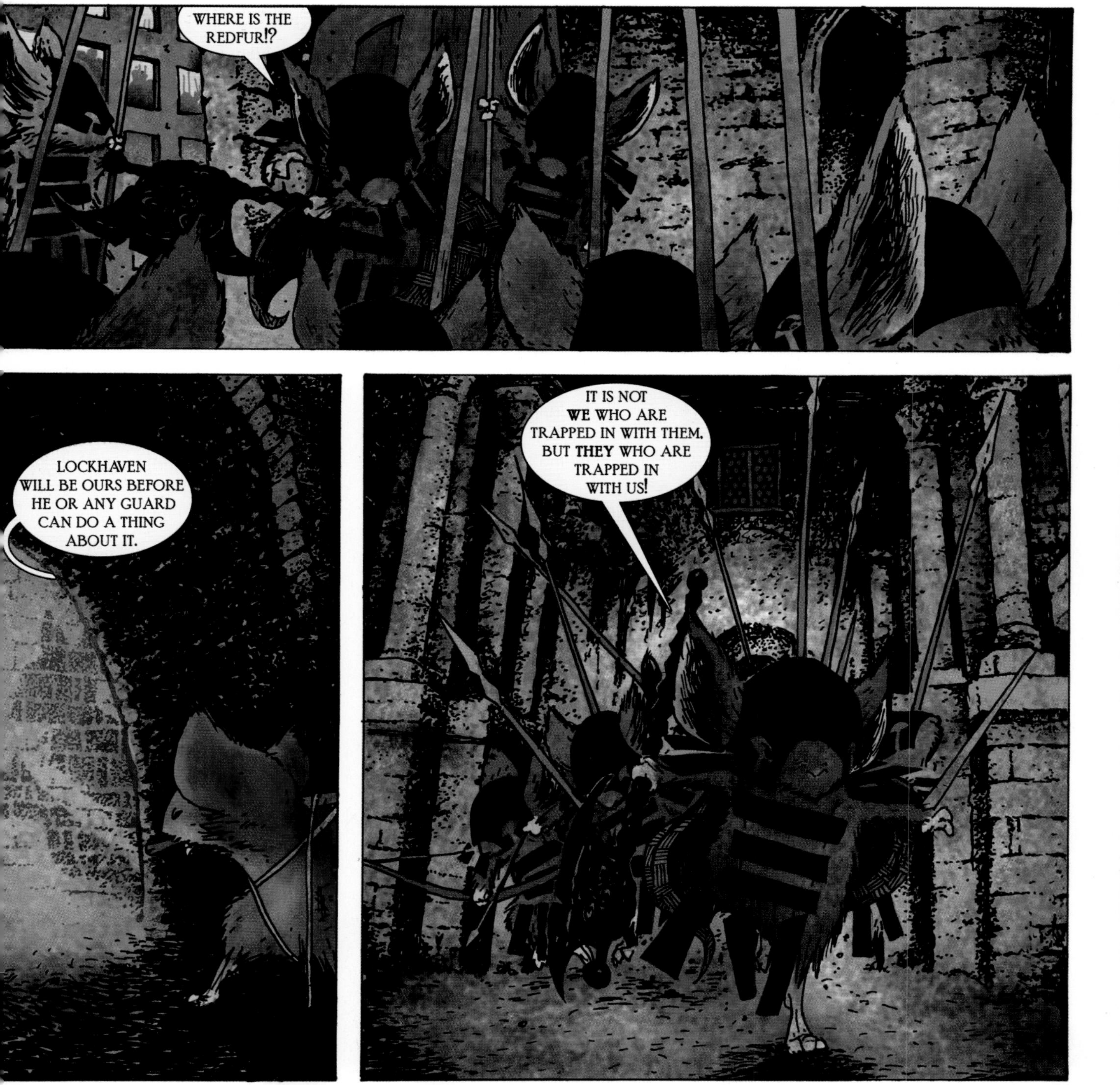
WHERE IS THE REDFUR!?
LOCKHAVEN WILL BE OURS BEFORE HE OR ANY GUARD CAN DO A THING ABOUT IT.
IT IS NOT **WE** WHO ARE TRAPPED IN WITH THEM, BUT **THEY** WHO ARE TRAPPED IN WITH US!

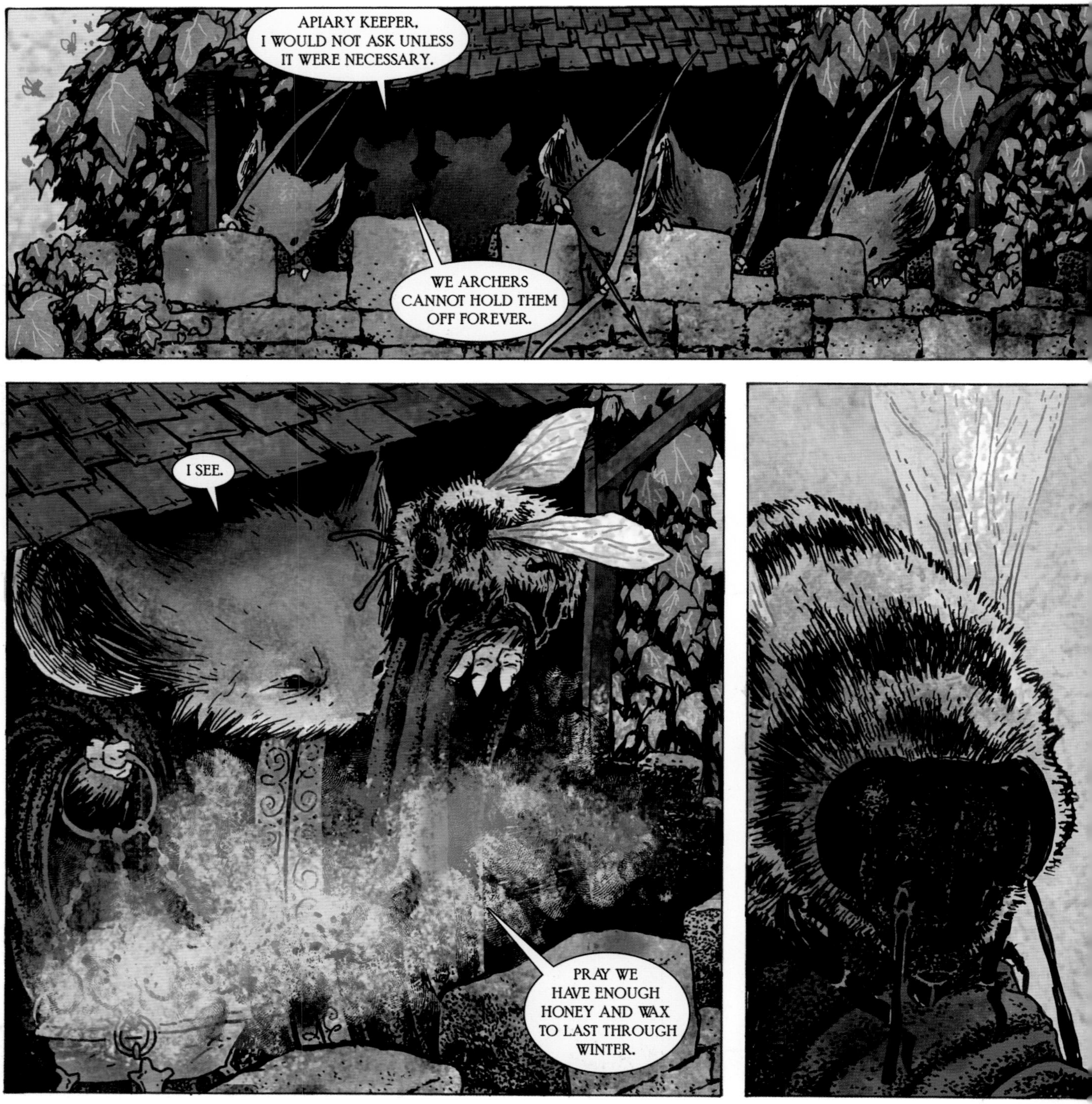
APIARY KEEPER, I WOULD NOT ASK UNLESS IT WERE NECESSARY.
WE ARCHERS CANNOT HOLD THEM OFF FOREVER.
I SEE.
PRAY WE HAVE ENOUGH HONEY AND WAX TO LAST THROUGH WINTER.

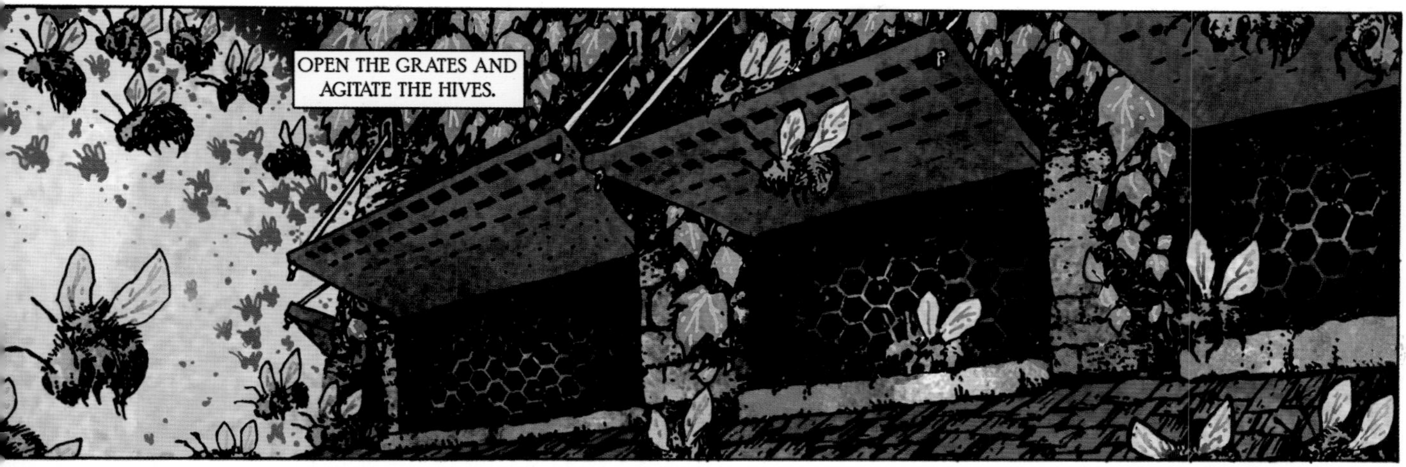
OPEN THE GRATES AND AGITATE THE HIVES.

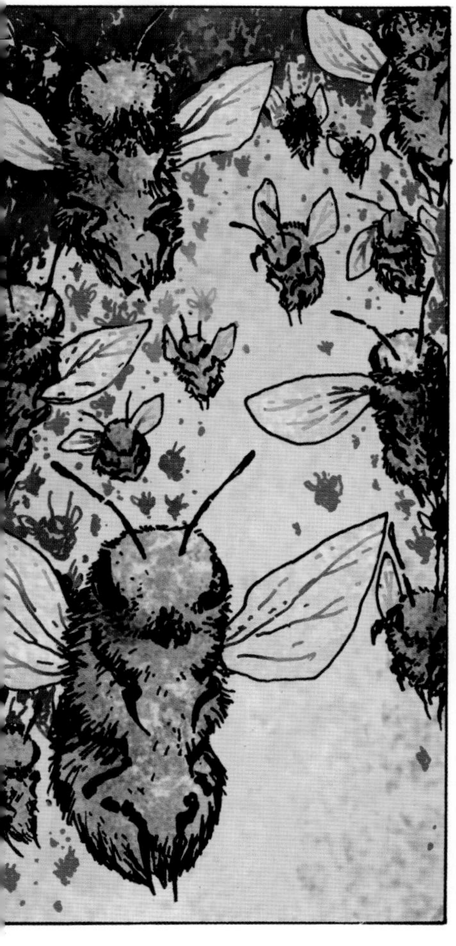

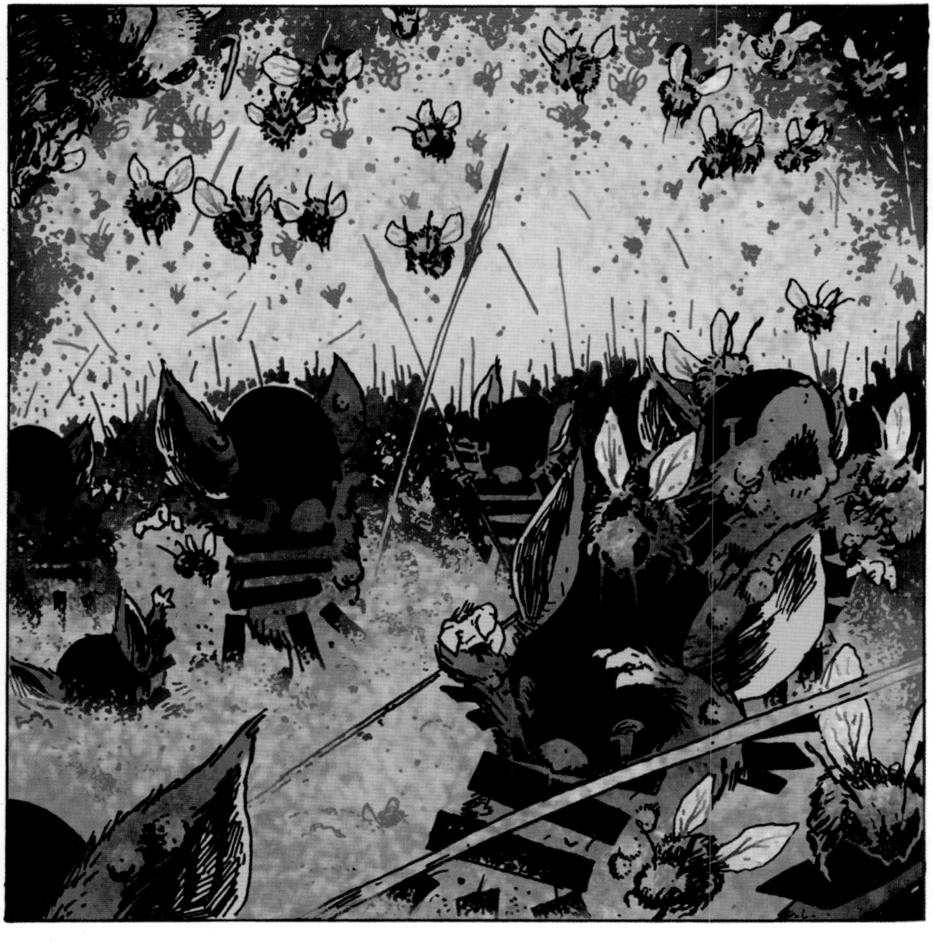

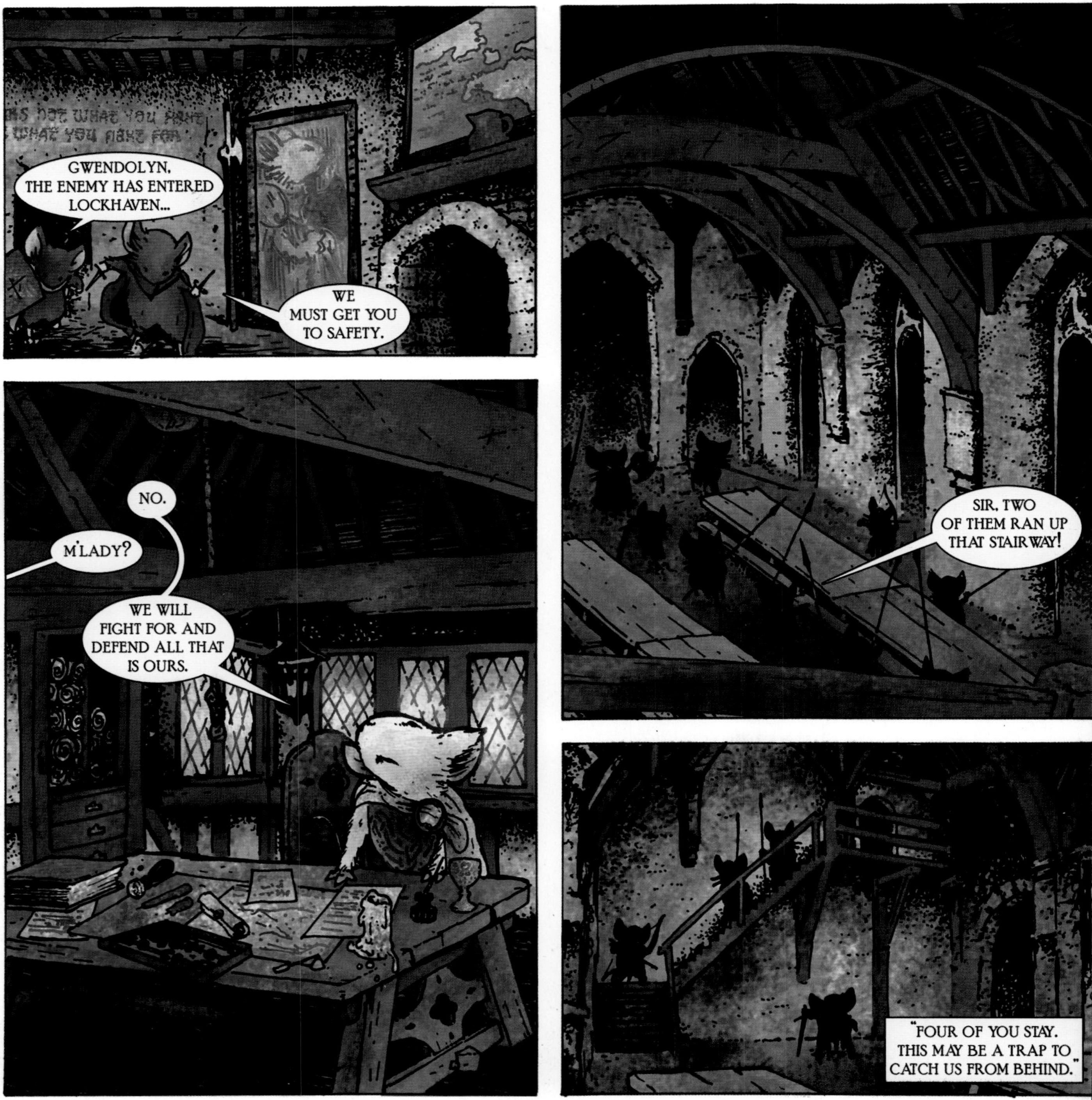
GWENDOLYN, THE ENEMY HAS ENTERED LOCKHAVEN...
WE MUST GET YOU TO SAFETY.
M'LADY?
NO.
WE WILL FIGHT FOR AND DEFEND ALL THAT IS OURS.
SIR, TWO OF THEM RAN UP THAT STAIRWAY!
"FOUR OF YOU STAY. THIS MAY BE A TRAP TO CATCH US FROM BEHIND."

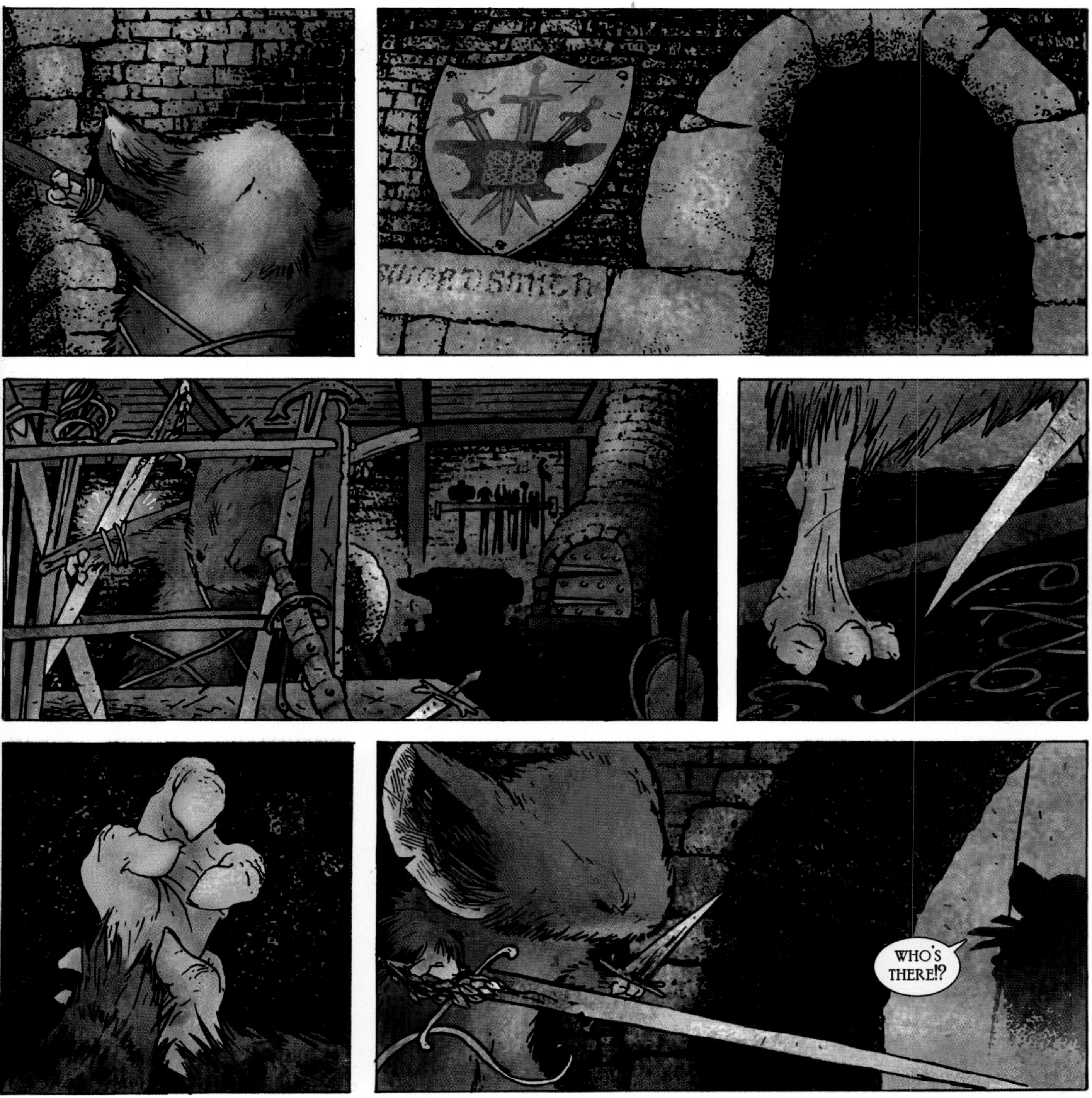
SWORDSMITH
WHO'S THERE!?

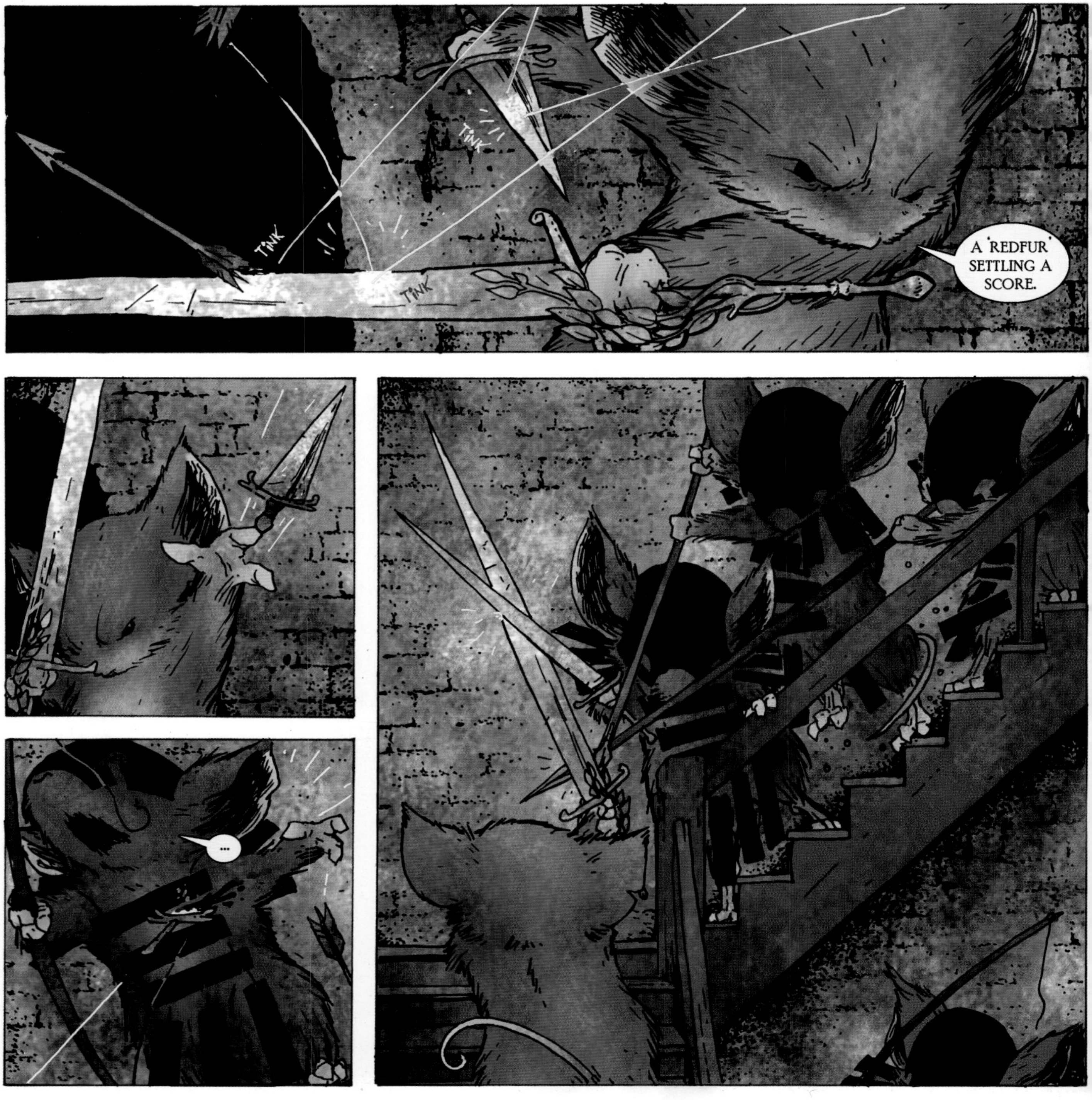
TINK
TINK
TINK
TINK
A 'REDFUR' SETTLING A SCORE.
...

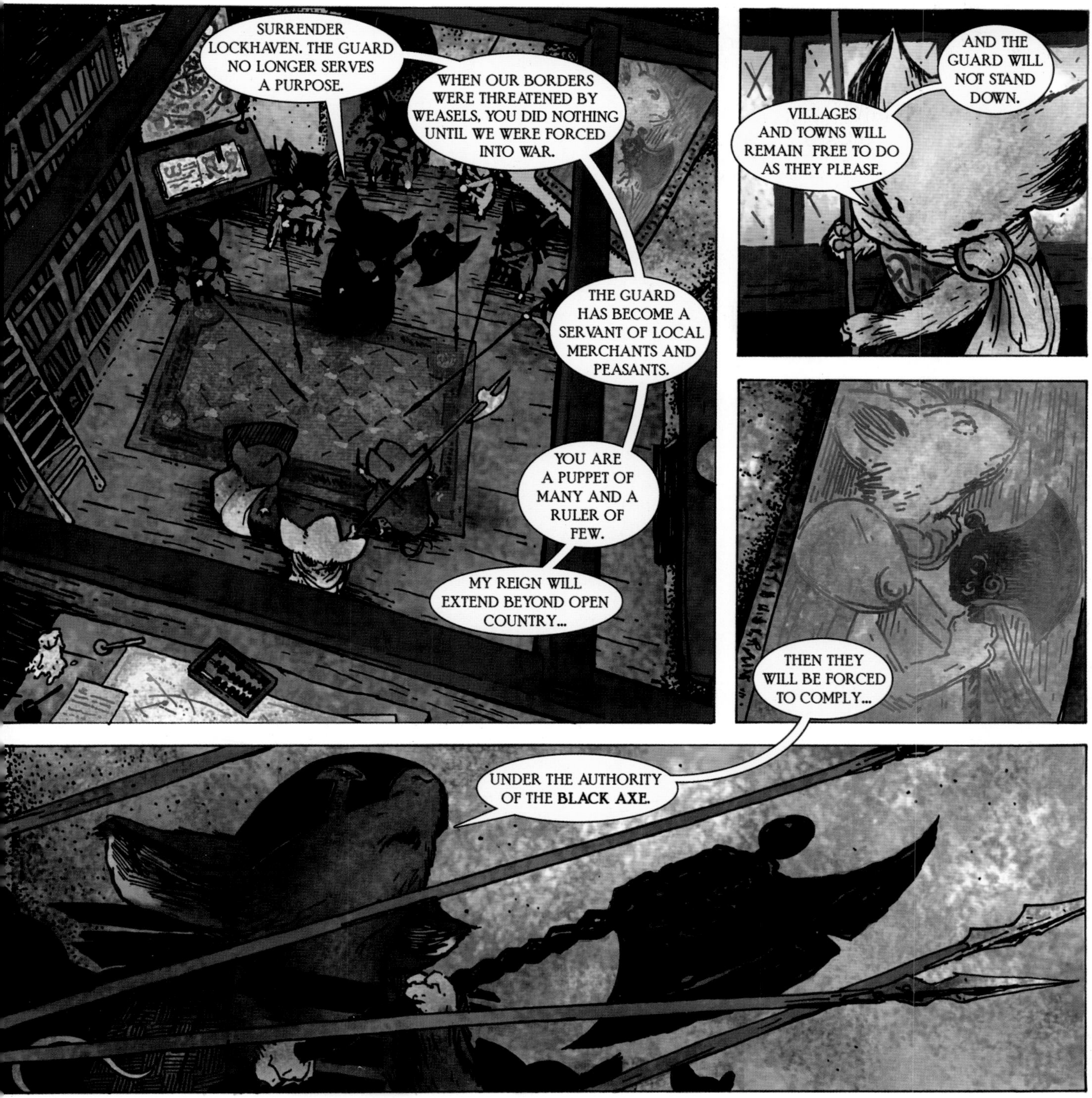
SURRENDER LOCKHAVEN. THE GUARD NO LONGER SERVES A PURPOSE.
WHEN OUR BORDERS WERE THREATENED BY WEASELS, YOU DID NOTHING UNTIL WE WERE FORCED INTO WAR.
THE GUARD HAS BECOME A SERVANT OF LOCAL MERCHANTS AND PEASANTS.
YOU ARE A PUPPET OF MANY AND A RULER OF FEW.
MY REIGN WILL EXTEND BEYOND OPEN COUNTRY...
AND THE GUARD WILL NOT STAND DOWN.
VILLAGES AND TOWNS WILL REMAIN FREE TO DO AS THEY PLEASE.
THEN THEY WILL BE FORCED TO COMPLY...
UNDER THE AUTHORITY OF THE BLACK AXE.

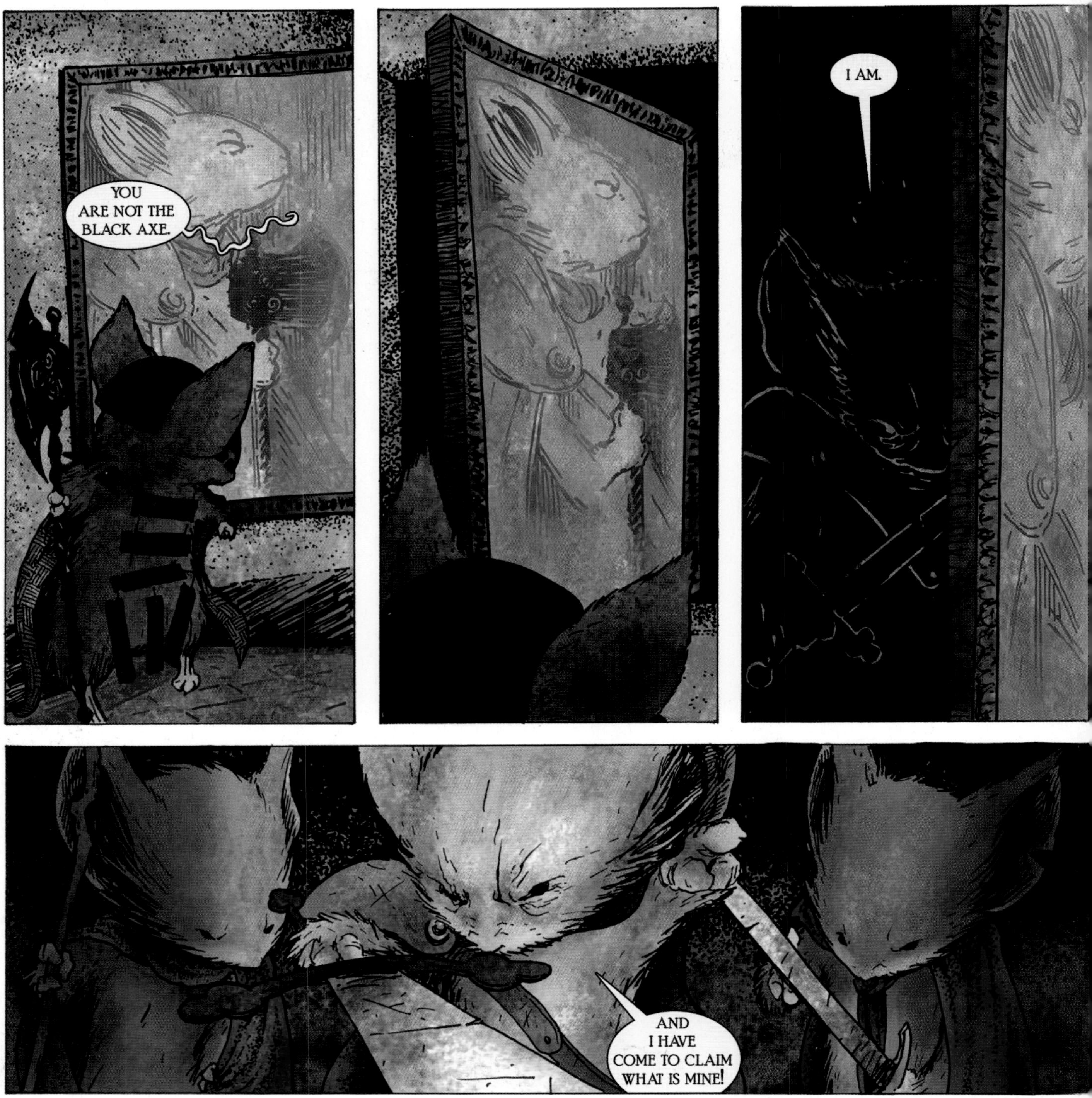
YOU ARE NOT THE BLACK AXE.
I AM.
AND I HAVE COME TO CLAIM WHAT IS MINE!

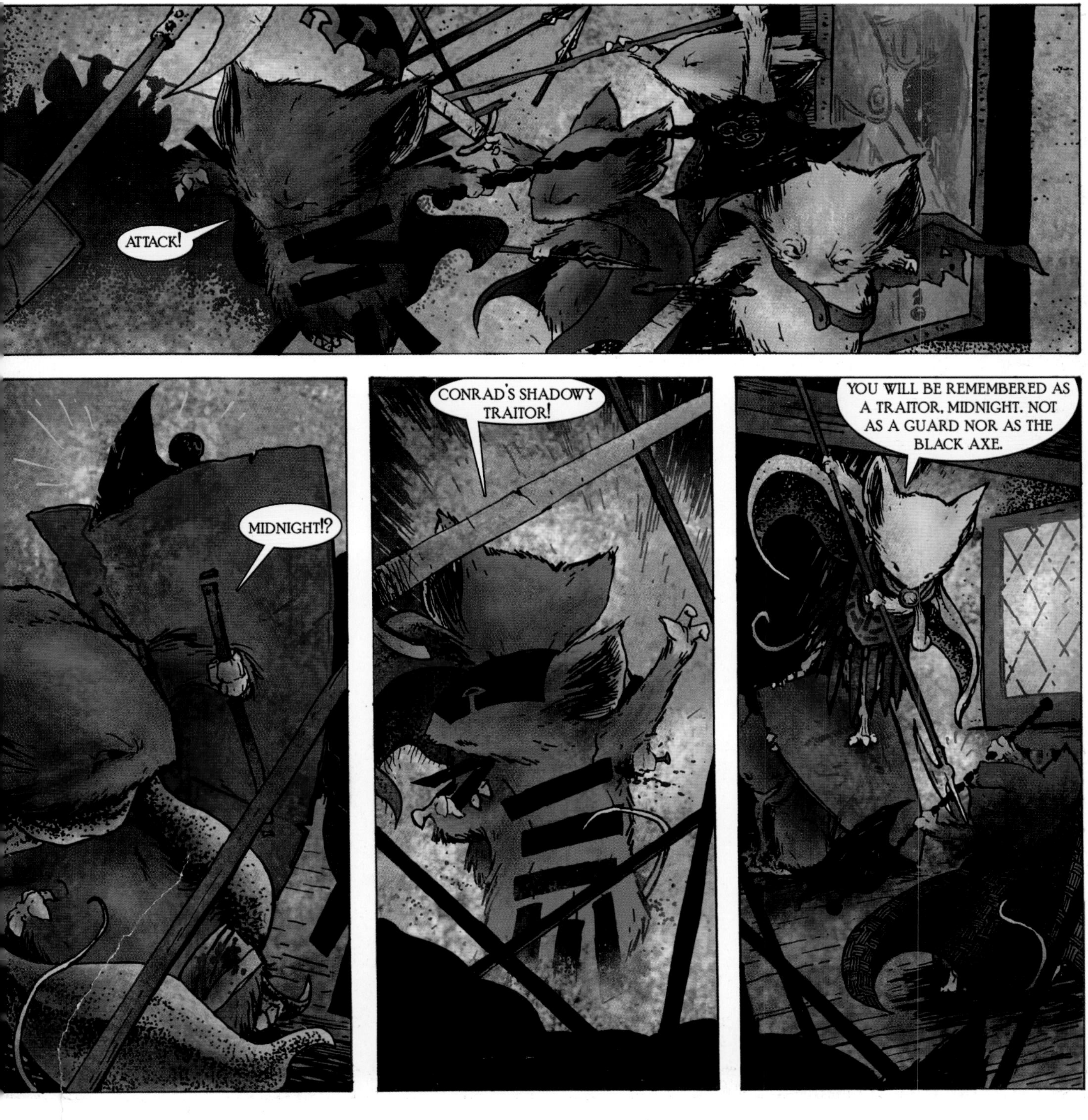

ATTACK!
MIDNIGHT!?
CONRAD'S SHADOWY TRAITOR!
YOU WILL BE REMEMBERED AS A TRAITOR, MIDNIGHT. NOT AS A GUARD NOR AS THE BLACK AXE.

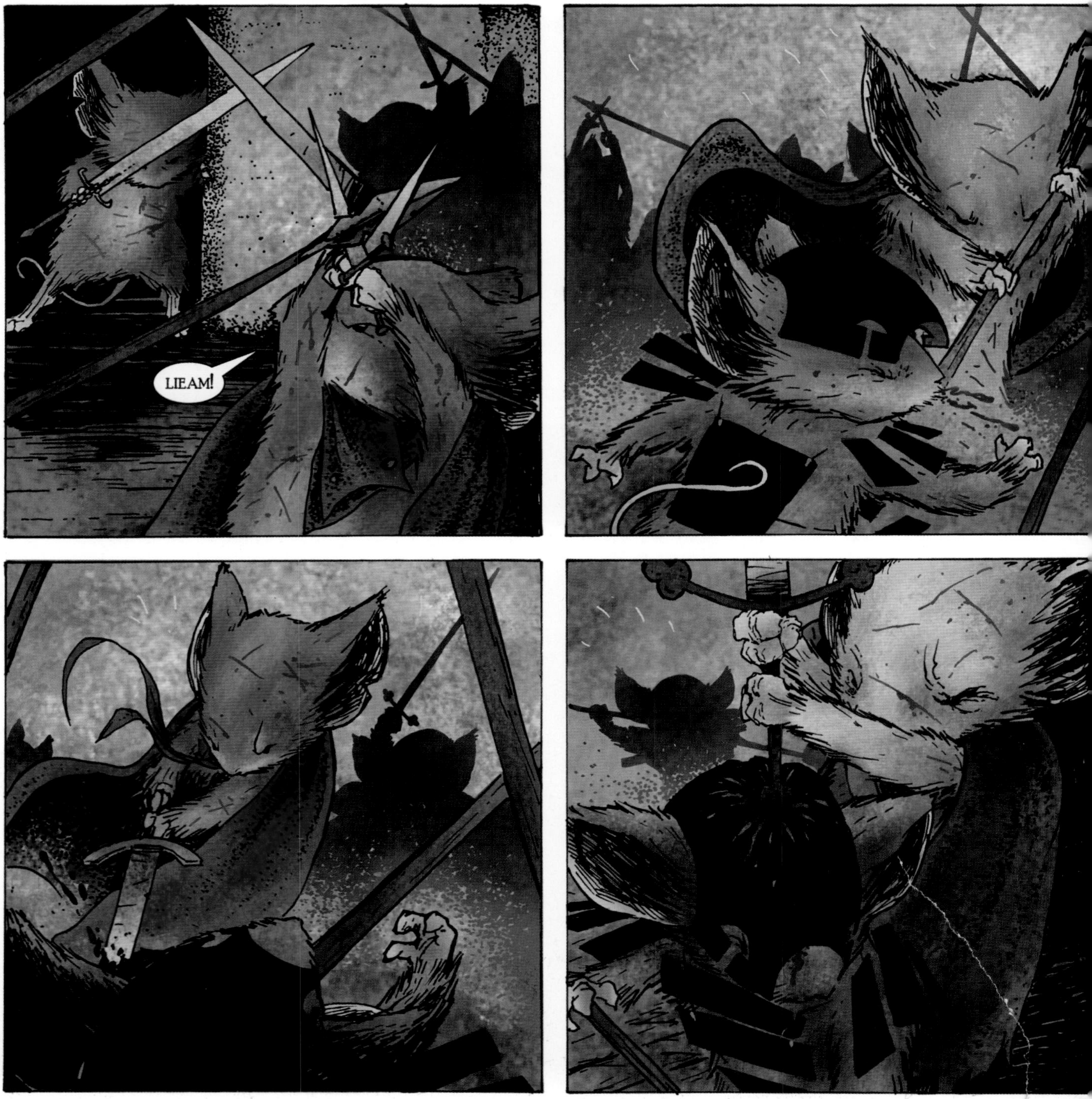
LIEAM!

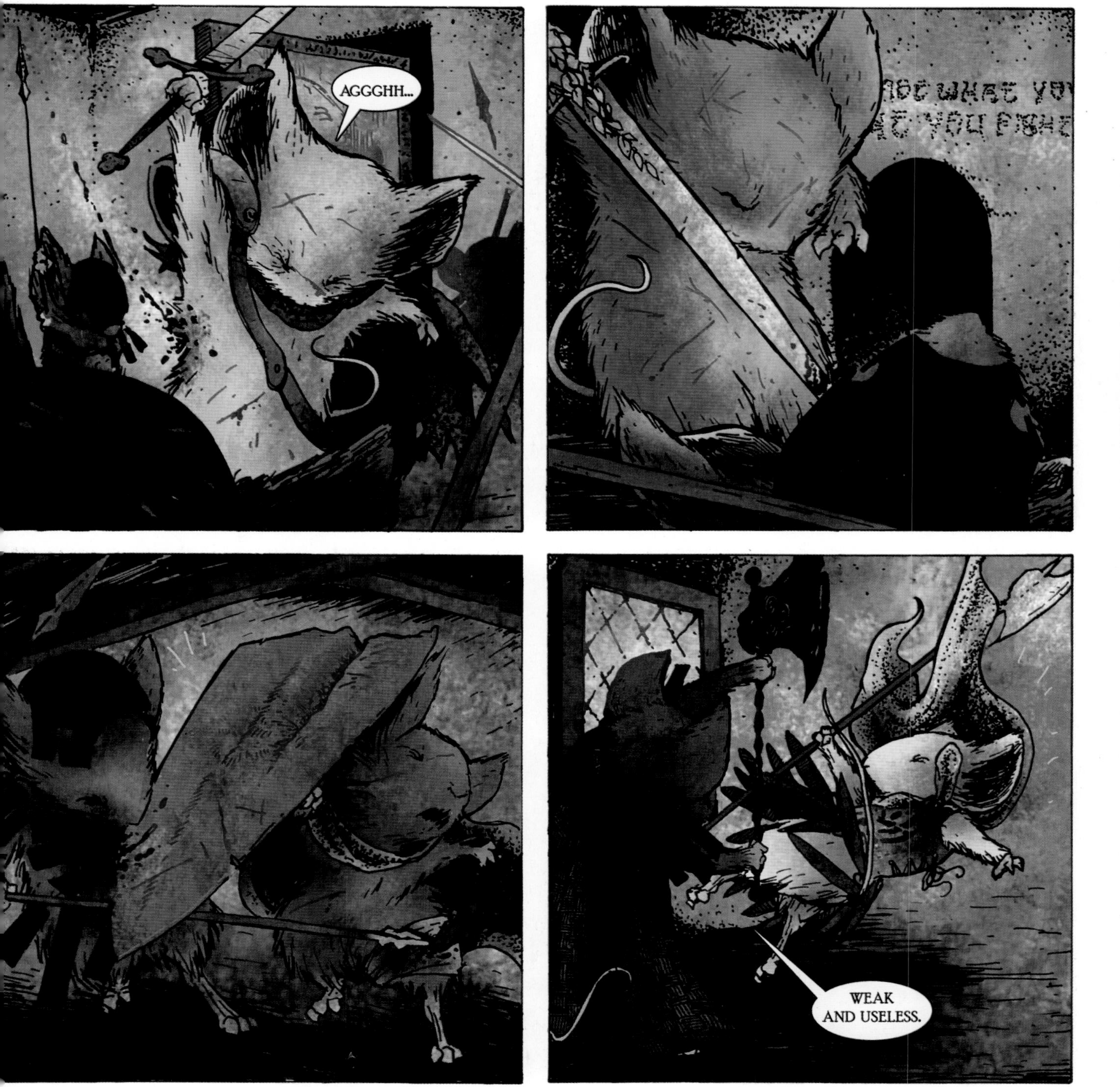
AGGGHH...
WEAK AND USELESS.

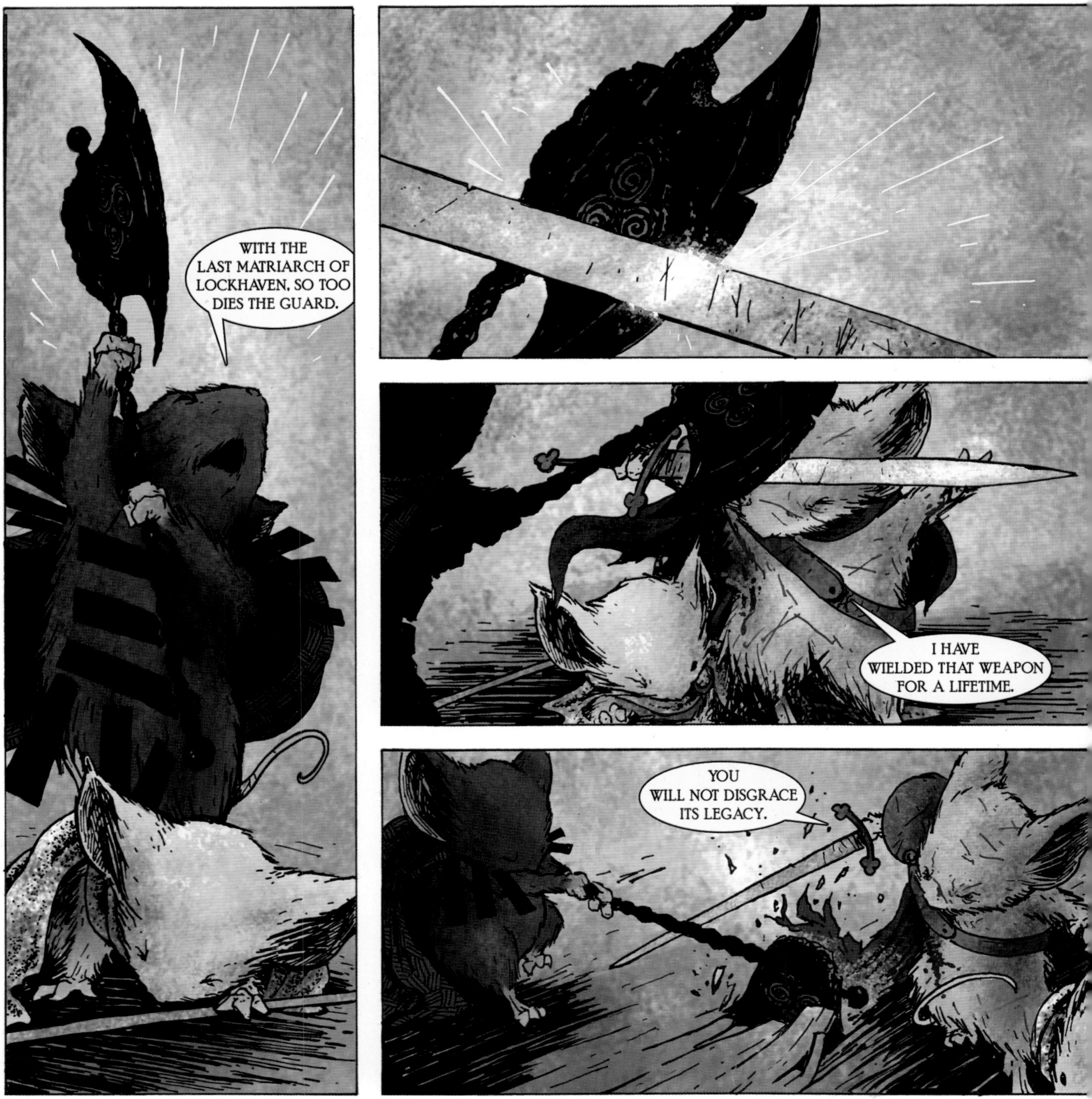
WITH THE LAST MATRIARCH OF LOCKHAVEN, SO TOO DIES THE GUARD.
I HAVE WIELDED THAT WEAPON FOR A LIFETIME.
YOU WILL NOT DISGRACE ITS LEGACY.

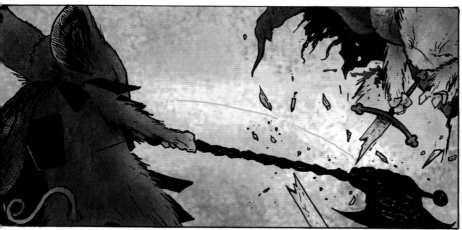
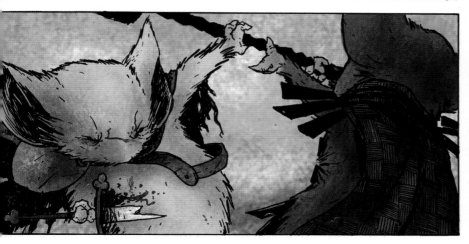

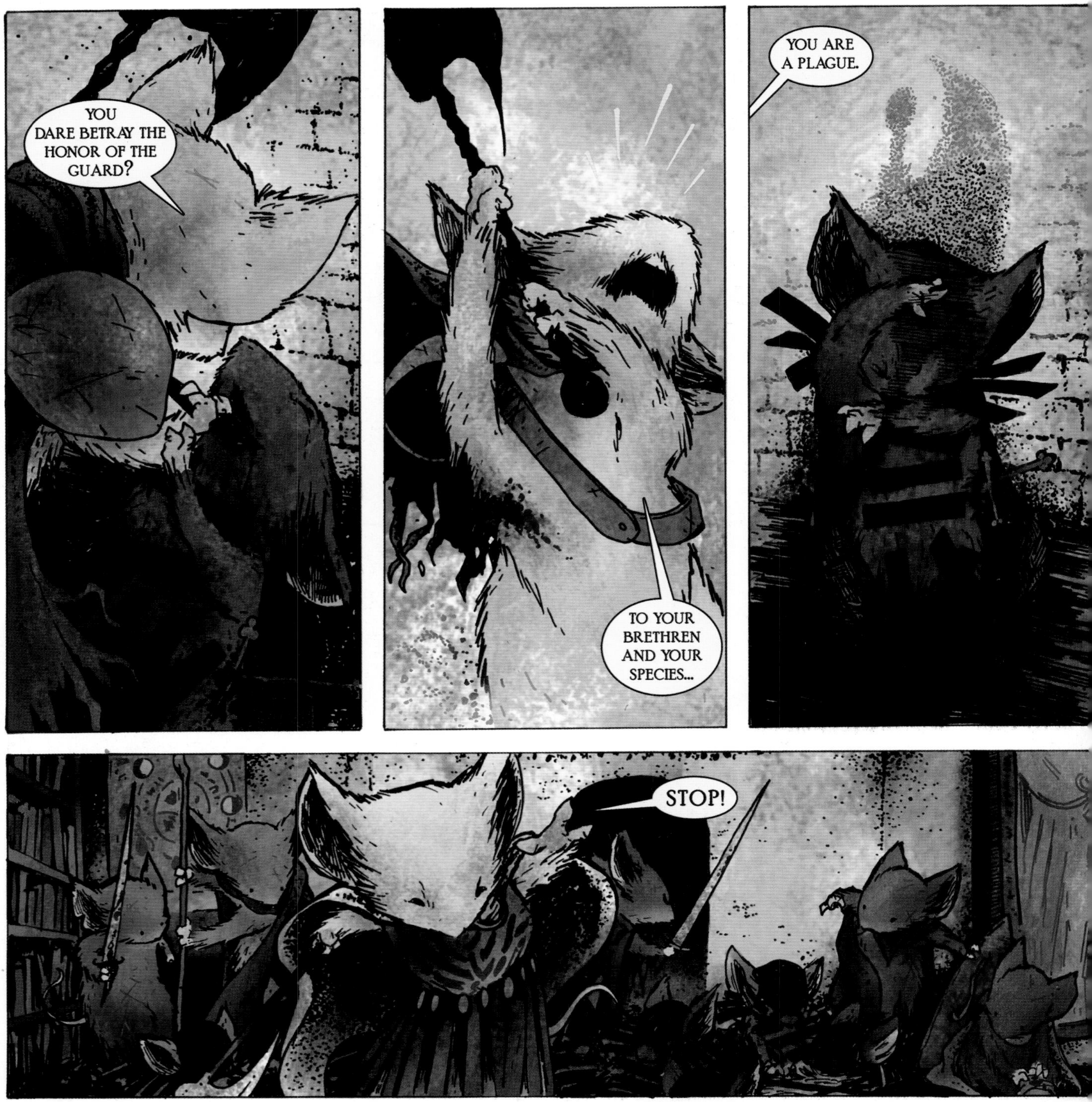

YOU DARE BETRAY THE HONOR OF THE GUARD?
TO YOUR BRETHREN AND YOUR SPECIES...
YOU ARE A PLAGUE.
STOP!

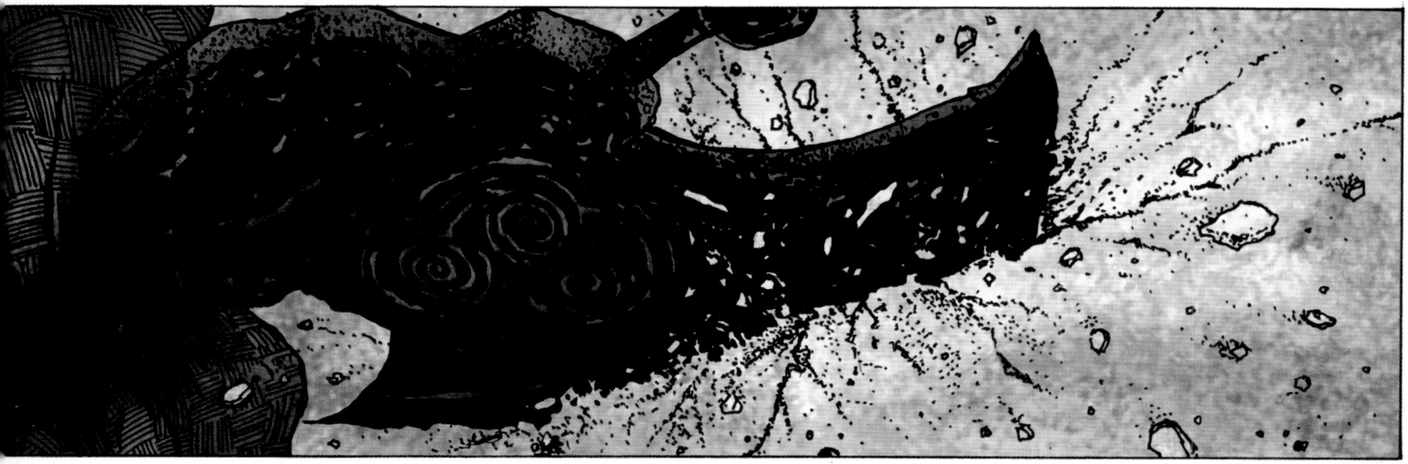

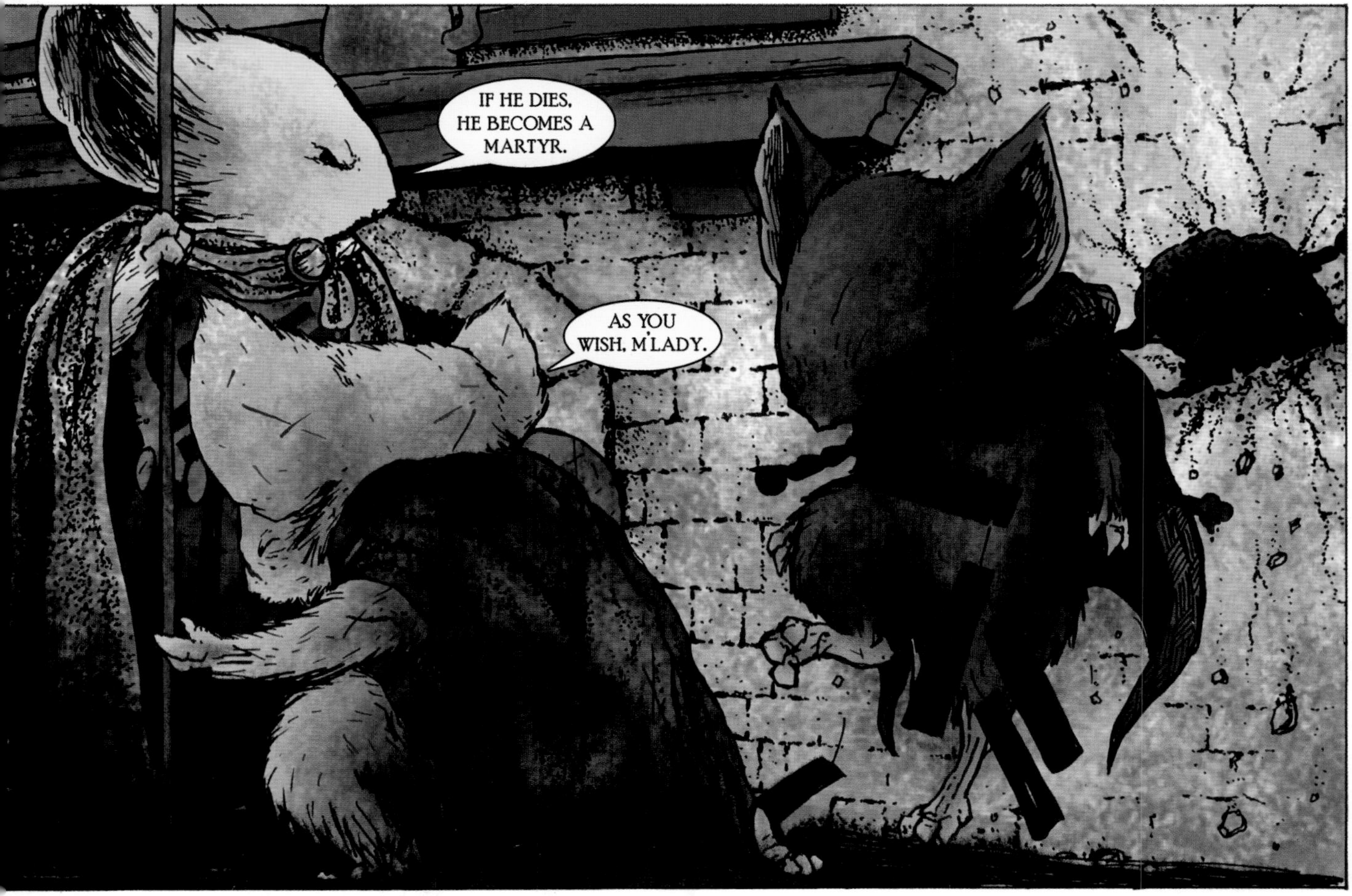
IF HE DIES, HE BECOMES A MARTYR.
AS YOU WISH, M'LADY.

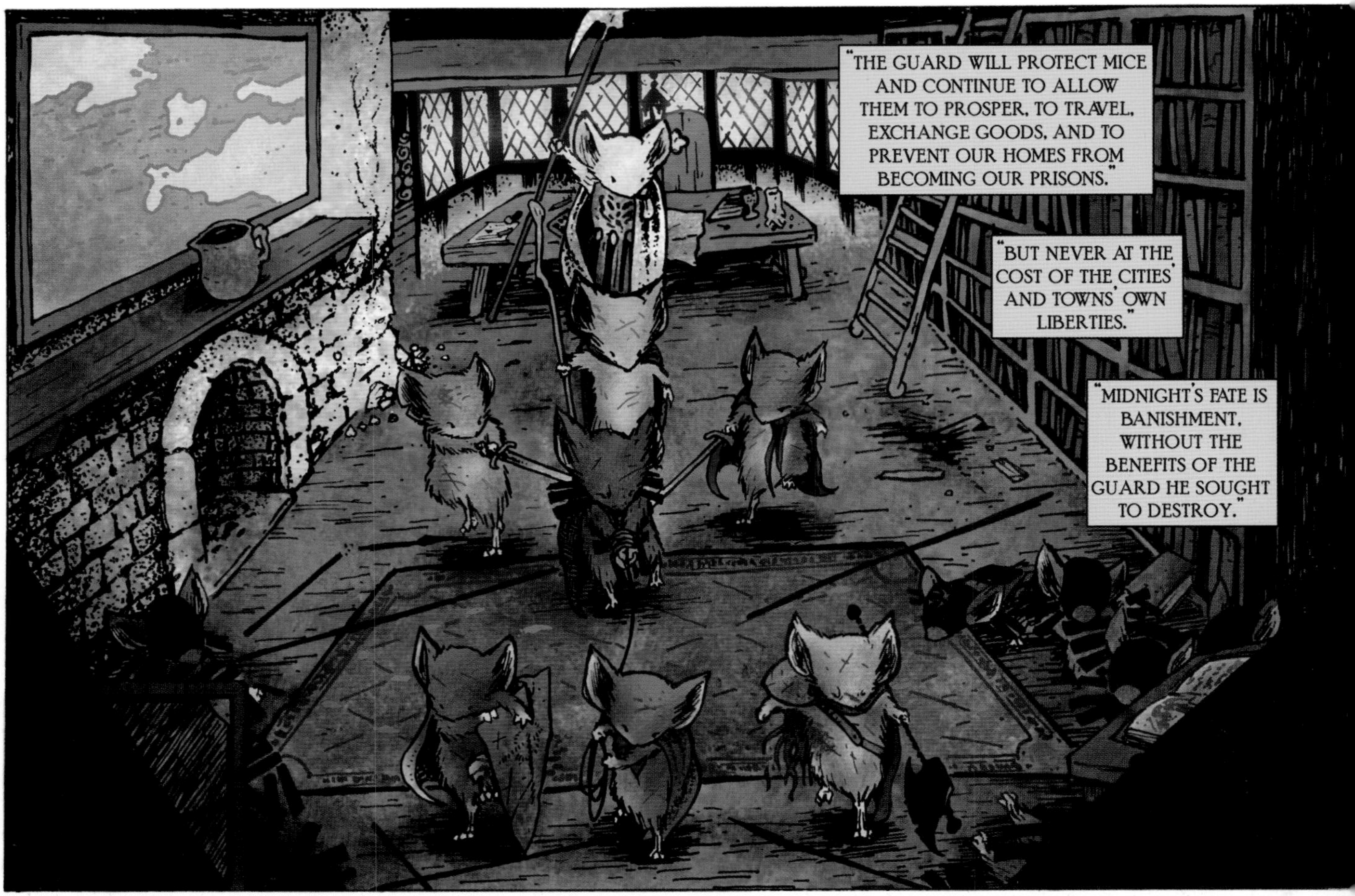
"THE GUARD WILL PROTECT MICE AND CONTINUE TO ALLOW THEM TO PROSPER, TO TRAVEL, EXCHANGE GOODS, AND TO PREVENT OUR HOMES FROM BECOMING OUR PRISONS."
"BUT NEVER AT THE COST OF THE CITIES' AND TOWNS' OWN LIBERTIES."
"MIDNIGHT'S FATE IS BANISHMENT, WITHOUT THE BENEFITS OF THE GUARD HE SOUGHT TO DESTROY."

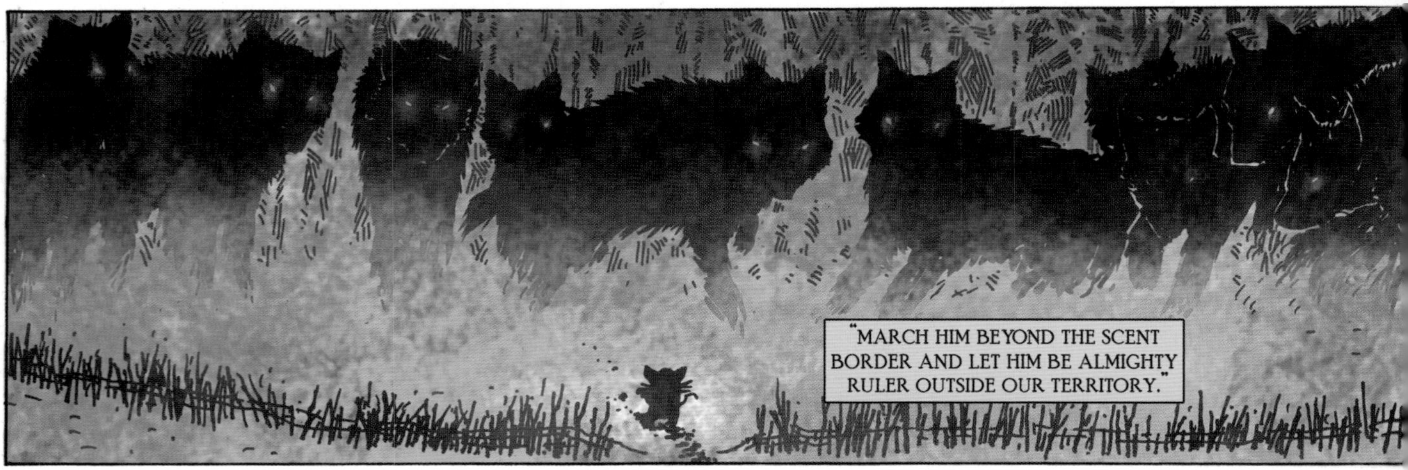
"MARCH HIM BEYOND THE SCENT BORDER AND LET HIM BE ALMIGHTY RULER OUTSIDE OUR TERRITORY."

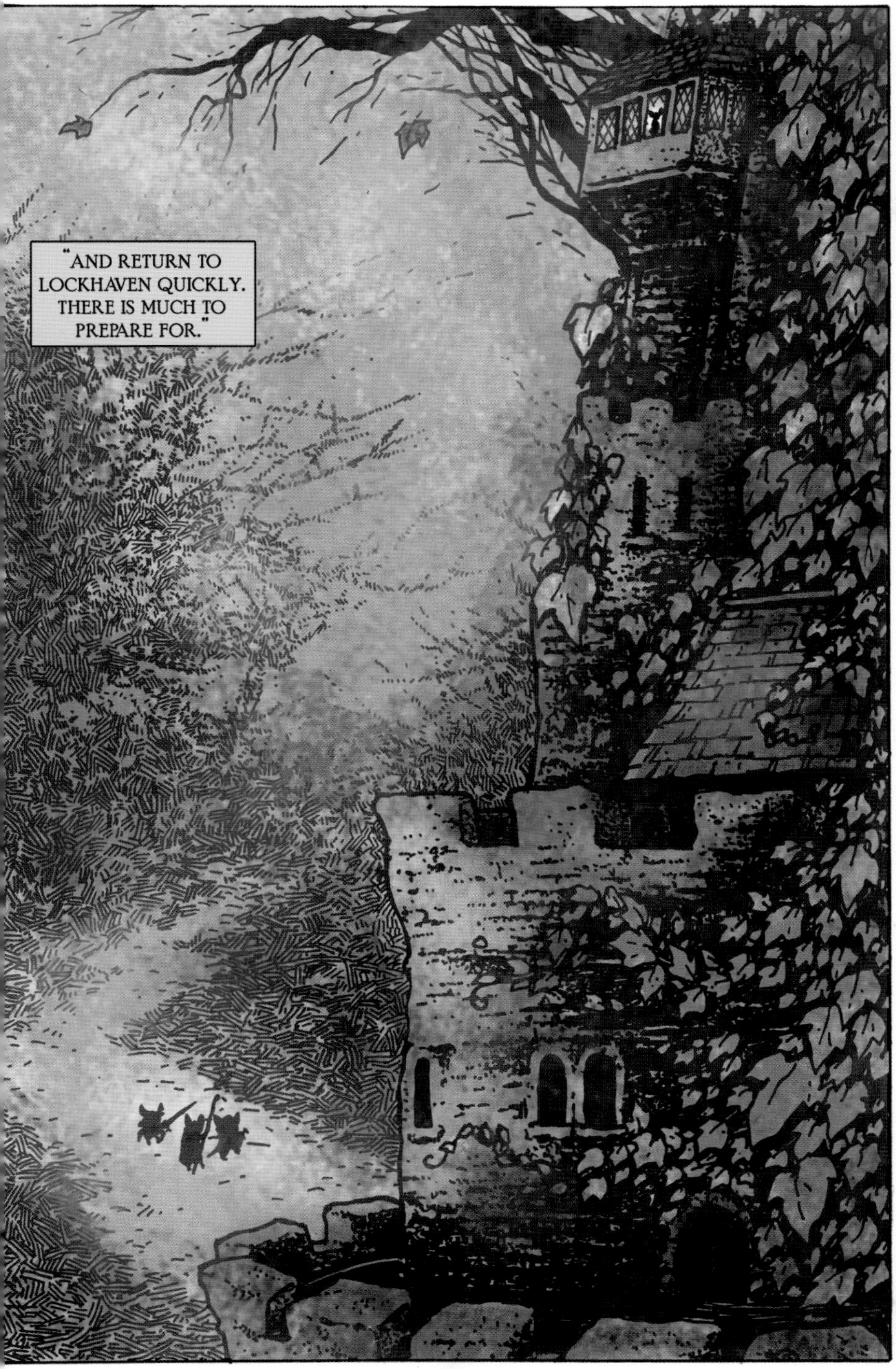
"AND RETURN TO LOCKHAVEN QUICKLY. THERE IS MUCH TO PREPARE FOR."

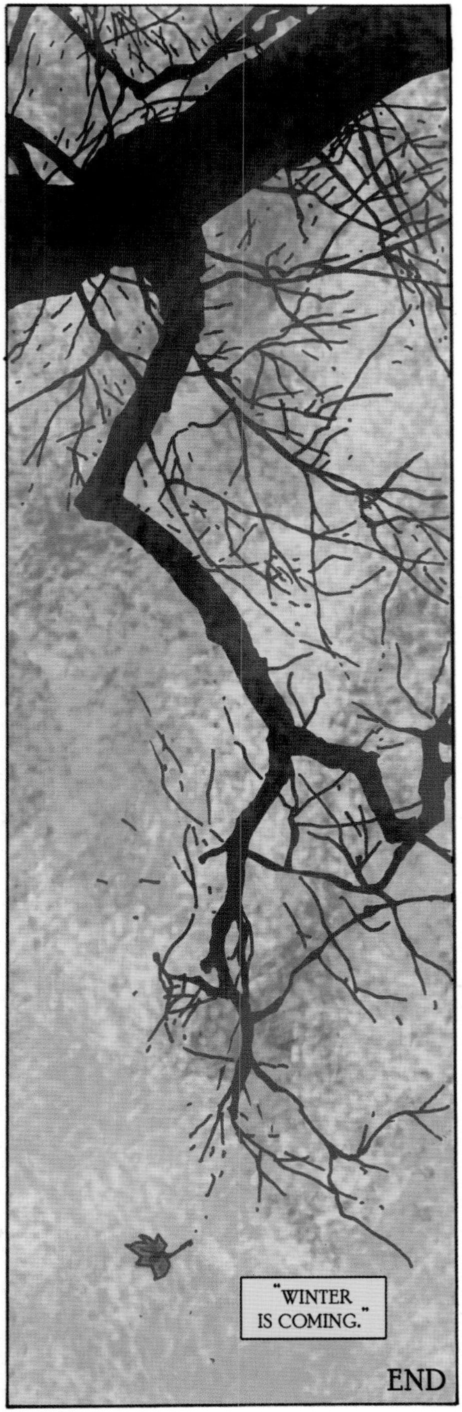
"WINTER IS COMING."
END

EPILOGUE

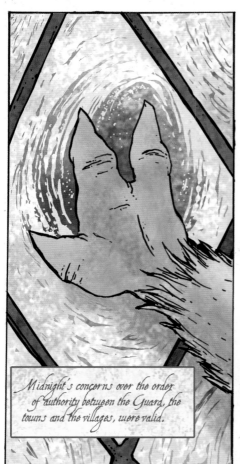

Midnight's concerns over the order of authority between the Guard, the towns and the villages, were valid.

Unfortunately, his solution was to rule from on high as an imposter in the shadow of the Black Axe, and slaughter those in his way.

Mouse should never raise blade against mouse. There are enough outside threats in this world.

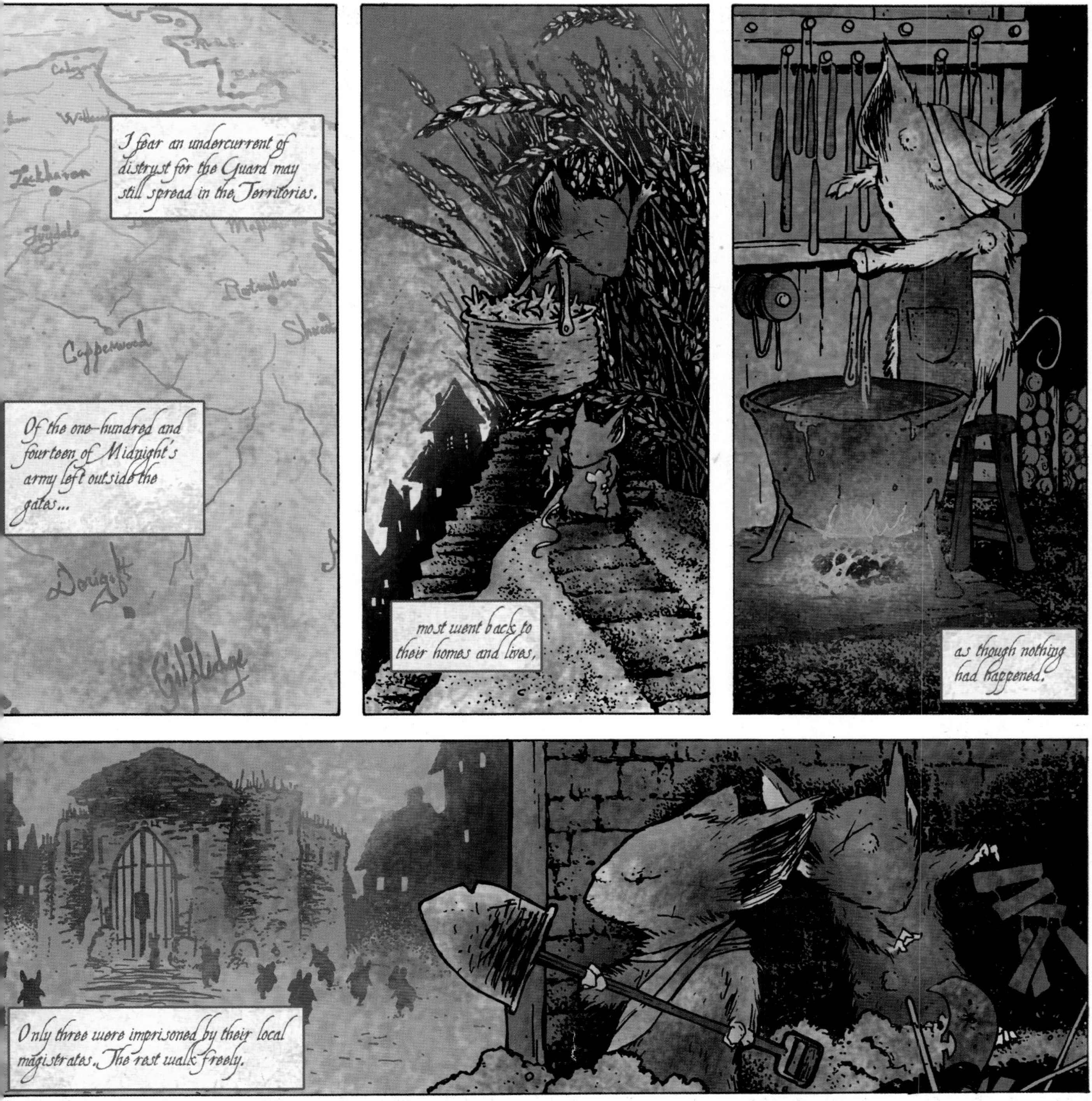
I fear an undercurrent of distrust for the Guard may still spread in the Territories.
Lockhaven
Copperwood
Gilpledge
Of the one-hundred and fourteen of Midnight's army left outside the gates...
most went back to their homes and lives,
as though nothing had happened.
Only three were imprisoned by their local magistrates. The rest walk freely.

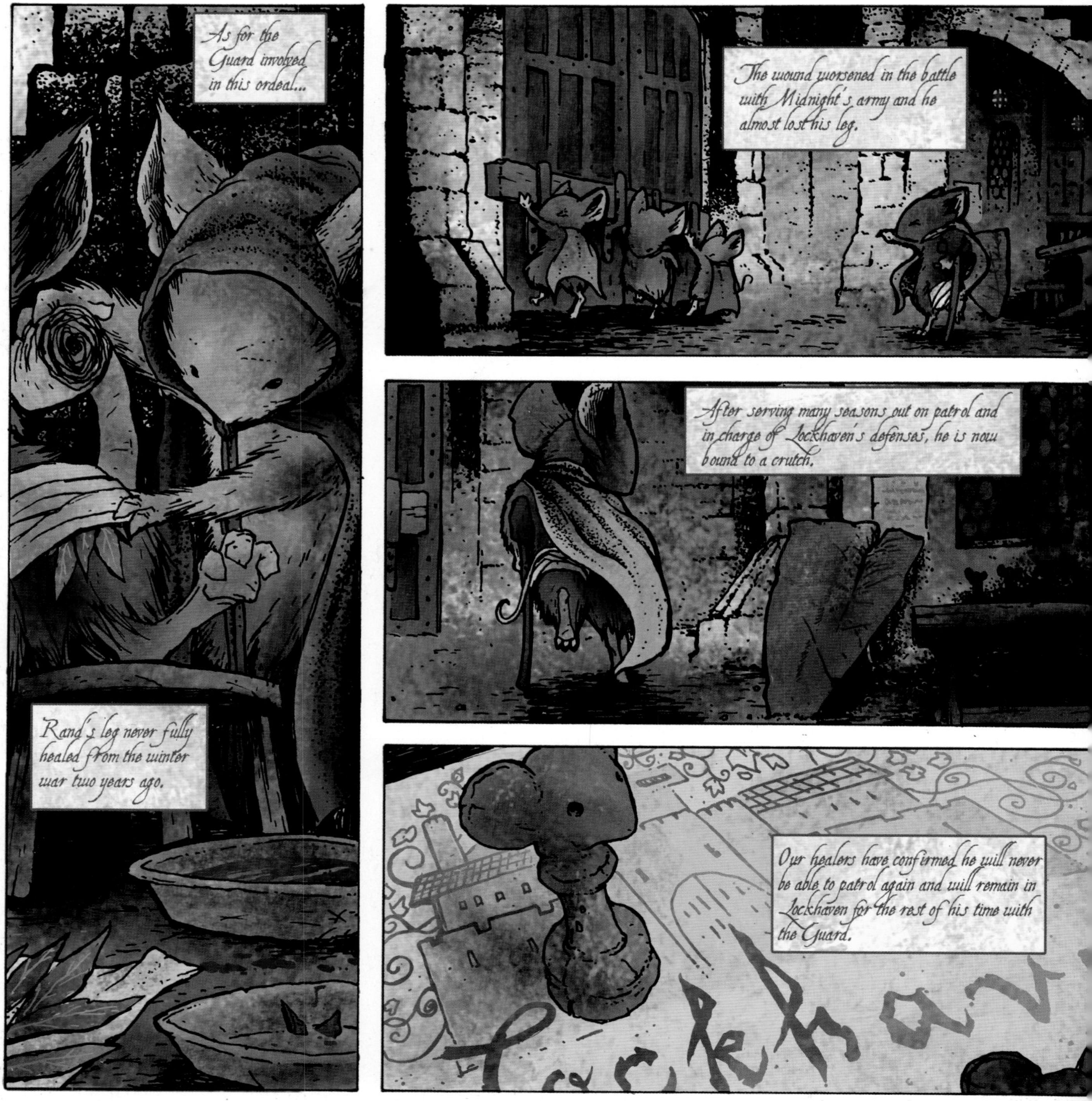
As for the Guard involved in this ordeal...
Rand's leg never fully healed from the winter war two years ago.
The wound worsened in the battle with Midnight's army and he almost lost his leg.
After serving many seasons out on patrol and in charge of Lockhaven's defenses, he is now bound to a crutch.
Our healers have confirmed he will never be able to patrol again and will remain in Lockhaven for the rest of his time with the Guard.

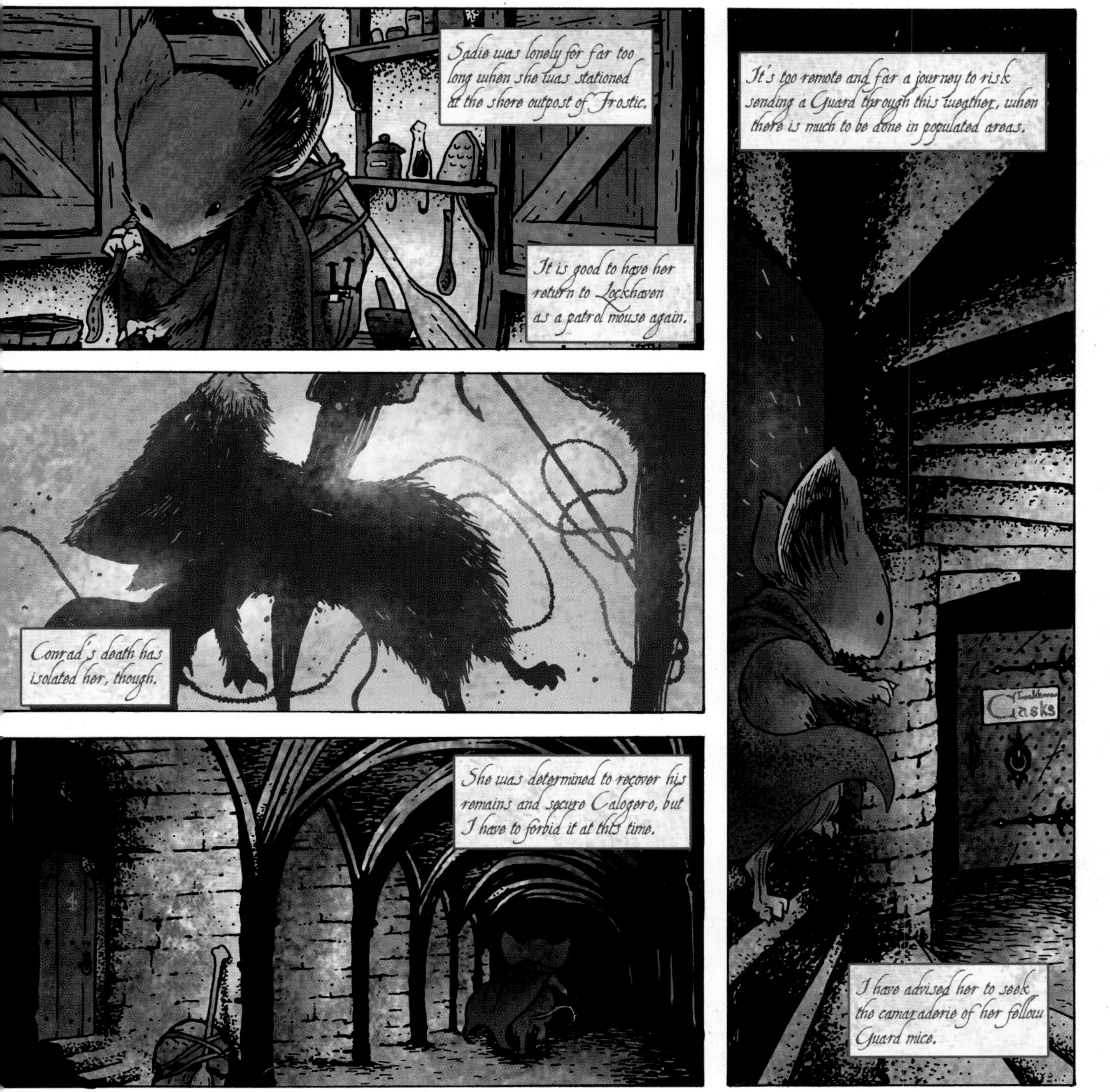
Sadie was lonely for far too long when she was stationed at the shore outpost of Frostic.
It is good to have her return to Lockhaven as a patrol mouse again.
Conrad's death has isolated her, though.
She was determined to recover his remains and secure Calogero, but I have to forbid it at this time.
It's too remote and far a journey to risk sending a Guard through this weather, when there is much to be done in populated areas.
Casks
I have advised her to seek the camaraderie of her fellow Guard mice.

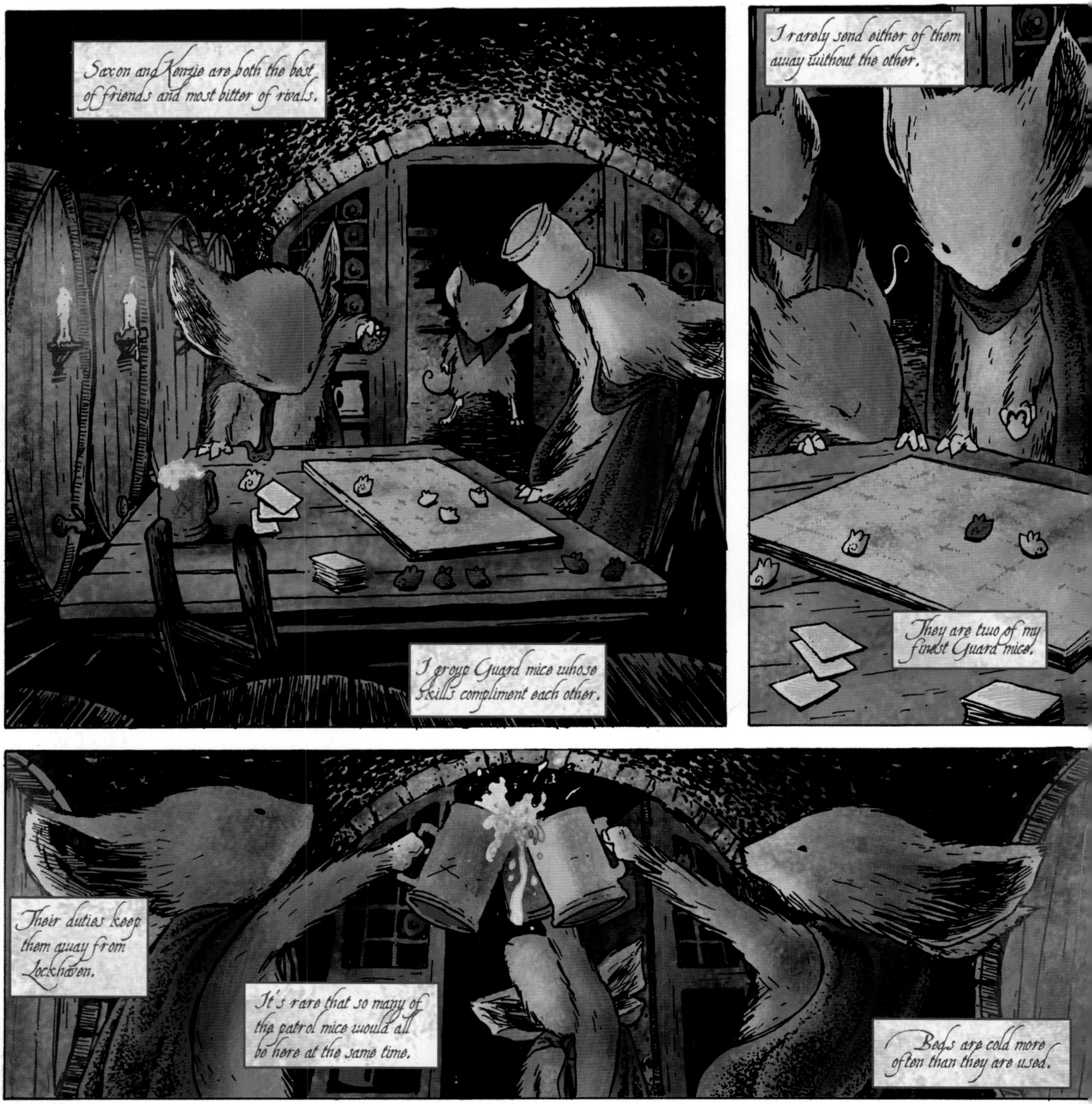
Saxon and Kenzie are both the best of friends and most bitter of rivals.
I group Guard mice whose skills compliment each other.
I rarely send either of them away without the other.
They are two of my finest Guard mice.
Their duties keep them away from Lockhaven.
It's rare that so many of the patrol mice would all be here at the same time.
Beds are cold more often than they are used.

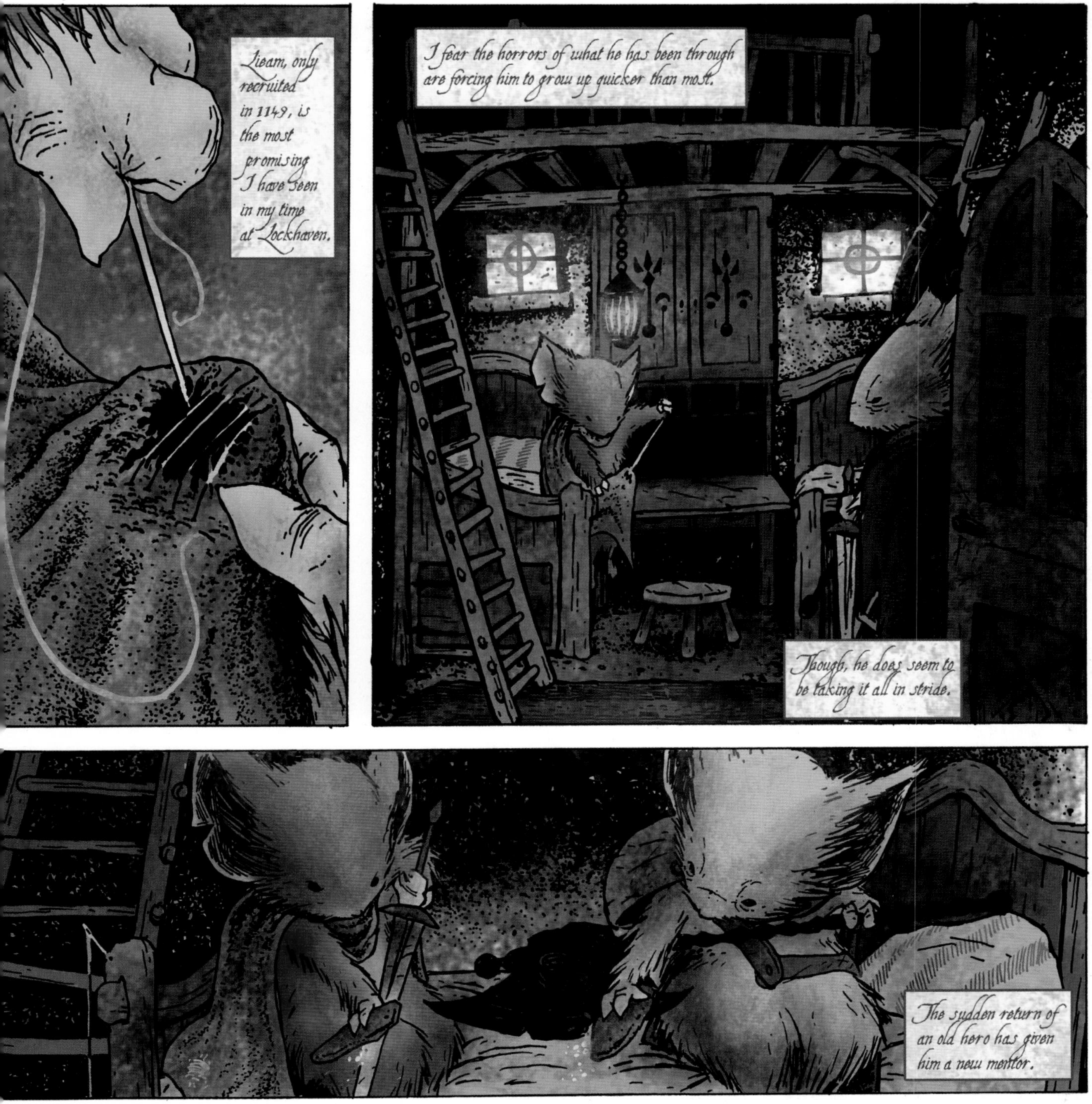
Lieam, only recruited in 1149, is the most promising I have seen in my time at Lockhaven.
I fear the horrors of what he has been through are forcing him to grow up quicker than most.
Though, he does seem to be taking it all in stride.
The sudden return of an old hero has given him a new mentor.

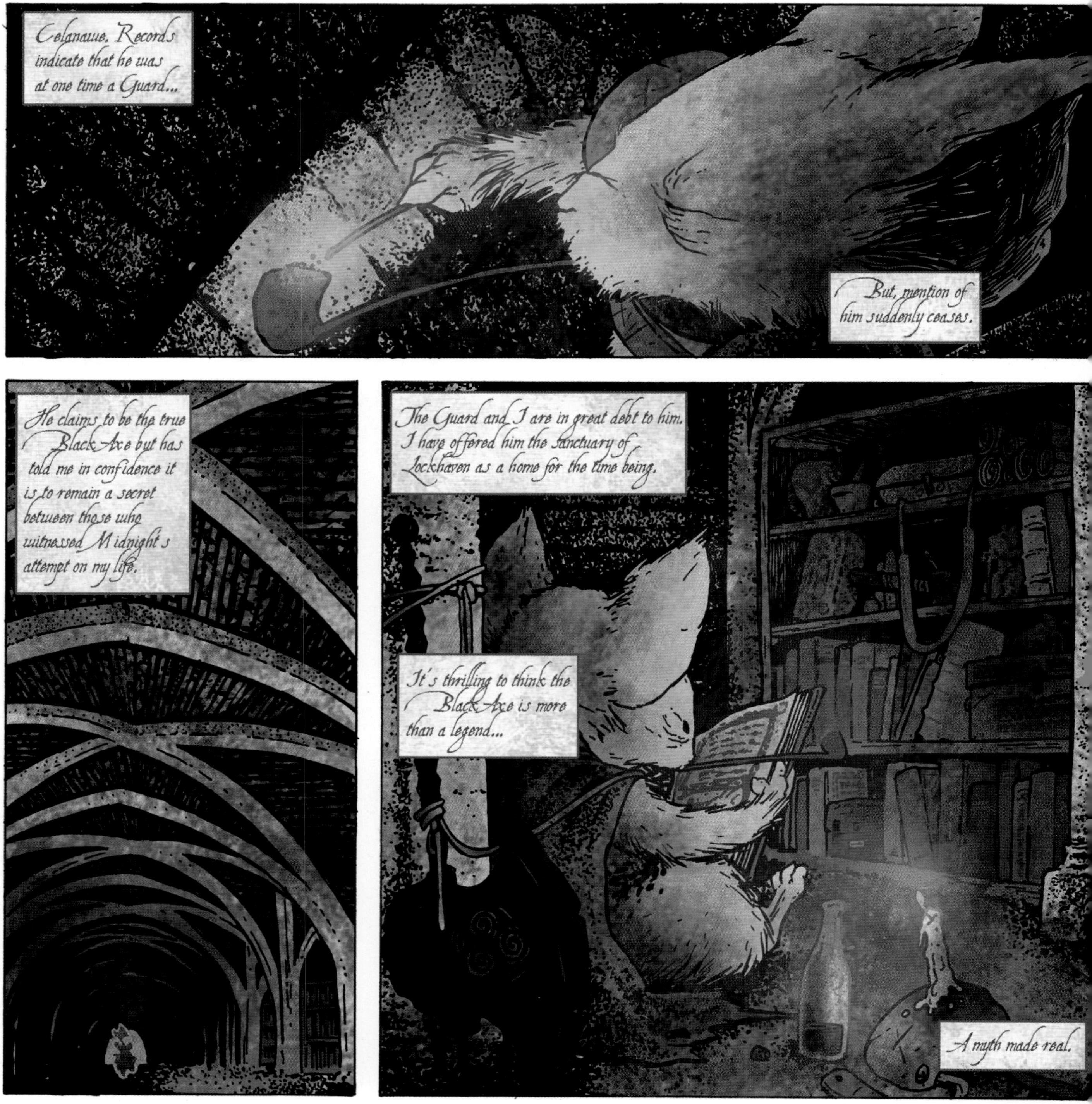
Celanawe. Records indicate that he was at one time a Guard...
But, mention of him suddenly ceases.
He claims to be the true Black Axe but has told me in confidence it is to remain a secret between those who witnessed Midnight's attempt on my life.
The Guard and I are in great debt to him. I have offered him the sanctuary of Lockhaven as a home for the time being.
It's thrilling to think the Black Axe is more than a legend...
A myth made real.

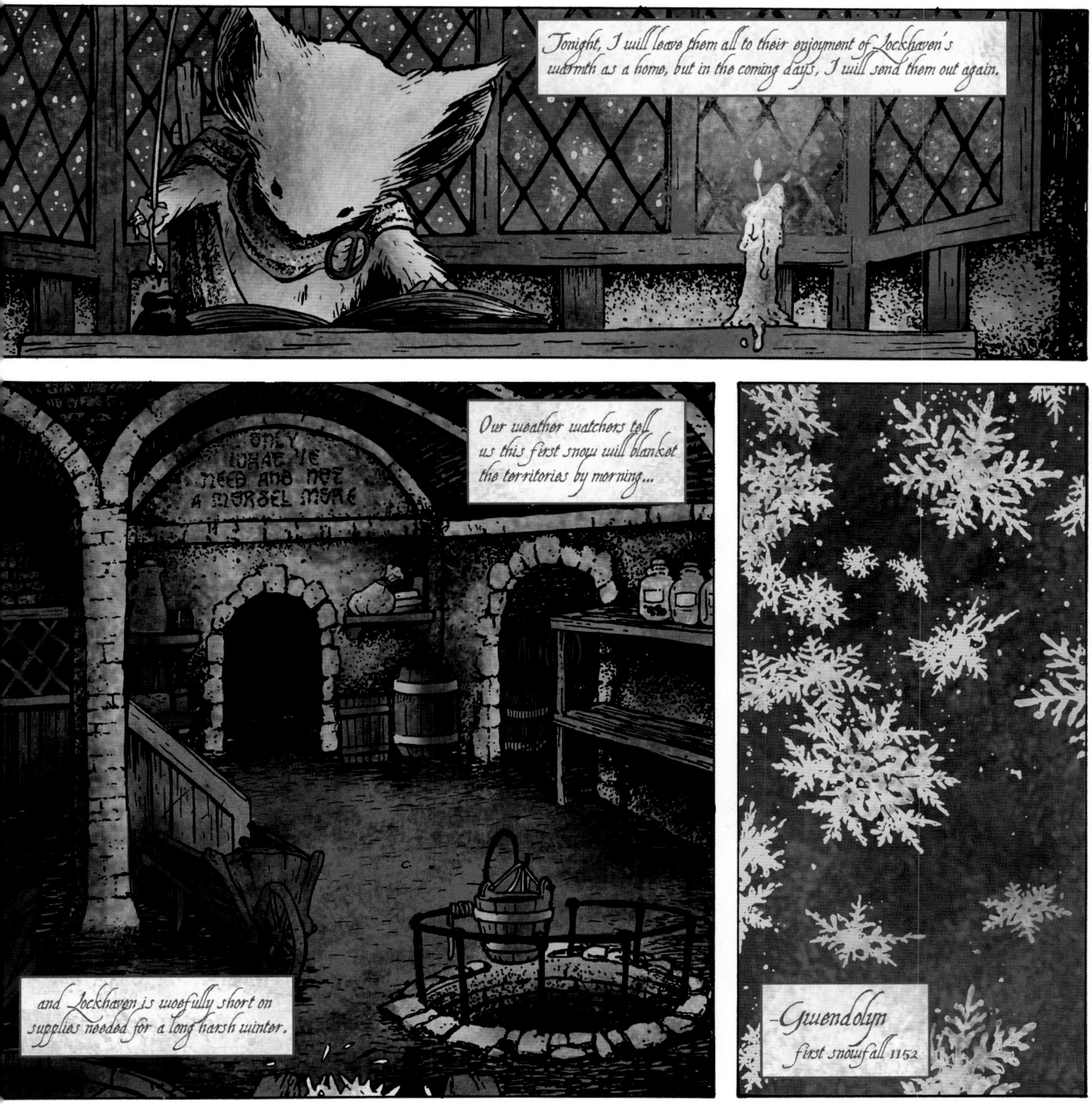
Tonight, I will leave them all to their enjoyment of Lockhaven's warmth as a home, but in the coming days, I will send them out again.
Our weather watchers tell us this first snow will blanket the territories by morning...
ONLY WHAT WE NEED AND NOT A MORSEL MORE
and Lockhaven is woefully short on supplies needed for a long harsh winter.
-Gwendolyn
first snowfall 1152

MAPS, GUIDES, AND ASSORTED EXTRAS

Mouse Territories 1150

A map of cities, towns, villages, and safe paths after the winter war
As measured by the Guard of 1149, Recorded by Clarke's Cartography
Fallen settlements listed & struck

Calogero

Dawnrock

Darkheather
Entrance

Whitepine

Chistledown

Wildseed

Elmwood

Lockhaven

Ironwood

Pebblebrook

Shaleburrow

Barkstone

Ivydale

Blackrock

Woodruff's Grove

Elmoss

Copperwood

R

Ferndale

Scent Border

Sprucetuck

Darkheather
Tunnels

Wolfpeck

Dorigift

Appleloft

Gilpledge

Frostic

Rustleaf

Port Sumac

Saint Bete

Wild
Country

Wolfepointe

arkwater

Lonepine

Grasslake

Burl

deharbor
Sandmason

re

Lillygrove

Oakgrove

Flintrust
Birchflow

Willowcrest

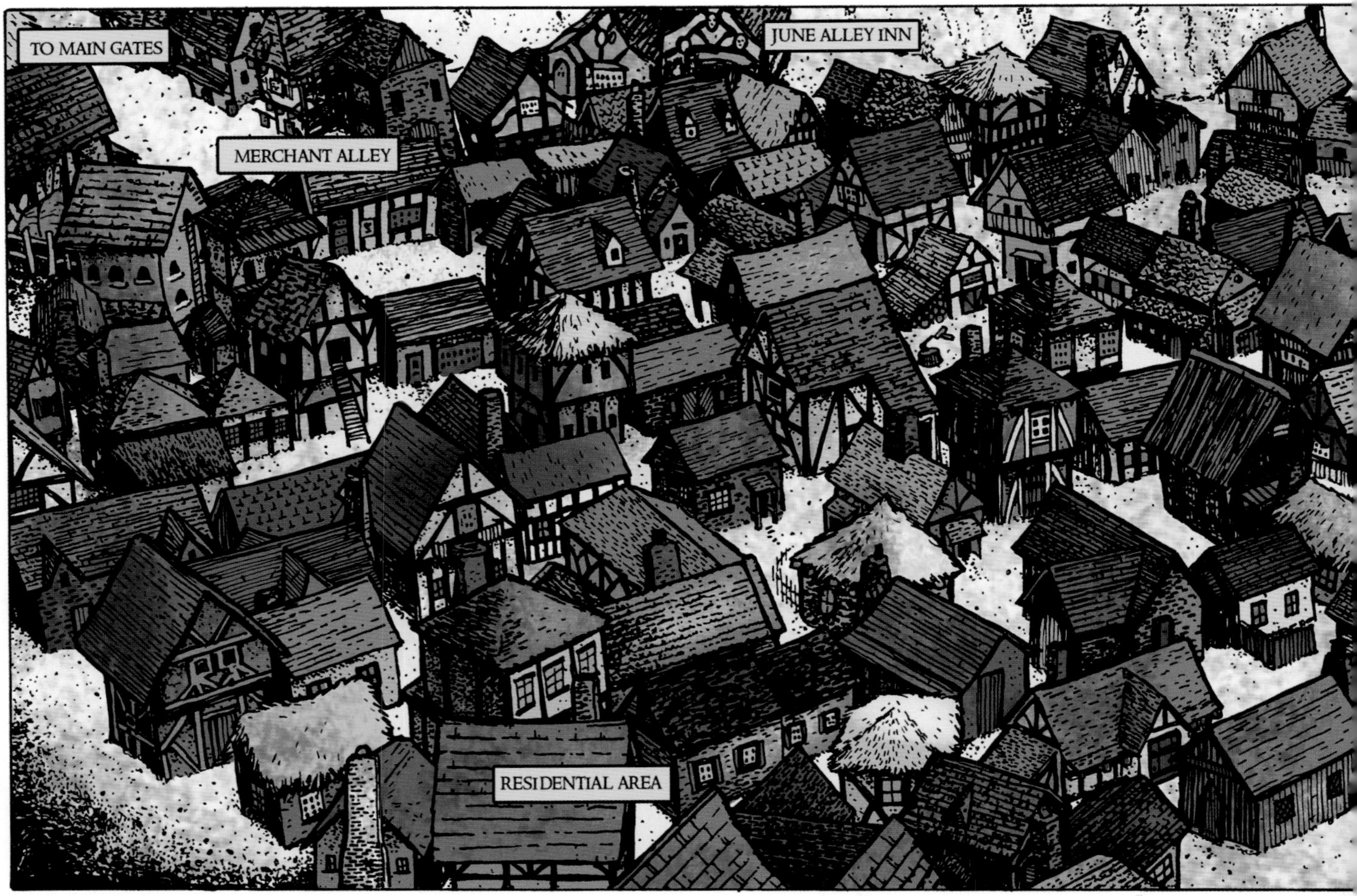
TO MAIN GATES
JUNE ALLEY INN
MERCHANT ALLEY
RESIDENTIAL AREA

BARKSTONE:

This town is located on the Western end of the Mouse Territories. Its gates were built into the trunk of a Locust tree backed up to an outcropping of stone. The town lies inside.

Known for being home to artisans and craftsmice, Barkstone is the destination for the best in glass, furniture, and other goods.

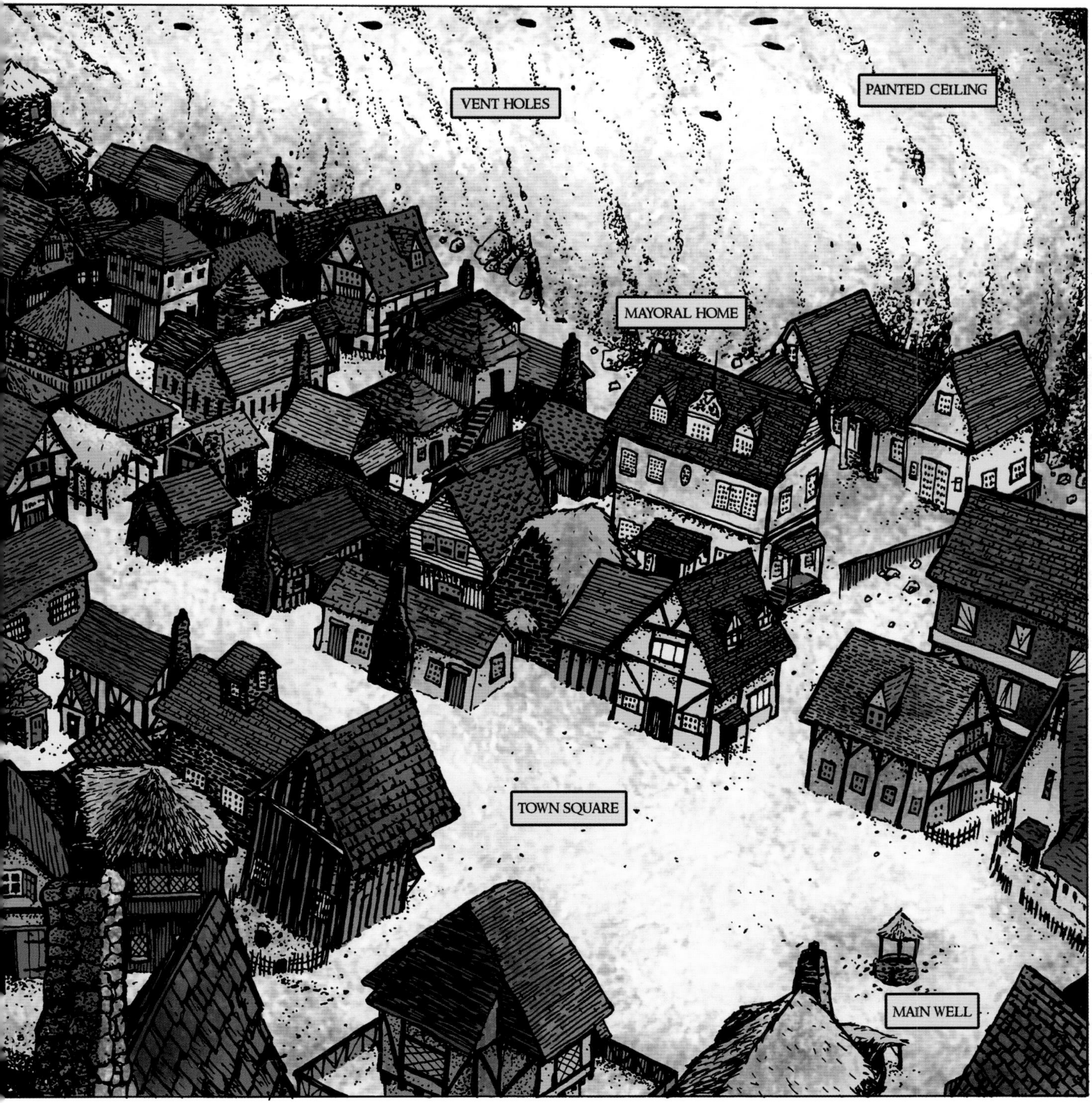
VENT HOLES
PAINTED CEILING
MAYORAL HOME
TOWN SQUARE
MAIN WELL

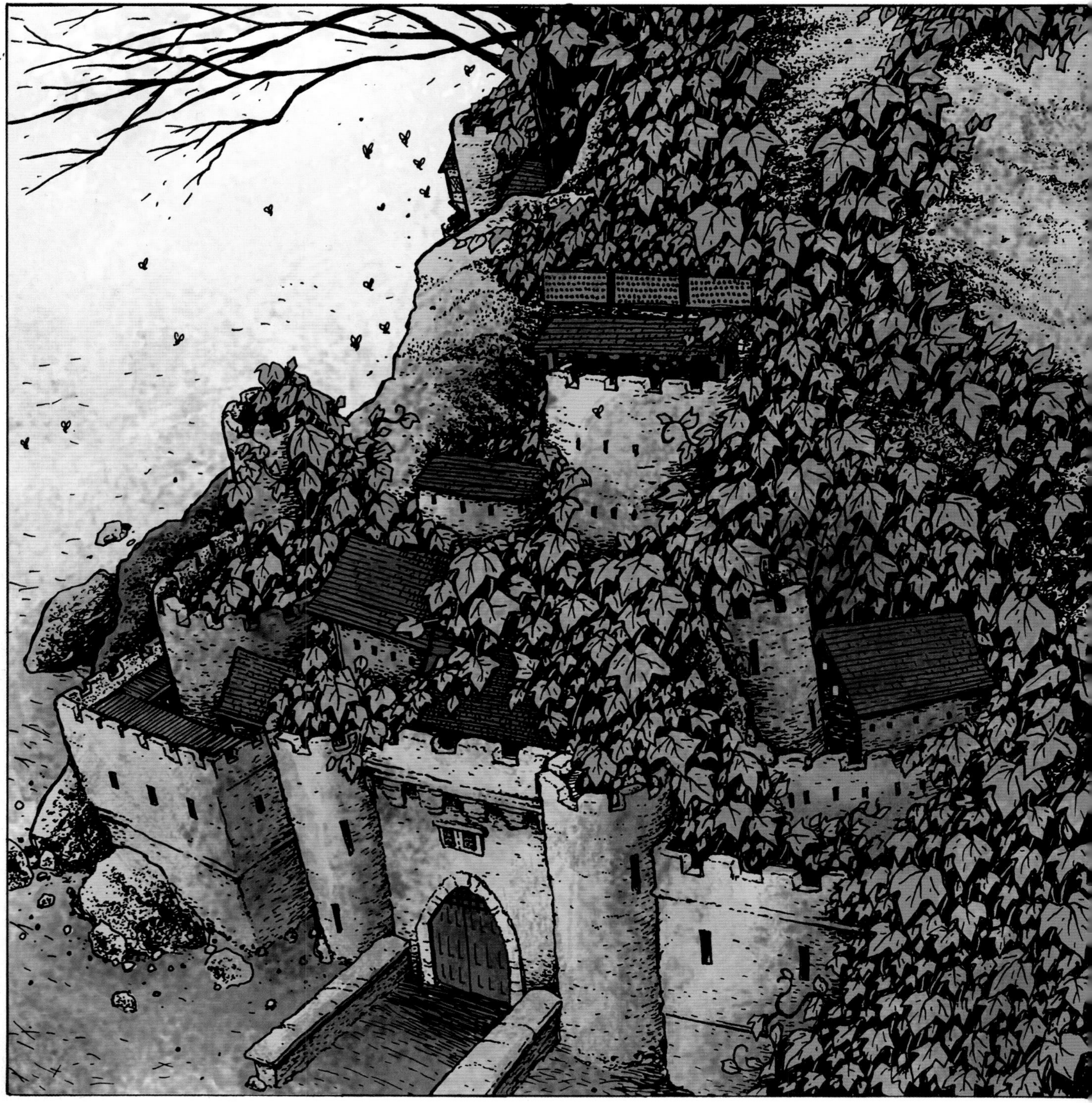

LOCKHAVEN:

Home of the Mouse Guard. Carved deep into stone, only the face of Lockhaven is visible from the outside. It is also protected by a thick layer of ivy. Lockhaven serves as a base of operations for the Guard and is not a true city. While there are mouse citizens that live there, they are only there as invited guests of the Guard to perform certain skills and labors:

WEAPONS & ARMOR:

A full time smith is kept on hand at Lockhaven to mend, sharpen, and create weapons and tools for the Guard. Occasionally this job is held by a Guard, but often it proves too time consuming for a patrol mouse.

COOKERY:

Staple foods are stored in abundance, while prepared foods are made as needed, as it is unknown how many or few will be fed on any given day. Lockhaven is known for Gabcroon: a dense bread filled with seeds, fruits, and nuts. It travels well and stays warm long after baking.

TEXTILES:

Woven and sewn fabrics are important to the mice of Lockhaven. The Guard are known for their cloaks, which need to be both warm and durable, as they are a Guard's primary piece of clothing.

APIARY:

Lockhaven is also home to a hive of bees. The mice harvest the honey for food and the wax for goods and medicinal purposes. To do this, the Apiary Keeper uses smoke to charm the bees. The bees also serve as a natural deterrent to other predators.

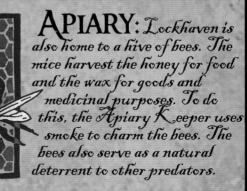

Common Mouse Trades:

Stone Mason:

Once chiseled into shape, stone provides a useful building material for mouse settlements. Masons quarry, shape, and lay mortar for the stone.

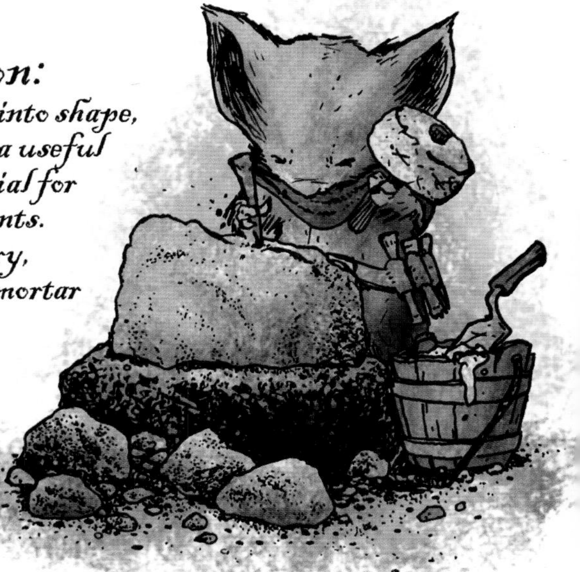

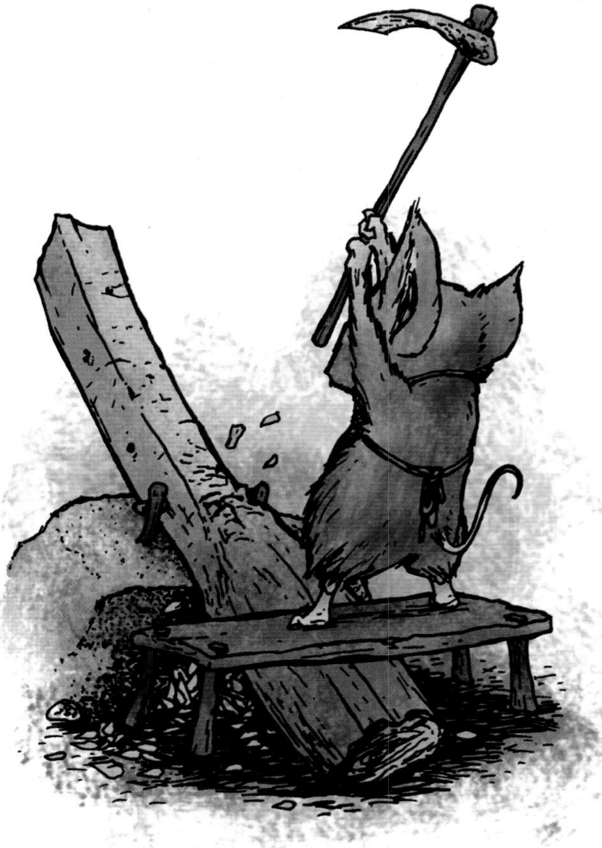

Carpenter:

From the smallest project to the largest, wood is a vital resource available to mice. An adze is used to square a timber for construction.

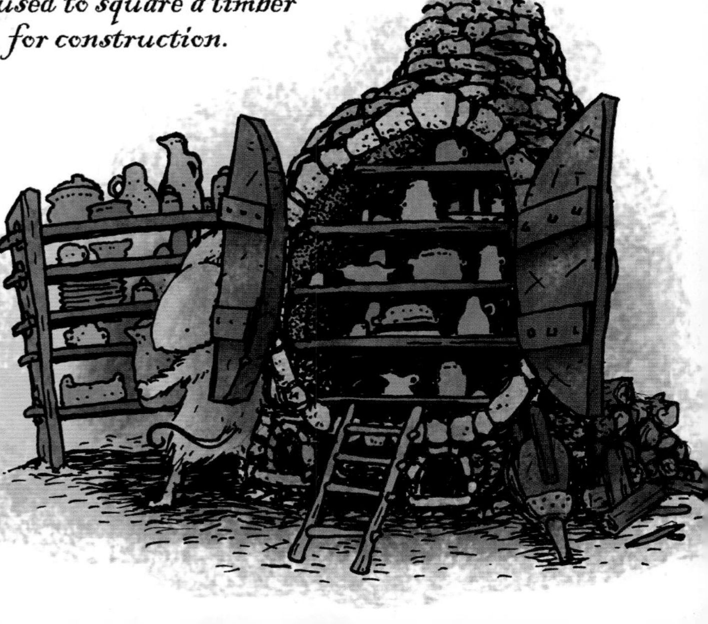

Potter:

Clay collected from under the soil is shaped and fired to create many food preparation and storage vessels. Kilns are closely tended in order to keep the temperature inside high enough to fire the clay.

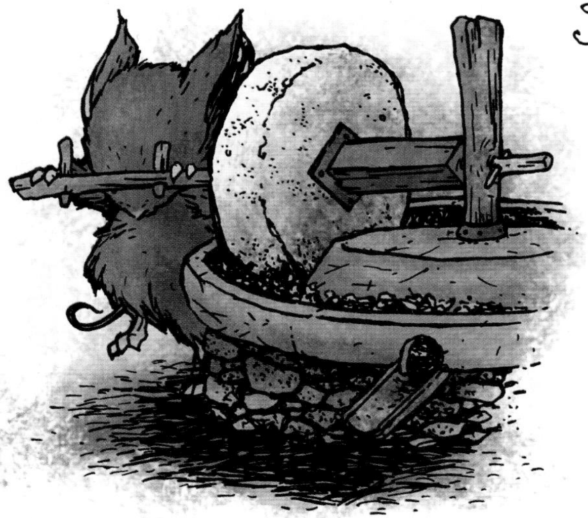

Miller:

Using the collected grain, a miller will use a stone gristmill to grind the harvest into a finer texture.

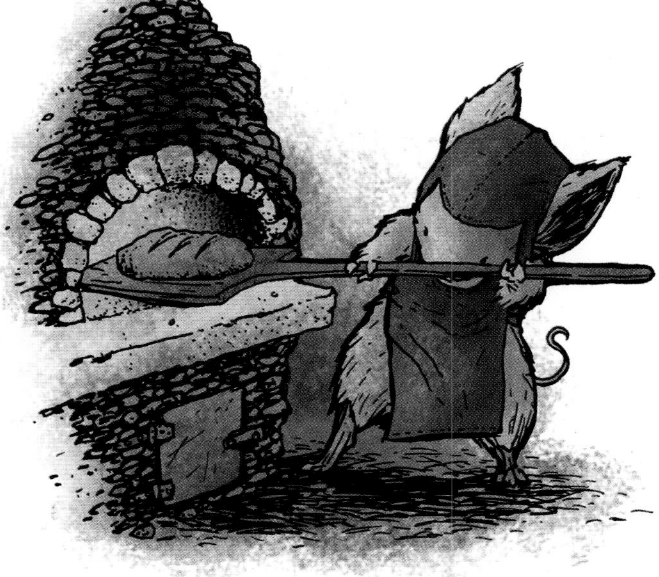

Baker:

Prepared foods can last longer and be stored and eaten more easily than raw grains. It also allows for the addition of seeds, nuts, and fruits to be added into a single-item meal.

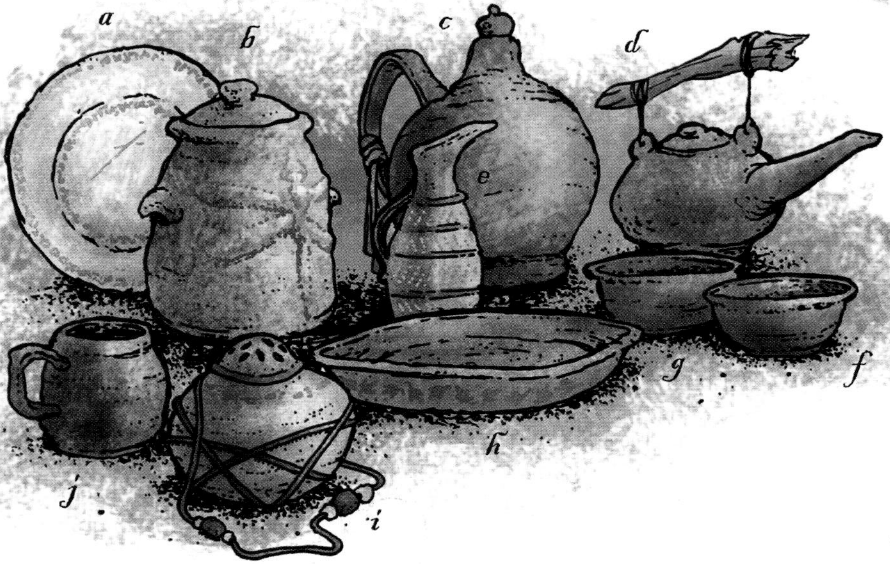
a
b
c
d
e
g
f
h
j
i

Examples of Pottery:

a: plate with painted trim.
b: storage jar with dragonfly motif
c: water jug with stopper
d: teapot with wooden grip
e: small decorative water pitcher
f: personal bowl
g: personal bowl
h: serving dish with leaf motif
i: scented smoking vessel
j: heavy drinking mug

A GALLERY OF PINUPS

BY ESTEEMED AUTHORS & FRIENDS

AS PRESENTED IN THE
ORIGINAL MOUSE GUARD SERIES

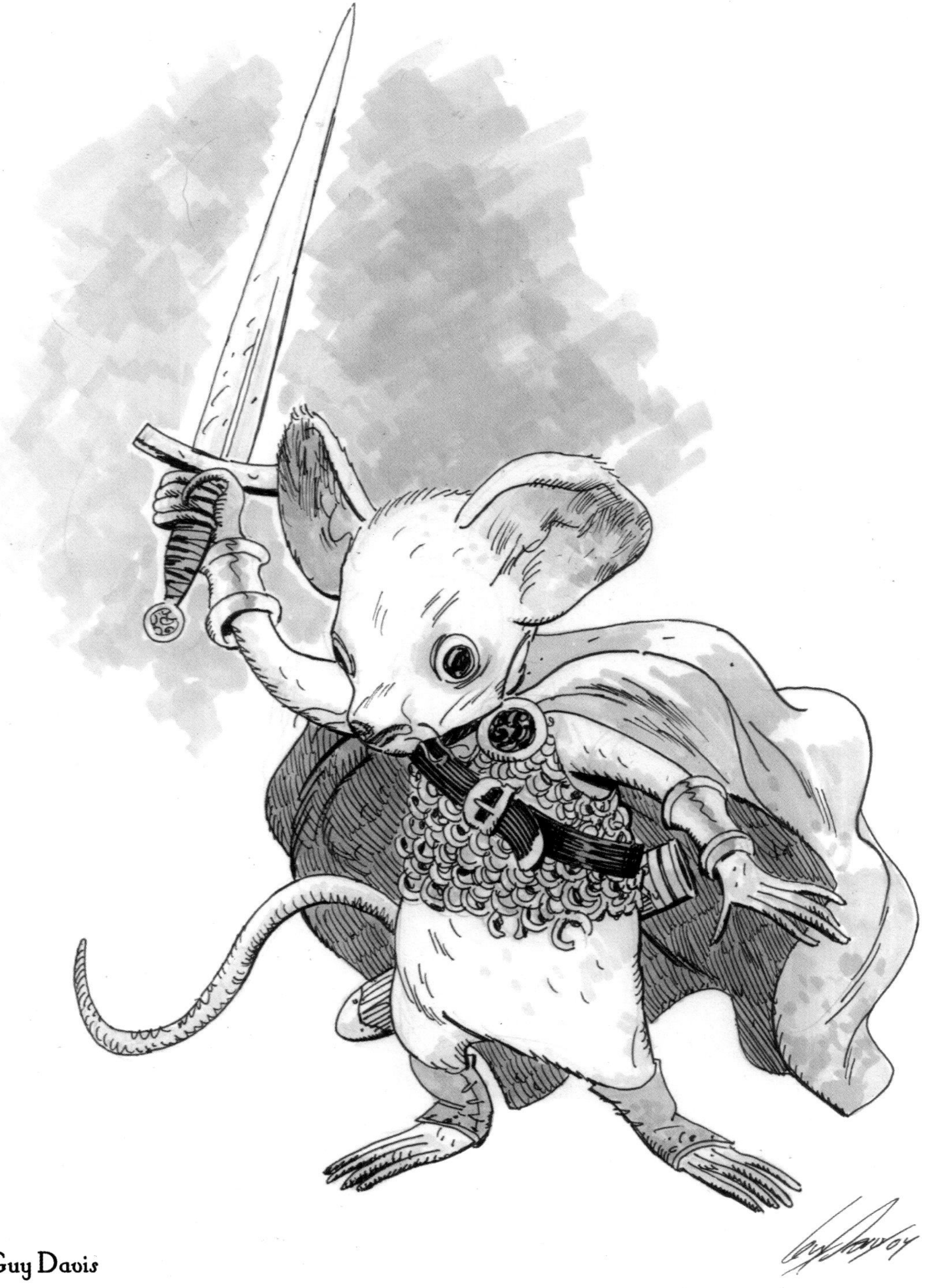

Pinup by Guy Davis

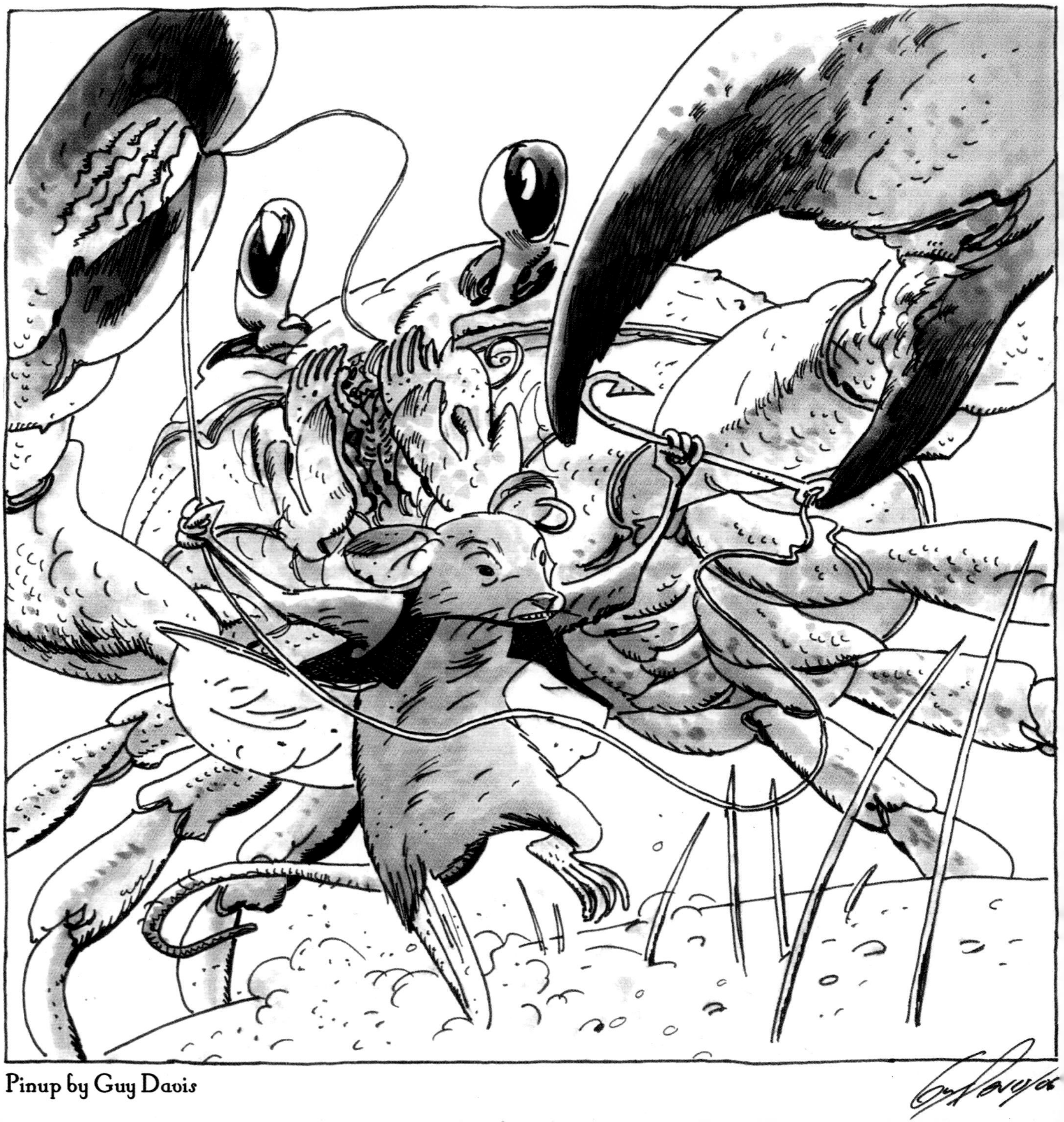

Pinup by Guy Davis

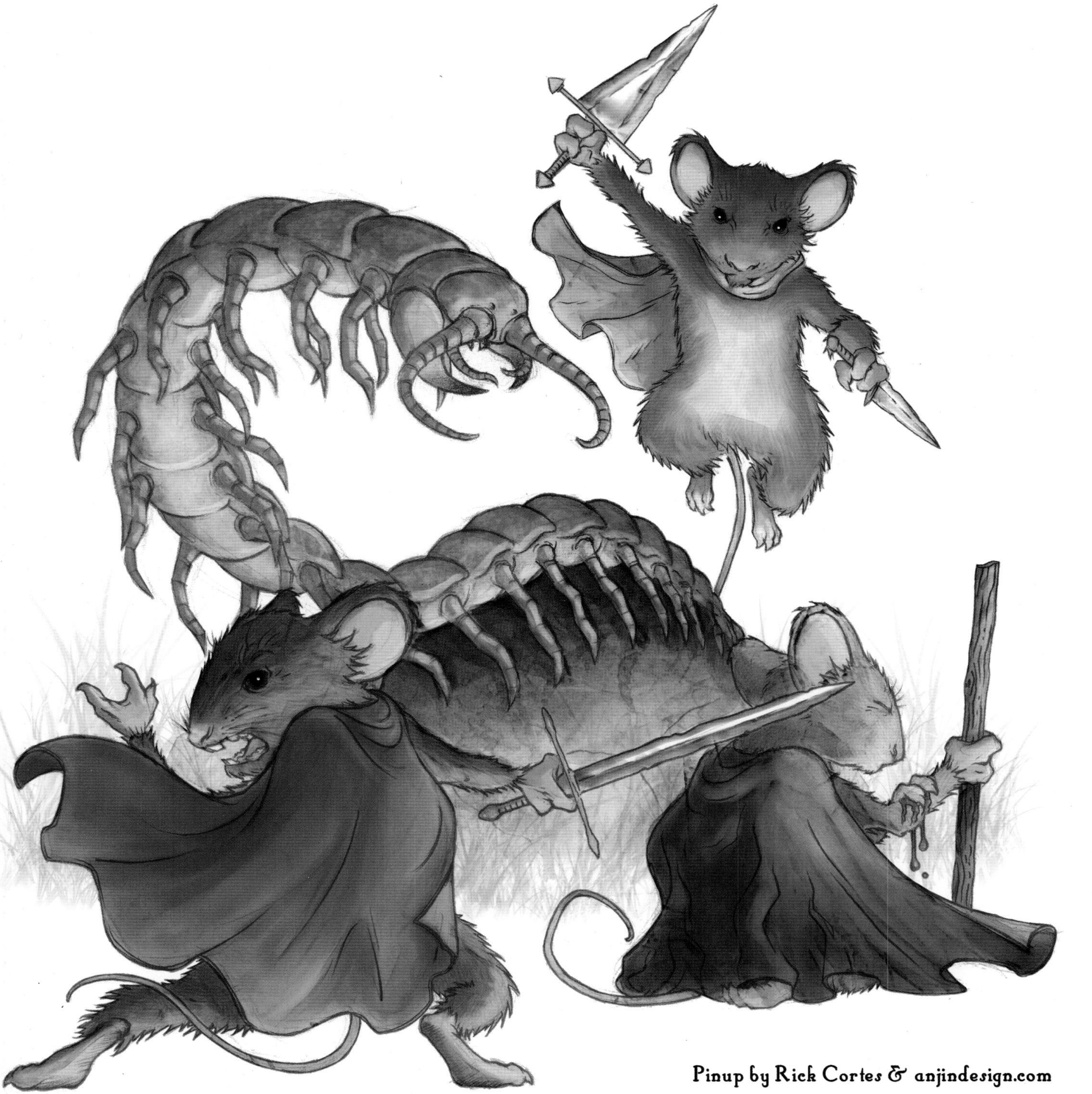

Pinup by Rick Cortes & anjindesign.com

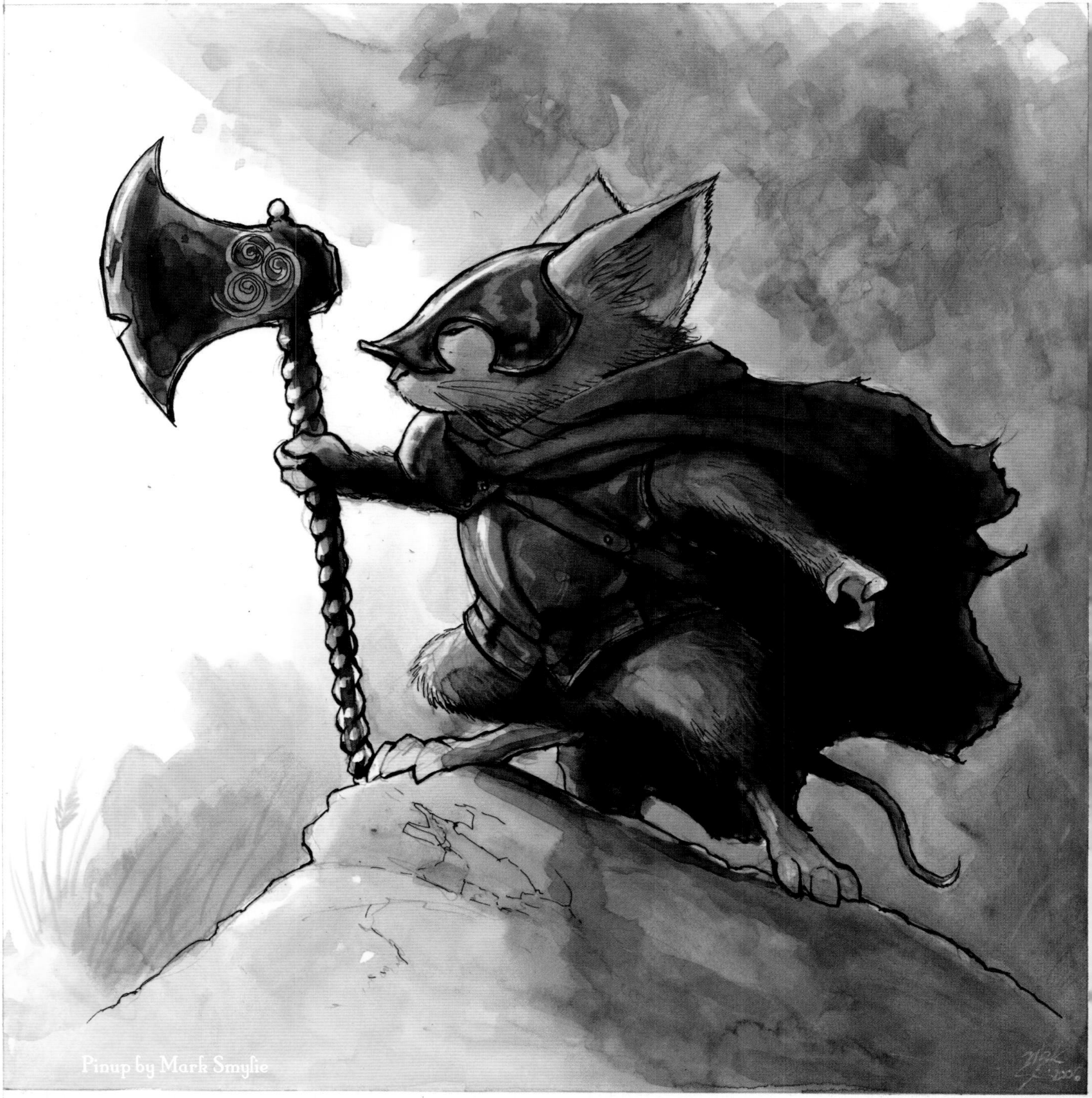
Pinup by Mark Smylie

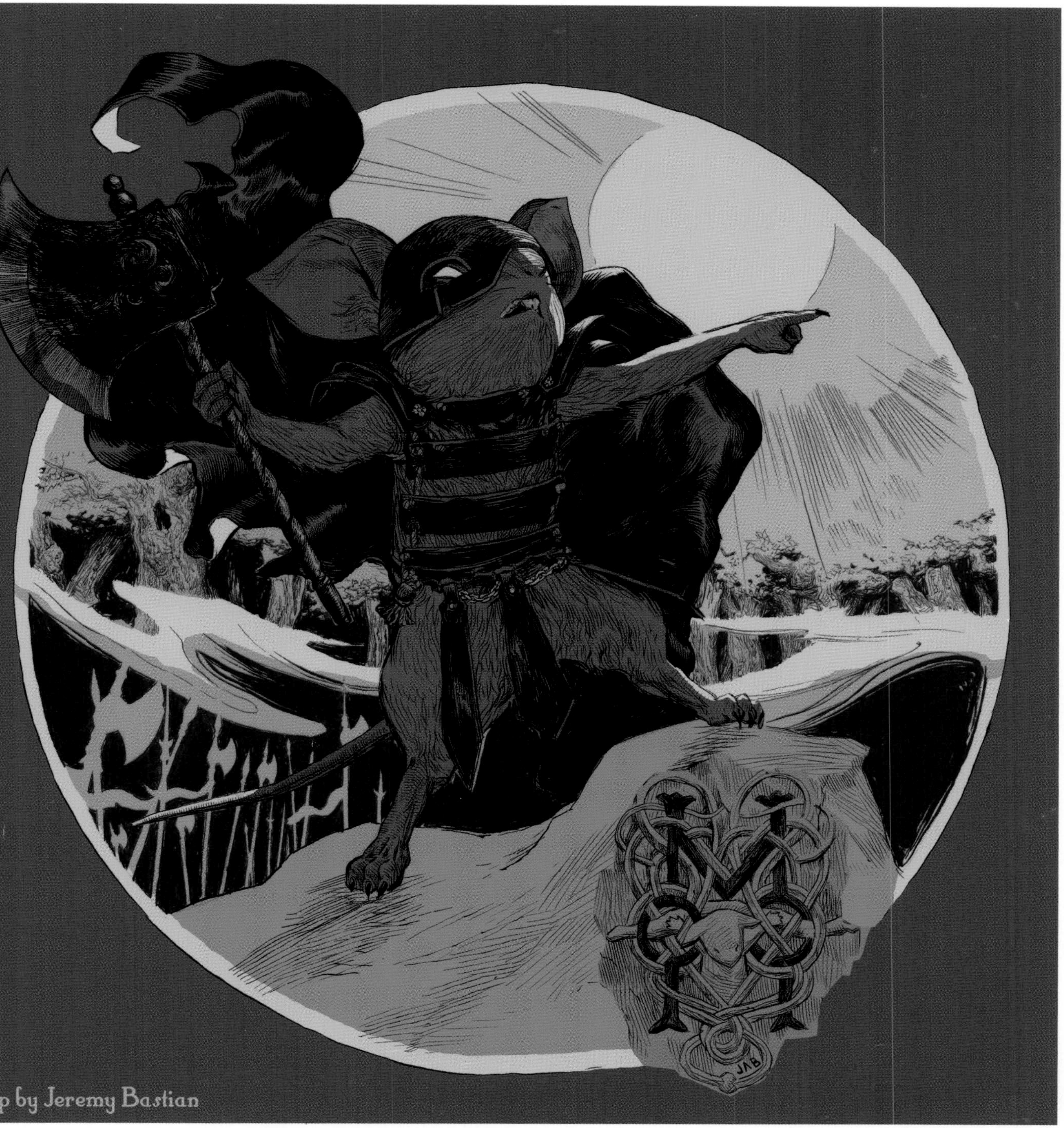
JvB

Pinup by Jeremy Bastian

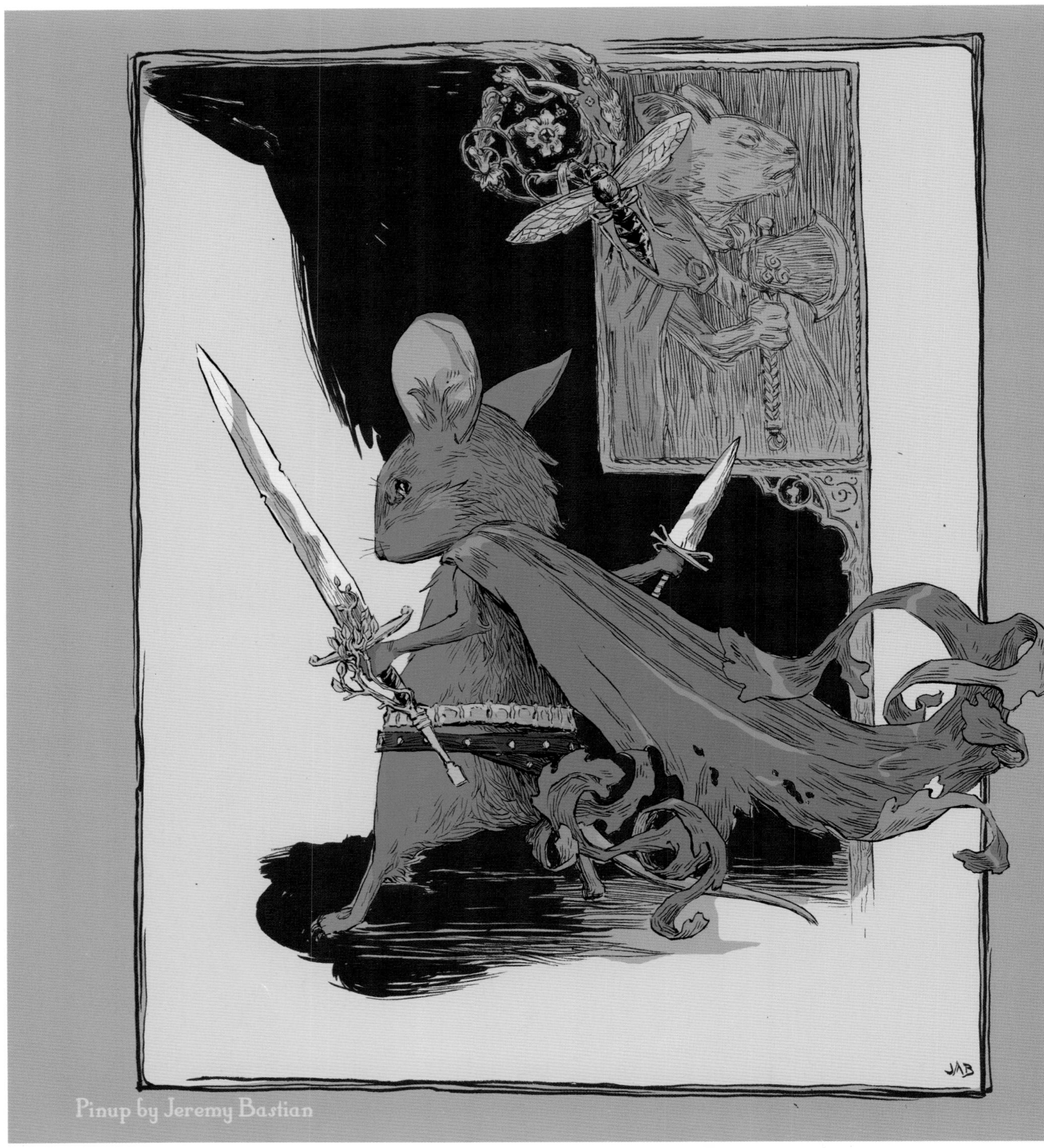
JAB

Pinup by Jeremy Bastian

THE NEXT BOOK IN THE

MOUSE GUARD
SERIES:

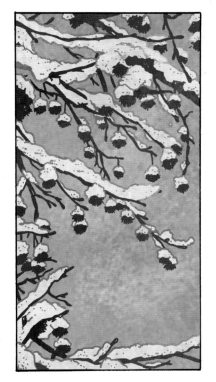

WINTER 1152

About the Author

David Petersen was born in 1977. His artistic
career soon followed. A steady diet of cartoons,
comics and tree climbing fed his imagination
and is what still inspires his work today. David
was the 2007 Russ Manning Award recipient
for Most Promising Newcomer, and in 2008
won Eisner Awards for Best Publication for Kids
(Mouse Guard Fall 1152 & Winter 1152) and Best
Graphic Album – Reprint *(Mouse Guard Fall 1152
Hardcover)*. He received his BFA in Printmaking
from Eastern Michigan University where he met
his wife Julia. They continue to reside in Michigan
with their dog Autumn.

Mouse Territories 1150

A map of cities, towns, villages, and safe paths after the winter war
As measured by the Guard of 1149, Recorded by Clarke's Cartography
Fallen settlements listed & struck

Caloga

Dawnrock

Darkheather
Entrance

Whitepine

Chistledown

Wildseed

Elmwood

Lockhaven

Ironwood

Shaleburrow

Pebblebrook

Ivydale

Blackrock

Barkstone

Woodruff's Grove

Elmoss

Copperwood

R

Ferndale

Scent Border

Sprucetuck

Darkheather
Tunnels

Walnutpeck

Dorigift

Appleloft

Gilsledge